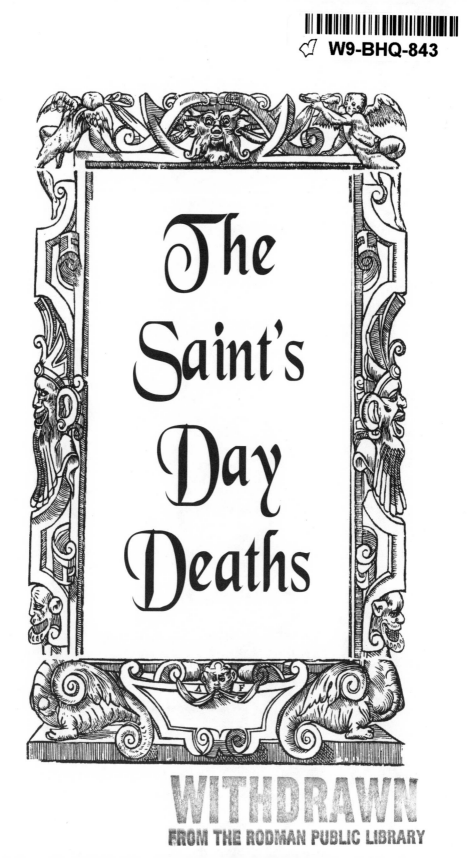

The Saint's Day Deaths

The Saint's Day Deaths

Albert Noyer

CREATIVE ARTS BOOK COMPANY
Berkeley, CA 2000

For Jennifer and J. Z.

Uni cuique dedit vitium natura creato.
Nature has conferred some vice on each created thing.
—Sextus Propertius

Main Characters

Treverius Asterius: Map maker in Pretorium cartography workshop

Blandina Cingetoria Asteria: Wife of Treverius; works with him in map workshop

Junius Asterius: Father of Treverius; Master of cartography workshop

Margarita Asteria: Mother of Treverius

Cyril of Constantinople: Wealthy merchant from Eastern Roman Empire

Quintus Albanus: Governor of the Province of Germania Prima

Publius Vertiscus: Pretorium Curator

Vetius Modestus: Presbyter at Mogontium

David ben Zadok: Son of Mogontium's Rabbi; owns cartage business

Penina: Wife of David ben Zadok

Suebius Nevius: Merchant partner of Cyril

Hortar: Associate of Nevius

Demetrius of Ravenna: Liaison at Mogontium for Emperor Honorius

Nicias of Alexandria: Garrison surgeon

Lupus Glaucus: Interim garrison commander

Gaisios: Vandal chieftain

Malchus: Prophet who believes he is one of the "Seven Sleepers"

Gaius Petranius: Director of the Theater of Trajan at Mogontium

Juliana: Actress-prostitute

Pumilio: Dwarf actor

Aethiops: Mute Ethiopian actor

Albino: Actor

Flavius Stilicho: Commander of the Western Roman Army

Glossary of Places

GERMANY
Aqua Flavia—Rottweil
Aquae—Baden Baden
Aquileia—Heidenheim
Belginium—Idar Oberstein?
Bingium—Bingen
Bodobriga—Boppard
Bonna—Bonn
Borbetomagus—Worms
Brocomagus—Brumath
Colonia—Koln
Confluentes—Koblenz
Dumnissus—Kirn?
Grinario—Kongen
Lopodunum—Ladenburg
Noviomagus—Neumagen
Speyer
Sumelocenna—Rottenburg
Tres Tabernae—Rheinzabern
Treveri—Trier
Vicus Aurelii—Ohringen
Voslovia—Oberwesel
(Mogontium is a fictionalized
Mogontiacum—Mainz, Germany)

FRANCE
Alesia—Alise-Ste-Reine
Andematunum—Langres
Argentorate—Strasbourg
Argentovaria—Horbourg
Aurasio—Orange
Axima—Aime
Cabillonium—Chalons-sur-Saone
Cularo—Grenoble
Dividurum—Metz
Lugdunum—Lyons
Matisco—Macon
Remi—Reims
Tullum—Toul
Vesontio—Besancon
Vienna—Vienne

SWITZERLAND
Augusta Rauricorum—Augst
Aventicum—Avenches
Basilis—Basel
Curia—Chur
Eborodunum—Yverdon
Equestris—Nyon
Genava—Geneva
Valens—Martigny
Vindonissa—Windisch
Vivescus—Vevey

ITALY
Augusta Praetoria—Aosta
Augusta Taurinorum—Turin
Classis—Classe
Comum—Como
Eporedia—Ivrea
Forum Livii—Forli
Mediolanum—Milan
Mutina—Modena
Novaria—Novaraso
Oscila—Domodossola
Ravenna—Ravenna
Vercellae—Vercelli

AUSTRIA
Brigantium—Bregenz

RIVERS
Arar—Saone
Arusus—Aare
Dubis—Doubs
Isara—Isere
Moenus—Main
Mosella—Mosel
Padus—Po
Rhenus—Rhine
Rhodanus—Rhone
Ruessus—Reuss

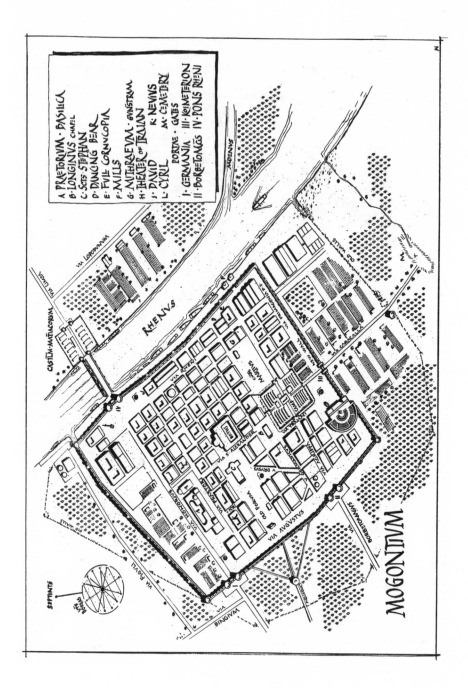

MOGONTIVM

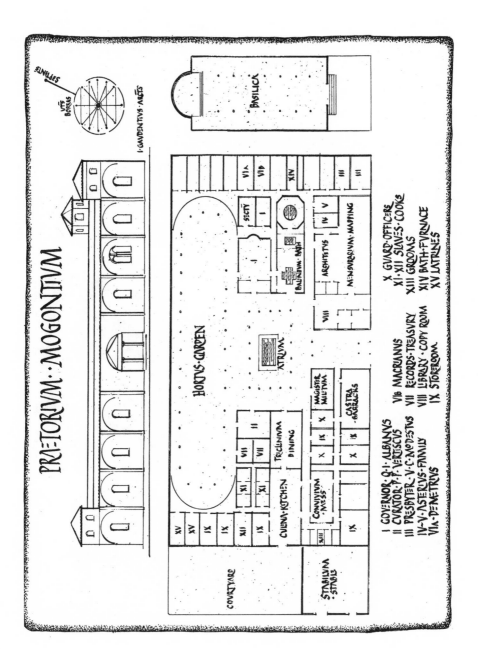

PRÆTORIVM·MOGONTIVM

BASILICA

HORTVS·GARDEN

ATRIVM

CVLINA·KITCHEN

TRICLINIVM DINING

CONVIVIVM MESS

MAGISTER MILITVM

CASTRA BARRACKS

COVRTYARD

STABVLVM STABLS

BALINEVM·BATH

ARCHITECTVS

MENSORARIVM MAPPING

I·GAVDENTIVS·ANSIS

VTE·BOREAS

SEPTENTS

I GOVERNOR·Q·I·ALBANVS
II CVRATOR·P·F·VETVSCVS
III PRESBYTER·V·C·MODESTVS
IV-V·ASERVS·FAMILY
VI·A·DEMETRIVS

VI·b MACRIANVS
VII RECORDS·TREASVRY
VIII LIBRARY·COPY ROOM
IX STOREROOM

X GVARD·OFFICERS
XI·XII SLAVES·COOKS
XIII GROOMS
XIV BATH·FVRNACE
XV LATRINES

The
Saint's Day
Deaths

chapter 1

Treverius noticed that the October air was colder than it had been in the morning and that the freshening wind smelled of rain. He glanced to the northeast. Dark clouds raced toward Mogontium, threatening to overlay the blue sky above the city with a broad black funerary shroud, yet Arbitos was still perched atop the roof of the old temple of Jupiter, struggling to mount a cross in place.

"Why is the man ignoring the storm?" Treverius muttered. "He'll be flung off by that wind." He cupped both hands and shouted, "Leave putting the cross up till tomorrow, Arbitos. You'll get blown into the Rhine."

The tile roofer looked down in the direction of the voice. "It's you, Treverius," he called. "When did you get back from Ravenna?"

It had been a week, but Treverius ignored the question. "Arbitos, you've got less sense than a raw apprentice. Have you seen that black sky behind you? All your men have already scrambled down the scaffold."

"Afraid of getting wet, I guess," Arbitos scoffed, but glanced over his shoulder at the approaching storm.

"Presbyter Modestus isn't in that much of a hurry to reconsecrate the temple, is he?"

"This won't take long," Arbitos hedged, "and it's worth the risk. Hades, he paid me a silver siliqua."

"Wonderful!" Treverius hooted. "Now you can have the finest funeral ever seen in Mogontium."

"I'll bet the silver against there being a fune . . ."

The rolling growl of thunder drowned out Arbitos's quip. When a gust of cold wind set the iron cross swaying in a crazed dance, Treverius saw the man almost lose his balance, then recover and reach out to steady the base toward its metal socket.

"Stubborn as a pack mule." Craftmasters were proud men. Since sarcasm had failed, perhaps logic would coax Arbitos down. "You once risked your life to save Cordus in that skirmish with the Suebi, but this gamble is insane."

"The presbyter wants this cross put up," Arbitos insisted. "Time we had a decent church in Mogontium."

"It doesn't have to cost your life." Treverius shook his head. His wife Blandina told him how the religious situation had changed in the past year. Those Arian Christians in town, who held a view of Christ's divinity that differed from Nicean teaching, had become more bold in challenging Modestus. The presbyter attributed their arrogance to the unexpected appearance of Gothic tribes across the Rhine who were Arian converts. Also, the wealthy merchant Cyril, a pagan sympathizer, was taking advantage of the uneasy situation to protest the rededication of the three-hundred-year-old Roman temple as a Christian church.

The lintel above the temple's porch columns caught Treverius's downward glance. The bronze inscription had been removed, but green patina still faintly outlined the words DIVI IOVI DIVI TARANI—To the Divine Jupiter, The Divine Taranis.

Emperor Domitian had donated the temple to Mogontium during a time when Roman priests still admitted local gods into their pantheon, yet even then no one could recall the Celtic god Mogon, after whom the frontier outpost was originally named. Taranis, a local tribe's sky deity, was substituted as a suitable companion for Jupiter.

A more recent compromise was the short transept wings that extended from each side of the apse. They were brick, rather than the grey limestone of the temple, because no one knew how to quarry stone any longer. This awkward addition and the temple's defaced pediment figures, columns and flanking half-columns, reflected the ravages of barbarian raids into the old province of Germania Superior. Frontier life had declined, and now the Gothic threat on the eastern bank of the Rhine gave rise to the threat of another imminent invasion among the city's nervous citizens.

A collective gasp of horror from bystanders jarred Treverius's attention back to Arbitos. He was crouched low, grasping the iron socket with both hands, his face drained of color.

"What happened?" Treverius asked a bearded, red-faced man in a greasy fur jacket.

"Cross was swinging. Almost knocked the idiot off."

"I've got to get him down." He grasped the man's arm. "Isn't Arbitos married?"

Greasy jacket nodded. "To Fredegund."

"Bring her here right away."

"I . . . I don't know," greasy jacket stammered. "She'll probably—"

"Get Fredegund, man!" Treverius ordered. "I'll check the crane to see if the rope will hold the cross's weight until she gets here." Treverius watched the man trot away, then went to the winch.

The handspike and capstan were well-secured by a ratchet, and the rope looked strong enough to support the weight of the iron, but, in the rising wind, the heavy cross at the top might begin to swing again. It could catch Arbitos and plummet him to his death on the stone paving below.

After Treverius stepped back, he saw Cyril of Constantinople hurrying from around the apse. *That's all Arbitos needs, a heckler to distract him. Cyril is probably the main reason Modestus wants the cross put up before the dedication of the church.*

Treverius had spoken with the rich merchant a few times. As Cyril boasted by his name, he came from the capital of the Eastern empire, but had inherited the family franchise for trading with local Celtic and Germanic tribes. Treverius had placed Cyril's age at close to sixty-five, old enough to support his claim of having served in the Rhine campaigns of the late emperor Julian. Presbyter Modestus claimed it was the influence of his apostate commander that had made Cyril an advocate for restoring pagan rites.

The merchant's full head of grey hair bobbed furiously as he threaded his way through the gawkers, pulling his fine-spun wool tunic and yellow-dyed cloak close to his body to avoid having them soiled by contact with grimy onlookers. Treverius noted that Cyril still affected the red leather boots of a senator, even though he was not entitled to the honor, and saw him push a bystander out of the way with the same ruthlessness that he had undoubtedly displayed against the Alamanni in their last raid.

Cyril was a few paces away when the gleam of a golden pendant caught Treverius's eye. *That ornament around his neck would pay Arbitos's wages for a year. And his clothes, mine as a cartographer. I'll grant that Cyril looks the part of the wealthiest citizen in Mogontium.*

"Map maker," the merchant said, without extending a hand, "I'd heard that you just returned from Ravenna. Yet you take time away from your charts . . . and beautiful wife . . . to witness this desecration of Jupiter's temple?"

Cyril's smirk made the merchant one of those few persons who look less attractive when they smile. Despite the man's sarcasm, Treverius decided to be agreeable.

"Desecration is hardly the correct term, sir. The building has been vacant ever since Theodosius ordered pagan temples and shrines closed fifteen years ago."

Cyril ignored the rebuke and held up his golden amulet. "Do you recognize two-faced Janus, the Roman god of beginnings?" He flashed the gilt metal to catch the light.

"I've heard of him." Treverius studied the twin bearded profiles. "Don't we still name the first month of the year after Janus?"

"Excellent! Yet, even if you do remember some of your heritage," Cyril warned, "the patience of gods like Janus and Jupiter will not last much longer."

"Sir?"

"The worship of Jupiter," he repeated. "Those of us who still have reverence for Roman ways ask only that the gods again be given equality with your Galilean."

"There are followers of the Galilean, as you call Christ, who are also proscribed. The disciples of Arius, for one."

"And rightly so, for not believing in your God's total divinity," Cyril replied.

"I'm surprised you agree."

"Perhaps you misjudge me, map maker." Cyril raised his eyebrows—still black in contrast to his grey hair. "Did you know that Pontius Pilate wrote to Tiberius about adding your Galilean to Rome's pantheon, but the Senate refused?"

Treverius glanced at Cyril's scarlet boots. "Because the senators had not thought of the idea themselves. And that letter is a forgery. It—"

"I see Ravenna at least has not corrupted you," the merchant interrupted. "Your blond hair is cut short. Is it true that, in the capital, men wear their hair as long as females, and women dress like shameless harlots?"

Before Treverius could answer the charge, a shrill voice sounded from behind him.

"Blessed Thais of Egypt! Come down, husband, or you'll widow me on the saint's feast day."

He turned to see Fredegund looking up at Arbitos on the temple roof.

"That's the man's wife?" Cyril snickered. "Let's see if he loves her more than his Galilean."

Arbitos made no sign of hearing Fredegund's plea above the growing shriek of wind. With one hand he had managed to grasp the iron socket that was fixed to the roof, and was struggling to swing the dangling cross over to it with the other. Treverius faced the woman.

"Fredegund, your husband is in my Limitans cohort. I've been trying to—"

"Limitans frontier militia?" Cyril interjected in scorn. "Commendable volunteers, I suppose, but not legionary material."

"Yet almost the only defense Mogontium has," Treverius shot back. With your patronizing arrogance, merchant, you should have been born wearing an emperor's purple. He turned back to Fredegund. "I've been trying to talk your husband down before the storm hits."

"He shouldn't be up there, putting a cross on the old temple," she complained. "That presbyter is just making trouble."

"Trouble?"

"Between Christians and the others. Come down husband," she called up again, "or I'll send your sons up after you."

To add urgency to her threat, a jagged streak of lightning struck nearby. Scarcely a moment passed between the chalky flash and a jarring crack of thunder that followed. Treverius saw Arbitos flinch in an involuntary reflex, but retain his grip on the socket. Yet the next flash could not be far away.

Pellets of hail and drops of cold rain began to design the paving stones with dark, round spatters. People watching Arbitos broke for the shelter of covered shops across the Via Severus Alexander. Treverius stayed, along with Cyril and Fredegund. He knew it would not be long before the wet terra cotta roof tiles became dangerously slippery.

"It's started to rain," Treverius yelled to Arbitos. "If you don't listen to your wife, I'll come up myself and drag you down."

"Your sons Basinus and Chuppa are on their way," Fredegund bluffed.

Arbitos, closing the gap between the cross and its holder, responded with a mocking grin. As he grasped the iron socket with his right hand, and strained to inch the base of the cross toward it, his hobnailed boot soles fought for traction on the curved clay tiles.

The next lightning bolt and thunder clap were so close that they blinded and deafened spectators. Treverius instinctively dropped to the ground on one knee. After he straightened up, he saw Fredegund clinging to Cyril. She was bawling in fright, but the merchant seemed too stunned to push her away.

Fearing the worse, Treverius looked up at the roof.

Chunks of broken terra cotta slowly followed after the scorched figure of Arbitos, his jacket and trousers smoking from the lightning strike. His body slid down the pitch of the roof, paused for an instant at the edge, then dropped to the stone paving below with a sickening thud that sounded as if a sack of sand had fallen. The cross was in its socket, leaning at an awkward angle like the soft iron of a javelin shaft pulled out of a shield.

After Treverius's shock ebbed, he ran towards Arbitos. Thank Christ that Blandina stayed at the map workshop and didn't see this.

Cyril recovered from his fear and tried to pry Fredegund's clutching fingers off his cloak. "Release me, woman," he shouted above her moans. When she finally let go and slipped to the ground, sobbing, he stepped around her and joined Treverius at the body of Arbitos. "Th . . .

the fool got . . . what he deserved," Cyril sneered, but his voice trembled. "Did . . . did he think his Galilean would protect him?"

Treverius ignored the callous remark and bent down to see if Arbitos was still alive. He had seen men suffer weapon wounds during training, but had never witnessed anyone struck by lightning. Arbitos lay on his back. The icy rain was turning to sleet. A puddle of dark blood spread from behind his head. The man's face was burned almost beyond recognition and his broken left arm lay twisted at a clumsy angle by the fall, like the cross on the roof overhead.

Kneeling, Treverius rubbed a hand on the wet paving to beat at sparks that smoldered on the dead man's clothing. The smell of scorched wool and flesh was nauseating, but he slapped at the glowing spots until most were put out, then straightened up. Moisture would soak out the rest. The white grains of sleet in the folds of Arbitos's clothing had begun to remind him of maggots he had seen on corpses.

"What did you say, Cyril?" Treverius glanced up at the twisted cross, then back at the merchant. "Did you ask me something?"

"I . . . I didn't know he was your friend." Cyril finally seemed moved by the death.

"Not really a friend, I knew him from Cohort Falco. I'm cavalry, he was foot. Never mind. I'll get someone to send for Presbyter Modestus. That's all I can think of to do." He looked toward Fredegund. She was still lying on the ground, her tunic whipped by the wind and a small drift of sleet granules already piled against her side. "Help her," Treverius called out to a woman watching from across the street. "And one of you men go find her sons."

No one moved or came out. Despite Modestus' s teaching against superstition, they're still afraid of being haunted by the dead. While Cyril stood by, Treverius unclasped his cloak, laid it over Arbitos, and tucked the wool material around his body to keep the cover from blowing away. Then he went to Fredegund and knelt down, brushing away the sleet. "I . . . I'm sorry," he stammered in an awkward attempt to comfort her. "Your husband was a brave man."

"He was doing God's work. Should have been safe." Fredegund looked up at Treverius with uncomprehending, red-rimmed eyes. "Shouldn't he have had Divine protection?"

He had no answer to her simple logic. Perhaps Modestus could explain or rationalize the contradiction. Treverius glanced back and saw the woman he had called start toward him, bringing a companion.

"Those women will take you home," he told Fredegund. "Someone will get Modestus to anoint your husband."

Despite the rising shriek of wind, Cyril was close enough to have heard the conversation. "Your presbyter should have been here to witness Jupiter's vengeance."

Cyril's brief tone of concern had turned cold as the Boreal wind. "What are you talking about?" Treverius questioned.

"Jupiter Fulgur. 'Jupiter of the Lightning Bolt.' The god's reprisals against the desecration of his temple have begun."

"Are you serious?" Treverius scoffed, looking up at the grey sky and veil of slashing sleet. True, an October thunderstorm was rare—more so if it brought an ice storm in its wake—but the poor weather was hardly an omen brought about by discredited pagan gods, as Cyril claimed. "Arbitos died because he was stubborn. Don't talk nonsense."

"Nonsense?" Cyril stamped his feet in wet boots and pulled the cloak more tightly around his body. "This is a beginning," he taunted, holding up the golden medallion of Janus. "Let us wait for the next incident at Jupiter's temple and see if you will also call that an accident."

Anger flushed Treverius's face beyond its redness from the raw wind. *A man has been killed and the only reaction in this self-styled pagan is to look forward to another death.* "Accidents happen on a building site. This one won't keep Modestus from converting the temple to a church."

"No? Let us see." Cyril turned away, walked a few paces, then spun around. "I tell you, map maker," he shouted over the gale, "there will never be a ritual held to your Galilean in Jupiter's temple. The gods and I will see to that." Hunching back into the sleet, he disappeared around the side of the new transept.

"I lose a year of work on my map of the province," Treverius muttered, "come back to threats of a barbarian invasion, then make an enemy of one of the most influential men in Mogontium. All that in my first week back. What's next?"

chapter 2

When Cyril was gone, Treverius glanced back at Fredegund. Her friends had slipped a cloak around the grieving woman, and supported her by the arms as they moved off in the direction of her house. Several men, whom he surmised were members of Arbitos's tile workers' guild, were tending his body. Modestus had not yet arrived, but he would probably arrange a funeral for tomorrow morning.

Treverius shivered without his cloak, yet felt a need to walk off both the shock of Arbitos's gruesome death and Cyril's savage threat. Instead of returning to the map workshop in the Pretorium, the governor's offices where he and his parents had quarters, Treverius turned right at the corner of the Via Alexander and Praetori. From there he skirted the brick wall of the basilica and headed toward Mogontium's Porta Pons Rheni. The massive gate at the end of the Via Honorius led onto a wooden bridge that spanned the Rhine to Castellum Mattiacorum, a fortified camp guarding the eastern approaches to Mogontium from Germania.

The river wall and gate's twin towers were curtained by a translucent veil of sleety rain. Looking at the fortifications, built before Christianity had taken hold in the town, Treverius thought about what Cyril's threat implied. In his sermons Modestus railed against crypto-pagans, charging that they were secretly holding illegal rites. Cyril was surely one such pagan, possibly their leader. Blandina had said the merchant was trying to exploit citizens' fears to proselytize. The local mercenary garrison held likely recruits—and the men had weapons.

A blast of sleet crystals stung Treverius's face. Not the ideal day for a stroll without a fur jacket and woolen trousers. He ducked low and turned his back against the wind. Weather has never been this bad so early in the fall. Cyril sees it as an omen of Roman gods suppressing Christians. Absurd, of course. Modestus may consider pagans and Arians spiritually dangerous, but the real threat are those Gothic tribes who suddenly appeared across the Rhine. What are their intentions?

Treverius blew on his numbing fingers. The wet northeast wind penetrated the woolen tunic and sleet stung his bare legs. Sidewalk and street paving stones were already slippery with a coating of rime, and drifts of grainy snow formed against the shuttered fronts of shops that had been closed for the day. He eyed the ice-glazed stonework of the high walls and the sentries huddled together in the shelter of the gate towers.

"Not much point in going on. I'd be better off catching up on the map work I missed. And telling Blandina about poor Arbitos."

* * *

That evening, Treverius was in the bedroom of the modest four-room quarters he and Blandina shared. He had eased the image of Arbitos from his mind by studying a copy of a map made by the ancient geographer Claudius Ptolemy. A century earlier the old province of Germania Superior had been divided at the 48th parallel into Germania Prima and Sequania, but a revised map had never been made. Now there was a dispute over the location of the border village of Argentovaria. Absorbed in re-checking the boundary, Treverius was barely aware of his wife when she exaggerated her shivering and called to him.

"C . . . c . . . come to bed, Trev. It's f . . . freezing in here. What is it you're reading at this hour, anyway?"

"Hmm, Blandina?" He placed a finger to mark his place at Lake Lemannus, the old southwestern provincial limit, without looking up from the parchment.

"I asked you what was more interesting than I am," she repeated.

"I'm just checking Ptolemy's grid of the latitudes for our map, dove."

"Must you do it now?"

"Strange," he mused, ignoring her question to scan the chart's width. "His world map only takes in one hundred eighty degrees, half a globe. Totally disregards what might be on the other side."

"Because everyone knows it's ocean." Blandina's voice was muffled by the blanket over her head as she complained, "Water, Trev. Cold water. Cold icy water, like this bed. Now get in here and warm me up!"

Treverius grunted, rolled up the parchment map, and slid it into its leather case. "There's the funeral for Arbitos in the morning."

"Such a horrible death." Blandina pulled the blanket down and looked over the edge. "You were quiet at supper Trev, didn't tell me much about the accident."

"It wasn't a sight I'd want you to remember." Treverius glanced up at his wife. She wore her black hair relatively short, to keep it off drawings, and the curly ends were secured for the night with a silver net he had given her. In the lamplight he thought her skin looked exquisitely flushed from the cold. Her blue eyes frowned, yet still made him feel as helplessly in love as when she had first looked at him. Was it too cold in the room to make love?

"So horrible," Blandina repeated. "To be struck by lightning while putting a cross in place."

"On a temple to Jupiter. It seems neither Jupiter, nor even Christ, was looking out for him."

"Trev, don't be blasphemous," she chided gently. "Wasn't Arbitos in your cohort?"

"A foot unit. He won the corona civica for saving a man's life, but that was before I came here. Cyril happened by just before Arbitos fell."

"Cyril?"

"That rich merchant, Cyril of Constantinople. Those rumors of his pagan sympathies are probably true. He objected to the temple being reconsecrated as a church and tried to connect the lightning bolt that killed Arbitos with one of Jupiter's old titles."

"But that storm came up suddenly from Goth-iscandza."

"True, and it's never been this cold in October. The Rhine could freeze over."

As if to confirm Treverius's prediction, a gust of icy wind rattled the door of the room and set the flame of his oil lamp dancing in a Dionysian frenzy. He looked toward the iron stove in the corner but decided against lighting the charcoal that late at night. Slipping off his wool shawl, he pinched out the lamp wick and groped his way in the dark to the bed. The mattress ropes sagged as he slid under the covers.

Blandina responded to his warmth by burrowing her back into the soft wool of his night tunic. She smelled of the laurel oil he liked, mingled with a slight, not unpleasant, scent of perspiration. Treverius's arm eased over her shoulder to cup a breast in one hand and gently stroke the nipple. After a moment, when he hardened against her, his fingers fell still.

"That felt good, don't stop." Blandina pressed against him more firmly. "You have been gone a year, you know."

Treverius hesitated. "Did you insert that wool-what do you call it?"

"Contraceptive pessary? No. You wanted to read, it seemed."

"I've told you how I feel about the risk of raising a child. Times are just too dangerous."

"When haven't they been on the frontier?" Blandina retorted sharply, easing away from him. "This time I suppose it's those barbarian tribes on the east bank?"

He reached over and stroked her hair. "I don't mean to worry you, dove, but we don't have enough of a defense to stop them from simply walking over the ice from Germania."

"Can't the governor send to Ravenna for help?"

"Quintus Albanus can try, but it's unlikely Emperor Honorius will strip armies there to reinforce our remote province."

"Remote, perhaps," she countered, "but Germania Prima is the Middle Rhine gate to the Western Empire. It just can't be left undefended."

"Albanus thinks he's been ignored ever since the capital was moved to Ravenna four years ago." When Blandina sidled toward him again, Treverius reached to knead her neck muscles. "He may be right, dove. Stilicho, Honorius's military commander, has never returned our men that he requisitioned for his wars in Italy. All we have between us and those barbarians is the mercenary garrison, an understrength militia, and the river."

"Old Father Rhine."

"As the Germani call it."

"I missed you, Trev." Blandina turned to face him in a stirring of the laurel scent.

"And I, you, dove."

"Whenever I felt lonely, I thought of when I first saw you at the palace in Treveri."

"You had come with your father to look at the mapping workshop," Treverius recalled. "Everyone stopped work and gawked, wondering, who was this slim, darkhaired woman with the serious blue eyes."

"And you?" she teased.

"Guilty," he admitted.

"I knew right away that you were the one I wanted to show me through the studio."

"And took me by surprise. I must have turned red as a pot of cinnabar ink."

Blandina laughed softly. "Not quite. Although my father did after told him I wanted to be an apprentice cartographer."

"It's hardly traditional work for a Roman lady." Treverius fell silent, remembering, then kissed her hair. "I was lucky that you found me as interesting as the work."

"Both lucky," she murmured sleepily. "And we've been married four years already."

"You'll be twenty-two, old woman, on next August first. The feast of your namesake, Saint Blandina."

After a moment his wife's regular breathing told Treverius that she had drifted into sleep. He wished he could do so as quickly, but his mind went back to his year in Ravenna. He had gone to study mosaic techniques for the new church decorations, and came back realizing that the Western Augustus and his government were isolated behind the marshes of the Empire's new Adriatic shore capital. Honorius seemed only interested in cocooning himself there, while hoping that provincial governors like Quintus Albanus could hold their frontiers with what mercenaries and local militia they could recruit.

As the warmth of his wife's body seeped into Treverius, his confidence returned. *We're almost finished with the map for the governor. Despite Cyril, the Curia will approve my sketches for the mosaics. And, Providence willing, the fron-*

tier may become safe enough one day for Blandina to give me a son.

* * *

Treverius was awakened suddenly by a sharp rap on the door. The bedroom had no window, but he saw a sliver of bluish light coming from the reception room. It must be near dawn. He swung his feet out of the warm tangle of bedding and onto the cold tile floor. "Hades," he muttered, "why didn't I light that stove after all?"

"Who is that?" Blandina asked, her voice muted by the bedclothes.

"Who is it?" Treverius echoed more loudly, as he struggled to pull on woolen trousers under his night tunic.

"Sebastian," a voice answered. "Secretary to Governor Albanus. He wants to see you."

"Hold on." Crossing through his small reception area next to the bedroom, Treverius felt relieved. At least it was not an alert for his militia unit.

Sebastian stood in the dim corridor holding an oil lamp. Its orange flame reflected off a boyish-looking face, although Treverius knew the man's age had to be near forty.

"Albanus wants to see me now? What watch is this?"

"A little after the first hour. The Governor is already in his office."

"Has something happened?"

"I only know that his phlegm humor is out of balance and he must speak at the funeral later this morning." Sebastian sounded annoyed. "Be prompt."

"Wait, give me fire." Treverius went back for a taper and touched it to Sebastian's lamp flame. After closing the door he lighted the bedroom lamp, then knelt to touch the taper against moss kindling in the stove.

Blandina sat up in bed and tugged the blanket over her knees. "What is it, Treverius?"

"The Governor wants to see me."

"This early?"

"Evidently." He blew into the nascent flicker until the flames caught in pinewood chips and sizzled into a blaze. "Get Agilan to build up the charcoal while I'm gone. I don't want you to be cold."

"Is this about our map, do you suppose? We are falling behind."

"Something like that could wait until after breakfast. This must be more important." Treverius flicked at the icy water in the bronze wash basin. "Just short of being frozen," he grumbled, then gulped a drink, scooped water onto his face, and dried on a swatch of linen.

"Maybe the governor wants to promote you," Blandina suggested, watching Treverius slip a long-sleeved tunic over his head and belt it in quick, annoyed gestures.

"To what? My father is Mapmaster."

After Treverius finished pulling on leather boots, Blandina laughed and handed him her ivory comb. "Run this through your hair, husband. You'd shame a barbarian, looking that wild."

*   *   *

Albanus's office faced the garden, around the corner from the Asterius family quarters that Treverius shared with his parents. When he reached the atrium he ducked against a gust of wind that pelted his tunic with sleet grains. The pool was streaked with triangular shards of ice. If the cold stays, it won't take the Rhine long to take on that look.

Leaves of garden trees, which had been green the day before, were now black withered strands being buffeted by the wind. Autumn blooms of lavender asters and orange marigolds, wilted by the deadly cold, sagged into drifts of sleet that almost buried them.

Treverius glanced at the opposite wall. The narrow bricks were coated with a layer of ice that made them resemble honey-glazed loaves in a baker's shop. It was going to be a miserably bad fall and winter.

Sebastian was waiting in the anteroom and opened the door to the governor's office without speaking.

Quintus Albanus was at his desk, his head hunched low as he inhaled the pungent steam from a potion in a red pottery cup. Even across the room Treverius recognized the pleasant aroma of a mint and thyme drink his mother made for sore throats. When Albanus looked up, the area around his eyes was dark from a restless night, and his nose looked red and swollen. It was obvious the man was feverish. He stood up, then winced in pain and clutched at his left thigh before quickly sitting again.

"Infernal leg wound's acting up," Albanus explained. "Appreciate your coming so early, son. Old Boreas has outflanked my phlegm humors." He swirled the remedy in his cup. "Nicias, the garrison surgeon, prescribed this potion as a counterattack."

Treverius nodded in sympathy. Sebastian looked into a bowl on the desk. "You should eat some of the millet porridge I brought, Governor."

"No appetite. Can't taste it anyway. You've been in my office before, son?"

"No sir." While Albanus took another sip of medication, Treverius looked around. The garden doors were shuttered so none of the early light came into the room, but flickering flames, from several lamps on a stand, seemed to give lifelike color and motion to a white marble bust set in a niche behind the desk.

"Know who that is?" Albanus asked. "Hordeonius Flaccus. Commander here when he was murdered by men of the Rhine legions who rebelled in the time of Galba. Recall any of the story?"

"Some, sir. Tacitus details the events. He—"

"Year of the Four Emperors. Seditious time for Rome."
Along with his way of speaking in clipped sentences,
Albanus also had a habit of interrupting others.

"But long ago, sir," Treverius countered to ease the
man's obvious agitation. "Some . . . three hundred years."

"Not long to me, son. Constant reminder of how
dangerous this post can be. Look here." He stood and
fingered the fragile linen of four tattered banners stacked
next to the bust of Flaccus. "From the cashiered legions.
First Germania, Fifteenth Primagenia, Fourteenth Gallica
and Fourth Macedonica."

"The one on the opposite side, sir?"

"Only faithful legion. Twenty-second Fortunata suppressed the rebellion." Albanus sat down again and took
a gulp of his lukewarm drink, then chuckled. "The story
still persists that the treasury of that Macedonica legion
is hidden somewhere in Mogontium."

"Old legionary talk, Governor," Sebastian scoffed.

Treverius knew the rumor. "Perhaps, but it would be
a sizeable sum. Booty. The mens' funeral fund."

"Chests of coin to pay the legionar . . ." Albanus's
words were lost in a bout of coughing.

"Couldn't you pass up the funeral in this weather,
sir?" Sebastian suggested. "You're not well."

"Impossible. The man was in the Limitans. I may be
civil administrator now, but with Vulcatius Bassus away
inspecting the Upper Rhine defenses, I'll give the eulogy."

"Sir, I've made notes on Arbitos's military service."

"Appreciate it, Sebastian. And don't let Boreas breach
your defense line," Albanus warned in a fond tone. "You're
my reserve legion."

Treverius was becoming impatient at the random conversation. What did the governor want with him that
couldn't wait until later? He glanced at Sebastian.

"Governor, you called Treverius in," the secretary
reminded Albanus.

"So I did. Go find those notes and send Ursillo in here with charcoal for the brazier. This room is chilly as a . . . a mausoleum."

After Sebastian closed the door, Albanus drained the herb dregs. "Cold." He coughed up phlegm and looked at the small painting of a woman he kept on his desk, then half-turned the wooden panel toward Treverius. "My wife Sophia. Died the year I was appointed governor here."

"I'm sorry, sir. I didn't know."

"Sophia always joked that I should end my career in a warm post, not the snows of Germania," Albanus mused, caressing the painted face with the back of a hand.

Why is he stalling again? Treverius noted that the governor's wiry hair had grown more grey in the last year, and deep creases in his face bracketed a mouth taut with anxiety. The new barbarian threat would not ease his state of mind.

"Well, son, I didn't ask you here to discuss my retirement. Sit on that camp stool." Albanus toyed with a silver medallion alongside Sophia's portrait, then looked up. "You've taken surveys of our old eastern frontier for your map of my province?"

"Yes sir."

"Had my men try to repair some of the forts across the Rhine. Vandal raids this summer forced them to stop. Now I have reports that Suebi and Alans have joined the Vandals. Alans aren't a Gothic tribe. What in Hades name are they doing around here?"

"I understand pressure from the Huns is pushing them westward."

"Huns? You heard that at Ravenna?" Albanus frowned and turned the medallion's inscription to the light. "Can you read this? Mogontium Felix. 'Happy Mogontium.'" After Treverius squinted at an image of citizens crossing the Rhine bridge to the opposite shore,

Albanus pulled the disc back. "Didn't need a fort on the east bank for protection back then."

"Sir, what did you want to see me about," Treverius asked, without voicing the cliche that times had changed.

Albanus turned Sophia's picture around to face him again. "You recently returned from Ravenna."

"Studying in a mosaic workshop, to make designs for the new church decorations."

Albanus's eyes took on the hue of a blued-steel blade. "I want you to brief me on the situation in the capital." After Treverius hesitated, the governor's hard stare softened and he leaned back with a nasal chuckle. "Just impressions, son. No palace scandals, no intrigues. I have Demetrius here to gossip about those. But I need the truth about how the Augustus intends to deal with this new Gothic threat. That clique of senators with Honorius seems more interested in setting up a third Rome in Godforsaken swamps than in securing the Empire's borders."

"I was in a mosiac workshop," Treverius pointed out again.

"I know that," Albanus snapped. "Son, you may be more interested in mosaics than machinations, but Commander Bassus and I are responsible for defending this stretch of Father Rhine. We need to—"

Albanus was interrupted by a knock on the door. Sebastian looked in. "Sir. Vertiscus and Cyril ask if they might walk with you to the funeral."

"When is it again?"

"Beginning of the fourth hour."

"Very well." Albanus stood up. "We'll talk of the matter later. Give you time to think. For now, you and your wife join us for the funeral. Meet at the entrance after you've had breakfast."

* * *

Rather than going back to his quarters, Treverius left the pretorium to retrace his previous day's steps along the Via Honorius toward the river wall. At the Rhine Bridge Gate he nodded to sentries huddled around a glowing brazier in the portal's shelter, then sprinted up the stairway to the top of the north tower.

On the east, dawn had brought a reddish tinge to the horizon, which now mirrored off the ruffled surface of the Rhine in a color that reminded Treverius of a smear of diluted blood. Behind, in the direction of the town, he caught a glimpse of the layer of grainy snow covering rooftops, before ducking behind the wall to avoid a blast of icy wind. A hundred paces away, on the rampart walk, sentries hunched around fires blazing in iron grates. Even indoor latrine duty would be preferable today, he thought.

Treverius looked east again, across the river to the Mattiacorum fort. Familiar barracks noises and the bluish color of the garrison's cookfires were signs that the Goths had not attacked during the night. Thank the poor weather for that, at least. Less reassuring was a haze of smoke that darkened the horizon far beyond, where three barbarian tribes were still camped in the area.

Along the Via Rheni, which paralleled the river wall, the slam of shop shutters signaled that despite the storm some merchants were opening their businesses. Bakeries certainly, from the savory aroma Treverius smelled on the wind, and a few stalls where grilled sausages were sold. He saw a trio of slaves hacking ice off a fountain in the square inside the gate, and heard the laughter of children welcoming the sleet as a chance to play new games on the slippery streets.

In the rolling hill country to the west, black smoke spiraled from smudge fires set in the hillside vineyards to temper unharvested grapes from the killing cold. Even at a distance vintners could be heard among the canes, cursing their mules up muddy roads to save what they could of the frozen crop. Normally, early morning was the time of day Treverius liked best, with its sight and sound mosaic of crowing roosters, carts rumbling over paving stones, the friendly shouts of merchants greeting each other—a promise of another day made new in the flash of a newborn sun. But today, Arbitos's funeral and the double threat of a frozen river and Gothic marauders on the opposite bank tempered his enthusiasm.

Though Mogontium was more rustic than Treveri, the Gallic prefectural capital thirty miles away where he was raised, Treverius had come to realize that the frontier had a raw appeal of its own, in the forested hills flanking the Rhine and the sweep of the great river swirling its way north to the Sea of the Germani. Mogontium had been relatively safe since the last Alamanni raid thirty-five years earlier, but Treverius knew the distant campfires could bring a sudden end to that peaceful interlude.

He turned away from the stormy panorama. It was time to find his wife and go to breakfast with her.

* * *

Blandina was already at a table in the pretorium dining area shared by the staff. The open room was fragrant with the smell of fresh bread, onions, and sausages frying in olive oil. Kitchen slaves sauntered to the tables with platters of boiled eggs and olives to accompany round, crusty loaves of bread and bowls of porridge.

"You look beautiful, dove." Treverius smiled as he pulled out a bench opposite his wife. Ageria had arranged Blandina's hair with a part in the center and a tumble of ringlets on either side. The dark cascade fell softly to her neck, and into the hood of the white fox-fur jacket she had put on over a full-length wool tunic. A slim torc of twisted silver wire graced her throat.

"Look at your red face!" Blandina laughed in the lilting way that made Treverius want to write verses about her voice. What had the poet Catullus penned about one of his loves? 'Godlike the man who sits at her side and hears that laughter which gently tears me to tatters.' "Where were you?" she asked, less musically.

"You knew the governor wanted to see me." Treverius playfully rubbed a cold hand on her cheek.

"Outdoors?"

"I went for a walk afterwards."

"In this bear weather? What is it like outside?"

"Nasty. Some shops are opening, but most people will stay home. It may affect attendance at the funeral."

"You'll need this." Blandina handed him his heavy cape over the table. "Where did you go, Trev?"

"The east wall overlooking the Rhine. I . . . I just wanted to see if those Goths were still out there."

"They are. I overheard some pretorian guards. Instead of their usual jokes about the poor quality of our mercenary garrison, they were quite serious about what it could mean." Blandina paused to sop a chunk of bread in olive oil. "What did the governor want?"

"Albanus wanted to know more about my time in Ravenna." Treverius leaned aside to let a boy set a bowl of boiled spelt-grits in front of him, thinking his answer was not a total lie.

"That early in the morning?" Blandina persisted.

Treverius shrugged, then ate a spoonful of lukewarm porridge and decided to avoid discussing the governor's concerns. "By the way, dove, we're walking to the funeral with the Governor, Vertiscus, and Cyril."

"Vertiscus, the Pretorium steward?" Blandina made a face. "I don't much like him. I've heard rumors that he's an Arian sect Christian."

"A man with his power creates resentment. What's the adage about not believing tales from an enemy's tongue? It's enough that Albanus is satisfied with the way Vertiscus manages things."

"Is it the Cyril you mentioned seeing at the temple yesterday?"

"Yes, and his nonsense about Jupiter may be more dangerous than that of any Arians. I could hardly get anyone from that superstitious crowd to come near Arbitos's body. A couple of women finally took his wife home."

"Poor woman. Trev, don't you think this Cyril seems a strange companion for Vertiscus."

"Going with him is probably a coincidence, but Cyril may try to convince the governor to halt the church renovation. I told you what he said after Arbitos died."

"About Jupiter being responsible?"

Treverius nodded, tore off a chunk of bread still warm from the oven, and used a silver knife Blandina had brought to spread honey on it.

"That's what I mean," she continued. "A suspected Arian sympathizer and a crypto-pagan who might be going to the funeral to cause trouble. Like mixing wine with . . . with this oil."

"Coincidence," he repeated through a mouthful of bread. "I wouldn't make too much of it."

Blandina flushed and slammed her own knife hard on the table. "Why is it that every time I express an opinion, we're not supposed to make too much of it?"

"Wh . . . what?" Treverius stopped chewing and stared at her.

"Like last night," she went on. "We could have made love, but you were evidently satisfied reading maps. Treverius, we've made love exactly once since you came back. Did . . . did you meet someone else while you were away?"

"Of course not, and lower your voice, woman," he hissed, glancing around to see who might be listening. "You know the saying, 'If the Tiber hears your rumor, it soon will be truth in Ticinum.'"

"My, husband, aren't we full of wit this morning?" Blandina retorted. "But Ticinum isn't on the Tiber. The town is Thermae Tiberis, where there are hot springs. In case you didn't know, it's a pun on bath house gossip."

"Sorry, dove," he murmured, then made a feeble attempt to placate her. "'More have regretted speech than silence.' Guess I'm one of them."

"Then, as they also say, 'Save your breath to cool your porridge.'" Blandina wiped their knives clean on a napkin and put them in her purse, then stood up and stared across the room without looking back at him. "Isn't it time we were going?"

Treverius thought better than to voice another adage about poultry, priests, or wives never being satisfied and always wanting more. "It's blustery outside," he warned instead. ""Flip your hood up over your head."

It was a one-sided conversation. Treverius flung the cape over his shoulders and secured it with an enameled silver brooch Blandina had given him. As he followed her to the entrance, two things she had said concerned him. Would Cyril disrupt the funeral rites by publicly trying to link the death of Arbitos with his drivel about Jupiter? And how bold had the Arians become over the past year? Modestus had closed their church, but the sudden presence of three Arian tribes could swing the balance and force Nicean Christians to negotiate a compromise— toleration in exchange for not putting Mogontium under seige. Civil disorder was the one threat Roman authorities feared most—from Honorius in his palace down to the most recently appointed camp centurion.

What a husband dreaded most, Treverius decided, was his wife's displeasure. Catullus knew about that, too.

"'Lesbia . . . stop launching these cruel sarcasms . . . and mocking the verses of the most humble Latin poet read in Rome,'" he mumbled, quoting the poet, after Blandina stepped into the hallway and beyond earshot.

chapter 3

Cyril and Vertiscus were warming themselves at the coals of a brazier, in a reception room near the entrance, when Treverius and Blandina saw them. Both knew the curator, whom they had placed at somewhat over fifty years old. Vertiscus had been raised in Mogontium, but an ancestor had been a chief of the Celtic Remi tribe, killed serving Julius Caesar during the Gallic Wars. He came from the same tribe as Albanus, perhaps influencing the governor's decision to appoint him pretorium curator. As such, Vertiscus was responsible for all aspects of the building's administration.

Treverius doubted that Blandina's dislike for Vertiscus was based on physical appearance, even though the man had a long narrow face and nose, smallish eyes, and thin mouth that rarely registered pleasure—horsish features, almost, with a curious fringe of white hair at the front of his head, blending with a darker mass of brown behind.

Governor Albanus, walking with a pronounced limp, came down the corridor with Sebastian.

"I'd heard the governor was wounded in the Frigidus River battle," Treverius whispered to Blandina. "Perhaps he'll talk about it one day."

She did not reply.

Albanus motioned the couple inside, nodded to Vertiscus, then grasped the merchant's arm. "Cyril. Good of you to attend the rites."

"Not at all Governor. Arbitos had done some work at my villa. Besides, I want to comment on the strange way he died."

"Strange?" Albanus echoed. "I suppose, in the sense that not many of us are struck by lightning. This is my cartographer, Treverius Asterius, and his wife, ah . . ."

"Blandina," Treverius reminded him.

"Yes. You know Vertiscus, son. Have you or your wife met Cyril before?"

"I spoke with him yesterday." Treverius reached for the merchant's hand.

Cyril absently returned his grip but stared at Blandina in her slim tunic, white jacket, and the black ringlets that framed the fur of her hood. The cold had given a natural blush to her cheeks no cosmetic could rival.

"How lovely you look, my dear," Cyril fawned, managing one of his stiff grins.

"That's kind of you to say." Blandina gave him her hand and flashed a smile.

"Did that husband of yours tell you we had a friendly discussion yesterday? I quite admire his spirit."

Treverius bristled. The old fox. 'Flatter a woman and she'll turn fool,' they say. Well, he doesn't know Blandina very well.

"Shall we go?" Albanus suggested. "Be a brisk walk to the chapel."

At the entrance the governor returned the sentries' salutes, then nodded for his two bodyguards, Marculf and Riculfius, to follow the group. He shook off Sebastian's hand when the secretary tried to help him down the stairs.

After Blandina stepped over a puddle and ducked into wind blowing from the river, Cyril managed to push in front and grasp her arm. Treverius gritted his teeth and dropped behind them to walk with Vertiscus.

"I'll keep my remarks short," Albanus promised, as he limped across the Via Pretori to the Alexander. "That chapel will be cold as a tomb."

"You realize, Governor, that the roofer's death was not an accident?" Cyril taunted.

"What? I was told the man was struck by lightning." Albanus looked back at Treverius. "Isn't that so, son?"

"Yes sir. I witnessed it."

"My point exactly," Cyril smirked. "Governor, you've obviously forgotten the significance of the date."

"Date? Anything special about yesterday, Sebastian?"

"The eighth of October? Nothing I recall."

"It was the seventh day before the ides . . . the feast of Jupiter Fulgur," Cyril said with a sneer of condescension. "Jupiter of the Lightning Bolt. You've forgotten your Roman heritage."

Albanus did not reply. *The old fool's gone beyond petitioning to restore pagan rites by insisting his gods have power,* Treverius mused. He wanted to run ahead, wrench the man's hand away from Blandina's arm, and tell him what he thought of his gods. *Easy, Trev. You've already made a fool of yourself today with your wife.*

"In the time of Julian, people remembered," Cyril continued, his tone accusatory.

"Surely, sir," Blandina countered softly," we recall Julian as an apostate emperor who persecuted Christians."

Good for Blandina, Treverius thought, pleased that she had contradicted Cyril. *She's not just trying to get even with me by flirting with a man older than her father.*

"My dear . . ." Cyril gave an indulgent chuckle, gripped Blandina's arm more tightly and followed Albanus to the sheltered side of the Alexander. "My dear, Julian only wanted to restore the gods as equals to your Galilean."

"Theodosius put a stop to that," Treverius exclaimed loudly.

"Yes," Cyril shot back without turning, "and since that emperor's desecration of the Altar of Victory at Rome, the decline of our empire has become as unstoppable as . . . as the ocean tides." He slipped an arm around Blandina. "You can't deny that, my dear."

"If your Jupiter loves Romans so much," Treverius called out, "why did he allow us to be beaten by the Visigoths at Adrianople?"

"That might be asked about your own three-personed deity," Cyril parried. "Surely one of them should have helped Emperor Valens prevail over the barbarians."

"The Augustus was a follower of Presbyter Arius," Vertiscus broke in. "An Arian Christian."

Cyril glanced back at him. "Exactly, curator, and Fritigern's Goths were also Arian. Christan sect against Christian sect."

"The Goths were starving, but our commanders offered them only dogs as food," Treverius argued. "One dog for one child of theirs, to be sold on the slave market."

He knew the barbarians had been provoked by Roman stupidity. His next point would clinch the argument. "And your almighty Jupiter let Valens pay the price with his life."

"The emperor's body was never found," Cyril countered. "Tribunes reported seeing him carried into the sky by Jupiter's eagles."

"Myth again. Our loss was tactical, not supernatural," Treverius insisted. "Valens attacked with exhausted men, instead of waiting for his brother's army to arrive. Hubris ensured his defeat."

"Enough bickering, friends," Albanus cajoled gently. "Let's put this aside for the sake of Arbitos. The chapel is just ahead."

The former temple to Mars, now Mogontium's only church, had been a gift from Vespasian to Legion XXII

Fortunata for remaining loyal during the Rhine rebellion. Constantius II had reconsecrated the building to Longinus, the centurion who pierced the side of the crucified Christ with his lance. Thus it remained a soldier's shrine, and legend expanded on the officer's ritual act of mercy. Blood and water were said to have run out of the wound, as symbols of the Galilean's divine and human natures. Some Christians saw baptism and the New Covenant of Redeeming Blood in the sign. Still others believed that Longinus suffered from an eye disease, and that a drop of blood had run off his spear to cure his sight. Votive offerings were still left inside the chapel by those afflicted with eye problems, and even by desperate women whose flow of menstrual blood was irregular.

Only a small cluster of mourners was outside, huddled together against the wind as they waited for the funeral rites to begin. Presbyter Vetius Modestus stood by one of the four columns of the porch, next to a deacon and the coffin.

The temple was smaller than that of Jupiter but made of the same dark limestone. Since returning from Ravenna, Treverius had admired the builder's use of symmetry and proportion. At the mosaic workshop he had been given an overview of Vitruvius Pollio's chapter on temple design. The Mars temple architect had used the ancient writer's proportion of a column height being eight times its width, with a two-column distance between. Treverius had measured the floor at ten paces by slightly over sixteen—the ideal Golden Mean ratio of the Greeks —yet the upper walls had been violated by windows cut on either side to allow light onto the altar.

Decades of harsh northern winters and barbarian marauders had defaced the building, but the storm softened its deterioration by a partial glaze of sleet.

Treverius was about to pull his wife away from Cyril when he saw Demetrius, the envoy from the court at

Ravenna, hurry from the edge of the group of mourners and speak to Albanus.

"It's commendable you came, Governor. This cold is keeping many away."

"Least I could do in the absence of Bassus."

"Trouble?" Demetrius probed. "The commander has been at Vindonissa a long while."

Albanus gave a non-commital shrug that Treverius understood. Demetrius wrote to Honorius regularly and there was no telling what he reported about Mogontium.

When Treverius looked toward Modestus again, the presbyter was struggling to keep a stole around his neck from blowing off. Cyril released Blandina's arm and went over to talk with Vertiscus. Treverius came alongside his wife and rubbed the back of her jacket.

"Modestus and Deacon Stephan must be discouraged to see so few mourners," he whispered.

"It's this cold," she replied.

"That's a factor," he agreed, "but from what I saw yesterday, superstition probably has a lot to do with it."

"About the supposed power of the dead?"

"Exactly." Treverius let Albanus edge past him to join Modestus on the porch. He saw the governor glance at the coffin, then brush the sleet off letters incised in the oak that should have read IC IX NIKA, an acrostic which proclaimed Christ's victory over death.

"These letters aren't Greek," Albanus observed.

"No, a Germanic rune alphabet," Modestus admitted. "Old beliefs are hard to forget. Arbitos's family thinks the runes will ward off evil. If you're ready, Governor, I'll start."

"Yes, do. Get us out of this infernal wind."

After Demetrius, Cyril, and Vertiscus had joined Albanus, Modestus nodded for the four men from Arbitos's tile-workers' guild to bring the coffin up, then led the procession into the chapel with Stephan. The two

churchmen began chanting a requiem verse, asking that
Arbitos be allowed to live in everlasting light.

When Treverius saw the dead man's family and their
friends hesitate, he went to Fredegund. "Domina, you and
your sons follow the coffin inside. We'll come in behind
you."

Basinus and Chuppa took their mother's arm and fell
in step behind Cyril and Vertiscus. As Treverius guided
Blandina past the bronze door he whispered, "Sorry,
again, for acting like a legion mule this morning."

She reached for his hand and squeezed it. As they
entered, near the end of the psalm of hope, the guttural
Latin of the frontier echoed in the cold chapel.

". . . et in lux perpetua lucat Ar-bi-tos."

The coffin bearers preceded Modestus past the Catechumen screen that separated those taking instruction
from the baptized, then skirted an octagonal baptismal
pool. Its surface was veneered with thin ice.

After the men put the coffin on a sawhorse stand, they
removed the lid and set it at a right angle to the opening.
Chuppa placed his father's shield, sword, and chain mail
shirt on top. Basinus laid a corona civica next to them, the
silver oak leaf award Arbitos had received.

Although Albanus and his entourage had taken places
fairly near the coffin, the other mourners stood well back.
Treverius glanced into the oak box. Arbitos was dressed
in a linen tunic, checkered wool trousers, and a wolf skin
jacket, with the fur side turned inward so he would not
acquire the beast's identity. His broken left arm cradled a
trowel, hammer, and tile chisel, tools his family thought
he might need in the Otherworld. A linen cloth covered
his face, not to hide the burned flesh, but to protect the
dead man from the Evil Eye an enemy might cast to disturb his eternal rest.

While Modestus thumbed through his Mass codex
on the altar, formerly a base for the cult statue of Mars,

Treverius kept a grip on Blandina's hand and looked around.

The chilly room smelled of mold and stale incense. He noticed a starling huddled on a moulding behind the altar, where someone long ago—with more zeal than talent—had painted a mural of Longinus. The officer stood in a stiff pose, wearing a plumed Gothic helmet, a mail shirt under a leather skirt, and Germanic trousers bound by thongs and tucked into sturdy boots. Treverius had seen the mural many times, but the outdated costume always amused him. Instead of the uniform of a centurion in the legions of Tiberius Caesar, the amateur artist had put him in his own clothing.

Longinus held the lance in his right hand, its tip glistening with the miraculous blood, while his newly cured eyes gazed up into a faded blue sky.

"Your paintings for the mosaics are much better," Blandina whispered.

"If I can get approval for them from the city council."

"Why wouldn't you?"

"Cyril is a member. He's bold enough to attempt a vote against reconsecrating the temple. That would include my mosaics."

"But Modestus sent you to Ravenna . . ." Blandina stopped. "He's starting the service."

The presbyter raised his hands to intone the hope that Arbitos would be part of the General Resurrection. "Jesus Christ who redeemed us, give your servant Arbitos remission of his sins. Grant him the promise which Blessed Paul made to the Corinthians, namely, that the Father who raised you from the dead will also raise us."

At the end of the prayer Treverius noticed several men skulk past the Catechumen screen and stand to the rear of the mourners. Treverius assumed they were friends of Arbitos delayed by the poor weather.

Stephan continued the reading. "'Your dead shall live and their bodies rise,'" he promised from Isaiah. "'Dwellers in the dust, awake and sing for joy . . . the dew is the dew of light, and on the land of the Shades will you let it fall.'"

The deacon's message of hope drew no response from those assembled, other than strained coughing and unconcealed sniffling. A few men cleared their throats and spit.

"'Truly, truly,'" Stephan went on, "'I say to you the hour is coming and now is, when the dead will hear the voice of the Son of God and those who hear will live.'"

After the reading Modestus stepped to the head of the coffin to give his eulogy.

Treverius once heard that he had been ordained by Ambrose, the late Bishop of Mediolanum, who had once dared to censure Emperor Theodosius. Modestus served in the bishop's diocese, then, twelve years ago, had abruptly appeared in Mogontium, the capital of a Rhine frontier province. Rumors circulated that Modestus had been married, a practice the Roman Church now discouraged among its clergy.

By age fifty-two Modestus had inherited a face that tended toward fleshiness, with a chin cleft and small, almost girlish mouth. His ear-to-ear tonsure and thinning blond hair gave him a slightly comical look, yet Treverius had seen his eyes harden in anger during sermons. He had evaluated Modestus as a somewhat disillusioned pastor who wrote pamphlets condemning heresy and superstition—which none of his illiterate flock could read.

Modestus began his eulogy by citing Arbitos's service in the border militia, then used it to stress the spiritual defenses that should be raised against false teachers like Arius. Although the Alexandrian presbyter had died seventy years earlier, a large Christian faction still accepted his view that Christ the Son was not co-eternal with God the Father. Arius had been condemned at the Council of Nicea called by Constantine the Great.

"The first emperor to die a Christian understood the danger of this heresy," Modestus reminded the assembly. "He understood what the Apostle Paul warned in saying we must not fear danger to the body, only what harms the soul. My brothers and sisters, I have been told there is a Gothic threat outside our walls. If so, it is a double danger, for these barbarians are followers of Arius, deceived by the false teaching of their renegade bishop, Ulfilas. Ulfilas . . . 'Little Wolf'' . . . an apt name for one who has devoured so many in the flock of Christ."

Treverius was not as convinced that the bishop was evil. Subtle doctrinal differences aside, Ulfilas had helped settle the tribes peacefully along the Danube River frontier, and invented an alphabet to translate the Christian Testament into the Gothic language.

"Therefore, brothers and sisters," Modestus exhorted the assembly, "as Paul advised the Ephesians, let us take up God's armor in resisting this spiritual evil. Fasten on the belt of truth. For a coat of mail wear integrity, and use salvation for a helmet. Take the words of the Spirit for your sword, the shield of faith for protection from the lance of falsehood thrown by Arian heretics . . . heretics who could be among us in this very chapel."

Treverius saw some of the people shuffle their feet, but could not tell if it was from a sense of guilt or simply to keep warm. During the eulogy he had noticed the newcomers thread their way through the assembly and stand closer to the coffin. Now they muttered to each other. He looked at Cyril, wondering if they were his pagan friends, but the merchant gave no sign of knowing the men. Yet why had Cyril come to the funeral? He said that Arbitos had done work for him, yet that would not place a man of his status under obligation to an artisan. He did spout his ridiculous ideas to Albanus. Perhaps there was no reason, other than a chance to do that.

After Modestus stepped back, he nodded for Albanus to complete the eulogy. He shook off Sebastian's help and limped to the left of the coffin, then up the rostrum steps.

"The governor looks terribly ill," Blandina whispered. "He should be at the pretorium, in bed."

"Sebastian tried to keep him away. The man's stubborn."

"More devoted to duty than his health."

"Commendable but foolish. Fever is nothing to trifle with. I saw men at Ravenna die of Swamp Fever in three days."

Quintus Albanus found his place and looked up at the dead man's family. "A grateful empire offers sympathy," he began hoarsely. "Arbitos. Ancestral tribe of the Nemetes. Roman citizen by his service in the Limitans. Awarded the corona civica for rescuing a comrade during a raid by th . . . the . . . Suebi." Albanus stopped, overcome by a bout of coughing before continuing, "Presbyter Modestus mentioned service in the Limitans. Without citizens like Arbitos in our militia, this province would have long fallen to barbarians." Albanus looked toward Demetrius. "Emperors from Caesar to Valentinian defended the Rhine, yet our present Augustus withdraws legions, hoping that ill-paid mercenaries, a few pretorian guards, and the Limitans will keep Germania Prima within the Empire."

"Dangerous ground for an attack," Treverius murmured to Blandina. "The fever's making him reckless."

"You told me it was true."

"Even so, discretion is called for with Demetrius here. I need to get the governor down from there. Quickly."

After almost dropping the note tablet, Albanus went on. "Modestus spoke of spiritual heresy, dangers to the soul. Mogontium also has known civil heresy. The Rhine rebellion. Murder of Severus Alexander by his mutinous . . . legions. Now we are faced . . . with . . . new danger across the . . . ." Albanus faltered.

"Governor," Treverius called out, "you'll feel better if you sit down." He brought the presbyter's chair to the rostrum, then grasped Albanus's arm to keep him from stumbling on the stairs. He did not resist being helped to the seat.

Modestus returned to the altar and asked the assembly to join him in the Profession of Nicean Faith. Treverius thought he had not recited the prayers of the congregation for the protection of Mogontium in order to shorten the rite for Albanus.

"'We believe in one God . . .'" The assembly mumbled the Nicean Creed in approximate unison, citing the role of God the Father in creating visible and invisible worlds, then proclaimed their belief in the nature of God the Son. "'And in one Lord, Jesus Christ, the one-begotten Son of God, born of the Father before all aeons.'"

Muttering among the strangers in front became louder. Modestus hesitated and looked their way, then continued in a stronger voice. "'God from God. Light from Light, true God from true God, begot, not made. Of the same essence as the Father.'"

"False! False!" the leader of the intruders suddenly shouted. "Homoiousios. Of similar essence, not the same."

"Those are Arians," Treverius whispered to Blandina, "not Cyril's pagans, as I thought."

"Jesus was anointed by God, as was David," another man heckled. "Like David, he is only a man."

"Presbyter Arius taught that, being men, we cannot hope to imitate God," a third called out, "but we can try to be as perfect as the human Jesus."

The Arians began chanting the Greek word for similar, which was at the core of their dissidence.

"Homoiousios. Homoiousios." Of similar essence.

The man Treverius thought he had seen before suddenly surged toward Modestus to snatch the missal off the altar. Shoving past Sebastian, he pushed Vertiscus hard enough to send the curator sprawling onto the stone paving.

When Treverius saw what was happening, he shouted to Modestus, "Get behind the coffin! Demetrius, alert the bodyguards outside."

Arbitos's sons wrestled the heretic to the floor, but another Arian grabbed the sword off the coffin lid and threatened Modestus.

"Abjure that blasphemous creed, Presbyter, or you'll die here for your God-Christ."

Treverius knew it would be his belt knife against the heavy sword, and he crouched low as the man advanced. Quickly pushing the shirt and shield off the lid, Treverius lifted up the heavy plank for protection, then stepped between Modestus and his assailant. Enraged, the Arian swung his broad-bladed weapon hard against the oaken board. It hacked out a shard of wood and glanced off Treverius's left hand in a spray of blood that speckled Blandina's white fur jacket. She screamed as the blow staggered her husband back into the coffin. It was knocked off its stand. The stiff body of Arbitos rolled out onto the floor with a sickening thump and the echoing clatter of iron tools.

Treverius regained his balance. He shouted for Blandina to get behind him, then used the horrifying distraction to ram his opponent with the coffin lid. Its hard edge caught the Arian in the throat, leaving him gasping for breath through bloody spittle. The sword slipped from his hand, hitting the stone floor with a ringing sound that echoed through the nave and set the starling fluttering in panic against the mural of Longinus.

When the other Arians saw their leader disabled, and the two guards running in with their swords unsheathed, they dodged back past the screen and scurried out the entrance.

Treverius squeezed his stinging fingers in his armpit, bloodying the tunic wool. Blandina tried to pull his hand away to see how badly it was hurt, but he held it back.

"I'm all right, just a flesh wound. Is the governor safe?"

Blandina looked back. "Yes. And Sebastian and Vertiscus seem not to be hurt."

Cyril, who had stood away from the brawl, taunted, "It seems that others aside from Jupiter are displeased with your presbyter."

Treverius ignored him to check on Modestus. The man was pale as the vellum sheets in the Mass book he clutched against his chest. "Did you know those men, Presbyter?"

"Some . . . some of the Arians I mentioned."

"They've become this bold?" Blandina asked.

"I closed their church here last year. Thought . . . most had gone up the river into Germania Secunda." Modestus stared beyond the open door in the front of the chapel. "The fact that there are several thousand fellow heretics among those Gothic tribes across the Rhine has made them bolder. If this could happen today, then God help us when the river freezes over!"

chapter 4

Treverius and his visitors, Modestus and Vertiscus, watched as Blandina mashed dried yarrow leaves into warm lard as an ointment.

"Thank Longinus that your hand was spared or your drawing days might be over," she said, spreading the salve over her husband's fingers.

"Then you could make all the maps," Treverius quipped. "I taught you so well that no one can tell our work apart."

"You were fortunate, young man," Modestus agreed. "That heretic's blow only scraped flesh off your fingers. I . . . I'm grateful you intervened."

"Governor Albanus would also like to extend his thanks for what you did," Vertiscus added.

"How is he this morning, curator?"

"Feverish. Nicias is treating him with some foul-smelling mustard concoction."

"The governor was limping badly when he went to the rostrum," Blandina recalled.

"His old leg injury flares up from time to time," Vertiscus explained. "Eleven years ago Albanus took an arrow in the thigh at the Frigidus River battle. Sebastian got him away. Saved his life."

"And how are you, sir?" Treverius asked Vertiscus. "I recall you were shoved down, but it all happened so fast."

"It will take more than a heretic's push to break these bones." Vertiscus pulled up a sleeve of his tunic, displaying purple bruises on his arm.

"Presbyter," Blandina said, "you pointed out in your eulogy that the teachings of Arius were condemned."

"They are, young woman, but some, like those Goths across the Rhine, still persist in denying Christ's full divinity."

"I suppose it's easier for barbarians to accept a God-like man, rather than a God who became man."

Modestus looked up sharply at Treverius. Blandina broke an awkward interval of silence that followed. "Did you find out the man's name, Presbyter? Where he's from?"

"He won't be telling us very soon. Your husband caught him in the throat."

"I'm sorry for that," Treverius said.

"Don't be!" Modestus made an impatient gesture. "These dissenters are Satans sowing weeds among the good seed."

"With respect, Presbyter," Treverius ventured, "I believe Cyril is a more immediate threat. His influence could stop work at the temple. After the accident he implied that Jupiter caused the roofer's death."

"Pagan stupidity," Modestus objected. "Resentment by their priests over loss of power. That Frigidus River action you mentioned, curator, was the last battle between pagan and Christian armies. Emperor Theodosius gained his miraculous victory through Divine intervention."

Treverius said nothing but recalled that his tutor, Serenus, had had a more secular explanation of the event. The Bora, a cyclonic wind peculiar to the mountainous battle site, suddenly materialized, sweeping down dust and debris, which blinded the pagan legions. Theodosius had used the tactical advantage to clinch victory; yet after his near defeat the day before, he truly had considered it an act of God's favor.

Blandina set aside the ointment bowl. "I'll bandage your fingers now, Trev. Hold your hand still."

While she wound a woolen strip around her husband's fingers, Vertiscus examined his bruises again. Modestus stood to look at books on a shelf in the simply furnished room. Aside from the bed, where Treverius lay propped by pillows, a clothes chest stood against one wall. On top were two bronze oil lamps and towels for the nearby wash basin. The stool where Vertiscus sat had been joined by a high-back wicker armchair for Modestus, taken from the reception room. An iron stove in the corner radiated a warmth that contrasted with the cold whistle of the wind in the outside corridor.

Treverius noticed Modestus skim past the *Geographia* of Claudius Ptolemy, Julius Caesar's *De Bello Gallico*, the *Germania* of Cornelius Tacitus, then thumb through the pages of a history of the Church by Bishop Eusebius.

Modestus looked up. "I'm surprised you own this, young man."

"It belongs to me, Presbyter," Blandina said, correcting his assumption. "A gift from my father. He's Pefectural Secretary at Treveri."

Modestus grunted, replaced the book, and looked at Treverius's bandaged hand. "You should probably rest now."

"I'm still shaken by the way Arbitos died," Treverius replied. "Cyril said it was the feast of Jupiter, Hurler of Thunderbolts, or some title like that. It's nonsense, of course, yet interesting that Arbitos was struck by lightning."

"Let me give you an opposite example." Modestus sat down again. "We'll soon celebrate the feast of Blessed Callixtus. In his time it was a statue of Jupiter that was struck by lightning." He nodded toward the bookshelf. "Eusebius records the event."

"I recall some of the story," Blandina said. "What happened, again, Presbyter?"

"Severus Alexander was emperor when a fire broke out at Rome and melted the hand on a statue of Jupiter. As reparation, the pontifex ordered sacrifices to be made. While the offering was burning, a bolt of lightning fell from a clear sky. It not only destroyed the statue but killed four of the cult priests."

"Even that's terrible." Blandina frowned. "Are you saying God was responsible?"

"They were pagans, my dear," Modestus hedged, "but it's not the end of the story. Who do you suppose was blamed for that coincidence?"

"Wasn't it the Christians in Rome?"

"Exactly, young woman. And Callixtus was martyred."

"But why would Cyril want to revive the worship of Jupiter, of a . . . a statue?" Treverius asked.

"Power, as I said earlier." Modestus snorted in contempt. "Let his pagan priests taste the bitter gall they once gave us."

"I have no particular sympathy for pagans," Vertiscus interjected, "but it does seem that Rome has faired badly since you presbyters advised our legions to 'turn the other cheek,' as the Galilean taught."

"So pagans maintain," Modestus replied, "but an African bishop at Hippo is compiling notes to refute the charge that Christians are responsible for Rome's decline."

"But look at our garrison here," Vertiscus persisted. "Poor morale, no place for the men to experience fraternal or spiritual advancement, as there was in the old legions."

Before Modestus could protest, Agilan entered and said that a man had come to see Treverius. David ben Zadok, son of the rabbi of Mogontium's Judean community, stepped in behind the boy. David nodded to the visitors, handed Blandina a covered dish, then grasped Treverius's wrist.

"How are you my foolish friend? I heard you tried to challenge a steel blade with your bare hand."

"Not quite, but thanks for being concerned." At twenty-seven, David was only two years older than Treverius, but his curly black hair and well-trimmed beard already hosted a scattering of white strands. "Take off your cape, David. How are your parents?"

"Fairly well." He unclasped a plain brooch and set his cloak of the edge of the bed. "Mother isn't fond of this cold, even though she's lived here long enough to get used to bad weather."

"And Penina?" Blandina asked.

"My wife is fine." He uncovered the sweet wine cakes he had brought. "She asked that I give you these, Treverius."

"Mmm, more than worth a few scraped fingers. Pass them around. Blandina, some Mosella wine perhaps?"

"Where's your mother?" she asked Agilan, who had lingered by the door. "Never mind, I'll bring a flagon. Come along, child. You're old enough to carry the cups."

After Blandina left, David looked at the two vistors. "Presbyter. Curator. I'm not intruding?"

"No, no," Treverius assured him. "We were just speculating on whether the lightning bolt that killed Arbitos was a coincidence, or the act of a god as Cyril claims."

"Some of what he said got to our side of town."

"David, does your Hebrew God use signs like that?" Treverius asked.

"Signs?" After a moment's hesitation, he replied, "Adonai, our God, as you say, was manifested in thunder and lightning when he gave Moses the Torah . . . our Law . . . on Sinai."

"The God of Moses is the God of Christ," Modestus added. "Perhaps we'll understand this better after Jerome finishes his translation of the Hebrew Covenant."

Treverius knew that David did not necessarily agree. He had discussed his people's view of Christians with Treverius, expressing puzzlement that they accepted a Judean carpenter from Nazareth as their concept of the Messiah. What had David called Christ? Jeshua ben Josep? He'd remarked that his people were still being blamed for the carpenter's crucifixion."Who were the men who caused trouble at the funeral?" David asked, changing the conversation.

"Heretics," Modestus snapped. "Dupes of Arius."

"Arians did disrupt the service," Treverius admitted, "but Cyril is trying to emulate his old commander, Julian, by being as serious about restoring paganism."

"Julian?" David whistled in surprise. "I know the late emperor is anathema to Christians, but we Hebrews respect him. He restored some of our citizenship rights and began to rebuild the Temple at Jerusalem."

"The Apostate was motivated by hubris." Modestus scowled. "Even the historian Marcellus admits that it was a vice of his hero."

"But the Judean has a point," Vertiscus agreed. "People are searching for the same stability they had under the old gods. Marcellinus thinks our disaster at Adrianople that we discussed on the way to the chapel was just another defeat, like Cannae, and that Rome will recover. But where are the Romans in our legions? Recruits are all barbarians now."

"They have been for some time, sir," Treverius pointed out. "From necessity."

"Yes, and the proverb goes, 'Trust not new friends or old enemies,'" Vertiscus warned. "Did you see the Goths' campfire smoke again this morning? Thousands are out there we hear, waiting for the opportunity to invade this province. All Gaul would be next."

"And Stilicho has not returned the men he levied for his war against the Ostrogoths," Modestus said. "Your unit is down to how many men, Treverius?"

"Cohort Falco? Half-strength. Perhaps a hundred fifty men."

"An alliance of these barbarian Arians and pagans would threaten the province." Modestus brushed at his tonsure, nervous. "Indeed . . . indeed, the entire Western empire."

Treverius sensed the unease in the room. "Presbyter, I had hoped to tell you about other ideas for the church decorations, but perhaps another time would be better."

"Yes, but the Curia meeting will be postponed until the governor recovers." Modestus stood and signed a cross over Treverius's fingers, "The Lord grant you healing. I must go."

"And I should attend to pretorium business," Vertiscus said. "Again, the Governor's thanks, young man."

Blandina came in with the wine flagon, followed by Agilan holding a tray of cups. "You're leaving? But . . . the cakes and wine."

"Another time, young woman." Vertiscus turned away toward the door.

"And I'll drop in again," Modestus promised. "Meanwhile, Christ keep you both."

Treverius noticed that neither man had acknowledged his friend before leaving. "David. What did you do to . . . to—"

"To be ignored?" He shrugged off the omission. "We Judeans are sometimes tolerated only because Christians believe our Covenant predicted the coming of the man they accept as Messiah."

Treverius watched Blandina hand David a cup of wine, realizing he knew little about his friend's background. "We've known each other how long, David?"

"Ever since you found out I owned a cartage business and your father commissioned me to build his surveyors' wagons. About three years."

"How long has your family been in Mogontium?"

"The Zadoks? Five or six generations. Actually, Judeans settled along the frontier long before that." David chuckled. "You know the old standards of the cashiered legions in Albanus's office? I imagine some of our men were among the rebels."

"Tacitus wrote that Hebrews emigrated from Crete to Libya. Is that true?" Blandina asked.

"He wrote a lot of nonsense about us. Our history goes back some three thousand years. Fortunately, Rome's attitude usually has been that 'ancient' somehow equates with 'good,' and has left us alone. Not that we haven't caused trouble from time to time."

"David," Treverius asked, after an interval of silence, "do you think Flavius Stilicho will bring back Bassus when he inspects our defenses in the spring?"

"Defenses? You mean our mercenary garrison?" David chuckled. "I hear that now it has a legion name. Fulminata, 'Lightning.'"

"Surely Cyril's doing, after all his talk of Jupiter," Treverius guessed. "His money bought the name, but Fulminata is still a mercenary unit that recruits any man willing to fight in exchange for money and rations."

"And loot." David absently swirled his wine. "It's a joke having Lupus Glaucus in command."

"The 'Grey Wolf' is a bad joke, even if a temporary one. What was Bassus thinking in appointing a brute like him as interim commander?"

"Maybe that the man's too stupid to be a threat in his absence?"

"That, and he was undoubtedly bribed to do so." Treverius munched a wine cake. "Mmm, tell Penina these are good. But, no, David, I have no idea what Stilicho will do. At the least he may leave what legions we have along the Rhine in place. He's slipped units out of Britannia for five years."

"Yet Stilicho's the best commander Rome has, despite Senate criticism at his having a Vandal father and Roman mother. Of course, being father-in-law to Emperor Honorius helps temper that." David drained his cup and put it down. "I should go. I suppose the best we can expect from those tribes on the east bank is that they'll ask Ravenna for permission to cross and be assigned lands in Gaul."

"A frozen Father Rhine is all the permission they'll need, David."

"Adonai forbid. Heal well, friend."

Treverius returned David's grasp. "My regards to your parents."

"And thank Penina for the wine cakes."

"I will, Blandina." David turned back to Treverius. "I should remind you that Nathaniel and I are on the council. If the temple matter comes to a vote, I'm afraid we'll have to abstain on religious grounds."

"I respect that, my friend."

"Thanks. Blandina, don't bother, I know my way out."

After David left, Blandina checked Treverius's bandage. "Does your hand hurt much?"

"Sore, but if your ointment keeps my black bile in balance, dove, I'll soon be able to get back to our map."

"Nicias wants me to alternate the yarrow with a poultice of plantain leaves and moldy bread." Blandina felt her husband's forehead. "Cool, but you hardly slept last night, did you, Trev?"

"The hand. And my mind kept picturing Arbitos falling off the roof. Also the hatred in the face of that Arian who attacked me."

"Try to forget. I'll bring you Ptolemy to read."

When Blandina bent over to adjust the pillows behind his back, Treverius nuzzled her breasts. "Friends again?"

"Friends." She pressed his head against her bosom. "But you do have this annoying trick of making me feel invisible from time to time."

"Not right now." He reached up to fondle her with his good hand, but she leaned away and laughed. "Correct, not now. It's getting close to the sixth hour. Ageria will be bringing your midday meal and making sure you eat." Blandina took down the volume of Ptolemy and absently flipped the pages. "Trev, you talked about how it was too dangerous to raise a child here."

"You just heard a discussion about that."

"Would you want to live in Ravenna, then? You must know the capital fairly well now."

"Too well, dove. I can do mosaics here as easily, with less back-stabbing for commissions. No, I like Germania. Ravenna was . . . artificial." Treverius reached for her hand. "Remember when we lived in Treveri? We found hot springs along the Nava River and made love in one so long that the couple we were with had to come looking for us."

"That was embarrassing. Do you want to go back to Treveri then?"

"Not really. Besides, we work for Quintus Albanus now."

Blandina handed him the *Geographia*. "It's getting chilly in here, I'll have Agilan add to the stove. Let's hope we get our autumn sun back quickly."

* * *

The normally fair October weather stayed raw. Northeast gales continued to blow sleet storms in from the direction of Gothiscandza. People dubbed them "The Gothic Winds," and added them to the list of crimes for which the barbarian tribes were responsible.

Treverius read Blandina the chapter in Vitruvius on the nature of winds. The architect wrote that the northeast wind put the body's four humors of blood, phlegm, black and yellow bile out of balance, so that phlegm came to dominate. Northwest gales entered the chest and brought coughing spells that often made the phlegm imbalance irreversible.

Modestus soon conducted two funerals a week, mostly of children or elders. Snow on the road leading to the burial ground outside the south wall was trampled to a muddy slush by mourners.

The grape harvest was largely ruined when juice from the surviving clusters froze in the fermenting vats. Barrels of beer shattered, as the frothy brew turned to ice and burst the staves. Root vegetables still in fields, and many in storage cellars, rotted before they could be eaten. So many cattle, sheep, pigs, and horses died from the shock of the cold that snow around the riverside slaughterhouses was stained red from the butcherings.

Treverius noticed attendance at Mass declining. Modestus told him that, in their desperation, people were reverting to superstitious practices. Older citizens who could still recall Roman and druid magic rituals were suddenly in demand, to recite spells that might counter the deadly weather.

Soon, animals were discovered sacrificed. At dawn, a time when druids said magic was at its most powerful, a number of cats were found gutted, except for their livers, and laid in a northeast direction on the frozen surfaces of public fountains. Even a butchered sheep was placed on the porch of the Longinus Chapel one snowy night.

Modestus told Treverius he was concerned that the frenzy might climax on the night of October thirty-first, perhaps with a human sacrifice. That was the eve of the Christian feast of the All Blessed, commemorating the dead, but also of the old Celtic new year festival, Samhain, when the dead were thought to roam free among the living. Modestus prepared a homily that cited Paul's letter to the Galatians with its warnings against sorcery.

* * *

By mid-October, Treverius heard that the Mattiacorum
garrison complained about game becoming scarce. The
forest seemed hunted out of deer, elk, and boar. Owners
of a number of snowbound outer farms came in to report
the theft of horses and cattle, or that their storehouses
had been looted of supplies. These incidents, frequent
glimpses of strange horsemen, and the persistent pall of
smoke in the Gothic camp to the east, prompted Albanus
to authorize a scouting party. The detachment did not
return. That ominous fact, and the continued bitter cold,
halted any effort to discern the barbarians' intentions.

* * *

Albanus was confined to the warmth of his room by
Nicias, who forced him to drink enormous quantities of
barley water to relieve the fever. More mint and thyme
potions, a cereal and egg diet, and daily soakings in the
warm pool of the pretorium baths soothed the governor's
body, but it took him over ten days to recover. He scheduled the Curia meeting for the twenty-fifth of October.

Treverius prepared his sketches of the decoration
scheme for the church. Modestus had decided to dedicate
the converted temple to Blessed Stephan, the first martyr
mentioned in The Acts of the Apostles. Even though the
mosaic tiles would not arrive from Ravenna until trade
routes opened in the spring, he wanted the work finished
for the feast of Stephan on December twenty-six of the following year.

* * *

Mogontium's ruling council, the Curia, met next to the
pretorium in the basilica where court cases were heard.
On the day of the council's meeting Treverius arrived
with Blandina. Modestus and Deacon Stephan were already there and motioned them to their table at one end

of the benches where councilmen sat. Treverius put down his artwork, images of holy persons painted on vellum skins that had been laced to wood frames.

"Stephan will help you display them," Modestus offered. "Your injured hand still looks stiff."

"Thanks. It's almost as cold as outdoors in here." Treverius blew on his fingers as he watched Blandina sort through the paintings.

She held one up. "I see you included a woman among the holy persons."

"Yes. Modestus wanted your martyred namesake, Blandina of Lugdunum."

While Stephan organized the pictures, Treverius glanced around the basilica. The narrow brick hall was without the side aisles often found in buildings of the type, but a row of clerestory windows, covered with thin alabaster, gave a soft light to the nave and apse. The sculpture niches in the semicircular space were empty of statues, except for two. One, a mutilated marble figure of Emperor Severus Alexander, reminded Treverius of the hapless Hordeonius Flaccus in the governor's office.

"Did your tutor mention Alexander?" he asked Blandina.

"Of the street with that name in Mogontium?"

"Right. Severus Alexander was the young emperor murdered near here by legionaries who were unhappy with his tactic of bribing barbarian tribes, instead of attacking them. His mother was with him. Also killed."

"The other statue is of Constantine's father isn't it?" Blandina asked.

"Yes, Constantius Chlorus. He was certainly a bearded bull of a man."

"I recognized him from coins my father showed me." She tugged her husband's sleeve as Albanus limped up the aisle. "There's the governor. He still seems ill."

Quintus Albanus, looking pale and haggard, took his place on a chair set on the raised floor of the apse. Sebastian sat at a small table to record the proceedings.

Vertiscus took a seat next to Demetrius, just as the envoy finished smoothing the wax on his note tablet. Most of the pretorium staff knew that Demetrius had come from Ravenna, but little else about him. Handsome, with a sensuous mouth and full head of well-groomed hair, he had become an immediate object of speculation. It was accepted that Demetrius was an informant for Honorius, but gossips wondered if he had been banished to the frontier for some indiscretion at court and was ingratiating his way back to the capital.

Cyril entered with another man and sat on a bench. "Who's that with him?" Blandina asked.

"An associate? I'm not sure."

"His east bank agent, Suebius Nevius," Stephan whispered. "Half-Germanic, and quite well off."

Good living had softened Nevius's features. He concealed a full mouth under a moustache of the same flaxen color as his receding hair. His small eyes glanced around in a nervous manner, like those of a foraging rodent.

Treverius recognized four landowners who had recently come in to have their property surveyed. Arinthos, Servilius, Pendatios, and Lupicinius consulted in anxious whispers, probably about the Gothic threat to their wealthy estates.

David came in, but sat apart from the other council members. Treverius signaled him a greeting.

Sebastian counted the members present. Almost as many were too ill to attend as were present, but he declared a quorum after Nathaniel, a partner of David's, entered the hall. When Sebastian nodded for the governor to begin, Albanus stood up. He winced and shifted weight from his injured leg, fidgeting with his baton of office.

"You're going to show your paintings," Blandina whispered to her husband. "I'm so excited."

"It's taken me over a year to get this far. Despite Cyril, I hope nothing goes wrong."

"This session of the Mogontium Curia is open on my authority as governor of the province," Albanus stated formally. "My intention was to have Presbyter Modestus present plans for mosiacs in the new church. However, in view of the hardship caused to our citizens by the unseasonable cold, I'm postponing that to a later meeting."

"What?" Treverius's stomach suddenly felt hollow. "Can he do that, Presbyter?" he asked in a barely concealed whisper.

"Not if I can protest."

"I agree, Governor," Cyril called out, before Modestus could speak. "I'm totally opposed to this desecration of Jupiter's temple."

"But we have the artwork ready." Modestus indicated the paintings. "I demand the right to show this work."

"Demand?" Cyril glared at him. "You and the map maker are guests here. Speak only when permitted to do so."

"I was invited to talk about the holy persons who will sanctify my church."

"Your church?" Cyril chortled. "The Galilean's followers will never profane Jupiter's house."

"We don't worship mute marble and bronze idols."

"But make a god of a crucified Judean seditionist."

"Enough!" Albanus ordered hoarsely. "Presbyter, your work will be shown at another session. Today we will consider relief from this damnable cold."

"I've wasted a year at Ravenna," Treverius mumbled, feeling as if a dark canopy had dropped to smother his future. "The mosaics will never be put in now."

"No, Trev." Blandina grasped his hand. "You'll have another chance."

"What is your proposal then, Governor?" Arinthos asked.

"First, that we vote funds for an afternoon meal for any citizen who wishes it."

"Where will it be served? By whom?"

"Pretorium kitchen staff. Set up a tent for shelter. Perhaps in the courtyard behind the stables."

"Citizens already have a bread ration," Pendatios objected. "Let them eat frugally, stretch the loaves."

"Other discussion?" Albanus looked around.

"A hungry citizen is a dangerous citizen," Arinthos pointed out. "I would vote for the proposal."

David raised a hand. "It's a mizvah, a compassionate plan, Governor. Nathaniel and I would so vote."

Others joined in a show of hands. Only Pendatios and Lupicinius declined and the proposal passed. Vertiscus was asked to supervise the meal preparations.

"I next propose that Lupus Glaucus and his men help with woodcutting," Albanus said. "Snow in the forest has made this difficult for our cutters. Fuel reserves are low."

"His men won't like it," Cyril called out. "They're soldiers, not peasants."

"Legionaries have always helped," Arinthos reminded him. "Why should these mercenaries be treated differently?"

Treverius guessed that most men had an answer, even if none expressed it. The statue of Severus Alexander was a reminder that legion rebellions could follow an unpopular order.

As the Curia members argued about the proposal, a man opened the front doors and hurried down the aisle. After he whispered to Pendatios, the councilor stood up.

"Governor," he stammered, his face ashen, "th . . . this man has brought word of another accident at the temple."

"Accident?" Cyril sat up from a slouch. "What happened?"

"Collapsed scaffold. The Masonry Master was killed."

"Chrysanthus?" Cyril scowled. "The fool. I warned him against working on a project cursed by Jupiter."

"Deacon." Modestus beckoned to Stephan and pushed away from the table. "We must comfort those who were hurt."

"I'll go too," Treverius said. "Blandina, take my paintings back to the workroom."

"Yes, map maker," Cyril sneered, gathering his sable cloak around his shoulders. "Go witness another hapless victim of Jupiter's wrath."

*   *   *

At the temple's south wall Treverius saw a tangle of shattered support poles, downed foot boards, and chunks of broken masonry scattered in the trampled snow. Chrysanthus's crushed body had been pulled from the rubble and covered with a cloak. Injured men lay unconscious, or sat on the broad stairs of the porch, moaning. The surgeon Nicias was there, treating wounds.

"What happened?" Treverius asked the nearest onlooker.

"The Master was on the scaffold helping take out blocks for windows. The thing gave way."

Treverius looked up. Openings had been made between the side half-columns by removing stones in the upper section of wall. A partially finished window would have been the last. He bent over to inspect the downed poles. Horizontal braces supporting the footboards are lashed to the uprights with rope in the usual way. Nothing seems frayed or cut. Why would the scaffold have collapsed?

"Are you convinced yet, map maker?"

Cyril's voice startled Treverius. He looked up to see the merchant staring down at him like one of his pagan deities.

"Surely," Cyril smirked, "twin deaths at Jupiter's temple in less than a month is no coincidence. First Arbitos, now the collapse of this scaffold."

"They were obvious accidents." Treverius straightened, noticing that Cyril had replaced the medallion of Janus with a silver disc depicting Jupiter holding a scepter and thunderbolt. The words IOVI CONSERVATORI encircled the god's image. "'Jupiter the Protector?'" Treverius gave a dry laugh. "You really believe your 'god' can influence human affairs?"

"You credit your Galilean with such powers. Why not a Roman deity?"

Treverius knew the idea was ridiculous, but had no ready answer to contradict Cyril's point. Christian philosophers had argued such questions with their pagan counterparts, who considered the followers of the Galilean to be apostate Hebrews whose Messiah had not supplanted the religion of Abraham, as he said he had come to do. It had been three hundred and seventy-three years since Christ was executed for sedition, but Church leaders were still trying to determine exactly who he had been. The Arian controversy was only one aspect of the confused interpretations.

"As I have told you, map maker," Cyril continued, less belligerently, "I wish only equality for my gods, not privileges. With this new Gothic threat, would it not be better to compromise than to fight each other?" He put a hand on Treverius's shoulder and forced one of his unattractive smiles. "There are ways in which I would support your mosaic project."

"Why is that?" Treverius was suspicious. Men of the merchant's status did not compromise with artisans. "You just tried to have the Curia block the project."

"Your mosaics would not be in the temple. The Arian church built by Constantius was closed by your presbyter. Speak to him about reconsecrating that building." Cyril pulled back his hand and tugged the hood of his sable cape over his head. "I have a meeting this evening with some men from the garrison. Think of my offer, map maker."

Cyril abruptly turned away. As the merchant picked his way around the rubble, hunched in his glossy cloak, Treverius was reminded of a weasel on the prowl and laughed despite the confrontation. A very wealthy weasel. That fur came through Constantinople from some remote Rus trading post. He watched Cyril round the corner of the transept and hurry toward his villa near the basilica. If he's suggesting that the new church be relocated, it means he's recruited others on the Curia to support his view. His gold alone could buy votes, but some councilors may also be secret pagan sympathizers.

Treverius looked around at the debris, then at the covered body of Chrysanthus and the injured men on the temple steps. Because of the cold, it had already been difficult to get workers to stay on the site. Now if men suspected the building was under a spell of sorcery, they would abandon the work entirely. The thought must have occurred to Cyril, too. Word will get out that he's told everyone on the council the project is cursed. It will be a miracle if anyone comes here tomorrow, even to repair the scaffold.

Why is Cyril meeting with men from the garrison? If he's trying to recruit legionaries to his paganism—buying their loyalty—Modestus's problems will escalate far beyond those he's having with a few renegade Arians. With Bassus away so long Governor Albanus's hold on the garrison could slip. The men will refuse to obey him and follow Lupus Glaucus.

"We'll have a deadly repetition of the Frigidus battle," Treverius muttered as he started back to his quarters. "Us against a powerful pagan garrison."

chapter 5

Suebius Nevius knew that his associate, Cyril of Constantinople, owned two houses at the eastern end of the Campus Martius. One was rented to Gundstram, a garrison centurion, and the other to women from Ad Cornucopian Repletam, "At the Full Cornucopia," a brothel on the Via Rheni.

The first level of Gundstram's house had no shop space, otherwise it resembled most of the half-timbered stone buildings in Mogontium that had not been finished with a stucco coating. There was a shed on the west side of the house, which Gundstram had ordered built for storing military equipment he used in training his men.

At dusk on the same day as the Curia meeting, Nevius and a merchant partner, Hortar, rounded the corner of the Via Rheni onto the Germanicus, heading for the centurion's.

"There's Gundstram's up ahead," Nevius said, glancing at the darkening sky. "The hour is right, too."

"What does Cyril want with us?" Hortar asked.

"To attend a meeting of men from the garrison. He said it was a fraternal club of some kind."

Hortar glanced at the darkened house. "We're not legionaries, why include merchants?"

"I wouldn't question Cyril too closely," Nevius advised. "Especially when he's made both of us rich and could make us poor again."

At Gundstram's, Nevius rapped at a side door with the handle of his dagger. The signal was answered by a burly legionary smelling of garlic and wine. When he admitted the two to an atrium, Cyril broke away from a group of soldiers and strode over to them.

"You did come," he said, grasping Nevius's arm. "Hortar, welcome."

"What is this association you want us to see?" Nevius asked, looking around and nervously fingering his moustache.

"Just a few men from Legion Fulminata." Cyril beckoned to Gundstram. "Are they all here, Centurion?"

"All present, sir."

"Good. This is Nevius, the associate I told you about. Let's take him down to the mithre . . . the meeting room."

As Gundstram led the way outside the other men followed. Nevius watched him unlock the bolt to the shed door, then order two legionaries to move aside an army baggage cart and pull open a trapdoor in the floor planking. Warm air, pungent with incense, rose from the opening. A flight of stairs led down into a dim space.

Cyril motioned for his two guests to follow the other men down the wooden steps.

After Nevius reached the bottom stair he recognized the distinctive smell of burning cannabis leaves, mingled with that of the incense. His eyes adjusted to the faint light of a small, curtained anteroom. Then, the grotesque sculpture startled him. A lion's head surmounted a nude, winged being that held a key in each hand. The coils of a huge serpent twined around the creature's legs until it rested atop its head.

"Wh-what kind of . . . ungodly monster is that?"

"The figure is Kronos, Infinite Time," Cyril explained to Nevius. "His four wings are the Seasons. The six coils of the serpent symbolize the path of Helios the sun among planets. Kronos holds keys that open the heavens at the solstice to admit souls into his realm."

Nevius eyed a banner behind Kronos on which gold letters spelled out LEGIO IV MACEDONICA. "What is that?"

"The standard of an old legion once disbanded for sedition," Cyril replied. "Men were sent home so quickly that the treasury was left behind. It's never been found."

"I've heard the silly rumor." Nevius pointed to another sculpture. "What . . . who does that kneeling bowman signify?"

"Our mithreum."

"Your what?" Hortar asked.

"Mithreum," Cyril repeated. "A temple to lord Mithras. Ours is named for Sagittarius. Rites are held once a month on a day named after Jupiter."

"Rites?" Nevius's glance shifted betweeen Cryil and Kronos. "What sort of rites?"

"We'll show you. Those men from the garrison are here to initiate a comrade into our cult. You and Hortar sit on the two stools."

After the other men took places along the wall, Nevius watched Cyril begin to pace in front of the figure of Kronos, noticing that one of the merchant's eyes was slightly larger than the other. In the flickering light of the lamp flames it glittered like an orange jewel.

"Men, in the past Roman legions were strong," Cyril began, a slight hoarseness in his voice. "Their power came from the mediation of lord Mithras with the sun god Helios. Mithras sacrificed Soma, the white bull, for our salvation. 'Thou hast redeemed us by shedding eternal blood,' the text reads. Nevius, as an Arian Christian you believe the blood of the Galilean is redemptive, but I say our legions have been weakened by your Christianity. What man here would also offer his wife, if his daughter were raped by a barbarian? Yet this is what your Galilean taught. No. Our kingdom is of this world and we will fight for it."

Cyril paused to wipe sweat from his face and brush strands of hair away from his brow. The pupils of both his eyes looked slightly dilated to Nevius, who was beginning to feel dizzy himself.

"The Galilean promised some vague heavenly mansion," Cyril continued, "but Mithras gives seven trials and seven ranks to his faithful. Paul boasts that all are free under his Christ, yet even a slave could rise in rank to be Pater . . . head . . . of a mithreum. Has any slave been made Bishop of Rome?"

Nevius knew that some had, but was skeptical of Cyril's claim. A slave who became Pater would still be a slave after he left the underground temple. Cyril's words were a signal. A man wearing a mask in the shape of a raven came from a curtained alcove to the right. He handed Cyril a white tunic, the floppy Phrygian cap of a freeman, and a golden sickle, then distributed short tunics to the men along the wall.

"Raven is the first of our ranks," Cyril explained while the man helped him slip the tunic over his head. "As a man rises in rank, so does his soul rise through the seven planetary signs."

Raven was joined by the men who had dressed in the alcove and came out wearing masks. Some represented animals, others a Bridegroom, Soldier, and Persian. The tallest man wore a golden radiate crown and was masked as Heliodromos, the personal courier of the sun god Helios.

After they had formed a circle around Kronos, Cyril put on the Phrygian cap and raised his sickle. "Divinity," he intoned, "whom men call Aeon, Kronos, and Saturn, you create and destroy all. You are master of the four world elements. We ask that you clothe us.

"Help us put on the armor of Righteousness,

"The helmet of Truth,

"The belt of Perseverence,

"The sandals of Thankfulness."

At the next litany, the men joined in.

"Arm us with the javelin of Moderation.

"The sword of Devotion, and the shield of Wisdom.

"Permit the lord Mithras to be our mediator with the great Helios. To him and Mithras we dedicate these rites."

"Pagan, yet I suppose commendable goals," Nevius murmured, glancing at Hortar and noticing beads of moisture glistening on his face. "You don't look well. Are you sick?"

"I . . . feel weak. My head is spinning."

"Courage, man," Cyril urged, grasping Hortar's shoulder. "We'll go into the mithreum now for the initiation ritual."

Nevius helped Hortar to his feet and followed Cyril through a drape that separated the anteroom from the temple itself. Beyond was a narrow rectangular cave, some thirty paces long, vaulted by a low arch. Blue paint flaked from a sky studded with yellow stars. Benches were hewn from rock on either side and covered with cushions. On the wall above the seats, faded murals depicted scenes from the life of Mithras, lighted by lamps on the benches. Incense smoke swirled from a bowl on an altar at the far end of the room. A man stood nearby.

Nevius felt a combination of awe and fear at the cavern cut inside Terra Mater. Sealed beneath the earth, its devotional altar hinted at arcane rituals that dared probe into mysteries and attempt to make a hostile universe manageable. He knew pagan cult members believed that the worship of deities—Jupiter and the other gods—matched the way merchants bartered with customers. There was a trade of incense, votive gifts, and prayers for favors received. And yet the litany of virtues the men had recited also pointed to a yearning for loftier ideals and goals.

"What is that altar used for?" he asked Cyril.

"The carving depicts lord Mithras sacrificing Soma, the white bull. Above him are personifications of the seven planets. Their meaning will soon become clear. Now, I must begin the ritual."

Nevius found the heated, smoky air oppressive and wondered if Hortar would make it through whatever ceremony would be staged.

Cyril brushed past the masked legionaries, who were forming a line on each side. He filled a bowl with water from a small well in the floor near the altar, then motioned for the garrison initiate to come with him to the Ravens. Heliodromos followed, holding a flagon and spoon.

"What is your name and rank?" Cyril asked the Ravens.

"My name is Raven. The rank is Messenger," they answered in unison.

"What is your planet?"

"Mercury."

After Cyril purified the mens' hands with water, Heliodromos poured an amber liquid from the flagon into his spoon, then into their palms, intoning, "May the water of Terra Mater and the urine of the sacrificial bull prepare your minds for an eternal rebirth with Mithras."

Heliodromos moved on, asking the same questions of the two other lower ranks. When the Courier reached Leo, the first of the higher ranks, he modified the wording.

"Since your sign is fire and unites you with Helios, your purification is not with water, but with honey."

Pouring a measure of the sticky syrup in their hands, Heliodromos prayed that the preserving quality of the honey might act to cleanse them. He repeated the ritual with the Persians. The last man in line wore a gold crown and held a globe and lighted torch.

"Messenger of Helios," the Courier ordered, "bring the sacrificial bullock to the Taurobolium."

A young bull was led to the area behind the altar, while the men masked as Leo disrobed the initiate. After an iron grate was lifted, the nude man slowly lowered himself into a pit underneath. The grill was replaced.

"Christ," Nevius muttered, also feeling nauseous, "they're going to slit the bull's throat. Initiate the man with its blood."

Hortar gagged and retched a spurt of bile onto the floor. The sight triggered the same reaction in Nevius. He groped his way through the curtain, staggered past Kronos, and slumped on the stairs, gulping in cold air from the shed above. Hortar followed a moment later, vomit dribbling from his beard.

Nevius leaned over to retch again. When he looked up, Heliodromos had come in and taken off his mask.

"Pub . . . Publius Vertiscus?" Nevius stammered in shock, recognizing the curator. "What are you doing at this pagan rite? Rumors say you're an Arian Christian."

Vertiscus ignored his question. "My sympathy if you feel ill. Our incense sometimes overpowers newcomers."

"I . . . I asked why you were here?" Nevius repeated.

"You and Hortar are Arian Christians. Since the Goths across the river are also Arians, the Pater . . . Cyril . . . thought you might work with us in mediating with them."

"Mediate?" Hortar mocked in a weak voice. "Barbarians respect power. How many legions does your Mithras have?"

"You miss the point, Hortar," Vertiscus replied stiffly. "The deaths at the temple were not accidental. Jupiter has begun reprisals against his enemies."

"You, too, curator?" Nevius laughed despite his queasy feeling. "Cyril may believe that nonsense, but you should know better."

"Cyril and I understand that the meek will not inherit the earth," Vertiscus replied, coming to sit on the stairs. "My aim is to strengthen garrison morale through the mithraic brotherhood. As you said, Goths respect force. I need your Germanic contacts across the river. Will you join us?"

"I want no part of your pagan rituals." Nevius stood unsteadily, ready to go back up the steps.

Vertiscus grasped his arm. "It will be too late when the Goths storm Mogontium's gates," he warned. "I have reports that a chief named Gaisios is one of the important Vandal leaders. Hortar, you speak Gothic. I want you to contact him, see what he wants."

"Not me!" Hortar cried. "I'm not willing to be taken hostage again."

"Perhaps these will convince you both to change your minds." Vertiscus stood, reached into his belt purse and selected two gold coins, then pressed one into each man's hand. "I must take off this ceremonial robe now."

Nevius waited until the curator had re-entered the mithreum, then went to the light higher up in the stairwell to identify his coin's portrait and inscription. "Servius Galba," he gasped when he recognized the old emperor. "This is an *aureus* from the time that Macedonica unit was cashiered. What's your coin?"

Hortar squinted at the lettering. "'A. Vitellius. Germ. Imp.'"

"Aulus Vitellius, from the same era. Could Vertiscus have actually found that Macedonica legion's lost treasure?" Nevius smoothed his moustache and chuckled. "For a share of that, I'd even kiss Kronos's ugly ass."

"You do that," Hortar replied. "Vertiscus wants me to cross the river and meet with a Goth who's probably just as ugly, but is alive and carries a sword."

* * *

By the time the legionaries left the mithreum after the ceremony, the incense and cannabis fumes had been vented through a terra cotta pipe that led up to the stove in Gundstram's kitchen. Vertiscus felt a bit giddy, but satisfied with the evening. As he divested himself of the Heliodromos robe and crown, he glanced at the still-quivering body of the white bullock lying by the grate. The gorestained towel, with which the initiate had dried himself of sacrificial blood, lay nearby. Fifteen men had come to the ritual and a new disciple of Mithras initiated. Lupus Glaucus had not been there, but, with the help of men who were already cult members, he was recruiting candidates for the next meeting.

"Do you think Nevius and Hortar will join us?" Cyril asked.

The question brought Vertiscus back to the moment. "If you ask whether or not the fish is caught, then, only the hook is baited. The coins will make them think it over. Have you known merchants who were not interested in making more money?"

"Your plan goes far beyond opening a new marketplace."

"True, Cyril." Vertiscus hung the Heliodromos mask on a peg alongside the others. "Have you seen the new map of the province Treverius is making?"

"No. What has that to do with your plan?"

"It's as if you were sitting on a cloud, looking down from Confluentes on the Rhine to Lake Lemannus, and west almost to Alesia. But my province . . . the New Gothia I envision . . . will not go that far. Only from the crests of the Arduenna and Jurassus Mountains to Genava. Easily defended."

"From the little you've told me, Curator, it's a dangerous plan," Cyril warned. "Lupus Glaucus and the garrison must be with you in this."

"And so we sacrifice to lord Mithras. Glaucus will recruit men through our cult."

"Why send Hortar into the Gothic maw?"

"That confuses you, Cyril?" Vertiscus took time arranging his tunic, reflecting on how much to tell Cyril at this time without alarming him too much. He needed the merchant's financing and contacts with tribes along the Rhine.

Vertiscus knew that his plan to form an independent province had several precedents. Twenty-four years earlier Theodosius had signed a treaty with Visigoths that allowed them to settle in a Roman province, under their own kings. Since then, two army commanders were declared emperors by their legions, but had been defeated with the help of these Visigoth allies. Even before that, Marcus Postumus, governor of Germania Inferior, had declared a separatist Gallic Empire and been recognized as its emperor by Rome. It had taken fourteen years to suppress his rebellion. A bid to be emperor would be suicidal, yet, in the present weakened empire, a break-away province could be feasible. With shrewd planning and Vandal help, it was almost a certainty.

Vertiscus chuckled as he fastened his cloak. He would let Gaisios know what the Visigoths had achieved, offer him a treaty that would make him a king in New Gothia, and his warriors part of a new army.

"Hortar? Gothic maw?" Vertiscus returned to Cyril's question. "Because Gaisios and his warriors will be the determining factor in the success of my plan. My friend, you'll soon have your revenge on the presbyter and his mosaic artist for desecrating your temple. New Gothia will be a step in stemming the Christian tide. You, Cyril, will succeed, where your old commander, Julian, failed."

chapter 6

Gaisios shaded his eyes with one hand, rubbed at an old knife scar on his cheek, and squinted into the setting sun. The orange ball had suddenly materialized from a rag of golden cloud to transform the walls and buildings of Mogontium into silhouettes of hazy umber. Bluish smoke drifted from the city to the southwest. Ahead, bisected by a scrub-grown island, the Rhine River took on a glow of reflected orange. Gaisios noted that there were farmsteads beyond the town, open spaces among the forested hills of Gaul that rolled in misty ridges towards a salt ocean he had heard about, but never seen.

As an icy wind ruffled the back of his wolf-fur jacket, Gaisios sniffed the frigid air and grunted. The weather would get even colder. The banks of the river that separated his tribe of Vandals from the western lands were already encrusted with jagged planes of ice. His tribal seeresses predicted that the broad surface would freeze over within the span of a moon.

"The land of the Romans in Gallia is rich," Gaisios commented, as much to himself as to his companion.

"There are few true Romans there," Hortar corrected. "These are a new people, Kelts and Germani, mixed with the Romans who came long ago."

"I hear they are ruled by an overchief who hides away in a village by the sea." Gaisios snorted in amusement and pulled the fur hood of his jacket higher over his head. "True?"

"Honorius has moved his capital to Ravenna, but—"

"Tell me of these new Romans," Gaisios interrupted brusquely. "Your father was king of the Alamanni, yet he allowed you to become their slave."

"Not a slave," Hortar countered in a testy voice. "I was given as a child hostage after Julian defeated us at Argentorate."

"Defeated? Your warriors did not fight bravely?"

"Our men were brave to the point of foolishness, but the Romans fought from behind shields like . . . like an army of tortoises. Six thousand Alamanni dead were left on the field, and many more drowned trying to escape across the Rhine."

"Tortoises?" Gaisios stroked his reddish beard and picked at the scar on his cheek. "How many tortoises were killed?"

"Less . . . less than two hundred fifty."

"What has this to do with your becoming, as you say, their hostage?"

"Later on, when the Romans crossed the river to punish us, my father was wise enough to make a treaty with them. I was given as a pledge to insure that the terms were kept."

"And you learned the ways of these new Romans?"

"Yes. Because I knew your Gothic language I became a friend of merchants."

"And hid safely behind the shield of their supply wagons?" Gaisios immediately sensed his new friend's annoyance at the rebuke. He touched his arm to soothe him and confirm a rumor. "A jest, Hortar. You were wise, like your father. But tell me more of this tortoise army. I hear Goths can enlist in it."

"They receive pay and weapons," Hortar said coldly. "After they serve, they are given land to farm."

"Can our chiefs become their chiefs?"

"A warrior named Flavius Stilicho is overchief of all their armies. His father was Vandal, like you, yet Stilicho married an emperor's neice. His daughter is wife to Honorius."

Gaisios thought the information good. "This Stilicho. He pits Goth against Goth to serve the new Romans?"

"His kinship with the emperor binds him to Rome."

Gaisios pondered the conversation as he studied the darkening town across the river. Bonfires flickered on street corners, and a softer glow of orange shone from unshuttered windows in houses and shops. Even at this distance he could smell the fatty odor of roasting meat and the fragrance of baking bread. The place would be a rich prize, yielding more booty than all his tribe's wagons could hold. "Did your Alamanni try to take Mogon . . . Mogon—"

"Mogontium." Hortar chortled. "Does one piss into the wind? No warrior wins a quarrel with stone walls."

The chieftain grunted. The high ramparts surrounding the town indeed looked unbreachable. "Who is king at this Mogon-place?"

"There is no king. Quintus Albanus governs in the name of Honorius."

Gaisios threw an arm around his companion and squeezed him in a hug that could turn as menacing as it was now jovial. "A jest, I said, Hortar. You will arrange a parley with this king for me and my subchiefs. I will ask about joining his tortoise army."

* * *

When Hortar told Vertiscus about the chieftain's proposal, he was elated and ordered Nevius to arrange a meeting between the governor and the Vandals.

Albanus was glad to hear of the request. It might be a way to avoid war and replace the men Stilicho had requisitioned for his field legions. He told Nevius that he would meet with Gaisios and his officers on the afternoon of November twenty-second, with Hortar as interpreter.

* * *

The human sacrifice that Presbyter Modestus feared might take place on the night of October thirty-first did not materialize. Only a few bonfires in the hills west of Mogontium marked Samhain. By mid November, the animals killings gradually ceased.

* * *

On the day of the parley, Gaisios abruptly told Hortar that he would go alone to see the king of the tortoises. He had heard about Goths being lured into Roman camps, made drunk, then slaughtered, and did not want to risk having his subchiefs killed. Hortar tried to reassure him but did not press the matter.

Gaisios put on his finest regalia to impress the new Romans. He slipped an elkskin jacket, trimmed with otter fur at the cuffs and hem, over checkered wool trousers and knee-length calfskin boots. Under the jacket was a gilt chain mail shirt belted with an enameled bronze buckle. He removed the cheek guards from his silver-trimmed iron helmet to better display his splendid reddish beard. The scarlet cloak over his shoulders was secured by a gold griffin brooch.

Hortar guessed most of the clothing was Roman booty traded to the Vandals by Visigoths, who had stripped the dead after their victory at Adrianople.

Gaisios finished dressing by securing a dagger to his belt in angry defiance. Hortar had said the Romans wanted him to leave his longsword behind.

November twenty-second had dawned cold but sunny, a welcome respite from the dreary succession of overcast skies and sleet-laden winds. Hortar had a transit pass valid for Gaisios to be in Mogontium for two days. At the eastern gate of Mattiacorum a sentry who knew the merchant eyed the visitor's rich clothing, and admitted the two men.

As Gaisios walked though the fortified camp to the Rhine bridge, he looked around. The palisade was wood, not stone, encircled by a moat, but the water was now frozen. Good. Groups of men in the tortoise army warmed themselves at bonfires, but only a few looked up when he passed. He counted ten rows of wooden barracks, estimating that each could house fifty men. Most of the buildings looked unoccupied. Even better. It was true that the garrison was weak.

Hortar pointed out the commander's headquarters, where the two main streets intersected. It was the only building made of stone instead of wood.

At the gate that opened onto the bridge, sentries checked the pass, then gave Gaisios two wooden tokens with DIES and the numerals XXII and XXIII cut into them. When he asked about the marks that looked like bird tracks, Hortar explained the numbers marked the two days they would be in town. The tokens were to be shown if they were somehow separated and Gaisios was challenged.

While counting the five hundred and sixty paces across the plank bridge to the Rhine's western bank, Gaisios saw that patrol galleys were already wedged in by ice whose edges were thick enough to support the weight of men fishing in the open water of the river's center. Beneath the span, small ice floes bobbed downstream on the sluggish surface. Water level was low from the dry summer. The river would freeze more quickly.

When Gaisios neared the high, turreted bridge gate and saw the crenulated stone-and-brick walls of Mogontium, he was stunned by their size. They had seemed much smaller from the opposite bank. Perhaps the Alamanni had been wise, after all, not to attack them.

The gate sentries were more suspicious than those at Mattiacorum and questioned Hortar about bringing a Vandal into town. While Gaisios waited, he smelled meat roasting inside the Mogon-place, but it had a spicy aroma he did not recognize.

Once admitted, Gaisios saw a large open square edged by piles of soot-stained snow. Vendors sat outside booths, trying to absorb warmth from the elusive winter sun. He led Hortar to the stand with the tantalizing smell. Fat, round lengths of some kind of food sizzled on a charcoal grill.

"Sausages. Meat seasoned with herbs," Hortar explained. "Try one."

Gaisios skewered a link on his dagger and bit off a piece. It tasted of sweet-smelling field plants and pepper. Looking around, he saw houses and shops to his left, along a street that bordered the river wall. Beyond the open space buildings faced a larger avenue. Outdoor stalls were grouped on the sunny side. They reminded him of trade fair booths, only this Mogon-place was more orderly.

"What is traded in those?" he asked.

"Meat, bread . . . wine, food. Anything you want. Those are warehouses next to the wall."

"Where-houses?" Gaisios did not know the word.

"Buildings where supplies are kept."

Gaisios grunted. He would remember that. "Why is a man standing on that tree trunk?" he asked, pointing to a tall column at the north end of the square.

"Ignorant barbarian," Hortar muttered under his breath. "That's not a man, it's a statue of Jupiter. The old overchief of Roman gods."

Gaisios turned away and spotted a fountain gushing a stream of water into a basin. There was a hot taste in his mouth from the round meat that he did not particularly like. He walked over and gulped a drink. After he straightened up, wiping his beard on a sleeve, he noticed several women standing in front of a shop across the street. They were dressed in hooded fur coats, which looked incredibly soft, but it was their faces that intrigued him. His own women colored their lips and cheeks with plant juices, but these had whitened their complexions and outlined their eyes with black paint.

One of them, whose blond hair framed the hood's inside, waved to him and opened her coat to show a sheer tunic of golden material. Even at the distance he could make out the triangle of her delta, and the swell of rouged nipples that bulged into the silk.

Gaisios quickly looked away. The golden woman had made his penis reflexively stiffen.

"Lupae." Hortar grinned.

"Lup-ae?" Gaisios repeated. He did not understand the Latin word.

"Ulfi, 'wolves,'" Hortar translated. "Prostitutes are nicknamed wolves. That blond one who likes you is Auraria. 'Goldy.' But let's go to the Pretorium. I'll show you the town later."

As Gaisios sheathed his knife, Auraria spread her legs, flounced the golden tunic, and gave a suggestive lick of her red lips. The other wolves giggled. Gaisios flushed in humiliation and turned away. How had the white-painted women been able to distract him so easily?

* * *

As Gaisios sat in the king's office and fidgeted with a lumpish bundle he had brought, the chieftain was uncharacteristically subdued. He had been awed, first by the walls, then by the extent of the town, and finally by the complexity of the king's house. He had glimpsed a garden with many trees, like an indoor forest. The long corridors and rooms indicated a single building that was larger than many of the villages he had raided. Even some of the guards were dressed as richly as he was.

Quintus Albanus wore a parade uniform for the interview—short cavalry trousers and linen tunic under a tooled leather cuirass, and kilt of red leather straps. When Gaisios noted that his own dress was more magnificent than this king's, he regained some of his confidence.

The governor was cordial but formal in opening the conversation. "Tell the overchief we are honored by his visit," he said to Hortar.

As Hortar translated, Gaisios glanced around the small room, wondering if the white enemy head behind the king's table was of an ambushed chieftain. He did not like small rooms where he might be trapped and not have enough space to defend himself.

"Tell the king I will only talk in a larger place," he told Hortar, rubbing at the scar on his cheek.

"Larger room?" Albanus shrugged after hearing the request. "We could go to the mapping workshop. Yes. Wanted to show him charts of the province and the empire, anyway. Impress him with their size."

Treverius and Blandina were transferring field notes to their map when Albanus came in with his guest.

"This is a Vandal overchief from their encampment across the river," Albanus called over. "Wants to enlist his men in our service. No point introducing you, but I want to show him the extent of the empire."

"We'll just keep working, sir," Treverius replied.

"Find that Augustan map of the Western Empire you've updated," Albanus ordered. "I'll show him that."

Gaisios eyed the larger room and lingered his gaze on the woman who was with the man, then grunted agreement.

After he was seated at a table with Gaisios, Albanus opened a cedarwood case he had brought from his office. Its red kidskin lining enhanced a gleaming, gold neck torc whose terminals depicted twin eagle heads. "Local Celts believe this neck ring can work magic," he explained, easing it across to the Vandal. "Protect warriors from danger."

After the translation, Gaisios slipped the torc around his neck, said something to Hortar, and laughed.

"What's amusing?" Albanus demanded, flushing. "He doesn't like the torc?"

"He . . . he does, Governor." Hortar also reddened. "It's just that . . . You'll see."

Still chuckling, Gaisios unwrapped his bundle and pushed a large oval drinking cup toward the king. Albanus picked it up and turned it in his hands. The vessel seemed to be made of thin ivory, with a silver lining and foot and handles of the same metal. Gaisios tugged at his torc, grinned, and gestured toward Albanus.

"He 's amused because you gave each other similar gifts," Hortar said weakly. "Both . . . both involve a human head."

"Head? How is that? His is an ivory cup."

"It . . . it's not ivory, Governor. The bowl is the skull of one of his enemies."

"Skull?" Albanus frowned. "He killed the man?"

"A great honor to receive," Hortar added hastily.

"I can imagine." Albanus coughed and slid the cup aside. "Now. How many men does he have who want to join us as auxiliaries?"

After the translation, Gaisios toyed with the torc at his throat, then whispered to Hortar.

"He wants to know the terms, how much you'll pay."

"That depends on his men. Fifteen, twenty years service is the norm. If they don't want to sign on for that long, I'm willing to compromise."

Gaisios barely listened to the translation. The golden band around his neck felt constrictive, and he had seen all he wanted to see in the room, except for the black-haired woman with lake-blue eyes. He pointed at Blandina, then leaned over and spoke rapidly to his new friend. After Hortar stammered an answer, Gaisios shook his head and slammed the cedar box hard on the table.

Treverius looked up at the sound. "I thought it was going well," he murmured to Blandina, "but barbarians have a reputation for being unpredictable."

"The man is a bit frightening. I wonder what set him off?"

"I have no idea."

"Hortar, is there a problem?" Albanus asked. "What angered him?"

"He said he wants to consult with his subchiefs, then give an answer at the next full moon. Right now, he . . . he wants to see what the woman is doing."

"Blandina? Fine, I want to show him some maps. Son, have you found that Augustan chart?"

"It's here on the table, sir."

"Good. Hortar, tell Gaisios to come see the territory our thiudan at Ravenna rules," Albanus said, using the Gothic word for emperor.

Gaisios stood close to Blandina while he looked at the markings. He had not bathed and, despite his fine clothes, smelled strongly of stale sweat and urine.

"The woman helps make these maps," Hortar explained. "Pictures of the land."

"Her marks do not look like men or horses," Gaisios scoffed, turning away. "Our women bear children."

Hortar did not translate.

"Is he hungry?" Albanus asked. "I've had a meal prepared in the Pretorian mess."

After hearing the request, Gaisios shook his head. He was not going to risk being poisoned by this cunning king who pretended to be a friend. And perhaps the gift of a strange neck band was some kind of sorcery designed to strangle him as he slept that night."I will go back now," he told Hortar, with a final leer at Blandina. He had decided that, for the moment, he wanted the golden woman he had seen near the fountain.

* * *

Hortar had rented a room for the night above a tavern that he favored on the Via Rheni, Ad Vrsam Saltantam. After showing Gaisios shops along the Alexander, the public baths, theater, and wood palisade of the garrison camp, Hortar guided the chief back to his lodgings for supper.

The tavern was identified by a crudely painted sign of a dancing bear. Its front was shuttered against the cold, so the two men entered through a narrow door on the alley side.

Greasy smoke from a pig roasting on an open spit, and the stale smell of old wine and vinegar saturated the eating room. The owner nodded to Hortar from behind a slate counter where he tended wine amphorae sunk in support holes. Behind him, a barrel held corma, a sweetened beer. Another dripped Narbonensis wine from a leaking spigot into a pitcher. Gaisios stared at hams, smoked meats, and links of the hot-tasting sausages hanging from racks. Three kinds of bread, boiled eggs, and pots of olives and pickled fish were arranged on tiers of shelves alongside the counter.

Hortar ordered two plates of thinly sliced smoked pork and a lentil-leek dish flavored with mint, honey, and vinegar. Millet bread and a jug of the Narbonensis wine came with the meal.

Gaisios tasted the lentils, pushed them off his plate onto the table, then ate the pork in silence. His mind was cluttered by everything he had seen that day, but especially by the woman who had taunted him at the fountain. He suddenly pulled off the neck torc, took a gulp of wine, and looked up at Hortar.

"The golden woman. Where does she live?"

"Live? Actually, the wolves' lair is next door."

"I . . . I want to see her." Gaisios reddened at the humiliation of having to beg like a slave.

Hortar bent over to scoop up the last of his lentils and hide a smirk. "Finish your wine. The entrance is on the side."

* * *

The brothel resembled the other buildings on the Rheni, except for a row of closed doors on the second story, and a balcony where the women sat in warm weather to attract clients. Nor was there a front portal. The entrance was discretely located in the alleyway adjacent to the tavern.

Lettering on the wall at the entrance identified the house, AD CORNUCOPIAM REPLETAM. Puns charcoaled alongside suggested the pleasures to be had. ENJOY LIFE'S CORNUCOPIAM. LET'S SCREW! Another scribbling, next to a drawing of skeletons copulating, was a comment on earthy transience. FORNICATING WON'T FEEL GOOD AFTER YOU'RE DEAD.

Gaisios followed Hortar into a small anteroom aglow with the light of oil lamps, and hazy from the fumes of perfumed incense. Several men, who were waiting on stools, did not look up when the two entered. After the cold outside air, the room felt oppressively hot. Gaisios gawked at statuary that showed goatlegged men having intercourse with young girls and other half-humans like themselves. One sculpture depicted a leering, long-eared, horned wizard mounting a she-goat who presented herself to him in a frontal posture.

As the Vandal gaped at a series of paintings on the upper walls depicting women taking dominant sexual positions on top of men, a throaty voice intruded on his ogling.

"Ah, Hortar and his sausage-eating friend. I was sure the fish was hooked." Auraria giggled. "Has he come to let us sample his sausage?"

Gaisios did not understand, but his face flushed to the color of his beard.

"I'm called 'Goldy,'" she told him. "Would you like to see how golden I really am?"

"He doesn't speak Latin," Hortar said. "Has no idea what you're saying."

"Treveri? Some Celtic, at least?"

"He only knows Gothic. I translate for him."

"No matter, our services require little rhetoric." Auraria winced and touched her nose. "Tell him he smells like a sewer, that he'll have to bathe first. I wouldn't even assign old Eurycleia to someone who stinks worse than Pan's goat."

After Hortar cleared his throat and translated as diplomatically as he could, Gaisios nodded a reluctant assent to the bath.

He thought there was something woman-like in the manner of the two men who washed him in a bronze tub, but submitted to their scraping and oiling. After Gaisios was dried and fitted with a ridiculously short tunic, Auraria appeared at the door of the room with Hortar.

"That's better. Tell him to come and choose what he wants from the lamps. Hortar, I assume you'll be paying? A silver half-siliqua, plus a follis for the bath and tunic."

Hortar counted out the two coins, muttering a complaint about the excessive price.

"I'll give him Hagnia," Auraria said. "She doesn't talk much either."

When Auraria led Gaisios into a small cubicle furnished with only a narrow couch, a thin, dark-haired girl was crouched over a basin, washing herself after an encounter.

"I've brought you a barbarian, Hagnia, but he's paid well. Have him point to what he wants."

While Hagnia quickly dried herself, Gaisios noticed that her black eye paint was smudged, and the white face powder creased by wrinkles on her forehead and around her mouth. She stood and smiled wanly, then took him by the hand and led him to a ledge, where the flames of six oil lamps flickered wildly in the sudden stirring of air.

Gaisios was puzzled when Hagnia giggled, took his index finger in hers and placed it on each lamp in turn.

"Epeléxe mia lamba," she said in Greek. "Choose a lamp. What do you want me to do?"

Confused, Gaisios studied the human figures molded into the clay tops, then realized each of the six showed couples in different sexual positions, from fellatio to sodomy. He suddenly understood what Hagnia had asked and looked back in alarm. But Hortar was not in the room.

He felt ill. The wine at supper, the thin painted woman, the heat in the small room, and its sweet smell nauseated him. Feeling close to panic in the confining space, Gaisios shoved Hagnia aside and ran back to the anteroom. With his penis visible in a state of erection, under the hem of the skimpy tunic, he was followed by the humiliating laughter of the waiting men as he bolted out the door.

Gaisios was in the alleyway. Shamed and uncertain of where to go, he turned to the right and saw that the alley led to the street that followed the river wall. He dashed toward the open space, paused to scan the deserted Via Rheni, then spotted a small door in the wall masonry. Running to the portal, Gaisios forced its securing beam off the brackets and stumbled though the opening.

He was on the wharf.

Two buildings were silhouetted in the bright moonlight. Beyond them and a stretch of shimmering white shore ice, he saw open water in the center of the Rhine that reflected broken dashes of moonlight on its choppy surface. Gaisios stumbled to the edge of the stone dock and leaned over the water to retch. But the acrid bile stuck halfway up his throat.

Directly below, under a thin glaze of ice, he saw a ghostly face staring back at him. Its white eyes were open in a sightless gaze. Blond strands of hair undulated eerily with the current—a ghostly frame for the drowned man's pale, puffy features.

chapter 7

The report of Clement's drowning was known before the end of Mass that morning. Catechumens in the assembly, who were not baptized and had left before the Credo, soon returned to gossip that night guards had pulled the bargeman's body from the river, and arrested a visiting Goth.

* * *

After the service Treverius's parents, Junius and Margarita, had invited Modestus to eat dinner with the family. The presbyter arrived at their quarters in the pretorium during the short winter tenth hour, before it became too dark outside.

"My father is talking to Macrianus, the judicial magistrate," Treverius told Modestus as Blandina offered him an aperitivus, a silver cup of wine flavored with wormwood, bay, and mastic.

"Yes, Macrianus asked me for permission to visit the drowning scene on the Lord's Day," Modestus said. "I agreed because of the nature of the accident."

"Horrible," Blandina commented, her brow wrinkling above blue eyes. "Do you know who the man was, Trev?"

"Father said it was Clement, a bargemen who travels between here and Colonia. We hired him in the past to take surveying wagons up to Confluentes. He's lived alone on his boat since his wife died."

"What exactly happened?" Modestus asked. "I presume it was an accident."

"It looks like that. The Catechumens reported that Clement's foot was tangled in a loop of rope with an anchor on the end. He must have been trying to push off and slipped."

"Is it true that the Goth we saw with the governor found Clement's body?" Blandina asked.

"So it seems," Treverius replied. "He's being held as a suspect in the death."

"The way he stared at me yesterday was frightening." Blandina shuddered and turned to set dishes on the table.

"You met this barbarian?" Modestus put down his cup and leaned forward in his chair. "Where? What was he doing here?"

"From what I overheard he wanted to enlist some of his men in our garrison," Treverius said. "I forget the chieftain's name but Albanus showed him the map room. It doesn't make sense. Why would he murder anyone?"

"The man's temper flared up during the meeting with the governor," Blandina called over. "He may have quarreled with Clement over something."

"Where is this Goth now?"

"Under guard in one of the reception rooms, Presbyter. Macrianus's interrogators want to talk with him."

"Tomorrow," Modestus emphasized, "not on the Lord's Day. And I don't like the idea of Arian Goths becoming part of our garrison."

"Nothing was decided. And Hortar reported that the man was too sick to kill anyone. Especially in that ridiculously short tunic from the brothel."

Blandina stared at her husband with a frown. "Treverius, how would you know it came from there?"

"Ah . . . I think the Catechumens mentioned it, dove . . ." Treverius was glad the door opened and his father came in.

"Presbyter." Junius slipped off his cloak and extended a hand. "I'm pleased you could dine with us."

"A chance to get better acquainted." Modestus returned the grip. "I only know that you came here from Treveri. Were you born there?"

"At Rome, actually," Junius replied. "My father obtained an appointment to the imperial cartography school for me. After working in Mediolanum I was sent to Treveri. I began training my son there when he was eleven years old."

"And you taught me well." Treverius smiled at his father. At age fifty-five Junius combed his greying hair forward in the old Roman style, but affected the beard worn by most men living on the frontier. Years of hunching over mapping tables had left him with a slight stoop and a perpetual squint.

"Wine, father?" Blandina handed Junius a cup. "We brought you a pitcher of last year's Mosella."

"Fine. Presbyter, Macrianus is grateful you gave him permission to visit the wharf where Clement drowned."

"'The Sabbath was made for man,'" Modestus quoted. "Did he find anything suspicious about the death?"

"No, he concluded it was accidental. Clement probably slipped trying to push off into open water. Health, Presbyter." Junius took a sip of wine, then continued, "The river near the mill wheels is kept free of ice, but the chopping crews sleep like the blessed dead. They claim to have heard nothing, nor to have seen a body there earlier."

"I'm becoming a little skeptical of the accident theory," Treverius said. "Even if Clement wanted to get his barge into the open water at the center of the river, he wouldn't have been doing it on the Lord's Day."

"Certainly not at that late hour," Blandina agreed. "It would be too dangerous."

"True." Modestus put down his wine and ran a hand through his thinning hair. "I've made an unusual connection with the date. November twenty-first is the feast of Blessed Clement, third Bishop of Rome after Peter. I prayed to his memory this morning at Mass."

"The same name? That is an unlikely coincidence."

"Even more so, young man," Modestus added. "Clement was martyred by having an anchor tied to him and drowned."

"What?" The death reminded Treverius of another accident. "Presbyter, remember that mason who was killed in the scaffold collapse at the temple?"

"Chrysanthus?"

"That's the name. You commented at the funeral that he died on his namesake's day. That makes three coincidences if you count Arbitos being killed on the festival of Jupiter."

"Blessed Clement was martyred for refusing to sacrifice to pagan gods." Modestus's green eyes narrowed. "What are you implying, young man?"

"Probably nothing, Presbyter, but Cyril of Constantinople is telling everyone that the temple deaths weren't accidents."

"Cyril is a rich old fool steeped in error, a frustrated relic of pagan Rome. I need to find out who these Arian sympathizers are."

"I didn't tell you," Treverius said, "but after the October Curia meeting, Cyril told me he would support our mosiacs if they were put in the old Arian church, instead of the temple."

"Arrogance is the child of wealth," Modestus snapped. "Does that pagan believe he can dictate to me?"

"I didn't think you would—"

Treverius was interrupted as his mother entered the room. Margarita wore a plain wool tunic with a white fringed shawl wrapped around her shoulders. Her only ornament was a ringlet of freshwater pearls circling a braid at the back of her hair.

"Domina Asteria." Modestus stood up. "I'm grateful for your invitation."

"Please, the honor is ours, Presbyter." She looked at his cup. "Have you wine?"

"Yes, Christ reward you. We were talking about your husband's background. You're also from Rome, Domina?"

"No, from Treveri. I met Junius there." Margarita indicated the curtained entrance to the triclinium. "We can go into the dining room now. Bertra will bring in barley soup. I'm afraid we're only having chicken after that. Markets are not well stocked because the cold has rotted harvests."

"Don't apologize, mother," Blandina said, smiling. "Trev wishes I could make anything taste as good as you do."

Bertra came from the kitchen holding a covered pan. Treverius pushed the curtain aside. His father's quarters were a mirror image of his own, except for the furnishings. Junius's dinner guests sat on comfortable, round-backed chairs, and ate from dishes on a marble-topped table, not the narrow benches and trestle board in Blandina's dining room. The wall was decorated with a scene of an ancient villa along the Mosella River near Treveri. Treverius liked to speculate that it might have been the estate where Livia, the wife of Augustus Caesar, had retreated to escape Rome's summer heat.

Bertra ladled a thick soup of spelt grits and minced pork brain into red pottery bowls. Margarita watched her son try a spoonful. "Is the fennel right? Not too strong?"

"It's fine mother," Treverius assured her. "Sit down and enjoy this with us."

"The pottage is excellent, Domina," Modestus praised, then turned to Junius. "It's unfortunate your son couldn't show the Curia his paintings for the new church mosaics. I'll insist we be allowed to do so at the December eight meeting."

"I'm sure they'll look at Trev's work this time," Blandina said.

"What's the theme, son, since you're not interested in drawing maps anymore?" Junius asked bluntly, without looking up from his bowl.

"I'm still interested, father." Is he going to start again? "It's just that you were taught to draw strip maps. They're fine for diagramming distances between towns—"

"Glad you approve."

"Hear me out. Strip maps give a limited view. A Ptolemaic projection shows latitude and longitude. More accurate land features."

"And when was the last time it was safe enough to cross the Rhine and survey these wonderful features?"

"Junius, the Presbyter is a guest," Margarita broke in gently. "Is this a time to discuss work differences?"

"No, my dear, it isn't." Junius glanced at Treverius with his habitual squint. "Go ahead, son. Tell us about your mosaics."

Treverius looked toward Modestus. "You wanted Saint Stephan in the center, Presbyter."

"Yes. I'm dedicating the church to Stephan, the first martyr. Four holy persons who were Gauls will be on either side of the saint."

"Treverius, have you told the presbyter about your year in Ravenna?" Margarita asked.

Now mother's going to begin on me. "A little. I'm not sure he wants to hear about it just now."

"Of course he does." Margarita signaled to Bertra, "Give the Presbyter more soup."

"What was the artisan workshop like?" Modestus asked, watching the servant refill his bowl.

"Our master was from Constantinople. Since Arch-bishop Ursus was anxious to have his chapel finished, we were allowed to work on minor decorations for it."

"Tell what you did when you first arrived."

"All right, mother." Why do parents forever think you are still your tutor's laurel-winning pupil? "First, we made copy pieces on vellum with ink and colors, then used tiles on practice mosaics. The tesserae weren't cemented so that we could use them again. Just small projects."

"Your final piece wasn't small." Blandina smiled imp-ishly. "Tell us about it."

Not her, too. "It was copy work, dove. Christ's beard-less head in a medallion. We joked that the Augustus could have been the original model."

"Did you see Honorius?" Modestus reached for a chunk of bread to wipe his bowl.

"Only once. At the Vigil of the Nativity Mass, palace workers were invited to stand near him. He gave us a sil-ver votive coin of his tenth year as Augustus."

"Generous." Modestus dabbed at his mouth with a napkin, then accepted a third serving of pottage.

"Tell us about the city, dear."

"Right, mother." Treverius pushed his bowl aside. "Ravenna is an administrative center for our Adriatic fleet at Classis."

"What's left of it," Junius commented, squinting at a chunk of pork in his spoon.

"Our threats are on land, father," Treverius countered, "from tribes like those on the east bank."

"If Honorius has a falling out with his brother Arca-dius at Constantinople, we'll need war galleys to break a blockade. I hear a rift has already developed between them."

"Junius." Margarita touched her husband's arm. "Let your son tell us about Ravenna."

"Fine."

"Part of the city has canals for streets," Treverius continued. "Some of the houses are built on piers, so you need a boat to get to them."

"You said there were marshes all around the city walls."

"Right, Blandina, and mosquitos that would daunt Hercules! Some of us rented a place closer to the sea, hoping the breeze would keep them away."

"Now that Ravenna is the Western capital, I imagine Honorius has begun a building program?" Modestus asked.

"True, Presbyter. The Augustus is repairing the original walls, and has begun work on a new palace."

Bertra brought in the second course. The chicken braised with leek and coriander had a pleasant herb aroma.

"It's not very much," Margarita apologized again, explaining, "The early cold."

"Mother, Chicken Fronto is my favorite," Treverius said to ease her concern. "Tell Blandina how Bertra prepares it."

"I'll send Bertra over, if you want," Margarita offered. "Treverius, you like it with more savory, but my herb garden froze in October. Everything was ruined."

"It will be delicious, mother."

Conversation lagged as everyone concentrated on the food. During the sweet course of stewed pears baked in a custard of eggs, honey, and grape syrup, the table talk turned to the possibility of an invasion by Goths over the Rhine.

"The river looks bad," Treverius said. "Only the center is still free of ice."

"We needn't fear a crossing," Junius predicted. "Not now, anyway."

"How can you be sure?" Margarita asked.

"This cold will keep the barbarians close to campfires. And if this Gaisios is trying to recruit his men into our garrison, it means his intentions are peaceful."

"Gaisios," Treverius repeated. "That was his name? I hope Macrianus settles the matter before the Vandals mount an attack to rescue their chieftain. I think he came here to scout out our defenses."

"Vertiscus said something once about not trusting either new friends or old enemies," Blandina recalled.

"And these Gothic Arians are double enemies." Modestus put down his napkin. "I'm afraid I must go, but my thanks for your hospitality. May Christ return it sevenfold."

Treverius walked Modestus to the outer door, then returned and sat at the table again.

"I'm glad the Presbyter came. He seems lonely."

"Wasn't he married at one time?" Junius asked.

"At Mediolanum, father," Blandina answered. "Before he came here."

"What happened to his wife?"

"Rumors are she died in childbirth. The baby, too. Sad."

"He may have asked to be assigned here to get away from painful memories." Treverius flexed his fingers. They still felt stiff six weeks after the sword blow.

"How is your hand, son?" his father asked. "Healed yet?"

"Practically, thanks to Blandina's care. I should be able to work with the mosaic tiles after they arrive in the spring."

"If they arrive," Junius remarked. "To get here from Ravenna they may have to be barged up the Rhone and Arar Rivers. Or down the Rhine. Does your Judean friend have reports about the ice in those rivers?"

"David? I haven't seen him lately."

"It could be early summer before barges . . . can . . . get through." Junius winced and stood up to stretch.

"Your back hurts again," Margarita noted. "You must lie down awhile, Junius."

"And we should go." Treverius motioned to Blandina. "I'm asking that councilors meet in the temple for the December session. That way they can see exactly where the mosiacs will be."

"I like that idea," Blandina said. "And the governor won't postpone your presentation again, Trev."

*   *   *

During the first week of December the cold became more bitter. On the day before the Curia meeting Treverius spoke with sentries of the morning watch, who reported that ice in the Rhine stretched from bank to bank. It was still too thin to support much weight, but they estimated that it would become a solid footbridge into the province by the date of the Nativity on December twenty-fifth.

Governor Albanus agreed to hold the council session in the new church. Slaves were sent to heat the unfinished nave. They tended the glowing braziers until the sixth hour, grateful to be a bit warmer for half of their work day.

Scaffolding rose in tiers behind the tables and benches set up for the councilors. Workers who ignored Cyril's warning about Jupiter's curse had completed plastering the apse walls up to the ceiling, but the freezing weather prevented them from continuing. Above that point concentric bands of raw brick vaulting waited for a white gypsum coating.

A dull light came from clerestory windows that were open to the weather, so when the councilors arrived, the nave was chilly again. They sat huddled in heavy cloaks, blowing on numbed fingers while they talked to each other, or watched Treverius and Stephan set up the paintings.

Sebastian recorded attendance. Even fewer men were present than at the November meeting. Although he was not a councilor, Vertiscus was there. He looked tired, and the curious fringe of white hair framing his horsish face was more broad. Demetrius sat to one side of him, impeccably groomed and poised to take notes for his next report to Ravenna.

Treverius thought the governor still looked ill, thinner certainly, and the creases in his face more prominent. Dark-circled eyes betrayed sleepless nights that Nicias's sedatives had failed to relieve.

After Modestus signaled that the artwork was ready, Sebastian nodded to the governor.

"Presbyter," Albanus began, "you are here to show plans for the decoration of the church of Stephan, formerly the temple of Jupiter-Taranis. Proceed."

"In view of this cold I will be as brief as possible," Modestus promised. "The themes I have chosen are Blessed Stephan and four holy persons who lived in Gaul. Treverius, show the first saint."

"This is Blandina of Lugdunum, martyred at the time of Marcus Aurelius," Treverius explained, holding up her picture.

"A woman?" Cyril snickered and looked around at the councilors.

"Map maker, isn't that your wife's namesake?" Sulpicius called out in a mocking tone. "Is that why you chose her?"

Cyril, next to Sulpicius, laughed and leaned over to whisper to him. Other councilors behind them chuckled at the implied favoritism. Treverius reddened and glanced at Modestus. The presbyter stood up to defend the choice, angry.

"Not only a woman, councilor, but also a slave. Her witness gives life to Paul's words to the Galatians, 'There is neither Jew nor Greek, slave nor free, male nor female, for you are all one under Christ.'"

Sulpicius shifted uneasily at the rebuke, but Cyril stood, fingering the image of Janus around his neck as he looked at the men. "I'm not only against a woman, I oppose the entire project. But since we are proposing to supplant Roman deities with an invisible God, why do we need these images?"

"The people will be inspired by the Blessed who witnessed for Christ."

"They confuse the person with the image," Cyril sneered, "and pray to that."

"A legacy of your pagan gods," Modestus shot back.

"Presbyter. Councilor," Albanus admonished. "Let us finish the presentation. You'll have your vote afterwards, Cyril. Continue, son."

Modestus sat down again, his face flushed from the confrontation. Stephan handed Treverius another painting.

"This is Hilary, Bishop of Limonum in Aquitania. He challenged Pope Leo, who had fallen under the Arian heresy, and restored the Roman faith to Gaul."

"Reopen the Arian church, presbyter, and put the mosaics there," Cyril heckled. "That should make the barbarians across the river feel welcome." Nervous laughter followed Cyril's jest.

"Enough, councilor," Albanus warned again. "Go on, Treverius."

Stephan replaced the painting of Hilary with that of a soldier. Treverius identified the centurion. "Sebastian was born in the Narbonensis province. I'm sure his martyrdom is familiar to all in the Limitans. He was a centurion in Diocletian's First Cohort, executed for refusing to burn incense to the Emperor."

"Riddled with arrows," Arinthos called out.

The councilors nodded. After Longinus, Sebastian was the best known legionary martyr.

Albanus leaned toward his secretary with the trace of a smile. "You needn't worry, Sebastian," he quipped. "The era of martyrs is over."

"The final painting is of Julian, Bishop of Suindinum,"
Treverius explained. "Tradition holds he was Simon, a
leper healed by Christ and later ordained a bishop by the
Apostles. He's considered the patron of hospitality, because he invited Christ to eat with him."

"How in the name of Jupiter did he get from Judea to
Gaul?" Cyril taunted.

"God guided Julian there," Modestus replied, standing again. "Now I'll talk about Blessed Stephan, patron of
the new church."

Treverius was listening to Modestus describe the martyred deacon when he recognized a white-haired oldster
named Malchus, who had shuffled into the nave. Despite
the cold, he was barefoot, and dressed only in a thin linen
tunic. Christ save us! Malchus is here to preach his apocalyp-
tic vision. Treverius knew the man was leader of a fringe
sect that believed the end of the world, and the General
Resurrection, would occur in twenty-seven years. He
had no idea of how old Malchus actually was. A youth-
ful complexion combined with snowy hair to suggest an
indeterminate age, which the prophet found useful in
preaching his message.

A few councilors, who also knew Malchus, snickered
as he walked slowly to the apse and stood on one side of
the stairs. Modestus continued describing the stoning of
Stephan until Malchus interrupted him by calling out,
"Ye foolish man. Why concern thyself with these vanities
when the Apocalypse is upon ye?"

"Who is that?" Arinthos asked before Modestus could
respond.

"I call him 'Malchus the Sleepyhead,'" Nevius scoffed.
"He claims to be one of the Seven Sleepers."

"Yea, I have proof that I fell asleep in the time of
Decius." Malchus held up a silver quinarius the emperor
had issued 155 years earlier. "And the scroll I have de-
clares, 'For indeed we have risen and are alive. As an
infant in the womb, so we were alive.'"

Treverius had heard at Ravenna that the Legend of the Seven Sleepers was sweeping the empire, and considered it another sign of the uncertain times. Even legends provided a framework of stability, however tenuous.

"Someone escort this lunatic to the street," Nevius called out.

Albanus ignored him. "Malchus, Demetrius has come from Ravenna," he said. "Tell him of your Sleepers."

The governor knows the quickest way to get rid of Malchus is to let him tell his story, Treverius thought, watching the self-proclaimed prophet shuffle to the apse wall.

Malchus took a lump of charcoal and scribbled the numerals VII XL CCCC XXXIII on the plaster. "Seven is the number of Completion," he rasped. "God rested on the seventh day and there are seven Sleepers. Forty is the time of Trial, one hundred, the Plentitude." He slashed lines under the four Cs so hard that his charcoal crumbled, but he went on, "Four centuries have passed since the Nativity, added to thirty-three years of the Savior's life is four hundred thirty-three. That will be the year of the Resurrection. The Apocalypse is upon ye!"

When some councilors laughed openly, Malchus addressed the ridicule. "Ye mock me, but when the Antichrist persuaded Decius to order the worship of idols, my six companions and I hid in a cave, begged for food. Then God put us into a deep sleep." As Malchus reached the climax of his story, he worked himself into a trance-like state, pacing in front of the council, oblivious to everything except his mission. "In the third year of Theodosius, the emperor was given a sign of the resurrection of the dead. God raised us for him to see."

"Theodosius died eleven years ago," Vertiscus called out, "and you would have us believe you are one of the risen Sleepers?"

"The emperor came to the cave and found the scroll."

"And where is this precious document now?" Vertiscus mocked. "Do you have it?" When Malchus did not reply, the curator looked over at Albanus. "Surely we deserve better than that this lunatic takes up the Curia's time."

"Yes." Albanus motioned to one of his bodyguards. "This man will take you home, Malchus."

"I'll see that he gets a warm cloak and boots." Stephan rose and went to the old man.

Treverius watched Malchus shuffle out with the deacon, recalling that the legend involved Church teaching. Theodosius settled a heresy that had denied Christ's Resurrection, so someone now making the claim Malchus did might be ridiculed, yet not entirely dismissed.

"If the old fool is gone," Cyril grumbled, "I repeat my opposition to the Presbyter's desecration. I move that this project be abandoned and the temple returned to Jupiter's worship."

Albanus called for quiet when loud murmuring followed Cyril's motion. "The Curia will vote," he said. "Anyone who agrees to the mosaics must pledge to pay for part of their cost. Those who support Presbyter Modestus raise hands."

Treverius saw eight men agree. After a moment's hesitation in which three councilors glanced from Cyril to Modestus, the men slowly extended hands. Cyril glared at them, clutching his Janus medallion.

"Governor," David called out, "Nathaniel and I are not opposed. We abstain for religious reasons."

"Noted. Eleven for. Those opposed?"

Cyril stood, a glower of defiance on his face. Nevius and Sulpicius slowly followed his lead.

"Three against. The project is approved," Albanus announced. "Record the vote, Sebastian."

"Jupiter will punish this assembly," Cyril screamed, "just as he did the roofer and stonemason. Compared to the god's anger, the 'Fury of the Goths' will seem a child's tantrum." He gathered his cape around his body, then stalked past Modestus and Treverius. Nevius and Sulpicius followed.

"Cyril has let fantasy rule reason," Vertiscus said, hurrying down the stairs. "I'll try to calm the man, Governor."

"Do that, Curator," Albanus ordered. "Have him realize our real danger is beyond a disagreement over wall decorations."

* * *

After Vertiscus followed Cyril to his villa near the basilica, the curator caught up with him in the atrium. The merchant was obviously agitated. Bluish veins stood out in his red face.

"Why are you here?" Cyril demanded. "You did nothing to stop the vote."

"Patience, friend," Vertiscus counseled. "Not a single mosaic is in place, and I would bet a gold solidus that none ever will be."

"And why do you say that?"

"Because of Hortar."

"The Alamann?" Cyril stared at Vertiscus with a gaze he thought as icy as the frozen atrium pool. "What does he have to do with it? Where is he, still among the barbarians?"

"Exactly. You recall Gaisios, the Vandal who came here in November to see the Governor? After the bargeman's drowning, Macrianus toyed with the barbarian for awhile before releasing him. Hortar is in his camp, advising him and his subchiefs."

"Advising him about mosaics?" Cyril chortled at his own sarcasm.

Vertiscus gave a forced laugh. "Friend, have you seen the river ice? I estimate that by the end of December it will be solid enough to support horsemen and wagons."

"What are you getting at, Curator? Have you found out more about the Vandals' intentions?"

"We've continued to meet in the mithreum. Lupus Glaucus is doing well in recruiting garrison legionaries to our cult." Vertiscus grasped Cyril's shoulder. "When Gaisios and his Vandals walk across the Rhine they will remember their friends here."

"Friends?" Cyril shook off the curator's hand. "I agreed to be part of this to restore pagan rights. Didn't you say your New Gothia will be federated with Rome as part of the empire?"

"If need be," Vertiscus hedged. "It depends on Gaisios and his warriors."

"On Vandals?" Cyril gave a scornful laugh. "Trusting a mercenary garrison is risky enough, but recruiting fickle barbarians will push the goddess Fortuna too far."

"You're tired, Cyril, have your servants prepare a bath," Vertiscus suggested. "I've predicted that not one mosaic tile will be cemented in place," he reassured him. "After I hear from Hortar I'll call a special meeting in the mithreum. The time will soon come, Cyril, when your Jupiter will again be worshipped in his old temple."

* * *

Advent, the period of liturgical preparation for commemorating the birth of Christ, had begun the week before the council meeting. Modestus had reluctantly agreed with Stephan's request to stage a Nativity drama, hoping the play might attract more congregation members. The deacon wrote dialogue based on the text of Luke's Testament, and set verses to music. Although Stephan held a Churchman's low opinion of actors, he contacted Petranius, the director at the Theater of Trajan, for help in providing actors and coaching parish members who agreed to take part in the play. Blandina had volunteered to sing in the choir of angels who announce the Christ Child's birth to shepherds.

That evening, despite a shortage of charcoal, Blandina told Agilan to light a fire in the bedroom stove. She had not attended the Curia session because of a rehearsal. Treverius sat near the warm stove, watching his wife arrange her hair for the night.

"How did your rehearsal go, dove?" he asked.

"Not too well, I'm the only one who can read the angels' words. The other women have to memorize." She turned toward him. "Trev, would you be part of the drama?"

"Me? Sorry, dove." He held up a hand in protest and explained, "I'm not making a fool of myself in front of all those people."

"Petranius doesn't want you to act. He thought you could help with the setting."

"Petranius?"

"The director at the theater. It's sad, Trev. He tries to be cheerful in spite of his hunchback and an old leg injury that's still painful. Would you help?"

"Blandina, when you look at me like that, I'd swim the River Styx if you asked. What would it involve?"

"Read Luke's description. Petranius wants that kind of outdoor scene."

"In the Longinus chapel?" he objected. "That's too small a space."

"The Vigil Mass will be celebrated there, but the drama will begin in the temple. Afterwards, we'll have a procession to the chapel."

"Old Malchus came to the temple while we were showing my work."

"Still predicting the imminent end of the world?"

Treverius nodded. "The governor let Malchus talk, but Cyril forced him to be taken out. Called the old man a lunatic."

"Cyril is without human feelings. I'm glad he won't be opposing you any longer."

"Don't be too sure of that. After the vote he looked at me and screamed that Jupiter would destroy us all. It was laughable, except that he was so enraged . . . irrational."

"That is really frightening. Why doesn't he like you?"

"Modestus suggested that my artwork threatens his influence in recruiting pagans."

"But after that vote he should have even less influence."

"Even fifteen years ago Cyril might have gotten his way, but now Theodosius's laws banning pagan rites are usually enforced. I'm surprised Macrianus isn't doing anything, but then, Cyril is the richest man in Mogontium."

"Bribed?" Blandina gave her hair net a final graceful tug, then came to straddle her husband's lap. She had put on a thigh-length night tunic trimmed at the neck and sleeves with a Celtic design. "I'm so proud that the Curia approved your art." She smiled, touching her forehead to his.

"It wasn't unanimous, dove. If Modestus hadn't been there, at least three other councilors would have voted against the project."

"Don't think of that now." Blandina sealed his lips with a long kiss. Treverius burrowed his face into her breasts, gently teasing the nipples erect through soft wool that smelled of Artemesia oil, until he felt himself harden against her thigh.

"Are you wearing the . . . the shield?"

In answer, Blandina tongued his mouth more deeply. Treverius pulled her by the hand to the bed without snuffing out the lamp. For once the room was pleasantly warm. Shadows of its furnishings, made alive by the flicker of orange flame, danced softly on the white wall. Treverius slipped the night tunic over his wife's head to cushion himself in her body heat, and savor the Artemesia fragrance.

They made love slowly, relieved that the uncertainty over the mosaic project was resolved, and temporarily forgetting the barbarian threat. Yet, afterwards, Treverius listened to his sleeping wife's breathing with a lingering unease. He did not share his father's belief that the Goths would stay in their camp. Cyril was hostile again. At least Vertiscus, after seeming to defend paganism on his visit after the funeral, had gone to reason with the merchant. Perhaps the more practical curator could convince Cyril —in his own best interests—to halt his harangues.

Treverius turned and eased a leg over Blandina's thigh, thinking of what she had said about the Nativity drama. It might be a welcome distraction, even creative, to design the setting Petranius wanted. Cyril was still telling everyone who would listen that the temple was cursed, yet nothing sinister could possibly happen in commemorating the birth of the Nazarene, whose Church had discredited the superstitions of the merchant's pagan past.

chapter 8

A pungent smell of pine sap permeated the half-finished nave of the new church when, early on the morning of December twenty-four, Treverius went there to give the details of his Nativity drama props a final check.

He had ordered workers to put yew trees on the bare scaffolding and extend other pines into the shallow transepts. Hay strewn on the floor added a sweet scent to the tangy fragrance of the evergreens. At the base of the scaffold a patched backdrop painting, set up by Petranius's actors, depicted the country around Jerusalem. Sand-colored hills rolled away toward domed buildings visible behind the city walls. On one side palm trees bordered a band of dark blue that was labeled FL IORDANVS. Three pyramids near the river were an imaginative, if incongruous, addition to the banks of the Jordan River.

Carpenters had completed a crude pen in the right transept, where a few sheep bleated restlessly in the unfamiliar enclosure.

High above the dark-green yews, at the top of the scaffold, an eight-point copper star, pierced with holes and lighted from behind by lamps, glimmered.

When Treverius noticed that the actors were about to begin their rehearsal, he moved back to the center of the nave, to get an overview of the drama in his setting. Hearing the front portal behind him open, he turned to see Stephan enter with Modestus. The deacon looked nervous. It was the first time the presbyter had come to see the set and rehearsals.

Treverius waited until Modestus had had a chance to look around, then asked, "Do you like it, Presbyter?"

Modestus frowned and shook his head. "Why so many pine trees? It's a veritable forest up there."

"Yews," Stephan explained quickly. "The Germani worship the tree because it remains green throughout the winter. Their priests consider it a link between the powers of heaven and earth."

"How so, Deacon?"

"The branches reach the sky and the roots touch the Underworld."

"Yet another pagan superstition. I don't like it. No."

"Our garrison puts up evergreens in the barracks at this time of year," Treverius pointed out to reassure Modestus. "Stephan hoped to attract some of the legionaries, which, in fact, he's done. Several congregation members who had drifted away have also returned, thanks to the deacon."

Modestus grunted. "Perhaps you're right. This gives the yews a Christian meaning. Who are those people over there in the apse?"

"The cast," Stephan replied. "Some are actors who came to help our people with their lines."

"Tertullian warned against actors. And isn't the theater in Quadrant Three? It's not a savory part of town . . . run-down shops, apartments. Another brothel."

"The actors will help the congregation live the story," Treverius told Modestus. "That was the deacon's intent."

"It will be quite appropriate, Presbyter." Stephan held up a mansucript. "I've written music to the words of Luke for the angels to sing."

Treverius noticed his wife waving from the second tier of scaffold boards. He signaled back. "That was Blandina. She's one of the angels who announces the birth to the shepherds."

"That explains the sheep."

"Correct, Presbyter. They—"

"Attention, grex!" a loud voice called out from in front of the apse. "Take your places."

"That's Petranius," Stephan whispered. "Grex . . . a herd of sheep . . . is theater slang for actors. Excuse me, I must be ready for the reading."

"Take your places," Petranius repeated in an impatient tone. "This is the last rehearsal before the service tonight. Put on your character masks. Alexandros, help those clods."

Treverius had never seen Petranius before rehearsals started. Even though Blandina had told him about the actor's disabilities, he was startled when he first saw the man limping and noticed the deformed hump on his back. Petranius had not seemed as cheerful as Blandina implied, but Treverius attributed his shifting moods to the strain of working with illiterate citizens.

When Treverius guided him closer to the set, Modestus commented, "Life has not been kind to the fellow. First his hunchback, then an improperly set broken leg."

"You know Petranius?"

"A little about him. He came from Aurasio, in the Narbonensis. Evidently fell from the stage of the theater there and was treated by a bungling surgeon."

"He looks like he's in constant pain. His face is so gaunt."

"Yet he must have been handsome once. That curly red hair, striking green eyes. Now his actors mock him as Gibber, 'Humpy,' when he's out of earshot."

"I thought the subsidy for theaters was cut off. How does his troupe survive?"

"Small admission fees," Modestus answered. "And I suspect his actresses work in that brothel next to the theater."

Petranius looked around with a scowl to see who was talking. Treverius raised a hand as a signal of apology. "Deacon," the director called out, without acknowledging the gesture, "begin your reading."

Stephan squinted at the words. "'Joseph also went up from Galilee for the census, out of the village of Nazareth into Judea, to David's city . . . called Bethlehem.'"

At this cue a man led a donkey, with a woman sitting on its back, to a table. One of the pretorian guards pretended to write his name on a scroll.

"Stop. No, stop," Petranius yelled, shifting weight to his good leg. "You there, centurion or whoever. Talk to him before you write. How would you know his name? This is a census, not a line into a public latrine. Again."

After the action was repeated correctly, Stephan continued, "'While they were there, the days came for her delivery.'"

"Get behind the trees with that beast," Petranius screamed at the man with the donkey. "She's not having the brat out here." He shook his head and limped forward to push Joseph into the yews.

"'And she gave birth to her first-born and laid him in a manger,'" Stephan read. "'And there were shepherds living outdoors and keeping watches over their flocks.'"

"Shepherds? SHEP-HERDS!" Petranius waved his manuscript at several men. "Get over to the sheep pen, you clods. You're supposed to be watching the beasts. Angels up there, get ready to sing. Deacon, continue."

"'And suddenly God's angel stood by them.'"

One of the angels sang ahead of cue. Treverius saw Petranius struggle to control himself. The man should remember that these are townspeople, not apprentice actors.

"Stop. Thalia's Girdle, stop." Petranius's voice had regained a measure of calm. "Your cue, angels, is when the deacon reads, 'But the angel said to them.' Again. 'And they became fearful. BUT THE ANGEL SAID TO THEM.'"

"'Gloria in excelsis Deo, et in terra pax hominibus bonae voluntate.'"

The chorus was approximately together, for having memorized words that none except Blandina could read.

"Good, good," Petranius praised absently. "Shepherds, now the conversations we've added. If one of you still forgets your lines, Alexandros or Albino will take over."

After the shepherds finished a hesitant dialogue about the miraculous event, with stammering, missed cues, and frequent fill-in by the two actors, Petranius was ready to assemble the group for the procession to the Longinus Chapel. He motioned to Albanus's bodyguards, standing near their horses. Marculf and Riculfius, with a companion, had put on his finest tunic, hose, and shoes. The three men also wore silver cavalry parade masks, sculpted with the faces of Roman gods.

"Astrologers, mount your horses," Petranius ordered. "Leave an interval for the star lantern between you and the last shepherd. You, child, with that star. Hold it up. UP! Where is that brat's mother? CHILD, walk ahead of the astrologers." He winced and looked at his notes. "Musicians, ready. Your cue is when the deacon reads . . . where are we? 'Let us see this thing, which God has shown us.' Yes, when he says, 'And they went with haste.'"

"The man needs the patience of Job," Modestus murmured, as Treverius led him to the front entrance where the procession would pass outdoors.

"Stephan has written a conductus that repeats the shepherd's conversation as they walk to the chapel," Treverius explained. "You'll begin the Vigil Mass there."

"Who are they?" Modestus indicated three women in heavy make-up at the head of the line.

"Petranius's . . . ah . . . musicians." In view of their part-time profession, I hoped you wouldn't ask. "I heard him call the two with flutes Callixa and Laodike. Juliana, I think that's her name, has the tambourine."

Before Modestus could ask more questions, the booming sound of a drum came from the end of the line. A dwarf, carried on the shoulders of a muscular black man, beat out the processional rhythm.

"Pumilio and Aethiops. The Black is mute," Treverius said, identifying the two. "Stephan needs the drum to keep time during the procession."

"Seems you know these actors quite well," Modestus commented dryly.

"I couldn't help learn some of their names while putting up the set."

The procession was in motion now, amid a cacophony of bleating sheep, clattering horses' hooves, high-pitched flute sounds, a jingling of Juliana's tambourine, and the reverberating beat of Pumilio's drum.

Treverius noticed a grim expression on Modestus's face. He wondered if the presbyter would allow the drama, then was surprised to see Juliana drop out of line. Despite the actress's whitened complexion, rouged cheeks, and darkly outlined eyes, she had not masked a look of fright. The woman beckoned Treverius away from the presbyter.

"I've asked about you," Juliana said in a hoarse whisper. "You work in the Pretorium, and I think you might be trusted. Can you come to my lupanar?"

"Your brothel? I . . . I'm married. To one of the angels." Treverius realized how ridiculous that sounded, but Juliana's boldness had taken him off guard.

"Not to screw . . . not for that." She giggled and touched at her henna-dyed hair in a nervous gesture. "The Golden Mask is behind the theater."

"Why then? Is something frightening you?"

"Someone may . . ." Juliana glanced over his shoulder. Treverius turned and saw Petranius glowering at her. "The Golden Mask," she repeated, and ran back into the line.

"A musician?" Modestus asked in a sarcastic tone, coming up to Treverius. "What did the Magdalene want?"

"She's frightened about something, Presbyter."

"Her immortal soul, perhaps?"

"Something more immediate than that, I think.

"The slut. Soliciting in my church."

"She wasn't," Treverius snapped, realizing that he might be defending Juliana because he had found the red-haired woman disturbingly attractive. Juliana had mentioned the pretorium. Did someone there frighten the woman enough to make her confide in a stranger before Petranius interrupted her? "Let's follow Aethiops out," Treverius said, quite sure he would never find out the answer.

*   *   *

The drama and procession to the chapel went reasonably well. In his homily, Modestus urged the assembly to spend the day of the Nativity quietly, and suggested that simple gifts might be exchanged to counter the lingering pagan custom of the old Saturnalia.

*   *   *

Dawn of the day after the Nativity, December twenty-six, spawned an overcast sky, with ragged lines of clouds scudding to the southeast on a cold blustery wind. Since it was the feast of Saint Stephan, the deacon's namesake,

Treverius had told him he would help clear the nave of decorations that morning. Blandina volunteered to help.

Warmly dressed against the wind, Treverius and his wife locked arms to cross the Via Praetori and turn into the Fori, which led to the old forum where the temple stood. This area opposite the Pretorium hosted the private homes of wealthy citizens. Few people were out after the Nativity observance.

Treverius stopped at the foundation stones of long-razed buildings that once had been at the center of Mogontium's public life. The outlines of several structures were visible, but only the temple of Jupiter-Taranis was still intact. "Tell me about the forum that was here," he teased Blandina.

"You think I've forgotten, don't you?" She pointed to snow drifting against the ridges of ruined walls. "There was a temple to Fortuna, a Curia building. The old basilica."

"Very good. What's left now?"

"A tavern and the public latrines." Blandina laughed and indicated two buildings.

"Almost right, dove." He faced her to the left. "Temple of Jupiter. Modeled after Agrippa's at Nemausus."

"That doesn't count. Everyone can see it's there." She shook his arm in mock annoyance, then broke free. "Race you up the stairs."

At the top of the flight Blandina turned to look across the snow-swept area below. Treverius bounded up and put an arm around her, then followed her gaze to the arch of Severus Alexander in the distance. It framed the bricked-up outline of a gate, which once opened onto the aqueduct distribution cistern and hillside vineyards to the west.

"It's hard to imagine a time when it was safe enough to leave the gates open," Blandina mused, rubbing his hand over her cold cheek.

"Or that the town was once called Happy Mogontium."

"Will it ever be that again, Trev?"

"Politics have changed since that forum was built.
We call ourselves a republic, yet since Diocletian emperors have distanced themselves from the people. Officials
still have the titles . . . senator, consul, tribune . . . but the
legions have appointed, what, eight emperors since Constantine? We'd be helpless if someone like Lupus Glaucus
turned his men against Governor Albanus." Treverius
watched a flock of crows alight near the arch and peck at
weed stalks poking through the snow. "Sorry, dove, I
don't mean to be an alarmist."

"Then let's talk about something else. Those actors
are a strange lot, but I liked being in the play. In spring
we should go to one of their dramas."

"You're not going to give up the map room for the
stage are you?"

"Guess!" Blandina ducked out from under his arm.
"And I saw you talking to that henna-haired actress.
What kind of plans did you two make?"

"Blandina, she was afraid of someone in the pretorium. Wanted to talk about it."

"Where? In her 'office'?"

"As a matter of fact . . . Look, I'm not going to the
Golden Mask."

"Now I'm teasing you." Blandina pulled him by the
arm toward the entrance. "We'd better go in, or Stephan
will be all through cleaning up."

Treverius felt Blandina shiver as soon as she entered
the nave. The air was cold, with a damp chill that was as
penetrating as the outdoor wind. The dim space still
smelled of pine sap and hay. All of the yews were on the
scaffold, but the grasses had been swept into piles. No
one was in sight. Treverius surmised that Stephan might
not have come, and that unsupervised slaves had prob-

ably left after only sweeping the floor. "Stephan," he
called out. "We've come to help. Deacon, are you here?"
The echo of his words was the only response. As Treverius looked around for a presence, Blandina grasped
his arm. He shared her alarm. "Deacon," he repeated
more loudly, then spotted what looked like a pile of crum-
pled clothes in the apse. "Is that one of the shepherd costumes?" He pulled Blandina toward the unshapely form,
then stopped in horror.

Stephan lay near the scaffolding, with blood clotting
on a gash at the side of his head. Bits of shattered brick
were scattered on the floor beside him.

Treverius bent down and felt for a pulse at his neck,
then glanced at the ceiling. "Christ, look up there." He
tilted his head to indicate a dark rectangular gap in the
vaulting. "A brick must have come loose and fallen on
Stephan."

"Is he . . . ?"

"No, alive. Go bring Nicias from the camp. I'll keep the
deacon warm until we get him to the garrison hospital."

*   *   *

After Modestus heard about the accident, he insisted that
Stephan be housed in his quarters because they were
warmer than the camp hospital ward. It was a futile comfort. Despite the medical efforts of Nicias, and the spiritual balm of prayers by Modestus, Stephan died three
days later without gaining consciousness.

*   *   *

December thirty-first, the day of the funeral, was clear
but bitterly cold. A small group of mourners hoped the
cloudless sky would herald a return to better weather,
even as they feared that the last night of the year would
be one of the coldest yet that winter.

*   *   *

After the burial, Governor Albanus dismissed his guards and decided to visit the garrison before returning to his office. He knew the men were celebrating on this eve of the new year. Tomorrow, they would renew their oath of allegiance to Honorius, receive bonuses of supplies and money, and take part in games of skill with their weapons.

Albanus found the men already in a festive mood, drinking more of their issue wine than usual, and bragging of how well they would do in the contests the next day. He walked through smoky barracks still decorated with yews and joined in the mens' jokes as he accepted goblets of their harsh army vintage.

It was almost dark when Quintus Albanus left the camp and walked—a bit unsteadily—up the Via Alexander. When he reached the Pretorium, the red-violet shade of the horizon had darkened to indigo, and the moon was being coaxed into Leo by the brilliance of the dusk star Hesperus. Crisp black shadows of the pretorium and basilica lay on the whitish ground, a cold contrast to the warm light glowing from behind window shutters in the portico arcade.

Albanus paused to admire the crystal face of the moon. As he gazed at the silent, mottled orb, he felt a sensation of being oddly secure. He knew it might be the effect of too much wine, yet he also realized that he had reasons to be pleased. His town and province had survived another year, with the worst disaster being the early winter and the damage done to crops and livestock. True, the circumstances of four accidental deaths were disturbing, but, since October, many other citizens had died of sickness. Cyril was spouting nonsense about pagan gods, but the real danger was to civic peace, and Arian demonstrations against the closing of their church had not materialized. The rough garrison seemed loyal, and Lupus Glaucus would be replaced when Bassus returned.

"Let them call themselves Fulminata," Albanus mumbled jovially to himself. "It might even help their morale if I told them they shared the same name as Julius Caesar's famed Legion Twelve."

With a last glance at the star-speckled sky, Albanus entered the atrium and returned the guards' salutes. He felt definitely drunk. Since he would have to rise early for the ceremonies and games, he decided to go directly to bed, rather than to his office.

The bedroom was still comfortably warm from furnace air circulating through hollow tiles in the floor and walls. Once in bed, Albanus thought of Sophia, as he always did. Tonight he felt sure that he would sleep soundly until morning, without a dose of Nicias's sedatives, except perhaps something for a morning headache.

*   *   *

Treverius awoke suddenly and sat up in bed. The room was cold. He saw Blandina hunched next to a lamp flame, thumbing through the pages of a book.

"Are you all right, dove?" he asked. "Your humors aren't out of balance?"

"No, I feel well enough. I remembered something about Stephan's death. I'm trying to confirm it in Eusebius."

"Confirm what?"

"Just a moment." Blandina turned a page and read. "Yes, here it is, in Codex Two."

"What is?"

"I'm not sure, another coincidence? Blessed Stephan . . . our deacon's namesake . . . was martyred by being stoned to death."

"Of course. Modestus was describing his death when Malchus interrupted our presentation."

"Is there a pattern in these deaths, after all, Trev?"

"Pattern? Modestus didn't think so, yet the way Clement was found drowned, then the mason killed at the temple, has made me wonder. And now, Stephan's death. They all do seem to fit a half-completed mold."

"Even Arbitos."

"Cyril did try to connect his death to the act of a god, but that's absurd."

"As absurd as the fact that they all died on a date of significance to them?"

"On target, Blandina." Treverius thought back. "We found Stephan near the scaffold. I suppose someone could have climbed up earlier and chiseled out a brick."

"Then hidden behind the trees."

"And struck him with it. But why? The man had no enemies."

"We really don't know that," Blandina contended. "Perhaps someone was unhappy about the way he distributed altar donations."

"This cold is enough to unbalance anyone, but . . . murder? I'll discuss it with Modestus tomorrow, although, frankly, I can't make a connection between a boatman, a stone-setter, and a deacon. Come back to bed, dove." Treverius waited for her to put the book away, then pulled aside the blanket. After she nestled against him, he whispered, "A happy New Year, Blandina. Let's hope the coming months will bring Mogontium better times."

"Starting with better weather," she murmured.

"At the least." He chuckled. "We'd better go to sleep, I have to get up early. David is coming over so we can watch the garrison games together."

"Aren't the men . . . you know, won't they drink too much tonight?"

"Probably." Pray to God those Goths on the east bank can't realize that the men might be drunk tonight. The wall sentries wouldn't be able to tell a warrior from a wolf if their life depended on it.

chapter 9

Across the frozen Rhine, in the dazzling moonlight, Gaisios stood atop a wagon and looked beyond Castellum Mattiacorum to the black buildings of the town it protected. Behind him, blending with the dark edge of the forest, a line of warriors three men deep waited impatiently. The pines also screened massed wagons holding Vandal women, children, and oldsters, along with the belongings they had traded or looted during their long trek from the Vistula River. The tribe's name meant "Wanderers," but his people were tired of roving and wanted a share of the rich lands in Gaul.

Taking the Mogon-place would be relatively easy after all. Hadn't Hortar told him that the warriors of the new Romans would be unprepared tonight? After a strenuous day of practicing for their games, the men would stay in their barracks and drink too much. They would be, his new friend assured him, tired, drunk, and unfit to fight.

Although the air was as cold as the steel on his sword, Gaisios was sweating. He thought of the winter solstice ten days earlier, when he had met with leaders of the Suebi, a tribe that knew the countryside well. They had brought chiefs of the Alans, a people who spoke little

121

Gothic and had to be understood through interpreters. Hortar had been there, assuring everyone that the warriors of the new Romans were understrength, because men had been drained off for Stilicho's army. He also boasted that he knew people of the Goth's own Arian faith in Gaul, who were ready to overthrow the Bishop of Rome and the weak Augustus at Ravenna. The chiefs had listened, then laughed. The war against the new Romans would be as easy as clubbing rabbits.

Gaisios took a deep breath of icy air that froze in his nostrils. After the parley the chiefs had consulted with tribal seeresses, performed rituals to their war gods, and sacrificed an older slave, before swearing to support each other in the attack. By an augury of marked twigs the Alans were given the northern lands. The Suebi won the south, and—as he knew they would—the magic sticks awarded his Vandals the Mogon-place and the country directly west.

The Mogon-place. Gaisios felt his rage surface once again, recalling the humiliation he endured there. He had been questioned about the drowned man the way one would a murderous slave. The golden woman had given him one of her cast-off whores, who then mocked him with enchanted lamps that copulated. Worse, he had panicked and run from the sorcery in the bewitched rooms where metal animal-men coupled with beasts.

He remembered how unbreachable the walls had looked. But what he recalled, above all, was the door through which he had run to vomit in the river. It had been unguarded.

Hortar, his new friend, had devised a plan for entering the Mogon-place. He showed his men how to build a battering ram, an oak log six paces long fitted with handles so that eight men could carry it. The head was a granite boulder that would not shatter before the door planks gave way. It would be pulled across the frozen river by a team of horses shod with lashed-on iron plates to provide traction. A cart would bring a wooden ramp to span the distance between the ice and wharf top, then the men would carry the ram up the incline and aim their blows against the bottom of the door. Other warriors would pull carts loaded with brushwood and kindle them into flame at the overturned boats. Once the gate was breached, buildings inside the town would be set afire, diverting any men of the garrison who might be capable of fighting.

* * *

Gaisios squinted at the full moon and raised his spread fingers to measure its distance from the horizon. It was two handspans high, the distance, Hortar said, when the eleventh hour watch would be on duty, sleepy and drunk. He nodded and his bodyguards gave the signal to advance.

As the hooting call of an owl passed down the line of warriors, they trotted their horses forward onto snowy fields. Carts carrying the battering ram, ramp, and brushwood lurched into the frozen ruts of the road toward the river. Behind them, hundreds of wagons creaked out of the forest shadows into the white moonlight. Several thousand people moved forward to claim a rich land where they finally could end their wanderings.

Passing along a road that bordered the garrison's frozen garden, Gaisios led his contingent of horsemen and carts to the south of the Mattiacorum fort. The ram was unloaded at the river and hitched to the horses. He felt a moment of panic after the animals shied at moving onto the ice, but his teamsters were able to coax them across the frozen river.

There was no watchtower at the south end of the new wall, where the door was located, and the two grain mills helped screen warriors from the nearest sentries, as they set the ramp into place. Most of the boats were turned hull-up on the wharf. The Vandals piled brushwood underneath them and against the wooden sides, then struck sparks into pitch-soaked torches. But, when the kindling flared into smoky flames, the gate crew was still struggling to carry the heavy ram up a ramp slippery with frost.

Gaisios looked back across the river and cursed. He had told his subchiefs that the signal for their men to attack would be the thud of the ram as it smashed into the door—a sound that would carry to the opposite bank. Now he saw the dark shapes of horsemen already starting across the ice, and heard warriors yelling guttural battle cries. He knew that few leaders were able to control their unpredictable men in an attack, but his anger ebbed as rapidly as it had flowed after he heard the thud of the ram reverberate along the wall, across to the eastern bank of the river.

Charging forward over wharf stones sparkling with frost, his men smashed through the gate's oak timbers on their third run. Gaisios ducked inside, threw the bolt beam off its brackets and shoved open the door. His bodyguards followed. Inside, he paused to look along the line of buildings across the street. Torches threw oval pools of light on walls and streets, but the deathly white glare from the moon made them pale by comparison. Gaisios saw a yellow glow behind the shutters of a nearby building. The brothel looked eerie, like a tomb white-washed by ghost light.

"There is the wolves' lair," he snarled to his guards, pointing to the building. "Smash in the door."

Their Frankish axes splintered the pine panel after three blows. The reception area was empty. Only the flame of a single lamp flickered wildly at the onrush of air, to illuminate the bewitched statuary.

"Find a golden whore," Gaisios ordered. He entered the hallway and kicked in the first two doors, but the cubicles were unoccupied. Halfway down, a girl looked out, saw him, and screamed. He pushed her aside, just as a naked man rose up from a couch with a look of surprise on his face. The chieftain slashed him down in a spatter of gore before his feet touched the ground, then Gaisios grabbed the girl by the hair.

"Where is the golden woman?" he yelled, but she did not understand Gothic and only sobbed in terror. He threw her onto the man's body and stalked out.

From the hall Gaisios heard shrieks coming out of rooms as his men looted the brothel. Frustrated, he returned to the anteroom. Two warriors were carrying out the statue of the copulating satyr.

"Sons of sows," Gaisios screamed, "you're here to fight." He made a vicious swipe at the nearest man's head with his blade, severing his ear and spurting blood on the other. The warriors dropped the statue and ran out.

Gaisios went back to the hallway, kicking in doors to find Auraria. In one room he saw a warrior with his trousers down, pushing hard into one of the terrified women. He struck the man's buttocks a stinging blow with the flat of his sword and ordered him out.

In the room he had been given for his visit, Gaisios found Hagnia sitting in the center of the floor. Her makeup was streaked from crying and she was shaking uncontrollably. He heard her plead with him in her strange language, but he paused only an instant, to turn her face away with the tip of his sword, before decapitating her in a single savage swing. Then, he swept the row of bewitched lamps off the ledge with his bloody blade.

When Gaisios came out, burning oil spread across the wooden floor behind him. Flames lapped at the bed's mattress and pillow. He saw his bodyguards and motioned them to follow him up stairs that led to a second floor. Gaisios had gone only a few steps when Auraria appeared on the landing. She wore a yellow silk tunic with holes cut out to give a teasing glimpse of her breasts and rouged nipples. After she recognized Gaisios, her brows wrinkled.

"Filthy Goth!" she shrieked, then spat at him. "May you burn in Avernus."

Instantly, a guard threw his lance at her. The thrust between her breasts flung Auraria backwards and pinned her body to the wall. A look of stunned disbelief was frozen in death. Gaisios made a cutting motion at his throat, which the guard understood. The woman's head, with its blue eyes and wheat-colored hair, would decorate his chieftain's saddle when he moved into Gaul.

With smoke forming heavy blue threads in the halls, and his tunic soaked with sweat beneath a bloodied fur jacket, Gaisios went outside to gulp in cold night air.

He saw that most of the buildings on the side of the street leading away from the walls were on fire, but the dark shapes of men running out of the garrison camp at the end of the avenue told him the new Romans had been alerted. He squinted at a barricade of carts being put up, to block the far end of the street, then ducked a catapult bolt that swished past his head and shattered the stucco wall behind him.

Gaisios crouched low as he ran back to the Via Rheni. In the ghostly glare he saw warriors carrying tables, chests, jars of wine, silver bowls, and leather bundles from homes where owners lay dead in their doorways. But spears and arrows were angling down from the river wall now, catching some of the looters as they jammed the narrow entrance and tried to get to the wharf and onto the river ice. The groggy sentries had finally been alerted by the blazing boats and mills, and the shadowy forms of shouting warriors swarming across the moonlit river.

Gaisios assessed his situation from the doorway of the burning brothel. The way was blocked to the south by walls, the buildings looted and on fire. He had to outflank the new Romans at their camp barricade, by attacking to the north, along the river wall toward the bridge, and entering the town proper from there. If he could regroup enough warriors, and order them to follow him in the direction of the bridge gate, he could rout the guards, then open the doors so his men on the bridge could enter in force.

The Mogon-place would be his.

*   *   *

Albanus had been enveloped in an erotic dream about Sophia when he was abruptly awakened by Marculf and told of the attack. Summoning Tribune Ronulfus and Treverius to his office, Albanus brought the men to a map of Mogontium on the wall. "Treverius, I called you here because you drew up this plan. You know the town better than I do."

"How did the barbarians get in, sir?"

"Reports say through the small mill gate."

"Where that Vandal found Clement," Treverius recalled. "Gaisios was here to scout our defenses."

"Orders, sir?" Ronulfus asked. "The pretorian guards are waiting."

Albanus studied his map. The mill gate was in Quadrant IV at the southeast end of the Via Rheni, with the garrison camp west of that, across the Campus Martius training field. "Runners report buildings here in Quadrant Four burning, but the garrison has set up a barricade at the Germanicus and Martius. If it holds, the Goths can't get through that way."

"It will give us time to organize the Limitans," Treverius said.

"Fortunately. With the garrison tied up at the Germanicus, the north end of the Rheni is undefended clear to the bridge gate."

"What of the side alleys?" Ronulfus pointed to the warren of streets in that quadrant. "The Goths could weave their way through to the Pretorium here."

"And I need your guards to defend the building."

"Sir, if I might suggest something?"

"What, Treverius?"

"David and his Beneregesh could block the Via Rheni."

"Who?" Albanus seemed puzzled by the names.

"The Judean contingent in the Limitans," Treverius explained. "They call themselves 'Beneregesh'—'Sons of Thunder,' in Hebrew."

"Good. Forgot about them. Can you contact their leader?"

"David has cargo wagons in a warehouse just south of the bridge gate. He could use them to set up a barrier across the Rheni. His men know all the alleyways in the Judean quarter and could ambush any Goths who filtered in."

"Can you find this Judean?"

"I've been to David's home many times."

"God with you then, son. Ronulfus, order your men to set up a defense line at the Germanicus, north along the Alexander to the Pretorium, then east on the Via Honorius to the bridge gate. If the Goths manage to enter northeast Quadrant Two, they'll be confined there."

* * *

Rabbi Zadok and his family were celebrating the last day of Hanuk when they were startled by the blare of distant trumpets. David ran out, joining other men who had also heard the alarm. The glow of flames at far-off buildings in Quadrant IV suggested that the warning signaled fire, but the sight of warriors at the mill door and sparks soaring above the wall sent him and the others running for their weapons.

Treverius, mounted on a horse, found his friend at the Rheni beginning to organize the Beneregesh. "David!" he shouted. "I've just come from Albanus. Have your men pull wagons out and block the Rheni. A barricade will keep the Goths from reaching the bridge gate and forcing it open."

"I'll get Nathaniel's squad to help."

"Send some men on roofs to ambush any warriors who try to bypass the barricade through your side streets."

"Trev, you should have been a soldier, not a map maker." David grinned.

Treverius threw him a mock salute, then reined his horse away toward the Via Honorius to find his unit. At the bridge gate, he saw that wall guards were decimating Vandal warriors who had crossed the bridge, but could only rattle their spears in rage against the massive portals. At least this situation seems under control. He rallied a few horsemen and went with them to see if they could help David at the barricade.

* * *

By the time Gaisios was able to cajole or curse enough warriors away from looting and assemble them into a band, he saw activity at the far end of the street, near the gate to the bridge. Torches bobbed in animated arcs. Men shouted above the rumble of heavy wagons being moved, and the splintering crash as they were overturned. Gaisios surmised that another barricade was being put up, but saw that it was not yet complete at the left end. If he could get his men there quickly, they might be able to outflank the wagons through the gap.

Gaisios cursed his band forward, but forcing looters away from shops on the west side of the Rheni took time. When he was some twenty paces from the line of wagons, a file of the new Romans jogged out from behind the barricade and took positions in front. At an order Gaisios did not understand they locked their oblong shields together. Now he was also faced with a blue wall decorated with two superimposed white triangles that made a six-pointed star.

The Vandal chief hesitated, recalling Hortar's description of the tortoise army that had defeated his Alamanni. His warriors stopped with him, rattling swords on shields and yelling frenzied battle cries—"the Fury of the Goths" —to unnerve the men behind the blue star-wall. Frustrated by the barricade and pondering his next move, Gaisios picked at his cheek scar until it bled. A few of his warriors moved closer to throw their spears. He saw the tortoise star-shields deflect them, and the lances thrown back in deadly arcs that impaled his men with their own weapons. When Gaisios saw his warriors fall, screaming in pain on the cold paving, the humiliation became too much. With a bellow of rage, he threw down his shield to attack the blue tortoises with only a sword.

Gaisios loped forward, conscious of the taste of his own blood trickling from the scar. He dodged lances that dropped his bodyguards on either side. They stumbled and fell, but he kept on toward the blur of shields. When he reached the blue wall, he hacked savagely at the nearest tortoise. As the man reeled back and fell, his companion's sword thrust out. Its edge slid along the side of Gaisios's chain mail shirt. After he staggered back and felt the wound, his hand came away with a smear of blood. Gaisios looked up in rage and saw that another tortoise had taken the fallen one's place.

Through his anger, Gaisios remembered the end of the barricade, which had been unprotected by wagons. He shouted for his remaining men to attack on the left, but horsemen now blocked the way with armored animals and long lances. One of his men screamed in terror. After Gaisios looked up at the riders, a chill of horror penetrated his sweaty tunic. Their faces were not human flesh, but silver metal that bore an expression of calm assurance, rather than of the hate and frustration he felt in himself.

The new Romans have sorcerers whose power can conjure iron horses and warriors into battle.

His superstitious fear was replaced by confusion when Gaisios saw clay jars arc over his mens' heads and smash on the ground around them. After olive oil splashed out and spread a slick coating over the stones, he watched his warriors slip and fall in helpless heaps. Distracted, Gaisios heard a lance head clink off one of his bronze wrist guards, then felt a sear of pain. One of the iron sorcerers had opened a gash in his forearm. Cursing, he dropped his sword to grab at the wound. With blood seeping between his fingers, Gaisios stepped back to look around under the bright gaze of an indifferent moon.

The end of the street next the river wall, where he had entered, was a barrier of flaming buildings that tinted the blue shields and iron faces of his enemy with a ruddy orange glow. Many of his warriors were now grotesque statues of the dead, sprawled in front of overturned wagons. The wounded bellowed as they struggled to pull lances or arrows from their bodies, even as their unhurt companions tried to stand again on slippery paving stones that glistened as if the moon had coated them with a mocking glaze of silver.

Gaisios bent and retched from frustration and pain. His bodyguards were dead. The Arian comrades Hortar promised had not come to help. His supernatural opponents had bewitched the ground so that warriors were unable to fight. Wiping his mouth with a sleeve, Gaisios reasoned that it would be wise to bypass the enchanted town, just as the Alamanni had. He shouted for his surviving men to break off the fight and return to the door through which they had entered the Mogon-place of sorcerers.

* * *

By dawn none of the Vandal subchiefs was able to control the warriors who were still in town. Those who had gotten out the wall door had piled their looted treasures in the wagons of kin, then circled Mogontium to move on toward the undefended farms and villas beyond the city.

Low on the western horizon, a pale, unfeeling moon still watched as Gaisios rested in a grove of barren oaks near the road. Fingering the blond curls that framed the pallid face of Auraria, he muttered, "Golden woman, your tortoise army kept me from taking the Mogon-place, yet a tortoise is helpless when turned on its back. There are rich towns ahead and the friends Hortar promised. I will recruit new warriors, then come back and overturn your tortoises, one by one."

*　*　*

As the pretorian guards rounded up prisoners, Treverius went to find Blandina. He finally saw her in the common mess room, helping Nicias take care of wounded, and ran toward her, still holding his parade mask. She looked up in relief.

"Thank Longinus, you're safe!" Blandina hugged her husband in a tight embrace, then noticed the silver face-piece sculpted in the likeness of Apollo. "You . . . you're not ready for a parade just yet, are you?"

"No. I told the men to put masks on, figuring the Goths might be superstitious enough to think we were some kind of unearthly metal demons."

"Clever."

"David had the idea of throwing amphorae of oil at the warriors in front of his barricade. When they lost their footing and couldn't fight, their chieftain ordered them back. I may have wounded his arm."

"Was it the Vandal we saw in the map room?"

"I couldn't tell, he was wearing a helmet. It was dark and . . . well . . . confusing."

"But you weren't hurt?"

Treverius shook his head. "Let's go outside and take a look from the walls. We may have beaten back their attack, but the barbarians' wagons are moving west."

Standing alongside exhausted defenders, the couple saw smoke drifting from the gutted Mattiacorum fort, and the hulks of homesteads that clustered near the burned palisade. A hazy blue cloud rose over the wall from the direction of the wharf mills. Inside Mogontium, flames still licked at the blackened ruins of burned buildings in Quadrant IV. Below the city walls, snow-filled fields were dotted with the dark shapes of wagons, carts, cattle, and horsemen, flowing on either side of Mogontium like water around a boulder. Pretorians and garrison legionaries alike watched the enemy pass in unaccustomed silence. They and the Vandals were too weary to jeer each other.

"How many are out there?" Blandina asked her husband.

"Warriors from perhaps three tribes. Old men. Women and children. This procession could go into the province for a week." When she did not comment, he put an arm around her. "You're thinking about your father."

"Will the Capital be as fortunte as we were in defending itself?"

Treverius hesitated. Do I lie to her? Treveri is thirty miles west. Its garrison may be at even less strength than ours because the city is further back from the frontier. No, I won't lie. It is possible that Treveri held out, as we did. "I think Cingetorius is probably safe," he said. "And when Governor Albanus reports this to Ravenna, Stilicho may return our levy of men."

"That could take months, Trev." Blandina wiped an eye with a sleeve. "Months."

"Try not to worry your pretty head about it."

"Pretty head?" Blandina pulled away sharply. "You're not taking me seriously again, Treverius."

"Just tried to shield you," he said in a feeble response.

"From the truth? My father is in the path of these Vandals. Shouldn't I 'worry my pretty head' about that?"

"Sorry, Blandina, I'm wrong. Let . . . let me put the truth this way. Our situation is like being in a small house, on a tiny island, in a stormy sea. Our enemies don't know how to build boats to get to us yet, so we can only hope that before they do someone will throw a bridge from the mainland to rescue us. You've read Marcellinus. After our defeat at Adrianople the Eastern army was able to force the Visigoths into accepting Federate status as allies. We don't have an army here, so these Vandals aren't going to ask Ravenna to offer them what they can just take." Treverius pulled her to him and nuzzled hair that smelled of smoke. "Blandina, nothing will be the same again for Mogontium or for us. Barbarians can't read maps and certainly don't appreciate mosaics."

She looked up and half-smiled at his effort to cheer her. "What will the governor do, Trev?"

"Albanus doesn't have enough men to pursue the Vandal wagons." Treverius looked up at the cloudy sky. "Ironic. This poor weather got them over here, but now it could become our ally."

"I don't see how."

"The Vandals will need shelter, so they won't destroy all the villas they raid. Destruction will be at a minimum when we take the province back."

"Will we be able to do that?"

"You once said Germania Prima was the eastern gate to the empire, Blandina. Ravenna won't let it stay broken. Unless . . ." Treverius looked away from her.

"Unless what?"

"I don't mean to worry you."

"Treverius, I'm not a child."

"Right. Blandina, Modestus pointed out that Vandals are Arian Christians. If they can find enough support in

Gaul from fellow Arians, they could increase the number of warriors in their army. A few years ago, at the Frigidus battle, rebel pagan legions were narrowly defeated by Theodosius. Honorius isn't close to being the emperor and commander Theodosius was. We're isolated on our island, Blandina. The best Governor Albanus can hope for now is to prevent panic among the citizens and have Modestus pray that reinforcements will arrive from Ravenna soon."

Treverius knew that the former might be possible but, given Stilicho's preoccupation in Italy, the latter was unlikely.

chapter 10

Governor Albanus took measures to assess the extent of the Vandal invasion. He organized a well-armed scouting detachment and, over the objections of Lupus Glaucus, insisted on leading the men himself.

On January tenth Albanus set out with Sebastian and a force of forty mounted pretorian guards to reconnoiter the country west of Mogontium.

* * *

In mid-January, while Albanus was away, Vertiscus decided to call on Cyril to reassure the merchant and discuss the effects of the unexpected Vandal incursion on his plans for New Gothia. The strain of implementing his conspiracy had begun to show on Vertiscus. His horsish face was thinner and the fringe of white hair more pronounced. A thin line of mouth, already coldly grim, now twitched whenever he spoke.

After a slave ushered Vertiscus into Cyril's reception room, the curator was immediately critical of its comfort. He thought it too warm, from heated air circulating in the walls and floor. While he was trying to conserve fuel by heating pretorium offices with charcoal braziers or stoves, Cyril was undoubtedly bribing cutters to keep him supplied with furnace wood.

136

As he waited, Vertiscus glanced around the luxurious room where the wealthy merchant met his clients. Brightness from the atrium and garden entrances was muted by wooden screens, which blocked out the cold weather, but also light from outdoors. To compensate, three lamps on a stand cast a glow on the pattern of the mosaic floor. Its checkered border design framed an allegorical scene of a hoary Father Rhine watching trade barges pass along his river. The mercantile theme was repeated on wall paintings, in which slaves loaded trade goods from boats onto the wharves of Mogontium. A marble table in front of an upholstered couch displayed a gilt statue of Mercurius, the Roman god of commerce.

Vertiscus loosened his cloak and dropped into a cushioned chair, musing that Cyril's taste for decoration indeed reflected his business life.

After a servant unfolded a section of the screen, Cyril slipped through wearing a knee-length tunic decorated with gold bands at the sleeves and hem, and blue woolen hose. He had set aside his red senatorial shoes for silk slippers, but the gold Janus medal dangled from his neck.

Vertiscus thought Cyril looked haggard. Creases in his forehead accented the grim look on his face. "Why the mask of tragedy, friend?" he asked, standing to grasp the merchant's arm. "Are you auditioning for a part in Sophocles?"

"Only a fool would look otherwise," Cyril snapped without even a stilted smile. "Quadrant Four half-destroyed. My warehouses looted. With trade halted along the river roads, shops are hoarding food. We're as helpless as if locked inside the Mamertine at Rome."

"Calm down, Cyril. Mogontium is not yet a prison."

"What would you call our situation, Curator? People are afraid to go outside their homes for fear the Vandals will return."

"The governor should be back soon with a report on conditions inside the province."

"Albanus? The man hasn't held a military command in years. Lupus Glaucus should have led that detachment."

"I need him here. All the pretorians may not return."

"Why did the Vandal fail?" Cyril asked with a sneer. "Didn't I warn you about barbarians?"

"True, I wanted the invasion later in the winter. And Glaucus hasn't recruited as many men as he will in a few months. When the Vandals attacked, the garrison was confused. The men defended their camp, instead of fighting pretorians."

"I told you all barbarians were unreliable."

"No, Cyril, Hortar picked a good time for Gaisios to attack. The garrison was half drunk, but I was impressed with the way the Pretorian and Limitans units fought."

"Perhaps Glaucus should be recruiting them."

Vertiscus ignored Cyril's sarcasm. "Pretorians, fortunately, don't fraternize with the garrison. There's little chance of a drunken legionary boasting about what he might know of New Gothia."

"Have you thought of a ruse?" Cyril asked. "The pretorian guards will have to be disarmed if we're to succeed."

"Limitans and Judean contingents too. David's men kept Vandals from reaching the bridge gate."

Cyril paced the room, nervously picking at the gold decorations on his sleeves and staring at the wharf scenes on the mural. "Did you come with more bad news?" he asked Vertiscus without looking around.

"The Vandal attack at this time was unfortunate, but the henhouse has been breached."

"You talk of chickens at a time like this?" Cyril gave a nervous chortle.

"Figuratively, the Province. But I have Hortar controlling the foxes."

"Hortar?" Cyril spun around to face the curator. "Enough riddles. Where is that stupid Alamann?"

"At Treveri, with Gaisios."

"Wh . . . at?" Cyril sputtered. "The barbarians have taken the Gallic capital? Then we are lost."

"Calm, my friend. Sit down. I'll tell you about Hortar's role." Vertiscus traced the marble veins on the table as he explained, "The Vandals will find farms and villas in Gaul. Towns. If they destroy them, they'll have no food, no place to settle families. This was not just a makeshift raid, Cyril, but a migration of entire tribes."

"Get to the point, Curator."

"Hortar is forced to negotiate an alliance with Gaisios sooner than I hoped. But once my New Gothia is a reality we'll teach his Vandals how to benefit from the land, not merely loot it."

"While Stilicho merely sits on his legions?"

"You haven't heard tavern talk? Even pretorians are wagering that now Stilicho won't come in the spring." Vertiscus faced Cyril. "You're correct about the panic in town, but it works to our advantage. Once citizens realize they'll get no help from Ravenna, it will make their accepting our alliance with the Vandals . . . my New Gothia . . . all the more palatable."

"That might restore some stability. Trade could resume." Cyril rose to absently caress the statue of Mercurius. "But what about Albanus? Citizens like him."

"Perhaps he shouldn't count on it. A runner came to the pretorium this morning. The governor will return before January's end to face the situation you just described. No, Albanus comes back to a quite different Mogontium than the one he left. Courage, Cyril. We should have heard from Hortar by then."

"I still don't understand why you're doing this. You have authority as pretorium curator and the governor trusts you. Why risk it all?"

Vertiscus turned away so Cyril could not see a rare expression of anger. "In the time of Emperor Julian my father was palace curator at Treveri," he said evenly. "Since father was a pagan, he had me educated by one of their tutors. I was twelve years old when Julian became Augustus and tried to restore our rights."

"You will recall that I fought the Alamanni in Julian's campaigns," Cyril reminded him. "I supported the pagan emperor."

"Yes, but unfortunately Julian was Augustus only three years before Christian officers he trusted assassinated him in Persia."

"Assassinated? Marcellinus reports that Julian was killed in an attack of Persian cavalry."

"The historian's exact words are, 'by a spear directed no one knows by whom,'" Vertiscus corrected. "Gratian succeeded Julian as Augustus and hounded pagans. My tutor was arrested. Father was exiled to Mogontium. After he died, I was fostered into an Arian family."

"Then the rumors of your being Arian have a basis?"

"A convenient blanket, Cyril, for concealing the truth." Vertiscus turned and picked up his cloak to leave. "Enough of my story. Suffice it to add that I made a vow to do all I could to avenge my father and the gods." He grasped Cyril's shoulder. "I'm fortunate to have you as an ally. I tell you, friend, our New Gothia cannot fail."

*   *   *

Governor Albanus led his men back to Mogontium on the twenty-fifth of January. Although he was exhausted and depressed, he immediately wrote a report to Honorius, detailing the results of his expedition.

He also added an account of a personal loss that had taken place on the twentieth of the month.

Quintus Iccius Albanus,
Governor of Germania Prima,
to Flavius Honorius,
Augustus of the Western Imperium,

Greetings.

With regret, Excellency, I report an attack on my province by Vandal Goths, an invasion on an overwhelming scale.

During the autumn I became aware of increased barbarian activity along our old eastern frontier. Scouts reported large numbers of family wagons gathered there. In November, Hortar, an Alamann raised here, brought in a Vandal chief, Gaisios, who wished to enlist men in my garrison. I acquainted him with the procedure, but he made no commitment. I have since learned that he was leader of the Vandal contingent that invaded us.

The Rhine crossing took place on the night of XXXI December while our men celebrated the renewal of their oath to your Excellency. The Vandals were able to breach a small door at the river wall. I suspected treachery from inside, but the warriors used a crude ram to enter.

Pretorian Tribune Ronulfus coordinated the defense with me. I ordered the southeast Quadrant blocked and established a defensive line, which held. Our Judean Limitans prevented access to the bridge by a barricade. This action should earn them a citation, as well as my cartographer, Treverius, who rallied the militia cavalry contingent. My defenses, and the tendency of barbarians to lose sight of a goal other than looting, won the day. By dawn, Gaisios could not control his men and withdrew. This is not to diminish the disaster.

The Mattiacorum garrison was killed or captured. All homes on the eastern bank were burned. Here, twelve structures and the legionary stables were destroyed, along with two grain mills and four patrol boats. Warehouses and the slaughterhouse outside the wall were looted but are intact. The barbarians' wagons continued to cross the Rhine for a week afterwards. Prisoners told us that the Suebi raided south and the Alans went north, into Germania Secunda.

On X Januarius I reconnoitered the countryside, found many villas burned, but decimated enemy forage parties. Captured Vandals reported that most of the tribe had moved on into Gaul. I crossed the Nava River, meeting strong raiding parties, but suffered only a few wounded, proving again that barbarians are no match for trained Romans.

On returning to the Nava the men formed hunting groups. It was here that an accident occurred which struck at me personally. Sebastian has been my aide since the Frigidus campaign. On XX Januarius I found a stand of willows sheltering deer. My hunting details formed into groups of four. Sebastian was invited to join one, even though he was more capable with a pen than bow. It began to snow, hampering visibility, and Sebastian evidentally became separated from his group.

Fearing search parties might become lost, I ordered a search delayed until daylight.

They found Sebastian during the third hour. He had stumbled into a trap set to kill wolves, a device consisting of a stretched bow and trip cord. This one was left unattended by a local who fled, or was killed by Vandals. The shaft caught Sebastian in the heart. Since saving my life at the Frigidus, he was my second eyes and ears. I shall miss him.

In view of my failure to stop the incursion of barbarians into my Province, I ask that your Excellency accept my resignation as Governor by return dispatch.

Done at Mogontium in Germania Prima.
XXXI JANUS AN AVG XI

* * *

In the aftermath of the invasion, Demetrius was also anxious to send a report to Ravenna about the dangerous situation. Albanus included the envoy's sealed dispatch with his own.

Excellency.

Almost everyone exists here as if the goddess Fortuna put them in a dice cup and mocked their destiny by throwing them onto a board of obstacles. The Rhine has been a treacherous ally. Rather than a barrier, the frozen river offered itself as a footpath to the Vandals. Now, the uncertainty of invasion has given way to survival. The Furies Rule! Fear is the overwhelming emotion: of the barbarians, of starvation, fear of the plague, even the Elements of Air, Water, Earth and Fire. Four deaths, aside from those of unbalanced Humors, have been attributed to them. Air, that is, lightning passing through the flux of Air; a drowning by Water; two fatal injuries inflicted by Earth. Fire was used by the Vandals to destroy part of the city.

Confusion as well as fear is evident in the many false doctrines being secretly or openly professed. We have crypto-pagans, crypto-Arians, secret Gnostics and Donatists. An old fool even claims to be one of the Seven Sleepers discovered by your Noble Father. After disrupting a funeral in October the Arians have been quiet. I am watching Suebius Nevius, a merchant who seems to display Arian sympathies. Also Cyril of Constantinople who, under the guise of state security, argues for the return of pagan gods. There is a rumor of old Mithraic rites among the mercenary garrison.

As for the invasion, all the Glorius Caesars and Augusti who ever took the field could not have stemmed this flood of barbarian hordes. Of course, had you been there, Augustus, matters would have turned out differently. Unhappily, the responsibility of governing prevented it. I shall deem it an honor to continue as your eyes and ears. Discreetly. As Ovid advises, 'He goes most safely who goes in the middle.'

Demetrius of Ravenna
XXXI Januarius

*   *   *

Junius became depressed after the invasion, unable to concentrate on the map room. Treverius realized the failure of his father's prediction—that the Goths would not cross the river—was largely responsible. Each day he took Blandina to work on their chart of the province, as a semblance of normalcy in a city isolated by attack.

*   *   *

On February first, Treverius came back from hearing the latest reports and rumors in the marketplace.

"People are close to panic," he told Blandina. "They're hoarding food, locking themselves in their homes. Half the shops along the Via Rheni are closed."

"It's gotten that bad, Trev?"

"When I left, an ugly crowd was protesting the governor's decision to stop serving afternoon meals."

"Because of the food Vandals looted from warehouses?"

"Right," Treverius replied. "They're also criticizing Albanus for not raiding the Gothic camps first. Or at least bribing their overchiefs to go elsewhere."

"Severus Alexander was murdered for doing that."

"Citizens have forgotten that Albanus did send scouts out in the fall. The men never came back."

"Trev," Blandina asked hesitantly, "was . . . was there any news about Treveri?"

"Only rumors that I don't want to repeat. I ran into Gaudentius, the architect. The governor will call a meeting to discuss rebuilding. And I saw Modestus. He said people spit on him in the street because his prayers didn't deliver them from the Vandals. Or even the weather."

"Horrible. What will this do to his plans for the new church? Your mosaic project?"

Treverius shrugged. "The Vandals unknowingly helped Cyril, but that's not the problem. Over the next few months the very survival of everyone in Mogontium is at stake."

chapter 11

The following morning Governor Albanus called Treverius to his office, to return the regional maps he had taken with him on his expedition. Treverius was disturbed at how tired the governor looked, and noticed that he had developed a nervous stammer.

"Luck . . . lucky to have these," Albanus stuttered, handing back the leather case of stained parchment charts. "Might've got . . . gotten lost, or my men ambushed."

"I was sorry to hear about Sebastian, Governor."

"Death f . . . feasts on war, son," Albanus replied quietly. "I've served Rome's army mo . . . most of my life. Seen men—Never mind. Trib . . . Tribune Ronulfus was killed, clearing the bridge of warriors. Did you know that?"

"I heard, sir. Things were chaotic for days."

"True that Lupus Glaucus ga . . . gave the pretorians trouble while I was gone?" Albanus probed.

"Modestus authorized a mass grave for Vandals who were killed. One of the pretorian officers ordered garrison legionaries to dig the pit in frozen ground. When they refused, Glaucus backed them up."

"In . . . insubordinate bastard."

"Heads were bloodied in tavern brawls that night. The men stay even farther apart now."

"What happened at the temple?"

Treverius surmised that the governor had already heard about the incidents from Vertiscus. Why was he checking the information with him? "Sir, only a few men returned to work after the raid. One of them, a carpenter named Felix I recall, was found in a storage shed with an awl through his heart."

"An . . . another murder?"

"His hand was clutching the bloody tool, so Modestus called it suicide. He refused to bury Felix in the cemetery."

"That when Cyril offered t . . . to cremate the body for the family in . . . in the old Roman way?"

"Yes, sir. At the burned-out legionary stables."

"That must have infur . . . infuriated the presbyter."

Treverius nodded. "And there was another death."

"At the temple?"

"No. After Felix was found the men refused to work. This was at a brothel. The White Swan."

"One of . . . of the women was killed?"

"Agnes. I understand there was dagger in her throat. Macrianus assumed a drunken client was responsible and didn't investigate."

"Lupanarae don't keep records anyway—" A rap sounded on the door and a young man Treverius had seen with Sebastian looked in. "Remigius, come in," Albanus called out. "Treverius, ha . . . have you met my new secretary? Friend of Sebastian."

Remigius nodded a greeting. "Governor, Lupus Glaucus is here to see you."

"W . . . what does that mule's ass want?"

"Sir, he says it's about the flood of refugees."

Treverius knew that while Albanus was away fugitives from the ravaged countryside had begun to arrive outside the walls of Mogontium. He had gone out to see if he could learn anything about the situation at Treveri. None were from the capital, but many told of how Vandals had forced them off their lands and kept their slaves to work the estates.

"Refugees? I'm making plans t . . . to bring them inside the town." Albanus frowned. "Send him in."

Treverius had never seen the centurion whom Bassus had appointed garrison commander in his absence. Remigius turned to summon him, but Glaucus barged into the office, a stocky brute of a man of average height, but obvious above-average strength. He wore a tight-fitting iron helmet and belted chain mail shirt over a leather tunic, and checkered woolen trousers. A long Germanic sword in a red scabbard was slung on his right side. He did not salute the governor.

"Centurion, what can I d . . . do for you?" Albanus asked amiably. "You here t . . . to verify reports of looting by your men during the Van . . . Vandal raid?"

Treverius knew the rumors were true, but saw Glaucus's jaw tense at being called a centurion, belittling his interim rank as legion commander.

"I had my men set up tents for th' refugees," he growled. "I heard you want t' bring 'em inside th' walls."

"In case of another Vandal attack. We could p . . . put the ten . . . tents up on the old forum. Easier to feed them there."

Glaucus's piggish eyes narrowed. "That rabble keeps coming and th' warehouses were looted. We barely got enough for us. I don't want 'em here stealing supplies."

"You don't want?" Albanus flushed and struggled to control his temper. "I'm gov . . . governor here, Centurion."

"And I run th' garrison," Glaucus snapped. "Aside from your fancy pretorians, we and th' walls are all you got t' keep out th' Vandals." He chuckled in a tone that was ominous rather than amused. "Chew on that piece of fish fat, Governor."

"You insolent s . . . spawn of a barbarian whore!" Albanus shouted as he stood up. "You're talking to a Roman officer."

Glaucus's porcine face contorted in rage. His hand slid to the hilt of his sword. Treverius sprang forward to clamp both hands around the man's hairy arm. The centurion glared into his eyes with the look of an angry boar, then forced a sneering grin that exposed stained broken teeth.

"Pretty fast, sonny," he said, shaking off Treverius's grip, "but don't touch me again." As Glaucus backed away to the door he taunted Albanus. "Roman officer? In th' past, legions ousted emperors. You think they can't get rid of governors?"

After Glaucus left, Albanus slumped down onto his chair. "Should've kept my temper," he whispered hoarsely.

"Was that last remark a threat or a crude joke?"

"Ab . . . about the legions?" Albanus shrugged. "He's got more legionaries than I've got pretorians. My men are bet . . . better trained, but . . ." His voice trailed off.

Treverius understood. A surprise attack could cost the guards their advantage.

"Glaucus going for his sword was probably a bluff," he said, "but I'm glad I was on that side of him."

"Left handed." Albanus glanced up at Treverius. "Thanks for holding him back. If . . . if my wife Sophia had given me a son, I'd want him to be . . ." He stopped and ran a hand over his eyes, then shook the sandglass on his desk. "It's only the th . . . third hour, but I'm tired already. Think I'll go to my quarters."

* * *

Albanus lapsed into depression over the events that had shattered his world, and shut himself away in his room to wait for the dispatch from Ravenna that confirmed his resignation. But, on the sixth of February, he roused himself and called the conference in the mapping room to discuss the destruction in Quadrant IV. Architect Julius Gaudentius, Vertiscus, Treverius, and Blandina were told to attend. After Demetrius learned of the meeting, he insisted on being present.

The room that cartographers shared with architects was the largest in the Pretorium. Long slanting tables lined the walls, where the small staff worked from surveyors' notes to draw charts of field divisions, street and road layouts, or copied Junius's strip maps. Treverius and his wife occupied a separate alcove, where they worked together on the provincial map.

In a smaller area some apprentices used pumice stone to smooth the animal skin surfaces on which drawings were made. Others ground mineral pigments for ink and colors, or boiled rabbit skins to make glue and sizing. The pretorium library occupied the eastern end of the room. Modestus acted as librarian.

A wooden model of Mogontium stood on a table in the office of Gaudentius, next to a miniature of the Church of Stephan, his staff's current project. On the wall, a grid plan of Mogontium showed the four quadrants into which the town was divided and their street layout. Broken red lines indicated where walls had been torn down over the years as the population declined from raids, and defense became more difficult.

The pleasantly distinctive smell of tanned vellum and goatskin hides permeated the room as the group sat waiting for Gaudentius's assistant to bring in the model of Mogontium.

"The Governor, poor man, still looks terribly ill," Blandina whispered to her husband.

"I noticed. He's obviously not sleeping well. Let's hope Nicias is treating him."

Treverius guessed that Glaucus had boasted in the public baths about his challenge to the governor's authority. Gossip about the insult would certainly be known to him.

"Has there been any reaction from Ravenna about the raid?" Blandina asked. "He must be worried about that."

"I doubt any dispatches could have come through yet . . . ah, here's Gavius with the model." Treverius nodded toward a young man coming from the architect's area.

The apprentice slid the model to the center of the table. Some of the buildings were painted red, including Castellum Mattiacorum.

"Wh . . . why in Hades name is . . . is part of it colored?" Albanus stammered.

"Those are the destroyed areas in Quadrant Four." Gaudentius held back a sleeve of his tunic and tapped the red sectors with a stylus. "After the weather improves the rubble can be cleared away and rebuilding started."

"W . . . we won't rebuild."

Gaudentius looked up sharply. "Not rebuild, Governor?"

"Mo . . . most of the people in that sector of the quadrant were killed. I'll ask the Curia for authority to m . . . move in the south wall. To the Via Germanicus."

"What of Mattiacorum?" Demetrius questioned. "It's our eastern defense against new attacks."

"Will we garr . . . garrison it with phantoms?" Albanus scoffed. "No, the question is whether or not t . . . to dismantle the bridge into Germania."

"Dismantle?" Demetrius sputtered. "The Augustus would not be pleased."

"Then let him order Stilicho to return my men!" Albanus snapped. "Treverius, y . . . your father said you had a plan."

"Sir, the buildings could be razed and the lots converted into gardens. In the spring we may have to plant as much food as we can."

"Vertiscus, wh . . . what do you think of the idea?"

"Governor, the map maker has a point. Feeding those refugees outside the walls has depleted our supplies. We may not be able to barge more in because of ice in the river."

"How are garrison stores, Curator?" Demetrius badgered, incising a note on his tablet. "Adequate. Yes? No?"

"Glaucus has the men on short rations."

"Isn't that dangerous?" Demetrius made a nervous brush at his hair. "Legions have rebelled for far less."

"He's aware of that," Vertiscus replied with a snort of annoyance. "This is February, the river is still frozen, and no one knows the supply situation upriver."

"Governor. In my dispatch I could ask Honorius to send supplies."

"Really, Demetrius?" Albanus chortled sarcastically. "Will they c . . . come with Stilicho in the spring? When is the commander due? Anyone recall?"

"April, sir," Treverius said. If he comes at all.

"Perhaps at mid-month," Blandina added. "Near the Feast of the Resurrection."

"Good timing. Stilicho can resurrect this town." Albanus ran a hand through his wiry hair, then rubbed his eyes, clearly exhausted. "I've recom . . . recommended moving in the south wall. Other discussion?"

"The Theater of Trajan?" Gaudentius asked stiffly. "Inside the wall? Outside? Why not just tear it down?"

"No!" Blandina cried. "The actors also need a place where they can make a living."

"Not a great loss," Demetrius smirked. "Their obscene plays only encourage citizen idleness."

"Outside the wall," Albanus said, ignoring the envoy's comment. "The garrison camp, too, if we follow the Via Germanicus."

"You're taking away a third of the town!" Demetrius threw down his stylus in sullen protest.

"Demetrius, you're new here. G . . . go look at how much smaller Mogontium has become in . . . in the last century and a half." Albanus made an impatient hand gesture at the wall map. "If that's all, I—"

"A moment more, Governor." Demetrius retrieved his stylus and forced a smile. "How many men did you lose?"

Albanus sighed. "Treverius. C . . . casualties?"

"Sir, everyone at Mattiacorum was killed, or is assumed to be a prisoner. We buried over a hundred of our dead."

"Aside from citizens, how many were from the garrison?" Demetrius looked up from writing. "Your border militia?"

"All the men fought well," Treverius replied, irked at the questions. "The dead were mostly citizens."

"It . . . it was all in my report to the Augustus," Albanus added, standing up. "Treverius, re-establish coordinates in . . . in the destroyed blocks. Have debris cleared for the gardens b . . . but salvage as many bricks as you can. Excuse me now, I . . . I'm very tired."

After Albanus and the others left, Treverius went back to his mapping table with Blandina. He stared numbly at the unfinished chart of Germania Prima and Sequania for a moment, then said, "You just saw our future in there, Blandina. A map of the province seems like a futile project now."

"We can't just stop, Trev."

"Indeed not, Domina," Vertiscus agreed, coming into the small space. "It would be a shame to halt work on your chart."

"That's up to the governor," Treverius said, surprised to see the curator.

"Or on your mosaic designs," Vertiscus continued, "now that superstition has stopped work on the temple. To be reduced to surveying gardens must be disappointing."

"The people of Mogontium have worse problems," Blandina countered.

"Just so, young woman. And one concern of mine is the governor."

"Trev and I, also. He didn't look well."

"I meant his lack of interest in governing." Vertiscus idly traced a finger around the outine of the province. "Did you know that he's petitioned the Augustus to be relieved of duty?"

"I didn't," Treverius admitted. "And yet he made some decisions just now about Mogontium."

"None dealt with the Vandals. His province is awash in a sea of barbarians."

"Haven't they moved on into central Gaul?" Blandina asked.

"Some subchiefs may have. Gaisios is at Treveri."

"Treveri? Then they did take the capital." Treverius put an arm around Blandina at the confirmation of what had been a rumor. "My wife's father is there."

"I pray the gods keep him safe, young woman." Vertiscus looked down at the map again and pointed to the symbol for a legion base. "Vindonissa? Where Bassus is?"

"Yes."

"How many miles from here, would you say?"

Treverius moved a wooden scale across the distance. "About one hundred seventy-five as an arrow flies. Longer by the Rhine . . . when the river isn't frozen."

Vertiscus took Treverius by the sleeve and turned him away. "Should the governor be incapacitated, I'm prepared to assume his office. I'd support your work here."

"I . . . we're grateful, sir," Treverius replied, surprised by the unexpected offer. "You know the administration of the pretorium better than anyone."

Vertiscus's thin mouth broke into a smile. "I'm pleased you realize that, map maker. Think of my proposition. I may need your help."

After the curator left the room, Blandina snatched at her husband's arm. "Did you hear that?"

"It is far-fetched that he should replace Albanus."

"Not that, Trev. He asked that the gods keep father safe. Could he be another pagan sympathizer, like Cyril?"

"You know the rumors about his being an Arian." He pulled Blandina to him in a tight hug. "Dove, I was sorry to hear about Treveri, but I'm sure your father is safe. Gaisios would keep him and the palace staff for ransom."

"I hope you're right."

"Just now there's not much we can find out. The weather is bad and we don't know the Vandals' strength. If we haven't heard anything by next month . . . spring . . . Albanus could send out a strong scouting force to Treveri."

Blandina nodded and wiped her eyes. "I'll help with that surveying he asked you to do."

"It's near the theater. Perhaps we could look inside."

"For your red-haired Juliana?"

"Why would I want a wolf when I'm happy with my dove?"

"I was teasing you, Trev."

"I know. I'm ready for something to eat, are you?"

"I suppose, but our staff food ration is low. Ageria said she was only making Lucanian sausage and turnips."

"Fine." Treverius tongued at the salty wetness near his wife's eyes. "You go ahead, dove, I'll be there in a short while."

Treverius watched Blandina leave. He wanted to be alone, to think about what had been decided at the meeting and what Vertiscus had suggested afterwards. He went to a window, detached a parchment covering, and looked out at the street.

Along the Via Praetori a gentle fall of snow blanketed the slate and tile roofs of Mogontium in a tranquilizing pall of white. The slope of the distant temple roof and angled top of the public baths mimicked miniature, snow-crested mountains. Across the Praetori, homes of wealthy citizens, Arinthos, Pendatios, and Musonius among them, now were patrolled by hired guards. He could see the men hunched in cloaks, their backs to the cold fall of flakes. Looting and robberies had increased since the Vandal incursion, even in wealthy neighborhoods close to the pretorium.

Treverius watched the dizzying flocules swirl down from a sky of dark clouds to settle on the window ledge. He brushed off the accumulation. The scene was beautiful, but, in the light of Mogontium's problems, he thought the snow-laden rooftops and wintery scene along the Praetori looked deceptively peaceful. Too much so.

Governor Albanus's proffered resignation was more disturbing than his decision to abandon the southern sector of Quadrants Three and Four. Perhaps the burned buildings ought not to be rebuilt. Deteriorated apartments around the theater should have been condemned long ago, but how would the garrison react to having their camp outside the wall and only protected by the stake palisade? Since Glaucus had become insolent enough to challenge the governor, this could create an excuse for ordering an outright attack on the Pretorian Guard. If it succeeded, Glaucus could declare military law and dismiss the Curia. Even though Vertiscus hadn't said as much, he seemed to hint at the same thing. It made sense that he had offered to keep the administration of the town going and outflank Glaucus while Albanus was ill.

Treverius looked up at the early evening sky. Despite the snow clouds, a faint flush of light was still visible.

February was one of the months he liked best. The winter solstice was past and the short hours were becoming discernably longer, bringing with them the promise of spring and the break-up of ice on the Rhine.

As he turned his glance toward the river, Treverius recognized Cyril and his associate, Nevius, coming out a side door of the merchant's villa. They turned into the Via Alexander, which led toward the legion camp.

"Wonder where those two are headed?" he muttered to the falling snowflakes. "Cyril must be worried about theft in his warehouses. I'll wager he's going to the camp to hire more guards." After the men disappeared behind the corner shop, Treverius turned away and clipped the protective panel back over the window opening. "At least Cyril's been too preoccupied lately to spout his pagan nonsense. He's probably decided that his own survival is more important than that of his ridiculous gods."

*   *   *

Cyril scowled as he opened the door of Gundstram's shed, then covered his nose with the back of his hand to escort Suebius Nevius down through the mithreum anteroom, into the arched temple.

Although Cyril was Pater of the cell, he did not like coming to the underground rooms and always hurried past the bizarre sculpture of Kronos. Not that the main temple was more pleasant. Its overlying smell of incense could not completely mask the lingering, putrid odor that came from the dried blood in the taurobolium. Why, he wondered, must this Parthian god Mithras eternally sacrifice the white bull in front of a gore-stained chamber to fulfill some cosmic destiny? Roman gods were worshipped by daylight, not in the darkness of an Avernian Underworld.

Glancing at Nevius, Cyril thought his associate looked uneasy. He had had trouble convincing him to come again, but when he reminded Nevius of the ancient coins Vertiscus gave out at the first meeting, greed had overcome mistrust.

While Gundstram lighted another lamp, Cyril motioned his friend to one of the stone benches to wait for Vertiscus.

"I don't mind telling you that I don't like it down here," Nevius complained, his glance darting between the low ceiling and flaking wall murals. "What does Vertiscus need me for? I told him I wasn't interested in his scheme."

"He wants to explain his New Gothia more clearly. With the Vandals unsuccessful, he—"

"Unsuccessful? We're being strangled here. I lost a looted three-month cache of supplies."

"As did I, Nevius, as did I."

"The Germani I trade with along the Rhine are gone. That leaves only people in Mogontium."

"And the refugees. Raise prices, as I did." Cyril snickered. "They have no alternative."

"And how long will those goods last? The river ice probably won't thaw enough by May to barge supplies in through Raetia. Besides, the Suebi invaded that area."

"A crisis," Cyril agreed. "I'm in the same barge."

"The invasion and now these mysterious deaths," Nevius went on. "Citizens are close to panic."

"Which works to our advantage," Cyril said. "We're making headway in showing people Jupiter's power."

"We? You forget I'm an Arian Christian."

"And toleration, Nevius, is the keystone of my New Gothia," Vertiscus said, sweeping in from the taurobolium vesting room. Hortar followed him, a step behind.

"Keystone?" Nevius repeated. "Make sense, Curator."

"In good time, friend, I'm glad you came. We have affairs to discuss, affairs that will affect our very lives."

"Is there some new danger?" Cyril asked.

"Isn't there enough of the old?" Nevius bit his lip under the moustache. "The cold weather. Vandals."

"The barbarians, at least, have moved west," Cyril remarked. "When Stilicho returns our men, we'll drive them out of the province."

"Really, Cyril?" Vertiscus asked. "Have you listened to what I've been saying these past months? Gundstram, what do you hear about the men he's supposed to bring back?"

"The barracks talk is that Stilicho will have only his personal guard with him."

"Absurd," Cyril scoffed. "He'll come with Vulcatius Bassus."

"I think not, friend. Hortar, you've returned from meeting with Gaisios. Where is the chieftain?"

"Gaisios is still in Treveri."

"And it's an outrage!" Cyril sputtered. "The Gallic prefectural capital in barbarian hands."

"Indeed. Tell our friends what you've been doing, Hortar."

"As you know, I'm at home in this region." Hortar grinned. "I've helped you deal with both the Germani and—"

"Get to the point, man!"

"Cyril, Cyril. Calm," Vertiscus soothed. "Hortar, let me explain. I'll be blunt. Friends, the Vandal invasion has convinced me that our Germanic provinces are lost to the empire."

"Germania Prima and Secunda? It's treason to talk like that," Cyril protested.

"Treason or truth?" Vertiscus retorted. "The field legions are with Stilicho. Our militia along the Rhine has been decimated by the invaders. We may seem safe behind our walls, as . . . as Troy once did. It took Troy ten years to fall, but I give us no more than ten weeks, once the Vandals decide to attack Mogontium again."

"Barbarians have no seige engines," Nevius scoffed. "The Visigoths couldn't even take Adrianople after their field victory."

"You've been in your account books too long," Vertiscus reprimanded softly. "That was three decades ago. Since then, Ostrogoths, to name one tribe, have learned to use catapults and undermine walls."

"Then we are lost," Nevius cried.

"I'll let Hortar continue." Vertiscus nodded to him.

Hortar wet his lips. "I'm telling Gaisios that, if he destroys our governing agencies, he won't benefit from the estates he's taken. A dead villa manager, dead slaves won't produce a mound of manure."

"There are revenues to be had from land taxes, duties on salt, wine, parchment," Vertiscus broke in. "The man doesn't want to destroy the province, only settle his tribe within it. Or, in what will be my New Gothia."

"There's a procedure in applying for Federate status," Cyril retorted. "You implied the Vandals would do so."

"Apply? Now that they're deep inside Gaul?" Vertiscus gave a hoarse laugh. "The fish is caught, Cyril. What I'm suggesting is that New Gothia become an independent province ruled by Romans and Vandals."

"That's surely treasonable," Cyril spat out in anger. "I agreed to be Pater of this mithreum to boost garrison morale, not betray Rome."

"Where . . . where would the garrison stand on this?" Nevius asked, probing.

"In a moment I'll let Gundstram answer," Vertiscus replied. "You're aware that Albanus is a sick man and has asked the Augustus to be relieved as governor."

"Relieved? I heard he held a meeting today about Mogontium's future."

"I attended it, Cyril. The destroyed buildings in Quadrant Four won't be rebuilt. He'll ask the Curia for permission to relocate the south wall along the Via Germanicus. A third of Mogontium will be abandoned."

"Another outrage! The man should be recalled. Can't you get Demetrius to petition Ravenna?"

"Slowly, Cyril. I mentioned to Treverius that I would support his work if Albanus became incapacitated."

"You're confiding in map makers now?"

"You weren't at the meeting," Vertiscus countered. "The governor favors him. That could be useful."

"The garrison?" Nevius asked again. "And where's Lupus Glaucus? Why isn't he ever at these meetings?"

"He'll be here in good time. But to answer your question. Gundstram, is the garrison with us?"

"Sir, men have always followed those who paid them."

"And who will pay when their salaries can't get through from Ravenna?" Vertiscus asked. "Local taxes are uncollectible because barbarians control the countryside."

"You're suggesting that you're wealthy enough to finance a new country?" Cyril scoffed. "As the saying goes, Curator, 'your ambition may be richer than your purse.'"

Instead of replying, Vertiscus untied his purse and tossed it to Cyril. After he slid the contents onto the bench, Nevius picked up three coins and held them to lamplight.

"These are like the ones you showed us last time. An aureus of Galba. This is a gold coin of Claudius Nero. Whose is the wreathed head?"

"I thought that would interest you," Vertiscus said. "The image is of Apollo. A Greek coin. Macedonian to be exact."

Cyril was almost afraid to voice what he thought the coins implied. "You . . . you've found the treasury of Legion Four Macedonica?"

"Let's say it could be at my disposal." Vertiscus scooped up the money with a smirk.

"Who else knows of this?" Cyril asked.

"Now, only the five of us. Albanus will be advised in good time. He'll join us in New Gothia, or Glaucus will see to it that his head sits alongside that of Flaccus."

"It . . . it's still treason."

"Not so, Cyril. When the Huns are at his eastern door, Honorius will realize that by buffering his frontier with New Gothia, we do the Empire a service." Vertiscus paused to stroke the flank of the bull on the Mithras altar. "Hortar will go back to Gaisios and convince him to join us, but now, Gundstram, take our friends up for a cup of good Mosella wine, not your legionary vinegar."

"Nevius, you go ahead," Cyril stalled. "I wish to ask a few questions about . . . about Mithras."

After the other men left through the anteroom, Vertiscus took Cyril by the sleeve. "You want proof of the Macedonica treasure, not of Mithras. Isn't that so?"

"I deal in realities."

"What you will see is no phantom." Vertiscus took one of the lamps and led the way to the space behind the altar. Cyril saw an iron grating in the floor, crusted with dark splotches of dried blood. Although the light was feeble, he could make out a stained mosaic floor beneath the grate. It was decorated with the same sacrificial theme as the Mithras sculpture.

Vertiscus handed Cyril the lamp, then knelt down and lifted the grate. After feeling around the edges of the mosaic, he lifted a section of the flooring, then another, and stacked the slabs alongside the opening.

When Cyril held the lamp lower, the light reflected off a layer of dull silvery plates. "Lead?" he asked in disappointment. "This is your treasure?"

"Put the lamp on the tiles," Vertiscus ordered instead of answering. "I'll need you to help me move these."

Cyril helped ease one of the plates over the other, then sucked in his breath. Underneath the lead, he already had caught the glint of silver and gold. Platters, cups, and votive images fashioned of the glittering metals lay on a broad bed of coins and jewelry.

"How deep is it?" he whispered in a husky tone.

"The legion burial fund alone fills seven chests."

Despite the dank air, Cyril was sweating when he leaned back from the opening. Strands of hair lay plastered against his forehead and dirt soiled his white tunic. He felt faintly nauseous, but finally stammered a reaction. "So . . . so they hid everything here in their mithreum and had no time to recover even a denarius."

"Those men who weren't executed bounded for home like frightened deer. Gundstram discovered the temple while building his shed." Vertiscus brushed dirt off Cyril's tunic and held his shoulders. "I need you and Nevius. Tell him Arians will have freedom to worship their Christ in New Gothia, alongside our gods.

"I see you as second-in-command to me. Nevius can deal with commerce. Glaucus can command the army, and Hortar will be our envoy to the barbarians." Vertiscus released his grip. "I tell you, Cyril, our Germanias have ceased to be Roman. They will never again be ruled by either Ravenna or Constantinople. I will see to that!"

chapter 12

Blandina held a surveyor's ranging pole as she stood in the open square at the theater of Trajan. The air smelled of charred wood from burned buildings. Treverius was a hundred paces beyond her. Snow had stopped falling during the night, leaving a canopy of white to soften the tangled outline of smoke-blackened beams and stone foundations in Quadrant IV, which stretched to the river wall as stark witnesses to the Vandal attack.

While waiting for Treverius to sight along the cross staff of a groma and establish a right angle, Blandina stamped snow off her boots and looked toward the theater that Marcus Trajan had donated to the city some three hundred years earlier, when he was governor of Germania Superior.

Weathered limestone blocks of the stage outer wall rose to three stories, its stark face relieved only by an arcade of abandoned food booths at street level. On the top, a few splintered poles still stabbed skyward from support brackets for a huge awning—long since rotted—that once kept the audience shaded from the afternoon sun. A subsequent governor, in an awkward effort to save stone, had ordered a new wall built into the theater's left side, then extended it beyond the curved seat area to enclose deteriorating houses in Quadrant III. The new wall blocked audience entrances on that side of the theater, leaving only two access tunnels open to the public seating.

Treverius motioned Blandina to the right. As she began to align her staff with his line of sight, a voice sounded behind her.

"Ah, one of my angels. You're hardly measuring here for the gates of Paradise, are you?"

She turned to see Petranius. Despite the cold his complexion was the sallow shade of a parchment sheet, and the lines in his gaunt face looked more harsh than they had in the dim temple. His reddish hair was uncombed, flecked with white strands that caught the light.

"My husband and I are surveying block limits for the houses Vandals destroyed," she replied.

"Destroyed?" Petranius chuckled. "One could say 'vandalized.' Use the tribe's name as a verb."

Treverius had seen the actor talking with Blandina and walked over to them.

"This is my husband Treverius," she told Petranius.

"Yes, I recognize him but hadn't made the connection with you, angel." He held out a hand. "You designed the Nativity set. Have you came to any of our plays?"

"I . . . I'm afraid not."

"No . . ." Petranius's face betrayed a wince of pain as he shifted weight from his injured leg. "Mother Church doesn't much approve of actors, even though She was founded on the awesome drama of the Crucifixion." He cocked his head toward the theater. "It looks rather pretty in its clean mantle of snow, don't you think? I was just going in for a rehearsal. Come meet my cast, make some new friends."

Treverius hesitated. Even though he had not gone to see Juliana at The Golden Mask after her invitation at the temple, the prospect of seeing her again was both attractive and disturbing.

Before he could reply, Petranius took Blandina by the arm. "Come along, angel, you might find us amusing. A diversion from all this vandal-ization."

As Petranius led the way to the first entrance on the right, Treverius followed behind, aware that the actor was trying to minimize his limp. The low, arched entrance tunnel was dank and smelled of urine. It led to a ramp that opened onto twenty rows of wooden benches facing a semi-circular orchestra level. The stage was dominated by a stone backdrop, divided into four sections by columns. Treverius surmised that the empty niches were for displaying statuary, like those in the basilica, but had been looted of them in long-ago raids.

Several people in the orchestra warmed themselves at a fire blazing in an iron box. When a woman looked up, Treverius recognized Juliana.

Petranius clapped his hands and called out, "Cast, I've brought new friends. On stage so I can introduce you."

"That's not necessary," Treverius mumbled. "We really should go back to work."

"Nonsense," Petranius insisted, "you said you haven't seen us perform, so we'll do a little improvisation. Hear that all of you? Albino, onstage."

A slightly built man, whose alabaster-pale skin and hair accounted for his name, sprang onto the wooden platform. He bent low in an exaggerated bow.

"Pumilio next," the director continued. "Friends, meet 'short and sassy.'"

The dwarf was lifted onto the stage by the black man Treverius had seen at the temple. Pumilio curtsied in mock homage.

"The sooty one is Aethiops," Petranius explained. "He's a mute, but handy for moving scenery or filling in as a slave, soldier . . . whoever." When Juliana was helped up the stairs by Albino, Petranius mimicked a fanfare. "The ravishing JU-LI-AN-A! Followed by Callixa and Erotia, two of my musicians, and Alexandros, our apprentice actor. His parents, of course, have totally disowned him."

"Better than totally disembowling him," Alexandros called back with a sneer.

"As I said, our profession is no longer held in great esteem. Mother Church thinks we should only look to the final drama of the General Resurrection, and swears it will be spectacular." Petranius waved, flagging over the seats, then sweeping the sky in dramatic gesture. "The orchestra opening up to swallow the damned, the Blessed rising to heaven without the help of that machine." He pointed to a crane, which lowered actors onstage or hoisted them upward during a performance.

"You did well with the Nativity drama," Blandina said. "I enjoyed being part of it."

"We're not that serious here, angel. Comedies by Terence and Plautus. Bawdy scenes. What the audience wants. We just keep adding to the plot until everyone is thoroughly confused, then some ridiculous deus ex machina sets things straight in time for dinner."

"Sir director," Pumilio called down to Petranius in a high-pitched wimper. "I'm freezing my tiny balls . . . sorry, Domina . . . my tiny ears off up here. What are we supposed to do?"

"A moment." Petranius led his two guests to the fire box, then eased himself up to sit on the edge of the stage. "Cast, you know I'm working on a play to entertain Stilicho when he comes in April. Let's parody the 'Savior of the West' a bit."

Treverius flinched. The commander's victories had prompted many to award him that title, but, given the number of legions that had declared their commanders emperors in the past, he knew the term was not popular with Honorius.

"Let's see." Petranius drew his cloak tighter and rubbed his chin. "The Goth he's fighting is named Alaric. Albino, we'll call you 'Garlic.' Alexandros, you do Stilicho."

"I don't usually do men," he mocked in a falsetto.

"Enough," Petranius warned. "We'll call you 'Stylus.' Stilicho is married to—"

"Serena," Juliana called out. "I'll name myself 'Serita,' a large jar."

"I've got a large something that would love to fill your large jar." Alexandros leered at her.

"None of that crude talk," Petranius cautioned again, "we have an angel here. But, good, Juliana, I like the name."

"What about me?" Pumilio whined. "Who am I?"

"You can be 'Pumilio-his-Penis.'" Albino chortled.

"I said enough!" Petranius snapped. "Pardon, angel. Pumilio, you're Arcadius, the emperor at Constantinople."

"How about calling me 'Arcane,' then?"

"Good, good. He's certainly involved in secret intrigues. Basic plot. We know Stilicho has cornered this Alaric many times, but he's always managed to escape."

"Or was bought off," Alexandros jeered.

"Petranius, do they need character masks?" Callixa asked.

"Not for an improvisation. Alexandros, you start."

"I'll need a sword."

"Mime it," Petranius cried in exasperation. "START, for Thalia's sake!"

"Jupiter's Balls, calm down," Alexandros muttered, then went to Albino and pretended to hold a sword against his chest. "Now I have you, you scabby-skinned, bushy-bearded, stinking barbarian son of pond scum."

"Oh Crate Gommander, I mean Great Commander." Albino affected trembling. "I fear your sword may strike one of my barbarian bones and dull its sharpness."

"Hmm. You're a well-seasoned warrior, Garlic. I see your point."

"It's your point I'm afraid of."

As Petranius clapped at the puns, Treverius saw the director relax and his face lose its mask of pain, as if he had created an artificial world to help deal with his disabilities.

"What will you take," Alexandros pleaded, "to go away so I can keep my sword sharp?"

"A handful of coins would be nice. Even an as."

Alexandros mimed counting coins into Albino's hand. "Get your as to Thessaly, then, but stay far away from my ass."

Petranius laughed at the vulgar pun on a small bronze coin. "Good, good. Now work with Erotia."

Albino went to the woman, pulled her to the stage floor and pretended to have intercourse. "Thessaly, I'm raping you," he gasped.

"Stop, Garlic, or I'll close your slimy windpipe!" Alexandros cried, striding over to choke him.

Albino looked up with a pleading expression. "Oh Crate Gommander. I fear you may injure your soft hands on my worthless throat."

"Yes, I see your point again."

Pumilio gave a squeaky chuckle. "An extremely small point, as Erotia found out."

Alexandros ignored him. "Garlic, how much will you take to go and rape Greece?"

"A bag of gold and I'll be off."

"Not on me, you won't," Erotia exclaimed, rolling out from under Albino.

"Good," Petranius called. "Now you, Arcane. Tease the commander."

"What's this I hear, Stylus?" Pumilio swaggered up to Alexandros and pulled his nose. "You're draining the imperial treasury with all this garlic you're buying."

"Oh excellent Arcane," Alexandros whimpered, "son of a god, sire of at least two gods . . . to whose cousin I happen to be married . . . I only meant to give employment to workers at the mint. Keep them off the public dole."

"Commendable." Pumilio clapped his hands. "If this Garlic shows up in Ravenna, you have my permission to open the treasury for him."

"But glorious Arcane, son of a god, et cetera, Ravenna is not yours. It belongs to your brother Honorless."

Treverius glanced at his wife. Blandina had hardly looked at the stage since the rape simulation, and he knew the parody on the two emperors was also embarrassing her.

Petranius looked his way and caught the signal. "Enough for now, cast." He lowered himself from the platform and limped back to the fire. "A bit raw, friends, but it's what our audience wants. You who live in the Pretorium . . ." Instead of finishing, Petranius smiled at Blandina. "Sorry if we offended you with our little games, angel."

"No, it's all right," she replied, "but we . . . we should go back to work."

"Of course, angel. I'll see you both out." Petranius turned to his actors. "Cast. Work on the Plautus we'll open with in the spring."

As the three climbed the ramp to the exit, Juliana abruptly came down the stage steps and ran after them. When she took Treverius by the arm and smiled at him, he noticed her breath smelled of wine. Juliana did not say anything, but after they came out on the square, she shook his arm playfully.

"I spoke to you at the temple, yet you didn't come to The Golden Mask."

"And he'd better not," Blandina called out from behind the woman.

"Oh, I'm sure you keep him satisfied," Juliana shot back. "But you work measuring fields. Actresses are forced to measure other things."

"Now, Julita, these are new friends," Petranius chided gently. "Rein in your remarks."

"What didn't you like about our little play?" she asked Blandina, ignoring the director.

"Blessed Paul advised us to honor emperors, not ridicule them," she replied. "But I suppose you only read your coarse scripts."

"On the contary. Your Paul also warned Corinthians that men should not touch women other than their wives."

"Julita! That's enough," Petranius repeated more sternly.

"No, let me finish. You two would be shocked to know who comes to visit me from the Pretorium. Even more so by the kind of services they want me to perform."

"I . . . I'm sorry," Blandina stammered. "I had no right to judge you."

"No, you didn't. Your Galilean pointed that out when he saved the adultress from being stoned to death."

Juliana fell silent, but clung to Treverius's arm. He turned toward the marker where he had left the surveying equipment: a crumbling brick-and-stone monument on which the long ago Rhine victories of Drusus Nero were commemorated. A relief sculpture of a Roman legionary was carved on the plinth. The soldier's face was exaggerated, like an actor's mask contorted to depict Brutality. Thick-set legs angled beneath an oval shield that hid his squat body. A javelin was at the ready, with two more of the deadly lances showing behind the shield. Treverius thought the figure looked almost a caricature of Lupus Glaucus.

"Bastard!" Juliana suddenly let go of Treverius's arm and spat at the figure. "A girlfriend of mine was murdered and those army swine did nothing to protect her."

"Now, now, Julita," Petranius soothed, stroking her hair. "You know Agnes was killed by a drunken client."

"Caco . . . Shit, Petranius." She pushed his hand away. "Some say that only an alliance with the Vandals will save Mogontium."

"Actors were born to parody politics, not formulate them," Petranius joked, shushing her lips with a finger. "You're tired, Julita. We'll not rehearse any more today."

"I'm sorry about Agnes," Treverius said in an attempt to calm Juliana. "I didn't realize you knew her."

"Treverius . . ." Petranius pulled him aside. "White Swan services wealthy men in town, so the magistrate didn't look too hard before abandoning his search. Agnes was, after all, a mere prostitute. A calling even lower than an actor's."

Treverius scanned Petranius's face for a sign of bitterness, but the director turned back to Juliana and winked at Blandina. "Goodbye, angel. I'm thinking of doing another Nativity this December. I'll want you to sing again."

"I . . . I'd like that, Petranius."

Treverius slipped his fingers between Blandina's, watching the director hobble away alongside Juliana until the two disappeared around a corner of the theater.

"What did Juliana mean?" Blandina asked, shaking her hand free. "Who told her about a Vandal alliance?"

"Gossip, dove." Treverius bent down to pick up the range pole chain. "Juliana has pretorium clients."

"I wonder who they are?"

"Probably some of the clerks. We hardly know most of the other staff." Treverius handed her the surveying instrument. "Here's your range pole. Let's keep on."

They finished their work in silence, distracted by the strange people they had met, those who lived in a world neither of them knew anything about. Treverius had no desire to visit The Golden Mask, but found it hard to shake the image of the red-haired woman who had held his arm so tightly.

* * *

By mid-February, Treverius was aware that Vertiscus was making decisions that were the governor's perogative. On the pretext of conserving wood the curator closed the public baths, an order that caused citizen resentment against Albanus. Vertiscus announced a resumption of public meals, which the governor could not carry out because of rationed food supplies, further alienating him.

Treverius knew that Modestus had lost part of his congregation through his failure to rationalize the deadly weather and Vandal invasions. Nevertheless, the presbyter announced the beginning of the forty-day penitential season, which preceded the Feast of the Resurrection, ordering those who still came to Mass to abstain from food and drink until the ninth hour on the second and fifth days of the week. Only a few catechumens, all women, were prepared for the Rite of Baptism.

Malchus added to Modestus's aggravation. The old man appeared at the Longinus Chapel with several disciples for the Service of the Ashes, the first day of the penance period. All were barefoot and wore tunics of coarse grain sacking. They brought their own ashes to rub on each others' arms and faces, displayed the silver coin of Decius, and badgered everyone entering the chapel to join their cult and repent.

* * *

A few days after beginning their survey of Quadrant IV, Treverius and Blandina were called to the governor's office. Albanus was standing by his wall map when they entered.

"Th . . . th . . . thanks for coming." His stammer was even more pronounced. "There's been a . . . a death near the theater." Albanus pointed to a rectangle on the chart. "Th . . . this house. The director wanted you to come. Sa . . . says he knows you."

"Petranius?" Treverius was surprised. He had not seen the actor since the day he and Blandina had gone into the theater.

"Petranius, that's the name," Albanus said. "He . . . he wanted you, too, Blandina."

"Who was it died, Governor?" she asked.

"One . . . one of his actresses. Mind going?"

"Of course not." Even as he agreed, Treverius felt apprehensive. "Again, where is the dead woman, Governor?"

"In th . . . the place where the actors live. La . . . last apartment on the Via Augustus. Take my bodyguard Marculf with you. It . . . it's a rough sector."

"Did Petranius say there was something unusual about the death?" Treverius asked.

"No. Jus . . . just asked that you get over there quickly."

With Marculf a few steps behind, Treverius guided Blandina along the Via Augustus, a street paralleling the west ramparts. The smell of woodsmoke from refugees' fires on the other side of the wall mingled with that of cooking food. When Treverius heard the wail of a baby and the laughter of children playing among the tents, he glanced at Blandina, knowing the sounds were probably making her sad, but she gave no indication of her feelings.

After passing the Porta Borbetomagus, Treverius stopped. A cluster of people were ahead at the end of the street, gawking at the actors' apartment, adjacent to the south wall. Aethiops barred the door. Petranius was next to him, looking tired, his red hair disheveled. Stooped and half-surrounded by the crowd, the director seemed a small, pathetic figure.

"He's fending off questions from those idlers. The dead girl must be inside." Treverius put an arm around his wife. "Blandina, are you sure you want to go in?"

"I'm sure."

Treverius saw Petranius glance in his direction, then push his way through the onlookers and hobble toward him without trying to conceal his limp or hunchback. Dark areas circled puffy, red-rimmed eyes. He looked as if he had not slept that night.

"Angel . . . Treverius," he wailed. "You came after all. Th . . . thanks."

"What happened? We were told only that one of your actresses died."

"Horrible, Treverius. It . . . it's Juliana," Petranius replied, his voice trembling. "Julita. My . . . my pet name for her."

"What? Where is she?"

"Upstairs. In the bath."

Treverius told Marculf to remain with Aethiops at the door that led to the second floor, then followed Blandina as Petranius led the way up a narrow stairwell whose treads were caked with mud. Chipped wall plaster was further marred by graffiti. A smell of onions and meat frying in rancid lard was not strong enough to mask an underlying odor of urine. The stairs were also obviously used as a latrine by children, or some tenents.

At the second floor landing Petranius pointed to the end of the hall, where Pumilio and Callixa stood outside a door. The dwarf moaned in a high-pitched whine. Callixa sobbed uncontrollably, dark streaks of dissolved eye make-up running down her face. After Petranius reached the bath entrance, he held Blandina back by a sleeve.

"No, angel, better stay here," he advised. "Let your husband go inside."

Treverius entered the tub room and felt his stomach churn. A high window covered with thin parchment gave feeble light to a small space that reeked of mold. The pine floor boards were warped from water that was continually sloshed on them. An overturned bucket lay against a wall stained dark by mildew splotches. His glance turned to a wooden bathtub on the right. "Christ, Jes . . ." Treverius gagged, choking off the words.

Juliana's nude, headless torso slumped against the lead sheeting of the tub's curved back. Her head floated in the pink-stained water between her knees, but the dead actress's face was mercifully hidden by her spread of dyed hair. Treverius's first thought was that Juliana, like Agnes, had been killed by a client. He glanced around the room for the weapon—it would have to have been an axe or sword—or some item of clothing, any clue that had been left behind by the murderer. There was only the water bucket and sickening mildew odor. He felt nausea rise in his throat, turned away, and leaned on a damp wall to retch into a corner. After another unbelieving look at the severed stump of neck, Treverius lurched out and grasped the door frame with a white-knuckled grip.

"This death is not an accident," he whispered hoarsely. "Juliana was brutally murdered."

"Trev, no!" Blandina sucked in a breath of disbelief. "How?"

"Don't go in. Petranius, who found her?"

"Callixa. She . . . she called Pumilio. He told me."

"Close the door and don't disturb anything," he ordered. "I'll have someone from the magistrate's office come by to investigate. Talk to neighbors."

"And will he care about another dead 'she-wolf'?" Petranius asked feebly, his eyes wet. "Sorry, I'm upset, need to be alone. Thanks, you . . . you're true friends."

* * *

That evening Treverius stared into his bowl of barley soup, pushed it aside, and took a nervous gulp of wine.

"I can't eat after seeing Juliana like that. I mean, the woman was decapitated, Blandina."

"Horrible. Even if someone wanted Juliana dead, why kill her like that?" Blandina came around the table to put her arms around Treverius.

He held her hand against one cheek. "We've always had killings, mostly tavern brawls, and there are more now with the refugee situation. People are tense, but you're right, why this?"

"I can't help thinking about Agnes. She was killed about a month ago."

"The only coincidence is the victims', ah, occupation."

Ageria looked in. Blandina waved her away, then went to sit opposite Treverius. "All of these strange deaths have been different. Almost 'creative,' if I can use that term."

"Interesting thought, dove. We speculated about them once before." Treverius absently ran a finger around the rim of his wine cup. "Arbitos was struck by lightning. That had to be Fate, but the mason's scaffold could have been weakened to make it collapse. Cyril came by before I could check."

"Clement's drowning?"

"Gaisios was cleared. Macrianus declared it an accident, so we just don't know."

"Deacon Stephan could have been struck with a brick and the result made to look like it fell from the ceiling."

"True, Blandina, the blood on the gash was fresh. But I didn't see anyone in the nave."

"Did you look? I went for Nicias, remember?"

"I was keeping Stephan warm." Treverius exhaled in frustration, drained by the horror of finding Juliana. "Dove, are we trying to read too much into these deaths? Random accidents, a suicide, the murder of two prostitutes. The answer may be that simple. I admit I was flattered by Juliana's attention but, to be realistic, she ran with the most vicious types in Mogontium, not people from the pretorium."

"Except as clients. At that last rehearsal you said she was frightened and wanted to talk to you."

"She didn't name anyone that day at the theater." Treverius finished his wine in one swallow. "If these are all murders, Blandina, I don't see a common motive. Juliana was just another luckless victim of 'earning the wages of vice.' Isn't that the way Saint Paul characterized it?"

"I suppose you're right. Poor woman. Oh, on a more pleasant subject. A servant came from David's awhile ago."

"Are they well? I haven't seen David since the barricade action, but I imagine he's repairing wagons."

"I've wondered how things in the Judean quarter have been affected by all this," Blandina said.

"I heard pretorians talking about a few incidents. Anti-Judean graffiti scribbled on their synagogue, random fires in shops. People need to blame someone for problems."

"Why the Judeans?"

"Right, especially after David's men prevented Vandals from reaching the bridge gate. What did the servant say?"

"She brought an invitation. David's father . . . Rabbi Zadok . . . wants us to join his family in observing one of their festivals." Blandina went to pick the note off the cupboard and handed it to him. "It's called Purim and celebrates a Hebrew woman named Esther. Could we go, Trev?"

"I suppose it's all right to attend one of their rituals."

"This evidently isn't a religious service. And Modestus has been invited, too."

"Modestus? Perhaps David's father wants to enlighten our presbyter and clear up some of the misconceptions Christians have about Judeans." Treverius handed back the invitation. "We'll go. Seeing David and Penina will be nice and it will take our minds off the horrors of the past two months. At least for an evening."

chapter 13

Treverius tried his best to force an investigation into Juliana's murder, the second gruesome death of a prostitute in a month. He persuaded Albanus, who ordered Macrianus to send an interrogator and question cast members, or neighbors in the apartment where Juliana was found.

The man reported that everyone he interviewed was either a consummate actor, or actually knew nothing about the death. Yet Treverius recalled that Petranius had admitted, shortly before Juliana's death, that some of her pretorium clients would not want their names known. Macrianus concluded that the dead woman was trying to extort money from a nervous client, who had hired someone to silence her. Since Juliana was a prostitute, the search for her killer was not pursued.

* * *

David's invitation had said that the celebration of Purim began at sundown, and asked his father's guests to arrive before that, during the eleventh hour. By the time Treverius and Blandina came to Rabbi Zadok's home, the couple had decided to stop worrying about the series of deaths and enjoy the company of their friends.

Modestus arrived at the same time. He rang the tintinabulum, a small bronze bell that announced visitors. A servant admitted the three guests and brought them through the atrium into a reception room.

David greeted them wearing a linen tunic decorated at the sleeves and hem with golden bands of Celtic knot-work design, and belted with a gilt-silver buckle. His red cloak was fastened with an enamel brooch he once told Treverius he had traded from the Suebi.

"Shalom Augusti, the Peace of the Augustus," David said, greeting his guests. "My father will be pleased you came, Presbyter."

"I was looking at your mural," Modestus commented. "Interesting."

"Yes." David chuckled. "Despite what you may have heard, Presbyter, some Judeans do decorate homes and synagogues. Our mural depicts the old Temple at Jerusalem, with a menorah and Moses at Mount Sinai receiving the Tablets of the Testimony."

"Paul reminds us, in his letter to the Hebrews, that your own Jeremiah prophesied a second Covenant. One to come after that of Moses."

"Perhaps he meant one written in men's hearts, not on stone, Presbyter. A beautiful thought. But let's go in to father. I've saved enough fuel to warm the triclinium for our festival."

David led the way through a short hall, which was curtained off to keep out cold coming from the garden. The dining room was large, with three couches on one side arranged around a table. Geometrical tilework patterns decorated a floor that was pleasantly warmed by heating ducts underneath. The walls were painted a soft apricot color and divided into panels by red floral borders. Center designs depicted ducks, quail, and pheasants browsing among fruited tree branches. A table and seven round-backed chairs on the opposite side of the room was where the Purim reading and meal would take place. The smell of chicken and cabbage filled the room.

When the guests entered, Rabbi Zadok and his wife Esther rose from a couch. David introduced his parents. "My father, Rabbi Azariah ben Zadok. My mother Esther. This is Presbyter Modestus. You already know Treverius and Blandina, father."

"Yes. Shalom, and welcome to our festival, Presbyter." Zadok reached for Modestus's hand.

"I appreciate your offer to be here, Rabbi."

"As do my wife and I," Treverius added. He had always thought David's father looked younger than his sixty years. Hair on the Rabbi's head and in his beard was mostly black, and his complexion ruddy. Zadok obviously had not spent his entire life shut away with books. David once remarked that his father had fought in Julian's Rhine campaigns against invading Germanic tribes.

"Presbyter. All of you. Take chairs," Zadok urged. "Perhaps my son could tell you about our festival while we wait for sundown."

"The start of our day and Purim," Penina explained, coming in from another room. "Welcome."

"My wife Penina," David told Modestus.

"I've seen you at the pretorium," he said. "I didn't realize you were such friends with the Asterius family."

"Ever since we came here." Blandina smiled. "David built our field surveying wagons."

Penina had put on a beige wool tunic with twin stripes down the front that were embroidered in a floral pattern. A fringed shawl covered her shoulders, its whiteness a contrast to the glow of her stunning olive complexion. Her almond-shaped eyes were outlined in dark ferric oxide, but there was no other coloring on her face. Penina's maidservant Cleo had pulled her mistress's black hair into a short braid at the back. A single white pearl on a gold chain hung around Penina's neck as an ornament.

"Something smells good," Blandina remarked.

"That's to enjoy later, after the reading." David indicated where everyone should sit. "Now. Purim is the last of our yearly festivals. Next month is our first, when we commemorate Pesah, the liberation of our people from slavery in Egypt."

"So that's your new year?"

"No, our year begins in September." He laughed. "Confused, Blandina?"

"I guess I didn't realize how separate your feasts are from our Christian ones."

Zadok stroked his beard and frowned. "Young woman, we are an exile nation, with our own ancient traditions."

"Yet loyal to the country where we settle," David added quickly. "Father fought against the Alamanni for Rome."

"Purim is about loyalty," Penina added, fingering the pearl at her throat. "It's the story of a Hebrew woman who became queen of Persia."

"She and her father saved the king from a murder plot," David continued. "My father will read in Hebrew and I'll translate for you. Basically, the king's first queen didn't enjoy being shown off like a prized heifer. Ahasuerus . . . that's the king . . . decided to dismiss her and make the most beautiful virgin he could find his queen."

Penina laughed softly. "David, was he afraid it might give wives the idea that they could disobey their husbands?"

"Wives, be subject to your husbands," Modestus mumbled under his breath, quoting Paul.

"It turned out," David went on, "that Esther, the ward of a man named Mordecai, was chosen. He warned her not to reveal her Hebrew origin."

"Why was that?" Blandina asked.

"Our people are not always welcome." Zadok's eyebrows knit together, then relaxed. "Go on with the story, son."

"Well, Mordecai stayed around the palace courtyard to make sure Esther was being treated well. One day he overheard a plot by servants to kill Ahasuerus. Mordecai reported the men to the praetor, but the king wasn't told."

Penina picked up the narrative. "It goes on to say that, after Esther became queen, a man named Haman plotted against her and Mordecai."

"Daughter, keep some of the story for the reading," Zadok suggested. "David, will you go outside and check the position of the sun?"

"We'll eat later on, after the reading," Esther explained, "but we have less because of the . . . the situation. I'm almost ashamed to be celebrating."

"It's not the first time Hebrews have been on short rations, my dear." Zadok patted his wife's hand.

Modestus shifted uncomfortably. It was true that Theodosius, some thirty years earlier, had exempted Judeans from his anti-heresy decrees, but Bishop Ambrose had opposed him, even suggesting that God would afflict the emperor, just as He had allowed the Hebrews to be afflicted throughout their history. Ambrose tolerated Judeans only because God had chosen this stiff-necked people to prophecy the coming of His Son. "You said this wasn't a religious observance?" he asked for reassurance.

"Not strictly, Presbyter," Zadok affirmed. "It's the only festival in which the name Adonai is not mentioned, except at the blessings. I'll begin with the Ma ariv, then, afterwards, read from the scroll of Esther."

Blandina smiled at his wife. "That's your name too, isn't it?"

"Yes." Esther blushed but was saved from embarrassment when David returned.

"The shofar signaled sundown, father," he announced.

Rabbi Zadok stood to cover his head with a fringed linen shawl that David called a tallit. After the rabbi intoned the evening prayer, he unrolled a worn white goatskin scroll and read from it. David let his guests listen to the unfamiliar Hebrew words for a time, then whispered, "My father is reading the three blessings where Adonai . . . the Lord . . . is mentioned. I'll translate the next two recitations.

"'Blessed are you, Adonai, Ruler of the universe, who performed miracles for our ancestors in this season.'

"'Blessed are you Adonai for giving us life, for sustaining us, and for helping us reach this moment.'"

After the blessings Zadok unrolled a larger scroll. He was about to read when David held up a wooden clapper. "A moment, father. Our guests don't know about the noisemakers. Penina, why don't you tell about using them?"

"Almost my favorite part." She took two blocks of wood and hit them together to make a sharp sound. "Every time the name of Haman is read, we make noise to fulfill the curse of his name being erased. In this case, it's drowned in noise."

David beat a rhythm on a drum. Esther tittered as she whirled a grager that made a harsh, clacking noise. Blandina took her blocks and hit them together, Treverius tapped on a drumhead. Modestus reddened and did not use his grager.

After a moment, Zadok raised a hand for silence.

"Remember to make noise when you hear H A M A N," David whispered. After his father began to read, David listened to the cadence of the words, then translated. "'After these things king Ahasuerus promoted Haman the Agatite, the son of Hammedatha and advanced him . . . above all the princes who were with him. And all the king's servants . . . bowed down and did obeisance to Haman.'"

Penina and Esther vigorously used their noisemakers when they heard the name. After watching a moment, Blandina followed with her wood blocks. Treverius tapped out a rhythm on the drum and motioned for Modestus to use his grager.

"'But Mordecai would not bow down,'" David continued as his father read. "'Then the king's servants said to Mordecai, 'Why do you transgress the king's command?' And when they spoke to him day after day, and he would not listen to them, they told HAMAN in order to see if Mordecai's words would prevail; for he had told them he was a Hebrew. And when HAMAN saw that Mordecai would not bow down . . . HAMAN was filled with rage.'"

David emphasized the despised name each time he said it. The noisemakers vigorously drowned it out. Continuing the story, David told of how Haman's anger prompted him to destroy all the Hebrews in the kingdom.

"'In the first month, which is the month of Nisan . . . they cast Pur, that is, the lot, before HAMAN day after day until the twelfth month, which is the month of Adar. Then HAMAN said to King Ahasuerus, 'There is a certain people . . . dispersed among the people in all the provinces of your kingdom. Their laws are different from those of every other people, so that it is not for the king's profit to tolerate them.'"

The long reading continued. Haman's attempt to bribe the king; his decree to all the provinces that the Hebrews were to be killed on the thirteenth of the month a year from then; Mordecai's distress on hearing the decree. But Esther tricked Haman into attending a dinner with the king. Haman accepted, then was asked to return for a second banquet. But when the sight of Mordecai distressed him, Haman ordered a gallows built on which to hang the old man. That night the king was restless. He ordered the chronicles of the kingdom read and finally learned that Mordecai had saved him from death.

At a banquet for Mordecai, Esther revealed the plot and told of her Hebrew origins. When the king demanded to know the instigator, she named Haman.

"'Then HAMAN was in terror. And the king found that the gallows . . . for Mordecai is standing in Haman's house.'

"'And the king said, 'Hang him on that.' So they hanged HAMAN on the gallows he had prepared for Mordecai.'"

When the section was reached where Esther asked that the ten sons of Haman also be hanged, David stopped to explain that the names were recited in one breath. Penina joined him in demonstrating.

"ParshandathaDalphonAspathaPorathaAdaliaArisathaParmashtaArisaiAridaiVaisatha."

Their intonation ended in laughter.

"I should tell you that the story has a grim ending," David warned. "Father."

The elder Zadok read about how the king nullified Haman's order to slaughter the Hebrews, but authorized them to take revenge. On the thirteenth day of the month of Adar, after the directive against the Hebrews was to be carried out, they rose against the Persians.

"'So the Hebrews smote all their enemies with the sword, slaughtering and destroying them, and did as they pleased to those who hated them.'"

Mordecai then sent letters to all the Hebrews, enjoining the people to celebrate the fourteenth and fifteenth days of the month of Adar with feasting.

Rabbi Zadok slowly rewound the scroll, then recited a final blessing of praise and thanks that God had championed the cause of the Hebrews.

Esther went to another room and returned with a plate of triangular pastries filled with stewed apples, and a small sealed pitcher of wine.

"It's customary to give small gifts to our guests," Penina explained. "The triangular shape represents Haman's hat."

Treverius beat his drum at the hated name. Everyone, including Modestus, laughed. Zadok nodded his head in appreciation.

While Penina readied the table for supper, Esther brought a silver flagon to her husband. David grinned, watching his father pour wine into matching goblets.

"This is one festival where we're allowed to get slightly drunk." He winked. "Or so we interpret it."

This celebration goes back eight hundred years, Treverius thought. David had once said that his people's history was some three thousand years old. Rome traced its founding to just over a millennium. Philip the Arab had celebrated the Millenary a hundred and fifty years ago with three days of games and gladiatorial contests. Junius had inherited a silver antoninianus, with the bearded emperor's portrait and the inscription, MILITARIVM SAECVLVM, "A milestone in the Ages." Christianity is half the age of the Esther story.

Treverius took a sip of wine and recalled the grisly revenge the king authorized. "David, I don't doubt the story," he said, "but that part about seventy-five thousand Persians being killed is hard to reconcile."

"A bit of Eastern hyperbole," he admitted. "Yet, how many Nervi warriors did Julius Caesar report killing in the Gallic wars? Fifty-five thousand? That was from one tribe. We're talking about a hundred and twenty-seven provinces."

"True. Historians exaggerate when their side wins."

Esther brought in a barley-cabbage soup. Everyone ate in silence, but, when a second course of braised chicken was served, Treverius proposed a toast.

"May the last of the Hamans have been hanged."

The elder Zadok joined in without comment.

"As Judeans," David remarked, cutting into his meat, "we're pretty well off here. Oh, we're often accused of staying to ourselves. But we can . . . literally . . . live with that."

"You work hard, why shouldn't you be well off?" Blandina asked. "Your home is like any of your class in Mogontium."

"I meant that we're tolerated about like you Christians were awhile ago."

"Rumors went around that weren't true," Penina added. "Like . . . well . . . that you drank the blood of children at your ritual suppers."

"That's a horrible lie!" Blandina's blue eyes clouded under a frown. "What's said about Judeans, Penina?"

"For a less grisly lie? That we worship pigs, since our Covenant forbids us to eat them. Or, that we hold donkeys sacred, because we don't eat hares."

"Why do they say that?"

"Both have long ears." David shrugged in a helpless gesture. "It's ridiculous, but some here in town believe it."

"My son is correct," Zadok interposed. "With respect, Presbyter, I fear that after you Christians make peace with each other, you'll turn on us."

"Nonsense," Modestus scoffed. "Why, we even accept one of your people, a Judean, as our Messiah."

Treverius realized that the conversation could quickly turn into an argument and decided to change its direction. "Penina, today you honored Esther and Mordecai. Do you observe the feast days of other Hebrew personages too?"

When Penina glanced at her father-in-law, Zadok nodded permission for her to answer. "We honor Moses. Abraham and his sons. Jacob. Is that who you mean?"

"In a way," Blandina replied. "Trev is saying that we remember those who witnessed for Christ. For example, Blandina is my name, but also that of a girl who was martyred long ago. Her feast day is August first. I was named after her."

"Another example might be Juliana, the woman who was found dead a few days ago," Treverius added. "She must have been named after a Juliana who was also martyred. Is there a Saint Juliana, Presbyter?"

"Let me try to recall a Juliana." Modestus tapped the table with his knife handle. "Yes, I . . . I believe there was a woman by that name martyed in Asia. She was beheaded."

Treverius felt a sudden chill. Can there be a connection with the way Juliana died? He pushed his plate back and stood away from the table. "Rabbi, I may have gotten an insight into some deaths. We must go to the pretorium library immediately."

"You cannot finish our festival meal?" Zadok looked puzzled.

"I . . . I'm sorry, Rabbi."

"Would this be a matter of life and death?" he asked.

"Quite possibly. What we discover about the dead persons' namesakes could be a clue to their murders."

Zadok nodded. "The Law allows even the Sabbath to be broken in such a case. Go with my blessing."

"Thank you. Presbyter, on the way to the library I'll explain what I'm getting at."

*   *   *

While Blandina lighted lamps, Treverius roused a servant and ordered him to bring a brazier for heating the chilly room. Even before the boy arrived, the three were looking through shelves for scrolls and books that recorded histories of persons involved in the early centuries of the Christian Church. While Treverius looked for a Juliana in the book Modestus passed to him, Blandina unrolled an Augustan map of the early Roman Empire, updated to include later provinces.

"Here," Treverius called out, after a few moments of searching. "Eusebius mentions a Juliana."

"Re . . . read it," Modestus ordered nervously.

"He writes that she was a virgin from Cappadocia."

"That's here in Asia." Blandina indicated the extreme right side of the map.

"Juliana gave Origen the commentary of Symmachus on the testament of Matthew," Treverius continued, "but Eusebius doesn't say that she was martyred."

Blandina groped in a bin among several scrolls. She pulled one out and read through the index. "Here. Under Bythinia. 'Legends of Bythinian Holy Persons' by Alexander of Nicomedia." Blandina read a few lines, then blurted, "This may be her! Juliana of Nicomedia."

Modestus took the scroll near a lamp and read, "'Juliana was betrothed to the prefect Eulogius, when she insisted on being baptized a Christian. Her enraged father had her stripped and beaten, then given to Eulogius, who refused baptism out of fear of Augustus Caesar. 'If thou art afraid of a worldly ruler, how much more should you be of a King who is eternal,' Juliana replied. Thereupon, Eulogius ordered her beaten with rods, then hung up by her hair.'"

"How horrible." Blandina winced. "What happened next?"

"'Eulogius ordered molten lead poured on her head, but she was not harmed.'"

Modestus read silently for a moment, then exclaimed, "Christ Jesus, listen to this. 'The prefect ordered Juliana plunged into a tub of molten lead.'"

"The . . . the tub I found her in was lined with lead sheeting," Treverius said, recalling how sick he had felt in the musty room.

Modestus's hands shook as he continued. "'But the lead suddenly cooled. Thereupon, Eulogius cursed the powerlessness of his gods to punish a mere woman, who had insulted them. He ordered Juliana beheaded.'"

"Is her feast day February sixteenth?" Blandina asked.

"Yes. Beheading was the method of execution then." Modestus dropped heavily onto a chair. "It seems these deaths have followed a pattern."

"Clement and that mason. Stephan. Sebastian." Treverius felt stunned, as if hit by a catapult recoil. "And now there's Juliana . . ."

"They all died on their namesake's day," Modestus rasped, covering his eyes with a hand that still trembled. "I haven't checked for Agnes or Felix, but I'd be sure of it. I was wrong. There was some significance in that."

"What's even more insane, they were killed in the same way the person was martyred," Treverius pointed out. "Sebastian was executed by men in his cohort, shot with arrows. Stephan was stoned to death. Juliana was beheaded."

"I mentioned the way Clement was drowned, tied to an anchor," Modestus recalled in a whisper. "I don't remember how Chrysanthus was martyred. Thrown from a height? I . . . I'll have to look it up."

"What about Arbitos?" Blandina asked. "His death seems to have spawned the others."

"That had to be a coincidence, just as we've thought," Treverius replied. "Cyril tried to link it to Jupiter, to stop the temple renovation, but these deaths have gone far beyond that."

"Why would anyone want to kill people in that manner?" Modestus wondered aloud. "It makes no sense."

"The reason must make sense to the killer." Treverius was relieved that the months of uncertainty might be over, but felt sorry for the presbyter. Slumped in his chair, Modestus looked aged and feeble, as limp as one of the straw practice targets on the Campus Martius training field. Treverius touched his shoulder. "I don't know the answer to why the deaths took place that way, Presbyter, but the most important questions now are . . . who will be the next victims, and how do we stop their murders."

Modestus nodded a numb agreement. "And the governor will have to be told in the morning."

chapter 14

"H... h... how dare this murderer v... violate my capital," Quintus Albanus stormed, snatching the medallion of a happier Mogontium off his desk. He glared at Modestus and clutched the silver disc until the tendons stood out on his hand and his knuckles were white. "F... find the one responsible, Presbyter."

Modestus stared at the floorboards without answering.

"Sir, we intend to do that," Treverius interposed. "I've brought—"

"I want this maniac caught," Albanus demanded, tossing the medallion back. "W... we've got, what, about nine thousand citizens in Mogontium, plus refugees? I can't make pu... public what you've discovered."

"Sir? But the people will need to protect themselves."

"Wi... with the Vandal invasion on top of th... this damnable cold, all I need is to add random murders to the panic. I won't do it."

"Governor, we've thought of a plan," Blandina said. "My husband and the Presbyter brought books that list names of martyrs to compare with those of citizens."

"One by Bishop Eusebius," Treverius explained. "Another is a Martyrium, a general book of martyrs."

Albanus stood and paced across his office, until he stood before the tattered standards of the rebel legions. "Gi . . . give me the names," he said, fingering the faded cloth.

"Sir, the earliest would be on March first. An Antonina of Nicaea was martyred by being sewn into a sack and thrown into a pond. Blessed Marinus was killed on March third. Theophilus, Adrian and Phocas on the fifth. Sir—?" Albanus, half-listening, had gone to stare at his map of Mogontium. No enemy ringed the immediate walls of the city, but Treverius realized that the governor's mind and spirit were under a kind of seige that his military strategies were unable to lift. "Shall I go on Governor?"

"Eh?" Albanus roused himself. "Oh. Names your wife found?"

"Governor, sit down first," Blandina urged. "In a moment you'll have a more clear idea of what we think we can do."

Albanus grunted a reluctant assent and sat behind his desk, again toying with the silver medallion.

"I've found Gregory and his brother Athanodore," she told him. "Born in Pontus."

"When is their feast day?" Treverius asked.

"March twelfth. It doesn't say if they were martyred."

"That may not matter. Someone poisoned could look as if they'd died in their sleep. Governor, I'd like to check the tax rolls and see how many people have the same names. That way we might identify those who could be in danger."

Albanus looked up from the medal. "Oh. Of course, son. Good. Want t . . . to see them now?"

"Sir, let us finish the names first."

Modestus glanced at Blandina's list. "Blessed Secundus is honored on March twenty-ninth. That's a common name here, tell us about him."

"He was a legionary, born near Augusta Taurinorum. Beheaded under the Prefect Sapritius."

Treverius recalled the chapel mural. "Isn't Longinus remembered in March?"

"On the fifteenth," Modestus confirmed. "During the penitential season."

"The Annunciation to Mary is on March twenty-fifth," Blandina continued. "Joseph's feast is on the nineteenth. The Passion accounts in the Testaments would cover March and April . . . betrayal by Judas, denial of Peter." She looked up at the governor. "Sir, there must be twenty names."

"I'll only d . . . deal with those in March," Albanus responded curtly. "Can't protect everyone in . . . in both the Martyrium and Test . . . Testaments."

"We're almost through," Treverius said. "I have Alexander on March eighteen. He died in prison."

"And Mamertinus, a Gallic holy man," Blandina added. "He wasn't martyred, but the story tells of his close call with a bear trap."

"A trap," Albanus sighed, slumping down in his chair. "Ju . . . just like my poor Sebastian. Son, I need something to act on. G . . . go check people on those tax rolls."

*   *   *

The morning's search at the tax office yielded eight possible victims, and the dates on which their murders might take place. Mamertinus was the most common name, followed by Secundus. Several traders, who were from the Eastern Empire, had the names Alexander and Gregory, but no one was listed as Athenodore. Nor Longinus, or Joseph. Modestus thought women named Mary were not in danger.

Treverius was not sure of what to do with the information, and still felt helpless in the face of the unknown killer. A guard could not be put on everyone with the same name but, as the governor had stated, even to warn potential victims was to risk panic among the citizenry. Rioting could follow, with Lupus Glaucus threatening military reprisals.

* * *

Modestus hoped he could keep to his liturgical routine without worrying about the next potential victim until March twelfth, the feast of Gregory. Instead, he was forced to counter a form of necromacy that suddenly appeared.

On market day of the second week in March, Modestus was walking along the Via Alexander toward the Longinus Chapel, when he noticed two old women on the sidewalk acting strangely. They held something in their hands, rubbing the object on the doors and walls of shops and mumbling what sounded like incantations. Modestus crossed over and faced one of the crones.

"Pax Christi," the Peace of Christ, Domina. What have you there?"

"A relic of Blessed Albans," the woman replied, continuing to scratch a greasy cross on the wall of a shop with a piece of bone.

Albans?" Modestus recalled that the holy man had been martyred at Mogontium in the previous century. "Where did you get that bone, grandmother?"

"The saint will protect my son's business," she hedged, avoiding his eyes.

"I asked where you found the relic," Modestus repeated less amiably, and reached out his hand. "Give it to me."

The old woman paused to squint at him, but clutched the relic fragment against her thin chest.

"Let me look at that bone." Modestus pried the piece from her gnarled fingers. It looked human, and shreds of attached tendon were fairly recent. He sniffed them. Rotten. Like soup bones at the butcher's stall. He recalled that he had forbidden refugees who had died to be buried in Mogontium's cemetery, for fear of contaminating the ground with heretic or pagan bodies. Soon after, reports reached him that wolves had unearthed corpses in shallow graves cut below the vineyards. Had someone seen an opportunity in the grisly plunder?

"This bone is no relic of Albans," he told the crone. "It is without spiritual value."

"And your praying hasn't given us a pisspot full of help, either," she retorted. "Vithicab promised that the saint who was martyred here would protect his city."

"Who is this Vithicab?" Modestus demanded.

"He has a booth outside the west wall." The woman snatched her relic back and hurried over to her friend, mumbling resentment at Modestus.

"We'll see about that," he muttered. "Indeed, we'll see, Vithicab."

Modestus went back to his rooms in the pretorium and took down a tattered copy of the Testaments from a shelf. Then he borrowed a whip that was tipped with lead barbs from one of Macrianus's interrogators.

Red-faced from both anger and the cold wind, with the whip tucked into his belt, Modestus held the sacred book high in both hands as he strode west along the Via Honorius, and through the Porta Germania. Turning left, he stalked among the rows of refugee tents and booths, chanting the verses of Aeterni Christi munera.

"'With joyful heart, let us sing a hymn as our tribute of praise to Christ's eternal gifts and the victories of our martyrs.'"

Children and a few curious women began to trail after the presbyter as he searched for the offending vendor. At a makeshift booth near the Barbetomagus Gate, Modestus saw a man frantically pushing small, whitish objects into a sack. He surmised that it was Vithicab, who had seen him coming and guessed the reason.

Before Vithicab could hide all of his bones, the presbyter was upon him. "Take these abominations away," Modestus shouted, holding up the text from Matthew that recorded Christ's anger at the Temple moneychangers. "You shall not make my house a place of trade." He swept the rest of the foul-smelling fragments off the table with the side of his Testament, then lashed out with the whip at Vithicab. "Viper! Spawn of Satan, deceiving the elect," he shouted, spittle flying from his mouth. "Beelzebub!"

All the frustrations of Modestus's ministry surged into the vicious flogging—his failure to instill enthusiasm in his flock for Christ's message, the fruitless process of weaning them from superstition, and now the added burden of horrifying murders. Not the least was the seeming indifference of his God to the barbarian victory, and the people's suffering during the harsh winter.

As Vithicab cowered under the beating, the commotion attracted the attention of two legionaries patrolling the gate. The men ran over to stop Modestus.

"Get this lunatic off me," Vithicab pleaded. "I was only giving them old hags a little hope."

One legionary wrenched the whip away. The other pinned the presbyter's arms to his sides, but he kept trying to kick over Vithicab's table in imitation of Christ's angry reaction at the Temple. Finally restrained, Modestus allowed the soldiers to escort him back to the pretorium, but along the way he continued an angry flicking at the ground with the instrument of his, if not God's, righteous justice.

Vetius Modestus did not look back to see Vithicab grinning as he rearranged his bones on the table once more.

* * *

After the feast of Gregory passed without incident, Treverius hoped there was no pattern to the deaths after all. Yet he was also uneasy. The killer might only be respecting the penitential season. He was with Blandina, as they broke their fast on the afternoon of March fifteenth. Ageria had made a meatless soup of stale bread boiled in watered milk, thickened with crumbled chunks of soft cheese. After pushing his bowl aside, Treverius recalled the recent incident with the sham relics.

"I can't believe those women were duped, but 'desperate ills, desperate cures,' I suppose."

"Modestus had a right to be furious," Blandina said, stacking his bowl with hers on a side cupboard.

"Especially since he's warned people about sacrificing animals, or paying any crone with warts to sell them a spell. Christ only knows what rites go on in the woods at night."

"Trev," Blandina asked, "who might be the next victim?"

"No one, I hope."

"You know what I mean."

"Today is the feast of Longinus, but no one in town has that name."

"There must be votive offerings at the chapel today," Blandina assumed. "Did Modestus say?"

"Actually, he was too angry . . . disgusted may be a better word . . . to hold a service this morning."

"I'll get the other names." Blandina went to the cupboard and brought back a small calendar sheet she had drawn up. "Alexander, the eighteenth. There are fifty men with that name, Trev. Can't we do something to help?"

"In three days? I could have Albanus post a pretorian guard at each house, but he hasn't even told the people. And he just doesn't have the available guards."

Blandina noticed Agilan hovering at the door. "What is it, boy? Come here."

Ageria's son handed Blandina a folded note. She read the message then looked up at her husband. "The governor wants to see us. Now."

"About?"

"He doesn't say. Wear a cloak, it's raw outside."

After Blandina slipped a cape over her shoulders, Treverius clasped it together, then kissed her. She laughed. "What was that for?"

"It's been so long since we had time for each other." Treverius stroked her hair a moment, then buried his face in her neck. "Blandina, we'll get through this."

"I know, Trev. And perhaps Albanus has good news about Stilicho's arrival for a change."

"Let's find out."

The weather was still unseasonably cold, but if a returning sun gave the illusion of a normal spring, no buds had yet formed on garden trees that had survived the winter cold. Drifts of dirt-stained snow still hugged the north-facing walls. Treverius saw the atrium pool clogged with moldering leaves and wondered if Vertiscus still bothered with such minor details of maintenance. He had enough problems rationing food and fuel, and keeping storeroom slaves from stealing supplies to sell in the refugee camp.

Neither Treverius nor Blandina had seen Albanus for almost a month. After Remigius ushered them into the office, they were shocked by the governor's slovenly appearance. His wiry hair was uncombed and a stubble of grey-flecked beard shadowed his cheeks.

A legionary from the garrison stood at one side of the desk. Treverius thought the man looked uneasy.

"I was told by Bructios here that something happened to Gundstram," Albanus said bluntly, without a greeting. Valerian had helped control his stutter.

"Gundstram, sir?" Blandina did not know the name.

"First Centurion at the camp," Treverius explained. "I trained under him. An accident in the barracks, sir?"

"His house on the Via Germanicus. No one can find Lupus Glaucus. If this is related to . . ." Albanus stopped with a glance at Bructios. "Will you two come with me?"

"Of course," Treverius agreed. "We're ready to go now."

Bructios led the way along the Via Alexander and past the Longinus Chapel. As Blandina had surmised, an assorted collection of meager offerings lined the stairs in the hope that Longinus would be helpful on his feast day.

East of the chapel the Germanicus was blocked by an extension of the camp palisade, which enclosed Lupus Glaucus's house. Treverius followed Bructios into an alleyway, then ducked around against an icy wind funneling in from the river. Blandina and Albanus hunched against the cold, reminding him that it was the ides of March. Julius Caesar had been assassinated on that date, but the occasion was scarcely remembered, except in tutors' lessons about the fate of the Roman Republic.

Two legionaries were slouched at the door to Gundstram's home. After the guards recognized the governor they straightened up and gave a clumsy salute.

Albanus ignored them. "Where is he, Bructios?"

"In the bedroom, sir. His wife found him."

The governor ducked in the door and passed through an atrium. After the legionary led the way into a half-timbered room on the right, Treverius blanched at what he saw inside.

Blandina gasped and buried her face in his cloak.

"In the name of Hades, man," Albanus cried, "why didn't you tell me he was found like this?"

Gundstram's body sagged against the wall, pinned to one of the timbers by a lance that passed through his left chest at heart level. A small stain of blood had dried around the entrance wound where the shaft had gone in. The centurion's eyes were closed, but his mouth was half-open, in an eerie twisted smile. Treverius thought it an incongruous detail in the violent tableau. He tried to ease Blandina out of the room but she shook her head.

"I . . . I want to stay."

Not the time to argue with her, he thought, and went to examine the body.

"Bructios, where was his wife today?" Albanus asked.

"Gone to help her parents, she told me. Left this morning and came back to cook the evening meal. I was the first man she saw after she ran out screaming."

"No help. Find anything, Treverius?"

"Still looking, sir, but I don't think the lance killed him." Gundstram's head was slumped to one side. Treverius touched it to test its flexibility. When he moved the jaw, he saw a flash of metal drop from the mouth, and heard a clinking sound on the floor. A coin had fallen, then rolled to a stop against the wall. Treverius picked up the silver disc without looking at the inscription and handed it to Blandina. "Put this in your purse."

"Where is Lupus Glaucus?" Albanus asked Bructios in an irritated tone. "This is one of his officers."

"Don't know, sir."

"Why would anyone do this? What kind of an officer was Gundstram?"

"Fine, sir." Bructios hesitated, then mumbled, "Ah . . . the men all liked him a lot."

"Might as well ask that door. Treverius. You said you trained under Gundstram?"

"A long time ago, sir. He worked us hard, seemed ambitious. Even built a shed at the back of his house to store equipment."

"Ambitious? Then he may have resented Lupus Glaucus as his commander." Albanus exhaled and ran a hand through his hair in frustration. "Bructios, have Nicias examine the body and report to me."

"Yes sir."

"Continue to post guards, but keep this quiet until Glaucus is located."

Treverius knew the advice was futile and suspected that, despite his warning, Albanus felt the same way. By dusk Gundstram's death would be a topic of speculation in every tavern in Mogontium.

* * *

It was still light when Nicias arrived at the pretorium and Governor Albanus asked him to bring Treverius and Blandina from their quarters. The old surgeon went around to knock on the couple's door.

"Nicias." Treverius was surprised to see the man. "You're here with a report for the governor?"

"Yes. Quintus asked me to bring you and your wife to hear what I found out about Gundstram's death."

"Good, I was hoping he'd do that. We'll come."

Treverius was pleased to see the surgeon, with whom he had only briefly spoken. Nicias was a slightly built man, about fifty years of age, with a beard and full head of hair that he claimed had turned dead white during the Frigidus River battle. His brown eyes reflected unspoken pain and compassion. Treverius knew Nicias had come to Mogontium with Governor Albanus after serving with him under Theodosius, but nothing else about the surgeon.

When Remigius admitted the trio to Albanus's office, they found the governor lying on a couch. Nicias wagged a finger at him.

"You're looking overly tired, Quintus. Are you taking your Valerian medication?"

"Nicias, I didn't ask you here to discuss my health," Albanus chided, sitting up. "You went to Gundstram's?"

"I did."

"And you found out?"

"The man probably wasn't killed there. Nor with the lance."

"I thought not," Treverius said, pleased at the confirmation of what he had observed. "Too little blood from the wound."

"Exactly," Nicias agreed. "The floor would have been pooled with gore."

"Then what did kill him?" Blandina asked.

"I found bruises . . . finger marks . . . on his throat."

"Strangled, then?"

"So it would seem, Quintus, but it couldn't have been easy. Gundstram was a powerful brute."

"Would Glaucus be capable of it, Nicias?" Treverius asked.

"Possibly. It took enormous strength to implant that lance in a beam and through Gundstram's body. But more than one person could be involved."

"Why Gundstram?" Blandina asked. "If this is connected to the other deaths, he wasn't named Longinus."

"It has to be connected," Treverius reasoned. "The centurion was the same rank and the lance is a symbol of Longinus." He recalled the money that had fallen from the man's mouth. "Blandina, where's that coin I found at Gundstrams?"

"What coin?" Nicias looked from one to the other. "And what other deaths are you talking about?"

"A siliqua, or some denomination, fell when I was examining Gundstram," he said. "It could be a clue to his murder."

"There've been other strange deaths, Nicias," Albanus added. "I've been trying to avoid causing panic among citizens."

"Let me see that coin." After Blandina searched her purse she handed the silver to Nicias. He held it to the light and made out the portrait of a pudgy-faced emperor and inscription. "'Nero Caesar,'" he read, then turned to the reverse. "A figure with a Victory. 'Augustus Germanicus.' This isn't current. Nero was emperor over . . . three hundred years ago."

"When our legions here rebelled," Albanus reminded him.

"There shouldn't be any coins around that are that old," Treverius said, feeling his scalp crawl. "Unless Gundstram, or someone, found the treasure that was supposedly left behind by disbanded units."

"Great Zeus, what a fortune it would be!" Nicias exclaimed. "Gundstram could have been killed for that."

"Something else seemed strange," Blandina recalled. "I thought I smelled incense in that room."

"Incense?" Nicias handed the coin back. "Perhaps Gundstram, or his wife, is pagan. There are a number of men in the garrison who are reportedly so."

"I didn't notice a Lares shrine to household gods."

"Nor I," Albanus recalled. "Gundstram's wife will have to be questioned. And Glaucus has some accounting to do."

"He's been recruiting men in the legion to some kind of association," Nicias said. "An effort to improve discipline, I suppose."

"Discipline," Albanus murmured, lying back and closing his eyes. "These murders must be solved before Stilicho arrives next month."

"Sir, we'll go." Treverius motioned to Blandina.

"As I will in a moment." Nicias took an empty cup off Albanus's bedside table. "Let me get you a stronger sleeping draught, Quintus. You need it after what you saw today."

* * *

After returning to her room Blandina ordered Agilan to bring a flagon of hot wine, mulled with myrtle berries, to ease a queasy feeling bothering her stomach. As she lay on the bed, propped up by pillows, Treverius stroked her arm.

"I'm sorry you had to see that today, dove."

"I insisted on going in." Blandina sat up higher and stopped his hand. "Trev, what's happening? Remember that day at the Drusus memorial when Juliana said something about the army not being able to protect her? She was right. She's dead, and the murderer has even penetrated army ranks."

He pulled away from her hold. "I don't know what more I can do."

"I'm not blaming you." Blandina grasped his hand back. "It's the governor who doesn't have a plan for countering these murders."

"Albanus did go to Gundstram's today. Still, it might be better if Vertiscus did take over. At least until the governor is himself again."

"Trev. I've told you that I don't like Vertiscus."

"And never given me the shadow of a reason. He's a good administrator."

"Call it a woman's intuition."

"Intuition?" He chuckled. "How many loaves of bread has that ever bought?"

"Scoff if you want, husband, but it's said a woman's instinct can be superior to a man's reasoning." Blandina let go of his hand, sniffled, and looked away.

Treverius turned her face back toward him and kissed at a tear. "A man can reach his limit. Albanus has. You were there when we first told him about these murders. He was so distracted he could barely follow what we were saying. Vertiscus at least kept a level head after the invasion."

"I don't want to talk about him. Who are the next persons in danger?"

"Men named Secundus, but we've already had one killing this month. Whatever his reason, I believe our murderer will wait until April, when Stilicho is here."

"I don't understand his motive," Blandina said. "These people weren't robbed or killed by someone who knew them."

"As far as we know. Gundstram might be the first exception. Albanus is probably right in thinking that citizens would panic if they knew what was happening."

"But he can't keep the Curia ignorant forever."

"True, Blandina, and it limits what we can do to protect the next victim. Christ! I should at least be able to tell men named Secundus that their lives might be in danger."

"Everyone in Mogontium would soon know, and that's what the governor doesn't want. I'm really frightened, Trev. When the person doing this realizes you and Modestus know about his method, he might try to . . . to—"

"Silence us?" Treverius squeezed Blandina's hand. "I'll be fine, dove. You, too."

"Perhaps by Secundus's feast day we could think of a plan to protect the others."

"Unless some other unforeseen calamity happens before that."

"Trev, what could possibly be worse than the disasters of the last few months?"

"Dove," he teased, to lighten her mood, "I wouldn't even be too surprised if the General Resurrection occurred next week."

"That would at least make old Malchus happy." Blandina's soft ripple of laughter momentarily eased the tension. "No, I'm serious, Trev. These murders have been going on for at least five months. Whatever the killer's purpose, I would think he's about ready to reveal it by now. And when he acts, I don't think he'll be stopped by the imminent end of the world."

chapter 15

In early April, shortly after a group of deserters from a Britannic legion had straggled into Mogontium, Treverius confirmed an incredible rumor that was circulating at the city's windy street corners and in its smoky taverns. When he hurried back to tell Blandina, he found her in their cramped pantry with Ageria, checking the month's staff food supplies brought by Vertiscus's aides.

"Blandina! Remember that jest I made a couple of weeks ago about the General Resurrection occurring soon?"

"I remarked that it would at least make Malchus happy. Why do you ask?"

"I've just come from the market. Malchus was there, babbling that Emperor Constantine is alive again and has crossed the Channel from Britannia into Gaul with his legions."

"The Constantine?" Her blue eyes widened in disbelief. "Constantinus Magnus?"

"Yes. Incredibly, Constantine the Great."

"But that's impossible, Trev. The emperor has been dead some . . . seventy years. This is just another one of Malchus's fantasies."

"Tell that to his followers, it's absolute chaos down there. They're claiming that the resurrected Augustus is marching into Germania Prima, with a shining army of The Glorified, to free us from the barbarians."

"Persons will clutch at any straw in a whirlpool," Blandina pointed out. "It's pathetic."

"Pathetic or not, they're remembering that Constantine once threw back two Frankish tribes from Treveri. Now they say he'll drive out Gaisios and his Vandals."

"What does Governor Albanus know about this?"

"He's pretty well isolated himself, but let's try to find out."

The couple found the governor's secretary in the outer office, fending off Arinthos and Pendatios, who were insisting on seeing Albanus.

"What's going on, Remigius?" Treverius asked.

"Nicias refuses to let anyone see the Governor," he answered nervously. "He's confined to his bed."

"No, I mean about Constantine supposedly being resurrected."

"Baseless," Arinthos scoffed, "but Malchus's fanatics want to throw open the gates for these phantom legions."

"The old lunatic has gone too far this time," Pendatios added. "When nothing happens, we'll have a riot on our hands."

"Let's stay calm," Treverius counseled. "Remigius, you must know something about how this rumor began."

Remigius hesitated, then went to lock the anteroom door. "A . . . a few days ago, some men from a Britannic legion came in. It seems that someone named Marcus, and then a certain Gratian, had declared themselves emperor on the island."

"Against Honorius? That's sedition," Treverius commented. "What happened next?"

"The report is that a centurion named Constantine murdered Gratian, and the legions proclaimed him emperor."

"So this usurper's coincidental name is the basis of the rumor?" Blandina asked.

"Citizens are desperate, Domina," Remigius replied. "He's taken the title of Constantine the Third."

"Now we have a civil war on our hands, on top of the other disasters," Treverius remarked. "Why didn't this Constantine stay in Britannia?"

"Gaul is a richer land to loot," Arinthos told him.

"In which direction is Constantine taking his legions?" Treverius asked Remigius.

"No one knows for certain."

"In any case, the third Constantine is obviously all too mortal. We can discredit one aspect of the rumor."

"But the people's slim hope with it, Trev," Blandina remarked. "How many more disappointments can they take?"

*   *   *

Vertiscus had doubted the report and had sent word to Hortar at Treveri to investigate. The information Hortar gathered was less eschatological than seditious. Britannic legions had declared Constantine emperor, crossed into Gaul, and defeated the Goths at Gesoriacum. But instead of going on to liberate the Germanic provinces, Constantine III had moved south and set up a rival government at Arelate. More disturbing for Vertiscus's plans, Hortar also reported that Gaisios was stalling in his support for New Gothia, waiting to see in which direction the new political winds might blow.

*   *   *

Gundstram's murder had pushed Governor Albanus into deeper depression. He only came out of his room to occasionally visit Treverius in the workshop, and stare at his map of the province. Blandina also guessed the governor had unknowingly come to fantasize her husband as the son Sophia had never borne him.

After the Constantinian hoax was exposed, further
shattering citizens' morale, Treverius persuaded Albanus
to call an emergency session of the Curia. He felt that
misinformation being circulated about the series of deaths
needed to be corrected, and the councilors finally told the
truth.

Vertiscus was told to attend. The curator contacted
Cyril, telling him that he would use the meeting as an
opportunity to discredit the governor—while pretending
to defend him—until he could step into the role.

* * *

The Curia meeting was scheduled in the pretorium to
avoid alerting citizens about the unusual session, but a
sullen crowd gathered to watch members go inside. Har-
rassing remarks were called out and clods of earth thrown.
After Tribune Riculfius ordered his guards to use their
shields and clear the entranceway, a few heads were
bloodied in the struggle.

Governor Albanus did not formally open the session,
and slumped in his chair to address the councilors. His
stutter had returned.

"I . . . I've called you here be . . . because of the deaths
of some citizens. Tre . . . Treverius, tell the Curia the circumstances."

Treverius glanced at Modestus, who nodded for him
to speak. "Ever since the murder of Juliana—"

"Who is this Juliana?" Arinthos called out.

"An actress at the theater."

"And she was murdered? Why weren't we told? What
has Macrianus found?"

"Arinthos," Vertiscus intervened, "this is indeed disturbing. Let the young man continue."

"Since her murder," Treverius went on, "we've discovered that other deaths haven't been accidents. Someone is killing citizens on their namesake's day."

"Meaning what?" Arinthos's voice had an edge of alarm now.

"People are being murdered in the same way that the saint after whom they were named was martyred."

"Tell us how Juliana was killed," Musonius demanded.

"She was beheaded in her bath."

Treverius's gruesome response generated babble among the councilors. Cyril motioned to speak. The usually well-groomed merchant stooped slightly and held his arms defensively in front of himself.

"Governor," he taunted, "Mogontium is no longer under your command, it is ruled by fear. This revelation about the murders underscores the fact."

"Your remark is inappropriate, councilor," Vertiscus sham-protested. "The governor is doing his best."

"No, le . . . let him speak," Albanus intervened. "Thi . . . this is out in the open now."

"Ever since October," Cyril went on, "I have tried to tell you that we are again the concern of our old gods. Jupiter has come to warn that unless he is given an equal place with the Galilean, we will be destroyed. Yet this very assembly voted to desecrate his temple."

"Only a fool would suggest that an idol is committing these crimes," Modestus called out to Cyril.

"Speak when you are given permission," the merchant shouted back. "This crisis demands action. I move that the temple be returned to Jupiter's worship."

"This is n . . . not why we are meeting," Albanus protested in a weak voice. "We are here t . . . to deal with these murders."

"Reopen the Arian church on the Via Praetori for Paschal services," Nevius demanded, ignoring the warning.

"There's one of your Arians," Treverius whispered to Modestus. "You've worried that they would ally themselves with pagans, against you. Nevius is doing it."

"These killings do seem to have a supernatural origin," Lupicinius argued. "What harm would there be in a pinch of incense to Jupiter?"

"I agree with Lupicinius," Musonius said. "The centurion's murder shows that even the army is powerless to stop the killer."

"What murdered centurion?" Arinthos asked, standing up.

"Gundstram, councilor," Treverius replied. "We—"

"Speaking of the army," Musonius cut in, "what's the latest rumor about the treasury of that Macedonian legion being found?"

Treverius thought he saw Vertiscus look visibly startled at the unexpected mention of the treasure.

"Just that, a . . . a new rumor," Albanus said. "I've had the camp searched. Noth . . . nothing was found."

"Of course you didn't find it there, in the most obvious place," Musonius scoffed. "It must be concealed elsewhere."

"We're digressing," Cyril called out, glancing at Vertiscus. "I've asked the council to vote on reopening the temple of Jupiter."

Albanus gave in to his request. On a show of hands, Nevius, Sulpicius, Lupicinius and Musonius supported Cyril.

"Your 'god' has failed again," Modestus scoffed. "Let that end the matter."

Cyril ignored him. "Nevius, explain your proposal for opening the Arian church."

"The Vandals are Arians," he replied, his rodent-like eyes scanning the men. "If we gave them recognition, they would be easier to deal with, Christian to Christian."

"They're heretics," Modestus objected. "I will not concede to error. Governor, we're here to talk about preventing these deaths."

"Yes. Nevius, this is an emer . . . emergency meeting. We . . . we've already digressed on the temple matter."

"Governor." Vertiscus signaled to speak. "This talk of Jupiter and Arius misses the mark. These killings point to a lunatic. You have handled the situation well and avoided panic, but people want reassurance. Treverius, you believe you have the cipher to the killings?"

"Indications are that the person died on his or her saint's day. We're trying to anticipate the next victims."

"What can you tell us Presbyter?" Arinthos called out. "Who may die in April?"

"With God's help, no one." Modestus scanned the list of names. "On April second we celebrate Mary of Egypt. She died a natural death. The fifth, Blessed Martialis, also in the Lord. Dionysius on the eighth, beheaded. Sulpicius was martyred at Colonia Agrippina on the twentieth. Georgius, beheaded on the twenty-third—"

"Wasn't he a tribune?" Musonius interrupted. "After what happened to Gundstram, put the garrison on alert."

Modestus ignored the suggestion and continued. "Blessed Mark, dragged to his death at Alexandria, remembered on the twenty-fifth. On the twenty-sixth, Marcellinus, beheaded. The next day we celebrate Anastasia, who was burned to death. Saint Vitalis on the twenty-eighth, buried alive. That is the list."

The councilors shifted uneasily, trying to remember friends who had the same names. Sulpicius looked especially shaken. His was a common Gallic name.

Demetrius had copied the names as they were read. "Have you a plan, Governor," he asked, "for capturing the lunatic who is doing this?"

"Treverius is wor . . . working with the presbyter."

"Sir, my wife is also helping." Treverius held up his list. "We began by culling similar names from the tax rolls, then eliminating those unlikely to be victims."

"Like who?" Sulpicius asked. "Give me an example."

"Well, Mary died of old age. Martialis also. Georgius and Dionysius have Greek names. No one here is called that. Anastasia was burned to death and Vitalis buried alive. We eliminated those. There would be no bodies."

Demetrius looked at his notes. "That leaves . . . Mark, Sulpicius and Marcellinus?"

"Yes sir."

"About how many people in all?"

"Perhaps two hundred," Treverius estimated.

"Have you discovered a motive?"

"We can discount the wrath of Jupiter," Modestus jeered at Cyril. "No, this seems to be the aberration of an ordinary person."

"But an educated one, to know all these details," Demetrius observed, jabbing the air with his stylus.

"We hadn't considered that," Treverius whispered.

"It could lead to our first clue," Blandina responded.

"Educated or not," Arinthos persisted, "he's trying to terrorize the citizenry."

"And succeeding," Sulpicius shouted. "I demand a legionary guard."

"G . . . guards for two hundred households? More in May? Im . . . impossible," Albanus protested.

"Councilor, Flavius Stilicho will be here this month," Treverius pointed out. "We need the men to protect him."

"If the Commander of the Western army was assassinated in Mogontium, Honorius would finish what the Vandals began," Cyril declared. "The city would be leveled as punishment."

"We must remain alert," Vertiscus counseled. "Will you post the names at the Longinus Chapel, Presbyter?"

Modestus nodded sullen agreement.

After the Curia adjourned Treverius turned to Blandina. "I'm glad Vertiscus is supporting Albanus in this, not trying to replace him."

"Perhaps I have misjudged him," she admitted. "Let's get those names ready for Modestus to post."

* * *

Vertiscus ordered Hortar to remain in Treveri and persuade Gaisios to commit his men to New Gothia, despite the unexpected incursion by the rebel Constantine. The curator was enraged at the prospect of postponing his plans, with the subsequent greater risk of having the scheme discovered, but he could do nothing except wait for a barbarian's decision.

* * *

Two afternoons before the Day of Palms, Treverius and Blandina went to David's house to discuss ways of finding clues to the murders. The chaotic Curia meeting had reminded Treverius that, although he might know the common thread that bound the killings together, he had not thought of a way to protect the next victims.

Penina met them in the reception room, wearing a belted white tunic embroidered with floral patterns. A band inset with pearls bound her long black hair, and the single pearl she had worn at Purim graced her throat.

"David is in the warehouse, preparing his wagons for the spring fairs," she told Treverius.

"He feels optimistic that trade will resume?"

"You know David. Once the snow has melted and roads are open, he'll be ready. Let me send a servant for him."

"No, don't interrupt what he's doing. I want to talk about ideas for blocking the next murder."

"He told me about that hectic Curia meeting. Let me get a cape and I'll walk over with you."

A warmish rain began to fall as the three made their way along the Via Rheni under an overhang of shop awnings.

"Your pearl is magnificent," Blandina remarked, fingering the gem at Penina's neck. "I noticed it at Purim."

"A gift from David. Penina means 'pearl' in Hebrew."

"Pearl?" Treverius stopped to examine the gem. "Margarita, my mother's name, means pearl in Latin. A pleasant coincidence for once."

At the warehouse, workmen were repairing wagons damaged in the Vandal raid. David greeted his visitors in the small office where he kept records.

"Shalom, friends. Don't tell me you're here to hire a cart to haul away the Macedonica treasure you just found?"

Treverius laughed. "A wish won't fill a sack, they say, much less a cart. No, I wanted to talk with you about ways of preventing the next murder."

"Have you found out anything more about Gundstram?"

"Nothing, David," Blandina replied, "but that smell of incense still bothers me."

"You think pagan rites were being held in his house?"

"Perhaps, yet the house is really too small."

"I discovered something when I was looking up names in the tax rolls," Treverius said. "Cyril owns the house."

"Cyril?" David whistled in surprise. "He advocates the worship of Roman gods. Could he be carrying out sacrifices there?"

"Perhaps," Blandina said. "Was Gundstram a Christian?"

"If so, of the Arian faith," Treverius suspected. "Or, for all we know, a crypto-pagan. The Neronic coin that fell out of Gundstram's mouth puzzles me."

"Put there in some kind of ritual?" David speculated. "Weren't Roman dead once provided with a coin to pay for their passage across the Styx?"

"There's a pagan connection," Blandina said. "Trev, could we get permission from Albanus to go inside the house?"

"I'll ask him," Treverius replied, "but I'd rather we weren't seen."

"Right," David agreed. "Gundstram's is within sight of the legion camp. There could be trouble if sentries noticed us snooping around."

"We could go while people are eating supper," Treverius suggested. "This rain should keep them indoors, too."

Governor Albanus authorized a search of the house and put his seal on a wax tablet to that effect. By the time Treverius returned to David's the rain had changed to a light drizzle that cloaked the houses and streets of Mogontium in a translucent greenish mist.

* * *

With hooded leather cloaks pulled up over their heads, the couples walked along back alleyways to reach Gundstram's. A few dogs barked at the sound of their footsteps, but the friends reached the edge of the Campus Martius without encountering anyone. Looking west, Treverius saw the garrison camp, its dark, angular palisade now blurred by fog. Everything seemed quiet. He surmised the men were in their barracks because of the weather, but knew there probably were guards on duty at the wooden ramparts.

Gundstram's was the only house in that part of Quadrant IV that had not been destroyed in the Vandal raid. Charred timbers, stone rubble, and salvaged bricks were piled near a basement foundation next door. The cavity was partially filled with wet earth, glistening in the dull light. Because of the rain, no one was at work.

Treverius pushed up the door's lock pinions with Albanus's passkey and slid the bolt free. The others followed him in, folding back their hoods in a spray of water that speckled the floor tiles.

The rooms looked much as they did at the time of the centurion's death, except that his widow had removed chests of clothing. Other furnishings were intact. Gundstram had been well paid as a centurion, and his household reflected both his wealth and the places where he had bought—or looted—his possessions: beds from Italy, tables of inlaid wood from the Asian provinces, and storage chests with intricate Celtic designs. Silk and fine wool tapestries and rugs decorated the walls and floors.

The timber beam in the room where Gundstram had been found still bore the stained scar of the lance point. Treverius ran a finger over the gouge. "This could have been a power struggle with Lupus Glaucus. It certainly would warn off anyone else who wanted to challenge him."

"Gundstram was obviously well off," David noted, "but they say ambition never takes a rest. What do you know about Glaucus?"

"Nothing," Treverius admitted. "I'd never heard of him before he was made interim commander. But then, the Limitans don't have much to do with the garrison. Let's look around."

The two men searched Gundstram's room, while Blandina and Penina poked through the others. When the centurion's room revealed nothing, David suggested they see if their wives had found anything. The women were in the dining area looking out a window at the rubble of the house next door.

"Any luck?" Treverius asked.

Blandina shook her head. "We don't really know what to look for."

"Do you still think you smelled incense that day?"

"Perhaps it was only an odor from the burned wood outside, near that basement."

"Basement." Penina tugged at Blandina's sleeve. "What's in the lower level of this house?"

"Good thinking, Penina," David praised. "Let's go see. There should be an entrance from the kitchen."

When they went in, the cooking area did not have an obvious door to a basement. A careful check of the walls failed to reveal a hidden entry.

"This house doesn't have two levels," David speculated.

"That would be unusual." Treverius glanced around once more. "Disappointing, but I think we're through here."

Outside, while Blandina waited for Treverius to relock the door, she followed a paved walk behind the house. It led to a small stone building some twenty paces away.

"What did he keep in this shed?" she called back.

Treverius looked over. "Carts, practice targets, catapults. Military equipment, mostly."

"The entrance faces the camp, so why is there a path to it from Gundstram's?" She bent down to look at the ground. "Trev, when would this have been used last?"

"September, after summer training. Why?"

"The new grass on either side of the walk is trampled down. Quite a few people have been in the shed recently."

"It couldn't hurt to look inside," David suggested.

"Right." At the shed door Treverius glanced across the muddy field toward the hazy outline of the palisade. Bluish cookfire smoke now mingled with the gray mist, but he saw no other movement and surmised that the guards were huddled under shelters, eating supper rations.

"This lock is different," David noted. "How can we force it open?"

"I saw something in the kitchen."

Treverius went back in the house and returned with an iron meat skewer. After he used the rod as a lever to pry off the brackets that held the bolt in place, David pulled the door open a short distance.

The dim interior of the shed was damp, its musty odor intensified by rain. The military equipment was laced with cobwebs. A single dirty window added a faint light to that which came from the door opening. Muddy straw was scattered on the floor around the army gear.

"Look for anything that seems suspicious," Treverius said, "but don't ask me what that might be."

After rummaging among the equipment, no one found anything unusual. Then Penina swept a hand over a cart next to where she was standing. "Treverius, didn't you say this was last used in September?"

"Yes, after the men's training ended. Why, Penina?"

"There are no cobwebs on this cart. It's been moved recently."

"Takes a woman." He grinned at David. "Help me push the thing aside."

After the cart was moved, Treverius found a trap-door in the floor, under a covering of straw. He eased up the wooden cover as David pulled on its ring handle. A rush of warmish, scented air rose from the opening. A flight of steps disappeared into darkness below.

"We don't have a lamp. Blandina, push that outer door open more so we can see what's down there."

The light was hardly improved, but Treverius led the way. At the bottom of the stairs everyone paused, waiting for his or her eyes to adjust to the dim light, when a rasping voice sounded from halfway up the stairs.

"Maybe y'd like t' join our little club?" Lupus Glaucus called down, his squat body silhouetted against the trapdoor opening. Despite the man's forced smile, his face reminded Treverius of the brutish sculpture that had upset Juliana on the Drusus Nero monument. "I'm legion commander. What're y' doing here?" Glaucus demanded in a less friendly tone.

Treverius showed him the wax slate. "We have the governor's permission to search Gundstram's for clues to his murder."

"It's you, map maker. Well, this is army property," Glaucus growled. "Albanus is civil. His word's not worth a leaky pisspot here."

"What kind of place is this?" Blandina asked.

"Just a legionary club." Glaucus affected a confidential tone. "Th' men like t' gamble a bit, even if that presbyter don't like it when they bet on dice and th' like."

"May we look inside?" David asked.

Glaucus's piggish eyes narrowed in a squint. "You're th' Judean. No, y'd have t' join t' see th' place. Now get out." He started back up the stairs, then turned to Treverius.

"Did . . . did y' find anything at Gundstram's?"

"No. Come on Blandina."

Treverius helped her up the stairs. David and Penina followed. At the entrance, they pulled up their hoods and stepped out into the mist, heading for home.

"Y'll pay for this lock," Glaucus shouted after them. "And I'll put y' in chains if y' come back!"

As soon as Blandina had turned from the Via Germanicus into the Rheni with the others she blurted, "Did you smell that room? That's where the incense is used."

"I noticed some kind of bizarre sculpture," Treverius said. "Did anyone have time to see anything else?"

"I noticed the figure too," David said, "and made out the glint of gold letters on a banner."

"David, could you read them?" Blandina asked.

"I'd swear on my oath to Honorius that they spelled out Legion Four Macedonica."

"The disbanded legion Albanus mentioned!" Treverius exclaimed.

"Then that's where the treasure could be hidden," Blandina said. "We have to go back inside."

"It won't be easy," David cautioned. "Now Glaucus will have the shed watched. Was he ever questioned about Gundstram's death?"

"If he was I didn't hear," Treverius replied, "but he was cockier than a rooster on a manure heap just now. In any event, we need to find out what's down there. Going in at the right time will be the problem."

"And getting out alive again." David gave a feeble grin. "No one would know where we were, and you heard Glaucus's threat."

*   *   *

When Treverius and Blandina returned to their quarters, their bedroom was cold. For a month the use of charcoal had been restricted to cooking; braziers and heating stoves had been made casualties of the Vandal raid.

There was little privacy in the pretorium, and Treverius's rooms abutted those of his parents. He and Blandina made love as quietly as possible. Afterwards, she lay with her head on his chest while he stroked her hair.

"That was nice, Trev, but I'm worried. That horrid Glaucus realizes we know about his hideaway."

"He called it a legionary club. It's possible. Didn't Nicias say he was trying to improve morale?"

"Just the same, we need to be careful. Especially after the way Gundstram was murdered."

"Dove," Treverius said to cheer up his wife, "when good weather is here, I'm going to suggest that Governor Albanus authorizes a scouting force to Treveri. We have to do something about finding out what happened to your father and the palace staff."

"Will you be part of it?"

"I hope to be."

"Then I want to go along, too."

"That's not a good idea, dove. It will be dangerous."

"It's my father we're talking about, Trev." She stopped his hand and looked up. "And if it's dangerous, I don't want you going either."

Stubborn woman. I've suggested to her that Cingetorius might be held for ransom, yet it's been almost four months since the raid and no request has been made. With Gallic estates and towns in their hands, the Vandals will have all the spoils they need, including the treasury and Imperial coin mint at Treveri. "Blandina," he said quietly, "perhaps we should wait until Commander Stilicho arrives to make decisions."

"The governor thinks we won't get much help from him."

"Maybe we are expecting too much, but I'm looking forward to meeting Stilicho. And seeing his Hun bodyguard. 'The Wolves of the North' are the best horsemen in or outside the Empire."

"Where did the tribe come from?" Blandina murmured, as she settled down against him and closed her eyes.

"Scythia, they're Asiatics. Marcellinus writes that the Huns forced the Alans to migrate westward, where that tribe allied themselves with Germanic Suebi and the Vandals who attacked us . . . Blandina?" Asleep. Treverius eased her head off his chest and onto the pillow at her side of the bed, then lay back to stare at the play of light on the ceiling from the flickering lamp flame.

He had kept from mentioning it, but was concerned that a charismatic Hunnish leader from Stilicho's guards, who had seen the wealth of Italy and Gaul, might defect and lead his men to fight for a share of it. Huns were allies now, yet their kings had alternately supported or fought the Eastern Empire's enemies.

But he had more immediate worries. The underground room discovered that day was puzzling, but Gundstram surely had to know about it.

Lupus Glaucus. The Grey Wolf looked capable of strangling a man who might challenge his authority, and certainly of decapitating a prostitute who had serviced, then possibly offended him. As Treverius reached over to pinch out the lamp flame, he had another disturbing thought. *What if Modestus and I are wrong? In the flush of excitement over seeming to find a connection in the murders, could we have been seduced by our own cleverness? I remember that Sophist philosopher at Ravenna, who could make a believable argument for or against anything. He'd prove the validity of a bystander's hypothesis, then cynically disprove his own argument.*

Treverius exhaled, too tired to speculate further, then turned to burrow into Blandina's warmth with a more comforting conclusion.

Stilicho is due to arrive any day. Despite the governor's fears, and even if some insane fanatic is murdering people, Stilicho will be safe, under heavy guard. Besides, I haven't found a martyr with his name. It's not even Christian.

chapter 16

Flavius Stilicho, Supreme Commander of the Western Roman Army, arrived on April twenty-third, after an arduous journey from Vindonissa, but did not bring Vulcatius Bassus, or the men he had requisitioned for his war in the south. Instead, a unit of seventy Goths and his Hun bodyguard had assured the Commander's safety on the road.

Once Stilicho was in Mogontium, Treverius noticed Governor Albanus relax, despite disappointment at not having his men returned. No suspicious deaths had occurred all month and only men named Marcus or Marcellinus remained on the list of possible victims.

Two days after Stilicho arrived, Quintus Albanus hosted a dinner in the Pretorian mess hall for the man who had been his superior officer at the Frigidus River battle. He included two Curia members, Arinthos and Pendatios, who remembered the commander from his last inspection tour, and Treverius's family because of Stilicho's interest in mapping the Western Empire.

Food supplies were low, but the cooks prepared dishes of grilled fish caught through open areas in the river ice. These were followed by roasted pork shoulder in a rue-pepper sauce, and a stew of pork livers and chicken cooked with mushrooms, wild narcissus bulbs, and turnips preserved in myrtle berries, honey, and vinegar.

Treverius was seated across the table from the Commander, next to Blandina and his parents. He thought Stilicho looked to be in his late thirties, yet white strands flecked his temples and well-trimmed beard. He wore his reddish hair combed forward and cut low on his forehead, in the style Emperor Honorius had favored when Treverius saw him at the Nativity Mass in Ravenna.

"We don't have venison or boar, Commander," Albanus apologized as he indicated Stilicho's seat. "We're pretty well isolated behind these walls, and the Goths hunted out the woods long ago."

"Quintus, after a month on travel rations, whatever you serve will be ambrosial," Stilicho said amiably, glancing around the table with piercing blue eyes. "Now introduce me to our guests."

Treverius noticed the man spoke Latin with a slight Gothic accent, the legacy of his Vandal father.

"Let me present Vertiscus, curator of the Pretorium," Albanus began. "This is Demetrius, our envoy from the Augustus. Councilors Arinthos and Pendatios remember you from your last inspection tour."

"Good to see both of you well."

"Cyril of Constantinople," Albanus continued. "He was in Julian's last campaign against the Alamanni."

"A pity the Apostate wasn't as fervent a Christian as he was a soldier," Stilicho commented dryly.

Cyril allowed him a thin smile. "Not everyone's opinion, Commander. Certainly not mine."

Albanus glared at the merchant, but continued to Treverius's father. "Junius Asterius oversees my map workshop with his son Treverius there. The two ladies are Junius's wife Margarita and daughter-in-law Blandina."

Albanus looked around the room. "Our presbyter was invited, but I don't see Vetius Modestus."

"Detained on a church matter, perhaps." Stilicho indicated everyone with a sweep of hand. "Please, sit down. I'm grateful you're here for Rome. The frontier isn't an easy assignment."

"What are your plans for our province, Commander?" Arinthos asked as he took his seat on the bench.

"Councilor, we'll take that up later," Albanus said quickly, turning to Stilicho. "I can well imagine your journey was tiring, Commander. What was your route?"

"Overland. The Rhine is still solid ice along its length through Raetia . . ." Stilicho paused to let a servant put a plate of fish in front of him. A Hun, who had taken a position behind the commander, snatched it up. Stilicho spoke to him, in what Treverius took to be Hunnic, then chuckled. "Uldin commands my personal bodyguard. Insists on tasting everything before I eat it."

"It's going to be that kind of touchy visit," Treverius muttered to Blandina. "Constant precautions for the Commander's safety."

Uldin sniffed, then pinched off and tasted a portion of fish. After he nodded and put the plate down, Stilicho commented on his guard's crudeness, "I'm afraid Huns have better fighting than social skills, Quintus. We could have used them at the Frigidus. I noticed you limping. Your old leg wound?"

"It acts up from time to time."

Stilicho gave a grunt of sympathy. "That young man who saved your life. Is he still with you?"

"Sebastian? No. Killed in an . . . an accident after the Vandal raid."

"Of course, I read your report. Sorry. The Frigidus was a dreadful slaughter, yet I seem to remember that Claudian wrote a poem about the action. Anyone recall it?"

When no one responded, Blandina spoke up. "I remember how it ended, Commander."

"Fine, young woman. Aren't the last stanzas about the Frigidus River being gorged with bodies?"

"Sir, it goes something like this:
'The Alpine snow bloomed red with blood.
The Frigid stream, now a crimson flood,
Rushed on with saddened mood, for
Every wave, so swollen with gore,
Wept at the ghastly load it bore.'"

"Very good." Stilicho tapped his knife handle against the table in applause. "Again, young woman, you are?"

"Blandina Asteria, sir. I work with my husband in the map room."

"Do you? I need charts that are up to date. I'd like to see you and your husband's work before I leave."

"Time permitting, Commander," Albanus interposed. "There's an entertainment scheduled for you in the theater."

"A play? Nothing too heavy, Quintus. No Sophoclian tragedies."

"No, no. The director isn't giving away the plot, but I think it has to do with your victory over Radagaisus."

"Yes, tell us about that," Cyril called out. "I understand all the Ostrogoth captives who were suddenly thrown on the slave market have depressed prices."

"A merchant's lament, perhaps, but not a soldier's," Stilicho shot back. "Yes, my men and our Alan and Hun allies did corner the bastar . . . the beast . . . outside Florentia. He should be on his way to execution in Rome by now."

"Some of the Limitans units you requisitioned from us were with you," Vertiscus probed. "Will you return them soon?"

"Alaric's Visigoths are still to be reckoned with," Stilicho replied, parrying the question.

"Didn't you offer Alaric 'a bridge of gold' to quit Italy?" Cyril sneered.

Treverius noticed Albanus stop in mid-bite, and Demetrius look up suddenly. What does Cyril expect to gain by his goading of the commander?

"It was actually pepper," Stilicho countered with an easy smile. "I wanted him to sneeze his way out."

"Spice up his life a bit, eh, Commander," Pendatios joked.

After laughter had relieved the tension, Albanus signaled for the next course. Uldin tried to taste the pork dish, but Stilicho waved him off. The group ate in silence until Demetrius asked about Stilicho's daughter Maria, who was married to Honorius.

"How is Augusta Maria, Commander?"

"Not well." Stilicho did not look up or elaborate.

"What's the situation with this rebel Constantine at Arelate?" Cyril asked casually.

"I've sent Sarus to deal with him."

"The Goth who defected from Alaric's army?" Cyril threw down his knife. "Really, Commander. First Bauto, then Fravitta, Gainas, Tribigild, and now Sarus. Will this litany of unpronounceable barbarian names in Roman service never end?"

Treverius noticed Stilicho flush—he should have been included on Cyril's list of Germanic commanders—then fix him with a cold stare. "Better an unpronounceable one in our service, merchant, than a pronounceable Eugenius or Constantine against us. Wouldn't you agree?"

While the group applauded Stilicho's rebuttal, Cyril gave a stiff grin before asking, "Has anyone heard the latest quip making the rounds at Rome? No? Then, what does S P Q R stand for now?"

"Actually, the Senate and People of Rome," Treverius murmured to Blandina. "What's his version?"

"'Special Privileges for Quasi-Romans,'" Cyril answered, without waiting for a response.

Only Vertiscus reacted with a dry laugh. In the uncomfortable moments that followed, Treverius was relieved to see Modestus enter the mess room.

"Governor, there's the presbyter," he said.

"Over here, Modestus," Albanus called out. "Your place was kept next to the Commander."

Stilicho stood to greet him. "I'm pleased you came, Presbyter."

"My apology for being late," Modestus replied, taking his seat. "I brought the Eucharist to a dying parishioner."

Treverius looked at him, fearful of another murder. "Who . . . who is it, presbyter?"

"Lucilius Maximus. Claims to be over ninety years old and to have been in the army of the great Constantine."

"Yes," Albanus recalled, "I had him speak to the pretorians a few years ago. Inflated his story until he, too, saw the cross over the Milvian Bridge."

"'In hoc signo, vinces,'" Modestus quoted. "That was the sign by which the emperor would conquer Maxentius."

"Our future was determined by a parhelion near the sun," Cyril scoffed, "and yet you ridicule pagan auguries?"

"Eusebius wrote that Constantine told him about the vision," Blandina said. "And he also saw a standard with the cross on it in his rooms."

Cyril glared at her but did not continue his taunts.

"Sad," Arinthos commented, "I knew Maximus. Another tile fallen from the mosaic of our Roman past."

"But councilor, a new design is being cemented in place," Stilicho pointed out. "Romans and the peoples coming in from Germania."

"Yes," Cyril sneered, "and creating a kind of barbarian quasi-monster."

"On the contrary," Treverius broke in. "The Commander is talking about a synthesis of peoples that is determining our future. We should understand that."

"Well said, young man." Stilicho looked at Cyril. "Rome will be the stronger for it."

Further comments were suspended when servants brought in a dessert course of stewed fruit and sweet wine cakes. Stilicho stood to excuse himself.

"Quintus, I'll make that inspection tour in the morning, but you must be curious about my bodyguard. I'll have Uldin order his men to demonstrate some of their riding skills. He bowed to acknowledge Blandina and Margarita. "Ladies. I look forward to seeing your maps, Blandina."

After Stilicho left with Uldin, Cyril looked around the table. "So that's the barbarian who leads Rome's armies?" he asked sarcastically. "The man can't capture one Visigoth chief with his mercenaries, but Julius Caesar conquered all of Gaul with only citizen legions."

"The situation is different today," Treverius protested, without concealing the irritation in his voice. "Rome wasn't a vast empire back then with its frontiers under constant attack by Goths or Parthians."

"You dare lecture me, map maker?" Cyril glowered, standing up. "When we're in New—"

"New times, Cyril means," Vertiscus said after a loud cough. "When Stilicho eliminates this Alaric and secures our northern frontier."

"Or defects Rome to join him, like other commanders have."

"Enough, Cyril!" Albanus ordered. "Your comments border on treason. Let's not spoil the commander's time here. I, for one, look forward to seeing his Hunnic bodyguard perform tomorrow."

* * *

Treverius was sure the Huns would create as much interest in the citizenry as their commander. In his history, Marcellinus had described the Asiatics as sub-human creatures whose principle food was meat that had been pounded into palatability under their saddles during the day's ride. These Huns were tall, with handsome flattish faces of a ruddy complexion, and eyes narrowed by a fold of skin. Rather than wearing the pelts of field mice that Marcellinus described, they sported brightly colored silk tunics decorated with silver and gold coins, soft sable jackets, and elegant calfskin boots.

The next day, wooden targets were set up on the Campus Martius and the Huns gave demonstrations of their equestrian and archery skills. Their composite bow, constructed of a wooden core backed with layers of sinew and cattle horn, could send an arrow through scale armor at over one hundred paces. The riders clamped legs around their mounts' bellies and, as their horses galloped past the targets, used both hands to send arrow shafts splintering through the boards.

Afterwards, a hundred men with money kept the brothel women occupied and tavern keepers busy resolving brawls.

*   *   *

Petranius's theater presentation was scheduled for the afternoon of April twenty-eight. Treverius introduced the crippled director to Stilicho, and he felt Petranius was impressed with the commander, who asked about the actor's leg injury but tactfully did not mention his hunchback.

Before the drama began, Petranius escorted Stilicho, Treverius, and Blandina through the storage rooms on either side of the stage. Dusty scenery flats painted on linen, tattered costumes, and grotesque character masks filled the areas. When Petranius arrived at the labyrinth of animal cages on the orchestra level, he explained that they were empty except for one, and proudly displayed a snarling yearling bear that he was training for summer performances.

Outside, when Stilicho commented on the hoisting crane at the right side of the stage, Petranius told him he would see it in use during the play.

*   *   *

The afternoon was pleasantly warm, with a vernal sun slanting its rays onto the backs of the audience. A light easterly breeze was buffered by the theater backdrop. About forty guests, including Lupus Glaucus, were already seated when Stilicho took his place next to Albanus on the orchestra half-circle. Uldin stood a pace away from the officers, scanning the audience.

Treverius sat with Blandina, David, and Penina in the first row of wooden seats. He saw other Huns patrolling empty upper tiers and the two exits, surmising that their Gothic companions were in town, patronizing as many taverns and brothels as they could before it was time to leave.

A copy of the name of the play and the actor's role was circulating through the audience. After Vertiscus finished reading it, a slave passed the parchment to Treverius and waited for him to share it with his companions.

A NEW AGE OF GOLD
By G. Petranius

Selegos: Romulus—One of the twin founders of Rome
Haimon: Remus—One of the twin founders of Rome
Albino: Jupiter—Chief god of the Romans
Pumilio: Garlic—A Visigoth chief
Alexandros: Stabilicus—A Roman Commander
Callixa: Serenita—Wife of Stabilicus
Aktea: Honoro—Western Augustus
Laodike: Arceo—Eastern Augustus
Citizens, slaves, etcetera.

The action tells of Rome's Golden Age, then moves to our present era.

"This is exciting, our first drama." Blandina plucked her husband's sleeve, then slid her hand into his.

"Stilicho didn't need to worry about sitting through a play by Sophocles," Treverius commented, reading the list of actors. "Did you see the names?"

"It's a parody of sorts, right?" David asked.

"To say the least. Arceo is obviously Arcadius, the Eastern Emperor, but the word means 'to hinder.' I suppose Honoro is preferable to Honorless for our emperor. Serenita, 'fair weather,' must be Serena, Stilicho's wife."

"And the commander is called Stabilicus," Blandina said, pointing to the name.

"That's not too bad, but how will he take it? We saw that these actors can be quite coarse," Treverius added, recalling their parody of the past February.

A creaking of gears in motion sounded from the stage, as the shabby curtain that was stretched across the platform was slowly lowered into its housing.

"There's Petranius!" Blandina squealed when he appeared onstage. "He looks splendid in his costume."

A scattering of applause greeted the actor's entrance for the prologue. Petranius had colored his face with garish makeup and wore a tunic of silver cloth. Bowing slightly to acknowledge the audience, he began reciting in a strong voice that belied his slim, twisted body.

"First, friends, a hearty welcome all,
Stilicho, Albanus, to all we call.
Come watch our play unfold its way,
Don't leave, please, we beg you stay.
Of a Golden Age we soon will tell,
That turned to lead and then to Hell.
The gods again will with us walk,
Romulus, Remus, return to talk,
And give advice we need to hear,
Of how we fell and why we fear.
But wait! A savior yet will come,

To show how glory can again be won.
No, I say too much. The actors pale.
They alone must tell the tale.
So give heed good friends and listen now,
Our story unfolds. Now, watch how."

As Petranius limped to the side of the stage to prompt
his actors, a rasping sound was heard from the crane's
winch when Selegos and Haimon were lowered to the
stage as Romulus and Remus. After their feet touched
the wooden floor, the twin founders of Rome looked
around in overstated bewilderment.

Rom: "What place is this?"

Rem: "For sure, 'tis wild."

Rom: "Let's find the Forum. It's there we'll see both
gawkers and talkers."

They walked to a painted backdrop of broken columns, then stopped in exaggerated shock.

Rom: "It's ruined! The Forum's rubble! Another civil
war?"

Aethiops came onstage and walked toward them.

Rem: "Wait. There's a slave."

Rom: "Or citizen."

Rem: "He'll tell us where we are. Ho! Citizen or slave.
What place is this?"

Being mute, Aethiops did not reply.

Rom: "Indeed, a surly fellow."

Rem: "Or king, perhaps, who speaks not to strangers."

Rom: "King of charcoal makers, from his sooty look.
Speak, or I'll thrash your dusky hide till it's white as the
snows of Germania, by Jupiter!"

Chuckling in the audience was overlaid by the grinding of the crane mechanism. Albino was lowered onstage
as Jupiter, wearing a gold diadem and carrying bronze
thunderbolts.

Jup: "Who called my name?" He hurled a bronze bolt into the floor. "Speak up, by thunder! Which of you twin turds called me? Who are you?"

Rom and Rem, in unison: "We're Remulus and Romus. That is, Romulus and Remus."

Jup: "Hmm, your names are familiar. I should know you but I can't place you. Are you priests? Sailors? Barbarians?"

Rom: "In a sense, all three."

Rem: "Sons of a god and Vestal."

Rom: "Set adrift in a boat then rescued."

Rem: "And suckled by a she-wolf."

Jup: "Indeed! Even a Suebi dare not lie like that." He looked around. "What place is this?"

Rom, in an aside to the audience: "That was our question! Imagine, we think like gods!"

Jupiter sees Aethiops: "You there, burnt-to-a-crisp. Has one of my bolts singed you?" Aethiops did not answer.

Rem: "He speaks not, even to a god!"

Jup: "I'll raise a whoop, Blackie." He threw a bolt at Aethiops's feet, who scurried offstage. "Ha! That showed the fellow. Seems only a month or two since I knocked another one off a church here, which was once my sacred temple."

Garlic entered from stage right, miscounting coins: "One, two, five, seven, three, eight."

Rom, Rem, Jup, in unison: "A TAX COLLECTOR!"

Garlic quickly dropped the coins into his pouch and hid it behind his back.

Jup: "You there, tax collector. Name this place."

Gar: "Mogontracium. Mognotocium. Montrogacium. Hades! It's a town in Ger-mania Prim-terior."

Jup: "A town that despoiled my temple. Tell me, tax collector, what gods do they worship here?"

Gar: "In truth, I think only one. A carpenter."

Jup, incredulously: "What? A carpenter god? You mean like Vulcan, the forge god? Or Mercurius, a commerce god? And only one, you say?"

Gar, confused: "Well, sort of one. You see, he's man made God. Or is it God made man? Anyway, he has father and a . . . and a . . . and a—"

Jup, interrupting: "His father's name is Anda? Definitely not a Roman."

Gar, still confused: "No, no. He's his own father. And also his own son. Oh, Hades, let the priests explain!"

Stabilicus strutted in with his nose lifted distainfully in the air.

Rom: "Who's this, a cook? His nose seeks out herbs to season with."

Sta, insulted, draws a sword: "Cook? Cook? It's your hide I'll skin and cook."

Jup: "Hold off, man. We're strangers here and meant no harm. Who rules this place?"

Stab: "Honoro is Augustus."

Rom, Rem, Jup, in unison: "TAKE US TO HIM!"

Sta: "He's not here. I, Stabilicus, am in charge."

Rom, in an aside: "A stable boy in charge?"

Gar chuckles: "As long as he keeps my purse filled."

Treverius noticed Albanus cough nervously at the reference to Stilicho's policy of bribing Alaric. The Commander, too, shifted uneasily in his chair.

Modestus tried to leave but was intercepted by one of the guards and sent back.

Sta: "What did you say, you miserable vis-ible Visigoth? Would that you were an un-visible miserable Visigoth."

Callixa walked onstage in a revealingly short tunic.

Sta: "Ah, Serenita my dear."

Rom, looking at sky: "No, it seems a bit cloudy. A chance for rain, even."

Sta: "You truly are strangers. Serenita is my wife, neice of an emperor, just as my daughter is married to an Augustus."

Gar, aside: "Which guarantees him 'fair weather.'"

Treverius saw that Stilicho's neck was flushed as he leaned over to whisper to Albanus. The governor nodded, then stood and called up to Petranius at the side of the stage, "Sorry, director. The Commander's time is short. He's scheduled to meet with garrison officers today for supper."

Petranius's body sagged. "You . . . you're not staying for the ending?"

"Afraid not," Stilicho answered, pushing back his chair and turning to leave.

"As . . . as you wish." Petranius bowed. "But hear my epilogue. It resolves everything in the play."

Stilicho paused, then snapped, "Quickly, director."

Petranius limped to stage center, motioning his actors away. "Spectators, today I hope we've pleased," he began, his voice now pitched strangely high and weak.

"Take no offense, all you we've teased.
If once we had an Age of Gold,
We can again, if all act bold.
Stilicho came to banish fear,
And bring us peace 'fore end of year.
It's him we praise and commend to you.
Now. If you think our play a worthy cause,
Kind friends, you all know what to do.
Now let us hear your loud applause."

Amid feeble clapping from the audience, Stilicho took out a purse and tossed it to Petranius. He deftly caught the bag, shifted weight, and bowed low to hide a grimace of pain and frustration.

When a grim-faced Albanus guided Stilicho towards the exit, Treverius and David fell in step behind. Blandina and Penina followed further back. Uldin shouted at four guards to come down and escort the group out, then for his other Huns to hold the rest of the audience inside the second tunnel exit.

As Stilicho and the others reached the darkened passageway, Petranius appeared from inside with a lighted torch to guide them through. Treverius was pleased. The director seemed to have regained his composure.

Uldin ordered three of his guards to go through the exit first and scout the square outside. Treverius saw them look around at the far end of the passageway, then signal for the group to come forward. Petranius hobbled a few paces ahead, holding his torch low to light the damp stone paving underfoot.

He had reached the center of the tunnel, with the others following behind, when a dull hammering sound was heard overhead. Two keystones of the arch suddenly gave way, tumbling down in a shower of mortar bits and dust. Petranius was hit on the shoulder and thrown backwards. The torch was knocked from his hand and fell, sputtering on the floor stones.

Albanus instinctively pulled Stilicho back by the arm. Uldin and his guard shoved Treverius and David against the wall and held them with sword points at their throats.

"No, let them go, I'm not hurt," Stilicho ordered and looked back. "Are you ladies all right?"

After Blandina nodded that she and Penina were unhurt, Stilicho bent down to check Petranius's injuries. The actor was conscious, but dazed, watching blood seep onto the shoulder of his silver tunic.

Albanus looked stunned, gazing in shock at the mound of broken stone. Treverius knelt down to sift some of the debris through his fingers. "Christ Jesus!" he exclaimed. "Remember I said Saint Vitalis was buried alive?

This is his feast day, but we had no idea something like this might happen."

Uldin ordered the other guard to run back through the passageway to alert his companions inside the theater. Treverius and David sprinted past their wives after him. When they reached the seating, they saw the Hun, who was not familiar with the theater's layout, looking around in confusion.

Treverius spotted a plank leaning against a seat and beckoned to David. The loose board had evidentally covered the keystones. A wooden wedge and sledge hammer lay near the opening where the stones had been. He peered into the hole and saw Blandina tending Petranius, who was slumped against the wall.

"How is he?" he called down. "Any bones broken?"

She looked up at her husband. "I don't think so. His shoulder and one side of his face are badly bruised, though."

Albanus held up some of the smaller debris fragments and looked at Treverius. "I don't understand. The stones seem to be pumice."

"I heard him, pumice." David brushed at some chunks near the hole. "It looks as if someone replaced the keystones with lighter ones made of pumice. They were held in place with the wedge, then it was hammered away."

"Good reasoning," Treverius said. "And Petranius took the stones intended for Stilicho. That should help redeem his play. Who would have pumice material, David?"

"Stone masons, carpenters. Even the shop that makes vellum, for scraping skins smooth." David looked toward the Hun. "Did you see anyone up here?"

The guard only stared at him.

"He doesn't understand," Treverius said. "Let's go back down. I wouldn't know where else to look either."

When they returned, Stilicho was refusing an apology for the accident.

"Nonsense, Quintus, you said you'd investigate the matter. That's fine." Stilicho bent to touch Petranius lightly on the head. "Take good care of our playwright here, he may have saved my life. There'll be a bonus for him." He straightened, put an arm around Albanus and smiled. "What have the garrison cooks planned for dinner? Danger always whets my appetite."

After Stilicho stepped around the pile of broken stones and went outside, he spoke briefly to Uldin in Hunnic, then walked across the square toward the legion camp with Albanus.

Treverius felt cold, despite the warm afternoon. "The Commander has catapult cables for nerves. Stilicho might have been killed, were it not for Petranius."

"We'll take him back to his room and call Nicias in to treat those bruises," Blandina said.

"No, I'm fine angel." Petranius slowly stood up, supporting himself on the wall and rubbing his injured shoulder. "I'm grateful the accident didn't harm the commander. This cursed theater is three centuries old. Needs repairing."

"It wasn't an accident," Treverius told him . . ."David and I discovered the arch keystones hammered away."

"What?" Petranius exclaimed. "I thought I heard you say something about Vitalis being buried alive. If this mad killer used my theater to assassinate Stilicho—"

"Petranius, you've had a nasty shock," Blandina broke in. "You need to go home and rest until Nicias gets there."

"Thanks, angel. I do feel a bit weak."

"All of us are shaken," Treverius said, "but at least the Huns will be on heightened alert now. While he's here, nothing more will happen to Stilicho."

* * *

At supper Treverius aimlessly pushed lentils around his plate, still shocked by the assassination attempt. "The Commander of the Western Army almost killed in Mogontium," he mumbled. "I should have been more alert."

"Don't blame yourself," Blandina countered. "Just thank God that Petranius led us out and isn't dead."

"If Stilicho had been killed, imagine the damage his Huns and Goths would have done to the town."

"Whoever is responsible knew that. Why would someone want to provoke a riot?" When Treverius shrugged, Blandina went on. "We didn't make the connection between Vitalis and Stilicho. Now I'm worried about you."

"Why should you be, dove?"

"You're named after the Treveri tribe. After we found a method to these killings, you didn't have a saint's name so I assumed you weren't in danger."

"My artwork isn't that bad!" He reached across and gave his wife's hand a reassuring squeeze. "Seriously. I can't imagine anyone interested in killing me."

"You're just trying to make me feel better."

"Blandina, there's a motive for these murders even if we haven't figured it out."

"I don't think that they're the work of a madman."

"They're too calculated," he agreed. "Whatever their purpose, the killings can't go on forever. I'd bet a gold solidus that the person . . . or group . . . responsible will act before summer is out."

"Did you see Lupus Glaucus at the theater?"

"Sitting apart." Treverius fashioned the letters L G on his plate with his uneaten lentils. "He's the only person whom we know has a connection to one of the victims."

"Gundstram."

Treverius nodded. "I think Glaucus was relieved that Stilicho didn't bring Bassus back. Once you've been a hammer, it's hard being the anvil again. Glaucus wants Bassus's post as Provincial Military Commander and he's had a year to plan for it."

"That's sedition."

"And with only our militia units to fight it." Treverius scattered the two initials with his spoon. "When Glaucus acts, he'll have the garrison on his side."

"Is he intelligent enough to lead such an action without help?" Blandina asked. "I recall that remark by Demetrius, about the murderer being an educated person."

"Demetrius himself is well-educated."

"True. And what do we know about him, other than that he's been virtually exiled from Ravenna? Going from the capital of the Western Empire to provincial Mogontium should rankle him."

"At all the murder sites we'd smell that perfumed oil he uses on his hair."

"I'm serious, Trev. He wouldn't do the actual killing, but he has the means to have them done."

"So we should suspect everyone who can read and write?"

"Fine. Be sarcastic, but I'm frightened. Stilicho was almost killed right under our noses."

"Above our heads, actually—"

"This is beyond your furcing jokes, husband!"

After both had laughed at Blandina's blurted vulgarity, Treverius said, "I didn't know you used army slang, dove."

"I've heard the pretorians use the word. What does it mean, again?"

"A furca is a set of crossed beams on which legionaries are lashed for punishment." Treverius paused, then continued in a serious tone. "Blandina, I've thought of a plan to protect potential victims."

"Tell me about it."

Treverius formed a square with the two knives and spoons on the table. "Say this is the garrison camp. I'd have the persons in danger report here on that particular day. Surrounded by over a hundred soldiers, they'd be safe."

"That would work."

"Hopefully. I'm going to tell Vertiscus and then the Curia at the May meeting. Getting some of the men to go in might be difficult, but if their wives are as persuasive as you are, dove, we'll not have another victim."

"Presuming Lupus Glaucus isn't involved," Blandina warned. "But no, my intuition tells me your plan is sound."

"Does it tell you if we'll get through the rest of Stilicho's visit without trouble?"

Blandina shrugged. "Can you read the mind of an invisible killer, Trev?"

"No, but his plan failed. It would take time for another attempt on Stilicho's life."

"You're saying we shouldn't worry?"

"Again, no," Treverius answered," but I'd like to know how our murderer chisled out those keystones and substituted pumice?"

"They already could have been loose, Petranius said the theater is in bad condition. And the actors aren't here all the time."

Treverius pushed away from the table. "I'm going to bed. Every new incident brings more questions than it does answers."

chapter 17

The next morning, after a restless night, Treverius led Blandina to the map workshop with little enthusiasm. The room was cold. None of the mapping or architectural staff was at work. As he stared numbly at the unfinished chart of Germania Prima and Sequania, Blandina called to her husband. He turned around to see Stilicho standing at the door. When Treverius went to greet him, he caught a glimpse of Uldin positioned in the hall with a sword in his hand.

"Commander, we're honored you came."

"I'm leaving for Ravenna as soon as my men secure the pack horses." Stilicho walked in and glanced around. "I promised your wife I'd look at her map."

"It's over here, sir," Blandina said.

Stilicho went to study the drawing. "Good overview of the provinces. We're here, near the northeast corner, and that's Vindonissa down there?"

"Yes sir."

After scanning the map a moment, Stilicho abruptly turned away. "I'm concerned about Quintus . . . Governor Albanus. I didn't see him at breakfast this morning."

"He hasn't been well," Treverius explained. "The garrison surgeon has been treating him."

"This damnable cold weather and the strain of the invasion." Stilicho picked up a compass and toyed with its legs. "I read Quintus's report, but convinced Honorius to turn down his resignation request."

"The governor had hoped you could give him some military help, sir. Vandals still control the province."

"I need my field legions to protect Italy, and this infernal rebel Constantine has drained off even more of my men." Stilicho looked up at Treverius. "Quintus seems to trust you."

"I hope to be worthy of it, Commander."

"He alluded to some unexplained murders that have citizens on the verge of panic. What's that all about?"

"I think I've discovered the cypher to the killings," Treverius explained, "if not the exact reason why victims are being targeted."

"That wasn't an accident in the tunnel," Stilicho emphasized. "I'd expect an assassination attempt at Ravenna, but not out here. What are you doing about these deaths?"

"Blandina and I are working with Modestus, trying to anticipate who might be in danger next."

"Better luck than you had with me." Stilicho half-laughed.

"I . . . we were looking for saints' names," Treverius mumbled. "I'll propose to the Curia that those in danger be confined in the garrison camp for that day."

"Good thinking." Stilicho broke into a slight smile. "Quintus tells me you're in the Limitans."

"Cavalry, sir. Cohort Falco."

"Your militia and Vulcatius Bassus's mercenaries may be the only defense the Rhine frontier will have."

"When can we expect Bassus to come back?"

"That merchant at dinner," Stilicho said, bypassing Treverius's question. "Cyril, was that his name?"

"Yes, sir."

"Do you think he was involved in the tunnel incident yesterday?"

"Cyril is one of the Romans who still resents the loss of pagan rights. He claims Jupiter is responsible for the deaths. Opportunism, yes. Murder? I don't think he'd go that far."

"Fanaticism is a dog that bites," Stilicho said grimly. "There's a faction at Ravenna that would like to have seen me buried in that tunnel. Treverius, I wouldn't underestimate this Cyril."

Uldin signaled that the men were ready to travel. Stilicho nodded and went back to the map. "With God's help we'll make over thirty miles today. Where would that be on your chart, young woman?"

"Here, sir, near Lopodunum." Blandina pointed along a road east of the Rhine. "You can cross the bridge at Borbetomagus."

"Good." Stilicho put down the compass, then grasped each of their hands. "These are difficult times for Rome. May Fortune be good to you both."

"And you, sir," Treverius said. "Safe travels."

After Stilicho left, Blandina slipped the compass back into its case. "He's a charming man. I liked him."

"Enough, I noticed, to make you blush like a new bride every time he spoke to you."

"Treverius!"

"Just teasing, dove, I was impressed with him too."

"Trev, I have a feeling we'll never see Stilicho again."

"I hope your intuition is wrong this time, Blandina, but what he just said about having enemies in Ravenna may be true. A man with his power breeds envy."

"I want you to listen to his advice about taking Cyril more seriously."

"Right. You know, it seems like a waste of time to work on this map. I'm going to find Vertiscus and tell him my idea about protecting potential victims."

* * *

As the weather turned warmer at the end of April, ice in the Rhine began to break up. At night, the noise of grinding floes resembled the groanings of demonic beings in Satan's realm, unearthly sounds that came from the direction of the river and kept children terrified and adults on edge.

The first three days in May celebrated the martyrdom of the apostles James and Philip, and the commemoration of the date on which, some seventy years earlier, Helena, the mother of Constantine the Great, had found the cross on which Christ was crucified outside Jerusalem.

Treverius heard from Nicias that Governor Albanus was too ill to schedule a Curia meeting, but that Verticus had called an emergency session for May first to publicize the list of potential victims for the month. In preparation Modestus asked Treverius to help compile the names.

As Treverius sat next to Modestus, watching Curia members file into the basilica, he noticed that David and Nathaniel's seats were vacant, then recalled that it was the Judean Sabbath. Had Vertiscus purposely called the meeting on a day when he knew the two men would not attend? He was also disturbed to see Lupus Glaucus posting a company of legionaries along the basilica's aisles. Did the curator expect some kind of trouble, or was he trying to intimidate the councilors? He had told Vertiscus about his plan to confine potential victims in the camp, but was puzzled because he had not been asked to present it at this meeting. Blandina was in her quarters with an upset stomach. Demetrius sat at his table. Treverius thought he looked worried, brooding.

When Vertiscus entered to preside over the meeting, he was nervous, and fidgeted with a rolled parchment as the councilors took their places on the benches.

"What's that in his hand?" Treverius whispered to Modestus. "And why the legion guards?"

"I'm not in his confidence. I was only told to be here with the names for May."

After the councilors were seated, Vertiscus tapped the parchment against his thigh and looked toward Modestus. "Presbyter, I have done my own research. Is not today the feast of both Blessed Philip and James the Just?"

"That is what I have here," Modestus replied.

"Yes, Philip was crucified in Phrygia. James remained at Jerusalem. As the brother of the Lord—"

"Not brother. Cousin, perhaps," Modestus corrected. "Blessed Mary remained a virgin. If James was a brother, why did the Lord commend his mother to the care of John?"

Vertiscus reddened. "You digress. My point is that the Judeans were angry because Paul, an apostate in their eyes, was at Rome to defend himself against their accusations. They turned their wrath on James."

Modestus became agitated at having his role so obviously challenged. And what was the curator's purpose in attacking Judeans? Treverius wondered. Is that why he chose a day for this meeting when David and Nathaniel would be absent?

"The faithless Hebrews tried to turn James against the Lord by threatening him with death," Vertiscus continued. "They forced him to the Temple dome and ordered him to preach against his brother. When James refused, they threw him down into the courtyard."

"So someone may die in a fall today?" Musonius asked.

"The fall did not kill him," Vertiscus lashed back impatiently. "On the ground, he was struck in the head."

"How many are named James in Mogontium?"

Vertiscus ignored Musonius to hold up the tattered scroll. "I have a secret letter of James, suppressed by the Bishop of Rome, just as an earlier one silenced Arius."

"We're not interested in letters," Pendatios shouted. "You said you had a plan for ending these murders?"

Treverius was startled. Is Vertiscus going to announce, as his own, my idea to confine potential victims?

"I do have a plan, Vertiscus replied. "Presbyter, who is on your list?"

"May six, Blessed John the Apostle. He was exiled to Patmos," Modestus replied. "May ten, Gordian and Epimachus, recently beheaded under Julian. The twelfth, eunuchs Nereus and Achilleus, beheaded under Domitian. Also, the child martyr Pancratius. May fourteen, Boniface, beheaded, and Urbanus on the twenty-fifth, martyred at Rome. May thirty-first celebrates Petronilla, the daughter of Peter, who died by fasting herself to death."

"And what are your conclusions, Presbyter?"

"Curator, if Treverius might answer for me?"

Vertiscus gave a curt wave with his scroll. "Let him be brief."

"We believe the feasts of Gordian, Epimachus, Urbanus, and Boniface are the days of danger," Treverius said. "There's no one here named Nereus or Achilleus. The exiled John can be eliminated, and certainly one would not kill a child. As for Petronilla, nobody could force another to starve themselves. In my plan, curator, I would—"

"Yes," Vertiscus interrupted loudly, "I have thought of a way to protect those in danger. It is so simple that our governor should have long ago implemented it himself."

"He is going to claim credit for the idea I told you about." Treverius began to stand, but Modestus held him back.

"Humility, son. It only matters that the plan succeeds."

"It's not about pride," Treverius hissed. "After pretending to defend the governor, now Vertiscus is blaming him for not acting. "Curator, I suggested the idea you're about to propose, both to the governor and Flavius Stilicho."

"Commander," Vertiscus called to Lupus Glaucus, "The map maker is a guest. If he disrupts the Curia, order your men to throw him out."

Glaucus straightened up. Two legionaries unsheathed their swords and started towards Treverius.

Modestus stood up quickly and ordered, "Put down those weapons. We're here to prevent bloodshed, not provoke it."

"Well said," Arinthios called out. "My brother is named Gordian. Is it your plan to assign him a guard on May tenth, Curator?"

"He will have a legion of guards," Vertiscus smirked.

"What? Make sense, man."

"I propose that those in danger stay in the garrison camp on their namesake's day. That way, they will indeed be protected by a legion of men."

It took a moment for the councilors to absorb the information, then they began to applaud.

"Excellent," Arinthos cried out. "I'll inform Gordian immediately."

Amid the babble of the councilors, Modestus turned to Treverius. "Let's hope for success. The test will be May six. Many men here are named John."

"I admit I'd forgotten about Gundstram," Treverius said. "If the killer is a member of the garrison, we've just provided a flock of ducks for the hunter to net."

*   *   *

With the thawing of river ice, ever smaller floes bobbed under the bridge at Mogontium. The floating blocks jammed the mouth of the Nava River at Bingium, where the Rhine took a sharp turn to the northwest. Further on, at Vosolvia, the river became narrower and the ghostly white masses seemed to hurry past rocky cliffs that many people believed were still the haunt of old Germanic gods.

Trees budded late because of the extended cold, but a haze of yellow-green gradually spread over the ochre fields and knarled vines on the slopes west of Mogontium. Vintners tramped paths of hardened mud to examine their surviving canes and prune those that could not be cut earlier. Although some plantings had been stripped of bark by hail and would not recover, encouraging reddish buds sprouted on most of the vines.

As swampy ground dried in the refugee camp, oldsters sat in front of ragged shelters to absorb the spring warmth and watch younger women scratch small garden plots next to their tents. Some men hired themselves out to others who had been bold enough to claim abandoned farm plots. Even children were put to work. Mothers sent them to beg from the vintners.

Along with the clean smell of freshly turned earth, the thaw also brought the stench of decay. Latrine trenches, which had been chipped from the frozen dirt, were filled in. Shallow graves were deepened. Headstones in Mogontium's cemetery, knocked over in resentment against those who would not allow the refugee dead a Christian place to sleep, were set up again.

In the early May sunshine, life seemed, if far from normal, perhaps capable of being controlled again.

* * *

The feast day of the Finding of the Holy Cross, May third, dawned with a clear sky and warm sun that quickly dried the previous day's rain puddles. At the morning Mass Modestus urged the few people in attendance to rejoice in the day that the Lord had made.

Fair weather had renewed the threat of a Vandal attack, but, since scouts reported no activity around Mogontium, Blandina cajoled her husband into a stroll through the refugee camps outside the west wall.

People had exchanged fur jackets for short-sleeved tunics. Some men constructed willow booths, from which to sell what they still had of their salvaged belongings. The stands extended beneath the ramparts around the Porta Borbetomagus, but Treverius noticed the crowd gravitating towards a display where the south wall adjoined the theater.

"It looks like some of Petranius's actors have set up a stage."

"Perhaps they'll do a play about the finding of the Holy Cross," Blandina commented.

"I doubt that. If so, it would be a parody." Treverius grinned. "But let's go take a look."

Aethiops, Albino, and Alexandros had set up a small stage and had hung the backdrop of Jerusalem that was used in the Nativity drama. After covering a table with purple cloth, they unpacked glass vials, pendants, and small wooden cases. The dwarf, Pumilio, arranged a cloth over a table on the stage, then scolded his companions.

"Can't you twin penises work faster? The sheep are waiting to be fleeced."

"Gnat's prick." Alexandros snickered and led his two companions behind the scenery to change into costumes.

Shortly after, the actor came out wearing the coarse tunic of a desert hermit with the hood pulled up to hide his identity. Aethiops wore the flowing kaftan and headpiece of a desert Bedouin. Behind him, Albino walked onstage in only a loincloth to show as much of his thin white body as possible. Callixa and Erotia appeared with a flute and tamborine. Laodike followed them, dressed in a sheer silk tunic with slits cut along the sides.

As her two companions played a popular tune, Laodike began to dance, moving in swaying steps that revealed a glimpse of her breasts and dark delta hair. Pumilio beckoned the bystanders closer, then trilled the lyrics of the song in a falsetto voice.

"'Kiss me now, and then a hundred more,
until, after a thousand kisses
and a hundred thousand still again,
you and I shall lose count.
And I gently undo the girdle of your virginity,
too long, oh, too long tied.'"

After the dance ended, Aethiops lifted Pumilio onto a crate at the edge of the stage.

"Our beauties will be back shortly," the dwarf promised. "Ah, I see a woman blushing. A modest Christian, as we all are." After men in the audience snickered, Pumilio winked. "Friends, our women dance only to reveal the charms Satan uses to seduce the faithful."

"What's on that table?" a man called out.

"Relics from the Holy Land, sir." Pumilio clambered off the box and affected a look of sadness. "Oh, to have lived in the time of the Savior or that of the holy men and women who were martyred," he moaned, waddling back and forth across the stage. "That is impossible, but we have mementos of their lives, of places where the Savior walked. Mother Church teaches us that it is good to honor such relics."

"Can they cure sickness?" the man called out.

"Ah, ye who want signs and wonders," Pumilio chided. "Only the Son of God can perform miracles."

"But can't the holy ones ask Christ for us?"

"How much he was paid to ask that?" Treverius wondered aloud.

"Shh, let's hear Pumilio's answer," Blandina said.

"Only to those with a pure heart," Pumilio fawned. "These relics were collected by Theophilos, 'One who loves God,' in the noble language of the Greeks."

"Let him tell us about them," a woman asked, pushing forward to watch.

"Alas," Pumilio sighed, "Theophilos has taken a vow of silence. Holy hermit, will you point something out?"

Theophilos touched a box next to a small wooden tile with XI painted on it.

"Number eleven?" Pumilio scanned a list Aethiops gave him. "Indeed a precious relic, Domina. Inside that olivewood box is a splinter of the manger in which the Christ child lay at Bethlehem."

"How did he get it?" the woman asked in a skeptical tone.

"A fair question." The dwarf pointed to Aethiops. "This Black visited the holy place. In kissing the blessed wood, he secretly took a piece in his teeth. But what a price he paid! Immediately struck dumb."

Another woman pushed forward and indicated a tile number.

"Seven?" Pumilio gasped in awe. "A . . . a clip of hair from the head of Mary of Magdala! Perhaps the very strands that dried the feet of the Savior."

"That one." The woman pointed to a silver cylinder.

"Nine? The thumb of Blessed Hadrian, brought from Constantinople. True, Holy Hermit?"

Theophilos nodded, then swung a small glass case in a slow arc.

"The hermit shows us a vial of dust from the Holy Sepulchre," Pumilio said, "walked on by the risen Christ."

"How do we know these aren't fakes?" a man yelled. "Like the ones that refugee sold last month? And I've seen that black brute in the theater."

"True, true," Pumilio agreed. "Aethiops was a prince of his country, cursed by his folly into the life of an actor." Hand trembling, the dwarf pointed to Albino. "The answer to your question, sir, stands in this poor wretch. T . . . tell them."

Albino fell to his knees. "You see me now, white as a maggot, but I was once black as the Ethiopian. One day in Rome,"—he spoke so softly that people came closer to hear—"I scoffed at a holy man who was showing a vial of the blood Christ shed at his crucifixion. I was instantly turned . . . as you see me now."

"But show us proof of the relics' power," a heavyset woman demanded. "Give us proof."

"Domina, even one of Christ's apostles doubted." Pumilio scanned the crowd. "Will someone with sickness come up? Anyone?"

The friends of an old woman with crippled hands urged her forward, and Aethiops helped her onstage. He took the reliquary with Hadrian's thumb and held it under her hand, gently closing his massive fingers over her twisted ones. The Black looked into her eyes, as he slowly massaged her fingers until warmth spread through both their hands and the woman relaxed.

"I didn't think a man that huge could be so gentle." Blandina marveled, watching Aethiops.

"He does seem kind," Treverius agreed.

"Do you feel pain now, grandmother?" Pumilio asked. After the woman shyly shook her head, he exulted, "Thy faith has made thee whole! Jesus be praised!"

As Aethiops helped the crone off the platform, Pumilio distracted the crowd before she could be questioned. "Indeed, citizens, one of these relics is false."

"What's he getting at?"

"Trev, the hermit is holding up glass containers of something dark," Blandina said. "I can't tell what it is."

"Theophilos has two vials," Pumilio explained. "One holds the blood of Blessed Philip, whom we honored May first. The other does not, but the labels have been lost. Which is which? Our Ethiopian prince, who walked in the Apostle's land, will determine the true blood."

Aethiops took the vials and slipped them under two pottery cups, then began to move them around each other in a series of deft movements.

"Blessed Philip," Pumilio intoned, gazing at the sky, "work through your servant Aethiops to show us your holy blood.

"Vial of truth, vial of shame.
Blessed Philip, show us plain.
Cause the false blood now to go.
Allow thy true blood still to show."

After Aethiops stepped back, Pumilio called to a man who had been watching. "Sir, I had reason to believe that the false blood was under the left cup. Do you know where the left cup is now?"

"It's there." The man pointed. "I watched it the whole time."

"Here?" Pumilio touched the cup. "And the vial is still under it?"

"You think I'm a fool? They're both still there."

"Not if my prayer has been answered. Aethiops, our friend says both vials are still under the cups."

After the Black lifted the left one, the crowd gasped. It was empty underneath.

Pumilio grinned. "Now the true blood of Philip," he boasted, revealing the other container.

"Are those relics for sale?" the man shouted, even before Aethiops held up the vial.

"Theophilos has taken a vow of poverty," Pumilio replied solemnly. "He accepts money only to continue his search for the holy relics."

As people pressed forward, waving their purses, Treverius took Blandina's arm to lead her back to the Borbetomagus gate. "They say hope will delude a fool. Those 'relics' were as authentic as the actors' imaginations, yet Modestus told me the Bishop of Rome will soon order relics placed in all church altarstones."

"Can you imagine what that will bring out? Trev, those were Petranius's actors, but I didn't see him. I wonder how he is?"

"Nicias looks in on him. Petranius was fortunate and so were we. If Stilicho had been killed his men might have elected another leader with ambitions of being emperor, as the legions did with Constantine in Britannia." Treverius fell silent, knowing that in the resulting civil war Goths would have hovered near the opposing armies like carrion birds, waiting for them to destroy each other. The Western Empire could not survive another rebellion.

At the arch of Severus Alexander Treverius guided Blandina onto a path that bordered the old forum, where the ruins had been spaded into plots. Leafy cabbage plants struggled to survive the remaining cold nights. Before turning onto the Via Alexander he glanced at the cross on top of the temple. It was still angled from the force of the lightning bolt that struck it seven months earlier.

Blandina followed his gaze. "So many horrors since then, but in a week, Trev, we'll know if your plan to confine possible victims in the camp will be a success."

"Men named Gordian and Epimachus. Then, for the rest of the month, only those called Boniface and Urbanus."

"I wasn't at the meeting," she said, "but isn't there one more name?"

"Pancratius? He was only a child. Diocletian had him beheaded, but I can't imagine our killer being depraved enough to go that far."

"What if he had something against his victims that we're not aware of?"

"The killer wouldn't have a grudge against a child. And we don't know if there even is a Pancratius in Mogontium."

"Still, I know how the parents would feel if they thought their son was in danger."

"I wouldn't even know their names, Blandina, children aren't listed on tax rolls." Treverius held his wife back to let a cart pass along the Praetori. "I've already told the Curia a child wouldn't be a target. Actually, the only women killed were prostitutes, hardly atypical."

"I suppose you're right."

"And with nicer weather more people will be outside, making it harder for our killer to hide." Treverius had another thought as he escorted Blandina toward the pretorium. "Besides, Pancratius is Greek. It's unlikely anyone here would call their son by that name."

chapter 18

Toward midafternoon on May twelfth, after watching men named Gordian or Epimachus enter the garrison camp, Treverius came back to the mapping workshop. His father was with Blandina, looking over the provincial map.

"How did it go, Trev?" she asked, running over to him. "As well as on May six?"

"There were probably a few men who didn't show up, but I'm pleased. Those who came should all be safe."

"This is the plan you thought of for protecting possible victims of that killer?" Junius asked.

"Right, father." He glanced at the worktable. "What is Blandina showing you?"

"She told me Stilicho was interested. Perhaps it's time I opened up to what you're doing."

"We'd be glad to have you help us, father," Blandina offered. "Wouldn't we, Trev?"

He threw her a disapproving frown, but Junius had gone back to the chart. After squinting at one of the degrees of longitude, he asked, "You've reckoned Mogontium to be on the twenty-seventh meridian east of the Isles of Canaria. How did you arrive at that ?"

"Based on Ptolemy and our own observations of the length of the summer solstice day here in Mogontium."

"Ptolemy measured one degree of longitude as fifty miles wide on the Rhodes meridian. Here." Treverius pointed to an island at the eastern end of the Mediterranean Sea. "This far north, we calculated forty-four miles between them."

"Did you resolve the location of Argentovaria?"

"It's definitely in our province, father," Blandina replied.

"Ptolemy placed the village a short distance above the forty-seventh parallel," Treverius elaborated, "but our calculations indicate it's a degree further north . . ." He stopped and looked toward the open window. The staccato sound that came in was somewhat muffled by distance, but he had heard it before—a racket of spears and swords being rattled against shields to unnerve an enemy.

"Trev, what's that noise?" Blandina asked, alarmed.

"I hope it's not what I think it might be." Treverius went to a window casement. Blandina and Junius joined him to look out.

A group of armed men, accompanied by a few grim women, came up the Via Praetori from the direction of the river. As the mob approached it was apparent the people were following two men and a woman. One man held a blanket-wrapped bundle in his arms. The woman was sobbing.

"I'm going down to find out what happened."

Treverius went to the pretorium entrance and Blandina followed. Riculfius was there, directing his guards to form a line that blocked the doorway. The man, leading the crowd, stopped six paces from the pretorians.

"Tribune!" he shouted. "I demand to see the governor."

"Albanus is sick," Riculfius called back. "What is your business with him?"

"My nephew has been killed." He pointed his sword at the bundle his brother carried. "That's my business."

"Dead? Then you need the presbyter, not the governor."

Treverius pushed through the line of guards to face the speaker. "What happened? Who are you?"

The man glared at him. "Bertchram. My brother Dagaric's boy was murdered."

"A child has been killed?" A spasm wracked Treverius's stomach. "Is . . . is his name Pancratius?"

"No, Pincis, but Nicias called him 'Pancras' because he liked to collect colored stones. It means that in Greek." Bertchram leveled his sword at Treverius. "Will the governor come out, or must we fight our way in to him?"

"He is ill," Treverius insisted. "Let me get Modestus for you instead."

"The governor," Bertchram repeated coldly, "or we'll sleep in pretorian beds tonight."

Laughter rippled from the men who had heard. Treverius looked at the armed citizens. They had deployed in a line that almost reached the length of the Pretorium front. In their mood, one wild throw of a lance at a guard could start the mob storming toward the entrance.

"Go back inside," Riculfius called out to Treverius. "Pretorians . . . lock shields."

The crowd hooted the tribune's order with shrill catcalls and a renewed rattling of weapons.

"In the name of the governor, return to your homes."

"Lupus Glaucus is our governor," one of the men shouted to Riculfius. Others took up the cry to the rhythm of sword beats. "Glau-cus! Glau-cus! Glau-cus!"

Demetrius came alongside Treverius at the entrance. "I was in the garden, heard the noise. What is happening?"

"I'm afraid the killer has been successful again."

"Today?" he asked. "Wasn't Achilleus protected?"

"It wasn't Achilleus."

"Then who?"

"Th . . . the boy on our list."

"No! Not the child," Demetrius cried. "Are those his parents with the bundle?"

"Yes. They want to see the governor."

"Come with me." Demetrius pushed past the guards with Treverius and faced Dagaric. "I represent the Augustus. What happened to your child?"

In answer, Dagaric gently laid his bundle on the paving stones. The closed end was soaked with blood. Two small tanned legs with sandals on the feet extended from the other. Demetrius gagged and brought a napkin to his mouth.

"Now can we see the governor?" Bertchram asked quietly.

"Nicias won't let him see anyone," Treverius repeated.

"Vertiscus then," Bertchram insisted. "The curator is the only one who has a plan to deal with this."

"I haven't seen him today." Treverius looked back at Riculfius, who shook his head. "Neither has the tribune. I told you I'd find Modestus."

Before Bertchram responded, Blandina pushed between the guards and came to the dead child's mother. "Treverius, tell the tribune that I want to bring her inside with her husband. We need to find out what happened."

Riculfius heard her and nodded agreement. As the guards parted ranks, Blandina escorted the woman and Dagaric through. Treverius and Demetrius followed.

"Disperse to your homes now," Riculfius ordered the crowd. "The child's parents can explain what happened."

At the door, Treverius glanced back. The chanting of Glaucus's name had died away, but the men were looking to Bertchram for instructions. At his signal, they slowly sheathed swords and lowered their lances.

"Tribune," Bertchram taunted, as Riculfius put his own weapon away, "when we come again, it will be with Lupus Glaucus and the garrison. For your head!"

* * *

The child's parents, Basina and Dagaric, refused Treverius's offer to send for Modestus. Blandina soothed them with mulled wine, then they told what had happened to their eight-year-old son.

"Pancras liked to go to the marsh near the river," Basina sobbed. "Where the ditch was before they tore down the old wall. There's tadpoles there."

"I work at the stock pens nearby," Dagaric added. "Didn't see nothing . . . and the cattle make noise."

"Who found your son?" Blandina asked.

"One of the stockmen."

"Could he have—"

"Muderic's a friend," Dagaric objected. "Went down to piss by the wall. S . . . saw Pancras and called me."

"There are reeds and bushes," Treverius recalled. "Parts of the old wall are standing and the marsh is screened by a thick grove of trees, east of the cemetery. A company of men could hide in there. When did your son go down?"

"Early. After eating his porridge," Basina wiped at her eyes with a sleeve and forced a half-smile of remembrance. "Took one of my cracked pitchers to catch the tads in."

"Found a handful spilled out next to. . ." Dagaric's voice broke. He covered his face with two grimy hands.

"So, while I was gawking at men going into the camp, our murderer was stalking Pancras." Treverius touched Dagaric's shoulder. "Modestus and I didn't think a child would be in danger. I . . . I'm sorry."

"Sorry?" Dagaric brushed at a wet eye with a dirty finger. "The governor doesn't know what to do about these killings. You and him need to be more than sorry."

"My husband is trying to protect victims by putting them inside the camp," Blandina said, but knew it was a lame excuse.

Basina peered at Treverius. "You're the one who helped Fredegund after her man was killed by lightning."

"Arbitos?"

Basina nodded. "I'm her sister."

"How is Fredegund? So much has gone on since then. We don't see her at the chapel."

"My sister will have nothing to do with that presbyter," Basina snapped. "And we'll not have our son buried by him, either. That rich merchant can give Pancras a funeral, like he did for Felix."

"Cyril? He's a pagan," Blandina objected.

"Fredegund has a little altar to Jupiter at home. In case Cyril's right about his gods."

Blandina glanced at Treverius. The woman's logic made no sense. Modestus's God might not have protected Arbitos, but it was "Jupiter's" bolt that had killed him.

"Those men calling out Lupus's name have friends in the garrison," Dagaric warned. "There's something going on that I'd bet will end these murders." He drained his wine and stood. "Come on mother. We'll take our son home and tell that merchant in the morning."

* * *

Vertiscus was meeting with Cyril and Lupus Glaucus in Cyril's villa, when the sound of the armed mob was heard outside on the Via Praetori. Cyril took a servant and went to investigate. He returned ashen-faced.

"A child's been murdered. The one Treverius thought wouldn't be in danger."

"That furcin' killer again?" Glaucus growled the question. "We need t' do something."

"Pancras. Yes, a pity," Vertiscus commented, "but these murders . . . whoever is committing them . . . are to our advantage. Did you hear that mob? Albanus's days as governor are numbered."

"Who would have expected that child to be killed?"

"Cyril, more is at stake than one small life," Vertiscus answered. "We're here to discuss ways of taking the pretorium and holding the governor hostage."

"What about Hortar?" Cyril asked. "Is he having any success with that Vandal chief?"

"Gaisios is stubborn."

"Fickle, you mean," Cyril retorted. "Untrustworthy, like all barbarians."

"I prefer that Gaisios be cautious," Vertiscus countered. "It could ruin us if his Vandals left the game after we've thrown the dice."

"What have you been doing?" Cyril demanded of Glaucus. "Where in Hades name is the garrison on this?"

"Th' men need t' be paid," Glaucus answered cooly. "I had t' drop hints about finding th' Macedonica treasure."

"Governor Albanus has reserve funds," Vertiscus said. "In a showdown, he could bribe the garrison with those."

"For a reward one of them might inform him about the plans for New Gothia," Cyril warned. "This delay could be our ruin."

"Calm, Cyril. Glaucus. How far along are your plans?"

"I got men t' lead an attack on th' pretorium, but we need t' surprise th' guards. Disarm 'em."

"Catch them with their shields down," Vertiscus agreed. "Cyril, I'm concerned about the delay too. I've decided that we must act by late July."

"The end of July?" Cyril thought a moment, then exclaimed, "That's it! August first is the Celtic Lugnasad festival. The day is celebrated with games, and Albanus presides over the events."

"Excellent." Vertiscus had caught the implication. "The governor and his guards will be distracted. Yes, excellent! I'll talk to Albanus about expanding the contests and having his pretorians take part. They'll be off guard. And unarmed."

Glaucus grinned at Vertiscus. "My men don't like them fancy soldiers. It'll be a slaughter."

"Fine, Commander." Vertiscus grasped an arm of each man. "Another planning session or two and we'll be celebrating New Gothia inside the governor's office."

"By th' way . . ." Glaucus chuckled hoarsely. "I caught that Judean and his friends snooping around th' mithreum. Scared th' shit out of 'em."

"What?" Vertiscus cried. "Wh . . . when was this?"

"Last month."

"And you tell us now, you stupid brute," Cyril snarled, grasping the neck of Glaucus's tunic. "What friends?"

Glaucus shoved his hand away. "Don't touch me, you prick!" he bellowed, unsheathing his knife and waving the blade in front of Cyril. "Your face will look like sausage meat."

"Calm, you two, calm. Put that blade away," Vertiscus ordered, recovering from his shock. "Who was there?"

"Th' Judean who owns th' wagons," Glaucus replied sullenly, sheathing his knife. "And that map maker."

"Treverius was with him?"

"With their women. I was heading back t' camp, saw th' lock forced. Th' four of 'em were on th' stairs. I said it was a legion club and ordered 'em out."

"Fine, Commander. You . . . you're dismissed for now." Vertiscus controlled a tremor in his voice. "Double your efforts to recruit the men to our plan."

Cyril watched Glaucus lope out. "That ignorant mule. Waiting this long to tell us."

"He said they were on the stairway. It's dark. Perhaps they didn't see anything and believed him about the club."

"How can we be sure? That Macedonica banner is in the anteroom. Treverius isn't stupid."

"No." Verticus's hand shook and he spilled part of the wine he poured into a cup.

"Perhaps your Jupiter has another lightning bolt, Cyril?"

"What are you suggesting, Curator?"

"A quip, Cyril. A jest." Vertiscus drained his wine in one gulp.

"That ape Glaucus is the one you chose to lead your army?" Cyril scoffed. "Julian would have had him tied to a furca and lashed to shreds for threatening me like that." He splashed wine into a cup. "I don't like what's happening. That Vandal is still stalling, and now that the mithreum is no longer secret we'll have to hide the treasure elsewhere."

"My thinking too. I knew I could count on you as second-in-command." Vertiscus chuckled. "As to Treverius, I've learned that he's planning to ask Albanus to send a scouting force to Treveri and go with it himself. I'll send word to Gaisios. Once the contingent is past the Nava River, a forest ambush should take care of our curious map maker."

* * *

That evening Treverius was depressed and went into the pretorium garden. Blandina followed and sat on a marble bench.

In a mauve twilight, he watched swallows swooping after insects for a moment, then abruptly bent down, scooped up a clod of earth, and flung it against the far wall.

"Hades! I even told the Curia that the child wasn't in danger."

"Trev, it's not your fault." Blandina patted the bench seat. "Come over here with me."

"This is totally out of control. Now children are being murdered and no one sees anything."

"Sit here," Blandina repeated in mock severity. "Talk to me about it."

Treverius pulled off a myrtle twig, then dropped down next to her. "I can understand that mob's frustration," he said, twirling the branch in his fingers. "Imagine if they could get Glaucus's men to act against the governor. They wouldn't stop at torching the pretorium."

"What about the victims for June, Trev?"

"I'm meeting with Modestus tomorrow to put together the list of names."

"How many are there?"

"I'm not sure yet. The June Curia session is on the first, but I don't imagine Albanus will preside."

"So Vertiscus will be in charge again?"

"I don't like the idea either." Treverius snapped the twig in two and tossed the pieces away. "He's planning something. At the May session he dropped his support for the governor. This time he might ask the councilors for a recall vote."

"Perhaps Demetrius could keep him in check," Blandina suggested. "And you said you were going to ask the governor about finding out what happened at Treveri."

"I know." Treverius slipped an arm around her shoulders and toyed with the neck of her tunic. "I could ask Demetrius to get authorization for an expedition."

"Good. You said you wanted to be part of it."

"With a wing of Limitans cavalry and part of David's contingent."

"I told you I wanted to go along, Trev."

He shushed his wife's lips with a finger. "And I said it was too dangerous."

"But not for you? Trev, I'll scream about going until I'm heard by that Lorelei maiden who's supposed to haunt the cliffs downriver."

"Blandina, we'll decide later."

"Now," she insisted. "Last time you wanted to wait until after Stilicho's visit. You're not putting me off again."

Still stubborn as a Lucanian peasant. Treverius pulled his arm away and clenched his jaw. "Right. I'll see if I can get permission for you to go along."

"Thank you." She nestled against his shoulder. "I . . . I want to find my father. And be with you."

"I know. Blandina, I'm worried about the governor's state of mind. Nicias told me he noticed a volume of Seneca's letters on the bedside table."

"The Stoic philosopher? Didn't he commit suicide?"

"That's what concerns me."

Both fell silent at the thought. A breeze rustled young leaves on the Linden trees and stirred the sweet scent of Convallaria lilies into the air. Hesperus, the evening star, began to host pinpoints of light as the first stars dotted indigo sky. After a high-pitched hum abruptly stopped, Treverius swatted a mosquito on Blandina's arm.

"Let's go inside," he said after picking the insect off and brushing away a smear of blood. "If you're that determined on going to Treveri, I'll have to find something suitable for you to wear."

chapter 19

After he had helped Modestus compile the list of names for June, Treverius estimated that half the people in Mogontium bore one of the martyr's names.

Curia members were stunned when he read the list at their June first meeting. Fourteen martyrs were identified, and as many names of persons who had been associated with their deaths in some way. All, except Basil and Barnabas, were common Latin names.

Primus and Felicianus had been beheaded. Vitus, another child, was celebrated on June fifteenth. Quiricus and Julitta, a son and mother, were killed by the praefect of Tarsus. The twins Gervasius and Protasius were martyred at Mediolanum. John and Paul, two officers who refused to serve Julian the Apostate, were honored on June twenty-six. Saint Peter, the successor of Christ crucified head downward, and Paul, the proselytizer of Gentiles, were celebrated on June twenty-ninth and thirtieth. The birth of John the Baptist added another day of danger to men with that name.

Even the presbyter's namesake was included. Blessed Modestus had been the tutor of the twelve-year-old Vitus, and martyed with the boy and his mother.

* * *

At the Curia meeting, Demetrius received the council's authorization for a cavalry sortie to Treveri. He reported to Governor Albanus, who placed Marculf in command, with David second to him in charge of twenty-four Judeans. Sixteen pretorians, and an equal number of men from Treverius's cohort, made up the balance of the contingent. Nicias was assigned to accompany the men and tend any wounded.

Since part of the mission was to determine the fate of the palace staff in the capital, including Blandina's father, Treverius argued successfully for her to go with him. June twenty-fifth was decided upon as the date for departure.

* * *

Huddled under a soggy cloak and with her hair pinned up under a cavalry helmet, Blandina waited in the shelter of the Germania Gate while the men formed into a column of two riders abreast. A warm drizzle hung in the air. The wetness had intensified smells, not only the loamy odor of plowed earth and the grassy fragrance of ripening hayfields, but also the pervading stink of decay that had overlain the air since the spring thaw.

Blandina shook off the raindrops and looked around. From openings in refugee tents crowded along the west wall, a few adults and children peered out to watch the preparations in the dreary dawn light.

In the near distance, along the sides of the river road she and the others would take to Bingium, she saw the yellowish limestone grave markers of legionaries who had once been assigned to the Mogontium camp. The wet stones glistened, throwing their inscriptions into sharp relief. Most of the monuments were tilted to one side. Some had been knocked over during periodic raids, or had their images defaced by sword and axe blows, but

Blandina liked to walk among them. She considered the memorials to be a mystical link with the past, a span of four hundred years, during which emperors from Augustus Caesar to Gratian had believed it was their destiny to bring civilization, the Pax Romana, to barbarian Rhenish tribes.

The youngest man she had found was Quintus Gavius, who had died at eighteen after only a year in the army. He had been born at Histonium on the Adriatic, trading life near that warm sea for death in the damp hills of Germania. Perhaps Gavius had rebelled at being a fisherman, hoping instead for a share of legionary booty. An unnamed brother had erected the stone. Blandina wondered if Gavius had been lured into Legion Fourteen by his sibling's tales of military adventure.

The stone of the oldest legionary was of Primus Aebutius, a veteran of Legion XIII Gemina, who had died at age fifty-five after twenty-two years of service. Blandina had calculated that the average age of the men at death was under forty years.

"Fall in the column, Blandina. You're riding with Nicias."

The shout from Treverius roused Blandina from her musings. She mounted and trotted her mare into place alongside the white-haired surgeon. He smiled at her.

"You're a plucky young woman. Let's hope we don't run into trouble."

"I pray not, but I'm glad to be riding with you."

"Quintus probably assigned me along so he would have some peace from my constant nagging," Nicias joked. "We're pretty safe in the middle of four wagons loaded with enough supplies for a month, and six Scorpio catapults to intimidate any barbarians we encounter."

"Aren't those the Imperial standards up ahead?"

"Yes, of Honorius. Quintus wants us to enter Treveri as if we were celebrating a triumph, not like some rag-tag forage detail."

Marculf signaled the advance. The supply wagons, centered between the vanguard contingent and the Judean rear guard, started up, jostling into twin ruts worn in the paving stones.

"A decent road," Nicias observed, "but we'll be paced by those slower wagons."

One mile or so beyond the abandoned pottery kilns north of Mogontium, the first of the walled villas that faced the river appeared. The stone building was surrounded by fruit orchards in bloom, and greening oak and birch groves set among clumps of dark green pines. Veiled by the rain, the farm seemed intact, but when Treverius broke from the column to inspect the site, he saw that the light-colored stones were blackened by smoke, and charred roof beams had collapsed into rooms. He reported to Marculf, then rode back to check on his wife.

"Everything all right, Blandina?"

"She's fine," Nicias responded first. "What did you find down there?"

"Looted and burned. I'm afraid it will be the first of many like that."

At the next villa Treverius led three horsemen to investigate. Several people were repairing the roof. When the squatters spotted the group coming toward them, they scampered down, ran to a skiff moored at the river, and shoved off into the current.

At best, Treverius thought, the strangers were escaped slaves. At worse Vandals who were the first of many returning tribesmen.

As the Bingium road bent southwest from Mogontium, it continued to parallel the course of the Rhine. Across the river the landscape rose in gentle hills, forested crests that were misted by a wispy, vaporous crown. The few riverbank clusters of fishermen's shacks looked deserted. Treverius surmised the hovels had been bypassed by the Vandals as they had surged over the ice, to raid Bingium and rich villas to the west.

To the left of the road, wherever the pine and oak forest gave way to stretches of stony soil, the hills were planted with vineyards, but now the canes grew wild and unpruned. There were glimpses of ruined villas and farms, scenes of devastation that jarred the men—mute testimony to the fury of the barbarian attack.

A stench of decay became stronger in the wet air as the contingent approached Bingium. The village was situated twelve miles northwest of Mogontium, where the Nava River emptied into the Rhine. With docks for unloading barges, its marketplace was a trading center for tribes settled in the hill country between the Rhine and the Mosella Rivers. Three and a half centuries ago a legion camp to protect the village had been built by Drusus Nero on the heights above the Nava. Nothing had been heard from the present garrison since the Vandal attack.

Marculf ordered Treverius and David to take two of their men each and scout the fort. When it came into view, the group could see that the palisade had been torched and the gate breached. The shattered portals hung in drunken angles from their hinges.

"Christ, the smell," Treverius exclaimed as he rode closer. "Put kerchiefs over your faces."

The desiccated bodies of legionaries, stripped of armor, were still slumped against the platform railing above the gate. One of David's men sent an arrow thudding into the wooden deck, startling ravens that were pecking at the cadavers. As the black birds flapped heavily into the air, their harsh, nerve-grating caws protested the unexpected intrusion.

"It looks like the men were replacing wooden timbers with stonework, but were attacked before they finished," Treverius said, eyeing the rampart.

"I'll scout around the perimeter," David suggested. "You look inside the fort."

Treverius clucked his horse toward the broken gate and dismounted inside the compound. The incessant drone of blowflies was the only sound, and their erratic flight the sole movement. He saw four rows of barracks gutted by fire. What had not been looted was still lying in scattered piles on the muddy ground, among the remains of corpses that had not been dragged away by wolves.

He glanced inside the shattered door to the commander's headquarters. The rooms had been ransacked, but not burned. Vandals had probably sheltered there before moving on toward Treveri. Nearby, the courtyard of the camp hospital was strewn with the bodies of patients who had managed to run out for a few more moments of life than the sick, who had been struck down in their cots.

Treverius felt ill. As he led his mount back toward the entrance, he saw David come through the gate on horseback.

"Bad in there?" David asked.

Treverius nodded. "The Vandals surprised the men celebrating the new year, just as at Mogontium. We'll have to halt, bury the dead."

"Is the stone bridge to the Treveri road standing?" David dismounted and walked to the rampart facing the Nava River. "Good. It's intact, we can cross." He turned back. "I'll have my men try to identify circumcised Judeans. We'll bury them according to our custom."

Treverius mounted his horse, sick at what he had seen and worried about his wife's reaction to the carnage. "I'd better see how Blandina is doing."

*　*　*

The drizzle stopped around the ninth hour, when a warm sun edged the retreating clouds with a halo of brightness that painted the grisly scene in an incongruous golden light. Marculf returned with his men and reported that the town of Bingium was destroyed. Many corpses lay among the charred rubble of shops and homes. Only an Arian chapel built over the old temple to Mercury had been spared. He agreed that the dead would have to be buried the next day, and ordered camp set up for the night on a wooded hill overlooking the Nava River. A detail of pretorians, with two of the catapults, was sent to secure the bridge.

After men hung their capes on tree branches to dry, they brought their horses and mules to the riverbank, letting the animals drink and browse in the lush grass. Fires, which first smoked from damp kindling wood, soon flickered into blazes for cooking an evening meal. David's unit was assigned the hill's western slope. After reciting evening prayers, the men prepared meals from their own supplies.

As the evening air became cooler the smell of smoke and roasting meat gradually overlaid the stench. Some men caught rabbits, skewered them on iron spits, and watched them sizzle over the coals in silence. Others quietly discussed what they had seen, or tried to forget the horror with familiar stories told in a louder voice. When Marculf's orderly passed out wood tokens for the night's sentry duty, subdued laughter marked an occasional objection.

As Treverius watched the sun set—a golden haze that stretched the long shadows of men and animals across the gilded grass—he saw David coming to join him and Blandina. Nicias and Marculf were already seated around the blaze.

"Are you well, Blandina?" David asked. "What you saw today was terrible."

"I couldn't eat anything," she replied softly. "Otherwise, well enough."

"I told her not to dwell on it." Treverius bent and kissed her cheek.

"I . . . I was afraid the same thing happened at Treveri," she said, then asked David, "Were your men praying? I noticed them cover their heads with shawls."

"Yes, it's called a Kaddish, a prayer for the Judeans we were able to identify among the dead. We'll recite it for a week."

"You may have to say it for longer than that," Marculf contended, giving the fire a poke that sent orange sparks twirling into the dusk sky. "No telling what we'll find between here and Treveri."

"These bodies should be buried quickly," Nicias added. "The Humors of Air and Bile are dangerously out of balance."

"That could cause plague?" Treverius asked.

"Exactly. The men should keep their faces covered to avoid taking in the malevolence."

The group fell silent at the thought of a new danger that could kill as surely as a Goth, if not as rapidly. Treverius glanced at Marculf. The man was the bodyguard sent with him to Petranius, when Juliana was murdered, but he had not spoken to him much. He had noted that, on the march, Marculf's eyes were never still, like a bird that was feeding on the ground and wary of every movement around it. As if to confirm the assessment, Marculf suddenly looked up from the fire and met his gaze.

"Marculf," Treverius asked, "are you from this area?"

"No, Jurassus foothills. Celtic Tigurini tribe around the three lakes."

"Tigurini?" Treverius chuckled. "I recall Caesar's Commentary mentions that your tribe once gave Romans a good thrashing."

"Five hundred years ago." Marculf gave a thin smile and eased a branch into the fire. "I'd heard that Romans commemorate defeats as well as their victories."

"What made you come to Mogontium?"

"Stilicho was looking for recruits in his campaign against the Alamanni. They were our enemies, too."

"What do you think we'll find ahead?"

"Even if the Vandals with Gaisios have moved on, there are sure to be others nearby under subchiefs."

"Do you think Gaisios is still in Treveri?" Blandina asked.

"He may be. While we're burying the dead tomorrow, I'll send a detail to scout ahead, then decide what to do after they report back." Marculf stood and brushed off his trousers. "I'm going to check the sentries. The password tonight is 'Tigurini.'"

Nicias went to one of the wagons to sleep. Treverius tried to reassure Blandina about what they might find at Treveri, until a guard ordered their fire put out. Wrapped in damp capes, they tried to find comfortable hollows in the ground that would fit their bodies. Gradually, the gurgle of the river, mingled with the shrill cadence of night insects, lulled the couple away from the scenes of horror that flanked them a few hundred paces away.

* * *

By the afternoon of the twenty-sixth of June, the grisly task of locating bodies in the camp and village ruins was finished. Rather than digging pits in which to bury the dead, the men had carried them to the V-shaped ditch surrounding the palisade, then covered them with dirt from the earth fill of the ramparts.

Judeans, whom David was able to identify, were buried in the east ditch, facing Jerusalem. Afterwards, he explained to Marculf that sunset would mark the beginning of the Hebrew Sabbath, so his men would prefer not to move out on the next day. Marculf agreed. His scouts had reported hot springs nearby, west of the Nava. The next morning he ordered groups of eight men to ride out and soak off the grime and trauma of the past two days in the comfort of the pools.

Treverius and Blandina found an isolated spring. After a short soak in the warm water, they made love. It was hurried, perhaps from an unconscious sense of guilt that they were together, while others were away from their wives and lovers.

* * *

When sunset ended the Sabbath, David and his men took advantage of the long twilight to pack supplies. The day had not been without incident. Marculf's scouts had pushed as far as Dumnissus, the westernmost town in that part of the province, and returned to report a skirmish with Vandal squatters who had taken over homes. Several warriors and two pretorians had been killed. Treverius surmised that Marculf was frustrated at having been held up three days, and knowing that his presence had been reported at Treveri. Yet he ordered most of his men to stay in Bingium another day, while he sent a stronger force ahead to reconnoiter.

Worried about her father, Blandina was depressed at the new delay. That evening, Treverius tried to distract her at their fire.

"This is June twenty-eighth. There were no murders this month, and there's no one named Peter. That's good news."

"Hopefully, the chain is broken." She leaned against his shoulder.

Treverius recognized two figures coming toward the circle of firelight. "Here's David and Nicias. Ave." Perhaps they could help distract Blandina from brooding.

"Is it too late to visit?" David asked.

"No, no," Treverius said. "Besides, I'm too excited to sleep. We're finally moving out in the morning. Sit down, both of you. We were just saying that no one was killed in June."

"And this is near the end of the month," David recalled. "That plan of yours seems to be working."

"The one Vertiscus gets credit for," Treverius commented wryly. "Tomorrow is the feast of Peter, but there's no one by that name in town. That leaves only men called Paul for the last day of June."

"And we didn't find many named after the Apostle," Blandina recalled.

"Did Modestus agree to go into the garrison camp?" Nicias asked.

"Not on your oath!" Treverius laughed. "He's not taking orders from anyone who isn't a bishop, but Riculfius made sure he stayed in his quarters."

Falling silent, they watched the pulsing glow of the coals and listened to the sizzle of pine sap bubbling from the end of the logs. A full moon had risen to silhouette the hills across the Rhine and reflect restless patches of light off the broad surface of the Nava. Treverius looked at Nicias. His white hair and beard reflected the ruddy gleam of the fire.

"Surgeon. I know you came to Mogontium with the governor, but you said you were from Egypt originally?"

"True, I was born in Alexandria. My father was a physician, so it was natural that I follow his profession."

"I don't know anything about that part of the world," Blandina admitted. "What's it like?"

"Exotic. Alexandria was the best place to study medicine. Academies at Rome, Smyrna, and Corinth prohibited dissecting corpses. Alexandria permitted it."

Blandina shuddered. "I've seen enough bodies here. Tell us what the city is like."

"Marvelously more cosmopolitan than Rome. Egyptian temples. The great lighthouse. Rome has nothing to compare with those. Or the library. That is, what was the library." Nicias turned away to trace a circle in the damp grass with a finger, throwing his face into shadow. "After Christian fanatics destroyed its scrolls and books, I left for Constantinople."

"Are the pyramids as huge as Herodotus claims?"

"Young woman, it's impossible to imagine their size."

"What was the most interesting to you?" Treverius asked, pleased that the conversation had distracted Blandina.

"As a surgeon, I would say it was the healing shrine to Asklepios at Petra."

"Petra? I learned a little Greek in Ravenna," Treverius said. "The name means 'rock,' doesn't it?"

"Yes, because Petra is a city carved of rock. Petrus . . . Peter . . . is the Latin form."

"Of course. Christ was making a play on words when he said his Church would be built on the 'rock' of his apostle Peter."

"Then could Petranius be a Latinized form of petra?" Blandina asked Nicias.

"Yes. It's probably a derivative."

"No one in Mogontium was named Peter, but—"

"Petranius!" Treverius exclaimed, connecting with Blandina's thought. "He could be in danger and Vertiscus wouldn't know that. Nicias, we have to ride back to Mogontium now. The moon is bright enough to see the road. We could trot the horses and still get there by dawn."

"I'll go with you," David said, "and ask Marculf to have Nathaniel assume my command."

"And I'm riding, too." Blandina stood up with the men. "We forgot about that poor child, but we have to make sure nothing happens to Petranius again."

* * *

The sun had risen as an incandescent sphere of orange, when Treverius saw the walls of Mogontium in the distance.

He guided his horse through the tangle of refugee tents and morning cookfires, scattering chickens and pigs foraging between the shelters. At the Borbetomagus

Gate he shouted up to the sentries for entrance. One demanded a pass, then recognized Nicias and ordered the portal opened.

Vendors, who were raising shop shutters on the Via Agrippa, were startled to see the four riders galloping their mounts toward the theater at such an early hour. Treverius wheeled his horse into the square and reined in at the entrance. Dismounting, he ran through the dark passageway and came out on the orchestra level, blinking at the orange light that washed over the tiers of seats.

Blandina ran up behind and caught his arm. David and Nicias flanked them, to stare in horror and disbelief at what was on the stage.

In the bluish shadow of the backdrop, a man was suspended from a cross set up in the center of the platform. He was nude, except for a purple cloak and the grotesque mask that concealed his face. Above the mask the spikes of a thorny circlet were visible on his head. The only movement was from a light breeze that ruffled the folds of the cloak.

Treverius and David sprinted across the orchestra half-circle and leaped onto the stage. "The mask is 'The Hebrew,'" David cried. "Is it Petranius? How can we get him down?"

Treverius looked around. "There's a ladder. Whoever did this must have left it. Quick, put it up."

David set the ladder against an arm of the cross and steadied it. Treverius climbed up and gently eased off the mask. "It is Petranius!"

The actor's head was slumped onto his chest and his forehead caked with dried blood from the thorn punctures. A cloth was stuffed into his mouth as a gag.

"Eleison. Mercy. Is the man dead?" Nicias asked, coming onstage.

"I don't know." Treverius looked at the arm nearest him. It was held up by a loop of rope. "At least he hasn't been nailed on. Can you see the other hand, David?"

"Also tied. There's a seat holding up his body. His feet are roped together."

"Get him down," Blandina screamed, close to tears.

Treverius eased out the gag and freed one of the actor's arms. Blandina steadied the ladder while David held up Petranius's sagging body so Nicias could pull his feet out of the hawser. After Treverius loosened the rope from the other arm, David laid Petranius on the floor and held up his head.

"He's fortunate, the punctures aren't too deep," Nicias observed, carefully working off the thorn band.

"Is he . . . is he still alive?" Blandina asked Nicias.

He felt Petranius's throat pulse. "Yes, he's living."

"Thank Christ." She wiped a sleeve across her eyes.

Nicias took a fleck of white powder from the actor's lips and tasted it. "Nepenthes. It's a narcotic. We must take the actor home."

"I'll go along," Blandina said. "I could help him."

"No," Treverius objected. "We found Juliana in that apartment building."

"I'm going with you."

"Very well. But the governor and Modestus should know about this. Both of you stay with Petranius until I come back."

* * *

When Treverius returned with the presbyter, Petranius was just regaining consciousness. His eyes focused on Blandina first.

"An angel," he mumbled. "Am I in Paradise?"

"Fortunately, not yet," Nicias replied. "This is only your room. How do you feel?"

"My head," Petranius moaned. "Worse than the effects of Lucanian wine."

"I know. I'll bring something to counter the effect of the narcotic and treat the puncture wounds."

"Do you recall what happened, man?" Modestus asked brusquely. "To be crucified like the Savior!"

"A part I didn't audition for, Presbyter."

"Sorry," Modestus mumbled. "What did happen?"

"I was writing in my office backstage," Petranius replied. "It was to be a surprise for you, Presbyter. Now, I'm convinced Christ wants me to finish the drama."

"What drama?"

"With respect to your late deacon, I wanted to improve the Nativity play he wrote last December," Petranius explained. "Expand the parts, make it more professional."

"Tell us what you remember," Treverius said. "It could help find who did this."

Petranius lay back and closed his eyes. "I worked quite late," he said softly, "then ate a little pork with some bread and wine we keep there. I don't remember much else. How did you find me? What brought you to the theater?"

"You can thank Blandina," Treverius replied. "She made the connection between the word 'petra' and your name."

Petranius reached for Blandina's hand and pressed it to his cheek. His eyes were moist as he looked at her, then at Modestus. "Certainly, actors are an irreverent bunch, Presbyter, but I do believe in angels. I'd like your permission to finish the drama." After Modestus hesitated, Petranius sighed. "I know, that performance for Stilicho. That may account for my, ah, punishment. Someone at the pretorium wanted to teach me a lesson."

"I think we should do the play," Blandina said firmly.

"Thanks, angel. By Thalia's pen, it will be inspiring. I'll expand dialogue, add the massacre of the Innocents—"

"Petranius, Petranius," Nicias chided genially. "Talk about that later. You've lost blood. You need rest."

"I want you to be in it again, angel." Petranius tightened his hold on Blandina's hand.

"You too, Treverius. There's a real part for you this time."

"Later," Nicias scolded. "I'm ordering you to rest."

Petranius slowly released Blandina's hand. "Thanks, friends."

After Treverius was in the hallway he took Nicias aside. "We should ask Riculfius to set a guard here," he whispered. "This was too close for Petranius to be left alone, especially after Juliana's murder. Whoever did this was able to drug his wine, then hang him on that cross. If it was done on orders from someone at the pretorium, they'll be able to get at him again."

"Yes, but I didn't want him questioned about it just now," Nicias said. "Petranius has gone through a trauma, an emotional shock."

"The killer could have bought off one of his actors," Treverius reasoned. "Nicias, you stay here until I get that guard over. Blandina, let's go back. This has been a shock to you too."

chapter 20

The following morning, June thirtieth, Treverius was discussing the awful discovery of the crucified Petranius with Blandina in their reception room, when a frantic rapping sounded at the door.

"Who . . . ?" Blandina stood up. "I'll get it, I sent Ageria to the markets for food." When she opened the door, Demetrius barged into the room. The usually well-groomed envoy was unshaven, his hair matted and uncombed.

Puzzled, Treverius rose to greet him. "Welcome. We—"

"Terrible news!" Demetrius interrupted. 'A runner came at dawn. Marculf's entire force was ambushed yesterday fording a river east of Dumnassis."

"What? How many casualties?"

"No one knows. The man says Marculf ordered him to report to the governor before the action was over."

"The Vandals knew about Marculf's force," Treverius said, "but an ambush takes planning."

"Exactly. Marculf was betrayed by someone in the pretorium."

"Trev, we . . . we would have been there," Blandina said.

"If you hadn't realized Petranius was in danger."

"The crippled actor," Demetrius scoffed. "Serves him right for that travesty he concocted for Stilicho."

"How do you know about Petranius?" Treverius asked. "The governor was to keep it quiet."

Demetrius snickered. "'Frogs drink and talk,' is the saying. Why not gossiping clerks?"

"The same ones who alerted the Vandals?"

"This would have to come from someone higher up than a quill sharpener."

"Do you suspect anyone, sir?" Blandina asked.

"May I confide?" Demetrius dropped into a high-backed wicker chair and rubbed his beard stubble. "I've sensed that you two have the basic guilelessness of rustics."

Rustics? Treverius suppressed his annoyance in humor. "Except when selling a mule, and I learned that in Ravenna."

"I've been concerned," Demetrius went on, without acknowledging the jest, "about the governor's apathy."

"As we have, sir."

"Quite, young woman. I've sent a dispatch to the Augustus, offering my services as Quintus Albanus's replacement to govern this province."

"You aren't alone," Treverius said. "Publius Vertiscus has told me as much about himself."

"The curator? I suspected he might have that goal." Demetrius frowned and rubbed nervously at his face stubble. "The Curia meets in five days. When the Marculf disaster is reported, support for Albanus will vanish like morning fog. That will encourage Vertiscus."

"Sir, why did you come to us," Treverius asked, "other than the fact that we're such wholesome rustics?"

"I . . . I meant that as a compliment. You've been looking into these murders. By late January, I had realized there was something up between Vertiscus and those two merchants."

"Cyril and Nevius?"

"Yes. Cyril has blocked the temple renovation. The other man agitated to reopen the Arian church."

"That doesn't make them murderers."

"No, I'm only suggesting that we stay alert at the Curia meeting. You'll have the list of July martyrs?"

"Modestus and I will read the names."

"Good." Demetrius stood up to leave. "Watch Vertiscus closely, I don't trust him."

* * *

The fourth of July dawned hot and humid, without a breeze to temper the oppressive heat. Sweat glistened on the faces of councilors as they came off the street and took their places in the relative coolness of the basilica. The names of July martyrs and the report from Marculf headed the agenda, but many of the men had already questioned Modestus and knew if they were in danger.

Old Malchus had babbled his way past the guards. He paced back and forth, muttering to himself while waiting for the meeting to begin.

Vertiscus glanced to see that the twenty men from the garrison he had ordered Lupus Glaucus to bring were in place along the right wall, and at the entrance, then called on Modestus.

"Presbyter. This heat is exhausting. You will read only the names of those endangered, not the dates. That information can be posted at your chapel."

"My throat is inflamed," Modestus replied hoarsely. "Treverius will read the names."

"Someone read them," Pendatios shouted. "Get us out of this sweat bath."

After Vertiscus nodded agreement, Treverius stood. "There are twenty-seven names. Felicitas was martyred under Antoninus. Then Januarius, Felix, Philip, Alexandros—"

"Leave out the Eastern ones," Vertiscus ordered. "There are none here with those names."

"Do you want Mary of Magdela?" Treverius asked with calculated innocence. "She was Judean but died in Gaul."

Before Vertiscus reacted, Malchus shuffled up the steps. "We Sleepers are celebrated on July twenty-seventh," he rasped. "The signs spoken by Daniel are upon ye."

"Enough, old man," Vertiscus warned. "Go back down."

Malchus ignored him. "The great Theodosius threw himself before us and declared that it was as if he had seen the Galilean raise Lazarus from the dead."

"Commander Glaucus, have your men take this fool outside," Vertiscus ordered. "His resurrection can wait until after this meeting."

Cyril and others laughed. Glaucus followed two of his legionaries, who began to shove Malchus toward the entrance. Blandina started after them, but the guards blocked her way. Treverius pulled her back, then, while the councilors' and guards' attention was on what was happening to Malchus, he slipped along the left wall, to the entrance.

"Let ye who are in Judea flee to the mountains," Malchus shouted, trying to shake off the men. "Ye who are in the fields, turn not back for a cloak."

As the soldiers laughed and pushed Malchus out the front door, Treverius saw the old man slip and fall down the four steps. One of his disciples ran to help him, but others picked up stones and threw them at the two guards. One rock hit Glaucus on the arm.

"Scatter th' bastards!" he screamed. "Use your furcin' swords."

"No!" Treverius shouted, hurrying down the stairs. "I'll help him home."

Glaucus stepped in front of Treverius, crouching low and ominously waving his sword, like a gladiator sensing a kill. "Stay out of this," he snarled. "Don't touch your knife, or your woman'll be ruining her pretty blue eyes crying at your funeral."

Helpless, Treverius saw the two legionaries strike out savagely with their swords. Malchus was slashed across the abdomen and fell again, bleeding on the paving stones. One of his followers was stabbed in the side. After two more were gashed on their forearms and ran, the others abandoned the old man and followed their companions.

Blandina came out of the basilica with a few councilors, just as Glaucus ordered his two guards to put away their bloody weapons.

Malchus, on the ground, breathed in gasps, clutching his side. Treverius bent down beside him and gently moved the old man's hand. Christ, his intestines. Malchus won't survive this wound for very long.

Vertiscus appeared at the door. "What happened here, Commander?"

"Th' old fool incited his followers t' attack my men."

"Incited? Glaucus, have one of them bring Nicias, double pace," Treverius ordered. "Malchus needs medical help."

"It was an accident," Glaucus called up to Vertiscus. "His men provoked mine."

"Report to me later." Vertiscus motioned him away. "Curia members, go back inside. We'll continue."

"Go in with them, Trev," Blandina said. "I'll stay with Malchus until Nicias gets here."

Vertiscus tried to finish reading the list of martyrs, but the men ignored him to discuss what had happened.

"The names will be posted," he shouted, starting down the stairs to leave.

Musonius intercepted him. "I heard about that actor being crucified. My son's name is on the July list."

"And m-my name," Felix stammered.

"I've been telling you it is the wrath of our Roman gods that brought us to this," Cyril yelled from his bench. "Appoint a priest to begin sacrifices and these deaths will stop. And the expedition the governor sent to Treveri has been annihilated. I demand Albanus be recalled!"

Treverius realized that Malchus had distracted Vertiscus and prevented him from giving a full report of Marculf's defeat, yet he might still call for a vote of censure and ask to be appointed interim governor.

Demetrius. Treverius ran to the envoy's table. "Sir, do something to restore order. You represent the Augustus here."

"Yes, correct. Honorius." Demetrius stood at his table, clutching his note pad and stylus. "Let me . . . Citizens. This scene is unbecoming to Romans. I . . . I will appeal to the Augustus."

Vertiscus glared at him and the Curia members stopped talking to listen. After a moment, Treverius realized that Demetrius was at a loss to continue, trembling as he opened and closed the wood cover of his pad, staring at the wax leaves.

"Ravenna won't abandon the Rhine," Treverius called to the men. "Honorius will send help."

"Even if he did, it wouldn't be here before October," Lupicinius countered. "The Vandals could attack again."

"Another four months of these murders?" Felix bawled. "I want a guard detail at my house on July tenth."

"And one for my son!" Musonius shouted.

"The Augustus will send men," Demetrius mumbled. "Albanus will—"

"Damn the Augustus and the governor," Felix shrieked. "I'm locking myself in my villa."

"No! You'd be safer in the garrison camp," Treverius pleaded. "Councilors, curb your panic."

Ignoring his advice, the men and Demetrius pushed past him and hurried out of the building. Treverius saw Blandina come back in and went to her.

"They've lost all semblance of reason. Let's get out of here." As he escorted her from the hall, he noticed Cyril and Nevius talking with Vertiscus. "What are they up to? Demetrius lost his nerve just now, but he may be right about those three."

"Never mind them," Blandina said. "Nicias had Malchus taken to the garrison hospital. He's in critical condition."

When the doors closed after the last councilor, Nevius turned on Vertiscus in anger. "A disaster," he jeered. "Where was your motion to recall Albanus?"

"Calm, Nevius, you saw what happened. Those men are terrorized. We need not risk a vote now."

"How so?"

Cyril answered, "I've been talking with the pretorians about the Lugnasad games, offering money prizes for the contests. They're eager to challenge the garrison."

"And they'll be completely off guard," Vertiscus said with a dry chuckle. "Our men will net them like birds in a hunter's trap. The Curia will have no choice but to agree to my leadership, and New Gothia."

"When is the next meeting in the mithreum?" Nevius asked, fingering his moustache. "I'll come."

"July twenty-seventh, four days before the Lugnasad," Vertiscus replied. "Glaucus will go over assignments."

"We'll give the men an advance payment," Cyril added, "which will be more than repaid by the governor's reserves."

* * *

At sundown that evening, after the Judean Sabbath was over, Treverius sent for David. After he arrived Blandina offered their friend a cup of sweetened wine.

"I heard it was chaotic today," David said. "Vertiscus calls these sessions on our Sabbath so Nathaniel and I can't be there."

"Malchus was slashed by Glaucus's men."

"I heard, Treverius. Is it bad?"

"Nicias doesn't think he'll live long," Blandina replied. "He's done what he can to make Malchus comfortable."

"Shame. A harmless old man."

Treverius handed David the plan of a chamber he had sketched. "This is what I wanted to show you."

David put down his cup and examined the drawing. "Some kind of temple?"

"I think so. I had a hunch about that underground room at Gundstram's. Something I'd heard in Ravenna about an Eastern cult among the legions."

"We checked in the library for information about a Parthian god named Mithras," Blandina said.

"Statius, Lucan, Porphyry, and more recently, Tertullian, wrote about his cult," Treverius continued. "Mithras was especially popular with Rhine legions. I think the room at Gundstram's was a mithreum."

"Where the rituals to this god took place?"

"Right, David. I drew up what the temple might look like." Treverius indicated the first chamber. "We probably saw the anteroom. The initiation involved a kind of baptism with blood from a sacrificial bullock."

"Where was that held?"

"Here, in a taurobolium at the far end of the main temple. There was a pit in the floor with a grating over it. The man knelt underneath, while the bullock was killed over his head and the blood spattered on him."

"Disgusting," David remarked, "but a mithreum would be a good place to hide treasure."

"Only cult members would know the temple even existed," Blandina added. "Tacitus wrote that the rebel legions were quickly disbanded and sent home in disgrace. It would have been worth a man's life to stay around the camp."

"That's why we need to go in there again." Treverius took back the drawing. "I don't think we need worry about Lupus Glaucus. He's hiding. Riculfius was sent to arrest him."

"Could someone else from the garrison be watching?"

"An absent master makes slaves slow."

"So they say." David grinned and took up his cup. "Exciting! To Four Macedonica and finding its treasure."

"I'm not going to tell Albanus this time," Treverius said. "I'll bring an iron bar to force the lock. We'll go in the morning, just before sunup."

* * *

Treverius, his wife, and David entered the shed before dawn and went through the trapdoor to the stairway. Each carried a lamp to light the gloomy anteroom and temple.

At the bottom of the stairs, the flames gave an orange wash to the sculptures of Kronos and the kneeling archer.

"Charon's Oars, what a monster!" Treverius rubbed a palm over Kronos's lion head. Behind the statue, a feeble glint shone from the golden letters on the old banner.

"'Legion Four Macedonica,'" David read. "We're on the right path at least."

"Here's a room." Blandina held her lamp to illuminate the interior of a curtained alcove on the right.

"What's inside?"

"Looks like a vesting room. There's a wardrobe against the wall."

"Too obvious to be a hiding place." Treverius studied his diagram. "I'd say this was an anteroom. The main temple should be behind that curtain."

Inside the arched cave, the lamps gave sufficient light to reveal the temple and white altar at its far end. The air was damp and penetrating, and the odor of old incense was not strong enough to mask the smell of mold.

"Carved out of solid rock." Treverius eyed the curved ceiling and brushed a hand over the walls and side benches. "You have to admire the legionaries who built this."

"The taurobolium must be behind that altar." Blandina shivered. "Could we look for it and get out? That horrible Glaucus might walk in on us again."

"It will take only a moment, dove." Treverius went behind the altar and saw the gore-crusted grating. "The pit is here. David, help me lift the grill. I can see a mosaic floor underneath."

Blandina watched the two men pull up the creaking iron grate, then she knelt to peer at the mosaic. "There's nothing down there. Let's go!"

"I need to find out for sure." Treverius felt around the floor's edge, then lifted a side. "There must be another space underneath. The . . . mosaic . . . is in sections and comes up," he grunted, pulling out a slab. A dark pit was revealed underneath.

"There's something on the bottom," David cried. "It looks like silver."

Too dull, Treverius thought, as he unsheathed his belt knife. He leaned into the opening and nicked the top of the metal, then slowly straightened up with a frown of disappointment on his face. "Lead plates. I guess our theory was wrong, or perhaps there never was a Macedonica treasure."

"What about that old coin in Gundstram's mouth?"

"Blandina, even Malchus has a coin from the reign of Decius that's well over a hundred years old . . ." Treverius stopped. "Malchus!"

"What is it, Trev?" Blandina asked. "What about him?"

"Why didn't I think of Malchus before? He might have seen someone suspicious while out proselytizing for his cult."

"Did you know he was staying with us?" David asked.

"No. Why is that?"

"He refused to stay in the hospital ward and asked to be housed in our Judean quarter. Penina agreed to take him in."

"How is he?" Blandina asked. "Any better?"

"My physician doesn't think he'll live out the month."

"We'll come over as soon as we can," Treverius promised. "Now, let's get out of this infernal catacomb."

* * *

On the afternoon of July twentieth Treverius and Blandina came to visit Malchus. David took his friends to the room where the old man lay.

Despite Penina's attempt to mask its foul odor with incense, the air in the close, hot space smelled putrid. Malchus was flushed, in contrast to the white stucco wall next to him. Perspiration glistened on his gaunt cheeks.

When Blandina wiped his face and thin arms with a wet cloth, his dull gaze followed her without expression, even when she gagged at the smell of death coming from his abdomen.

"Let me ask him something." Treverius leaned toward the old man. "Why did you choose to come to the Judeans?"

Malchus turned his head toward him. "Ye are as blind as the rest," he whispered hoarsely, opening a blue-veined hand to show his silver coin. "Just as Emperor Decius persecuted us, know ye not that the Hebrews are reviled?"

"True. Even Constantine lapsed in his toleration—"

"The Chosen of God completed His plan for salvation," Malchus rasped. "In calling for the Nazarene's death, they summoned his resurrection."

The brief effort exhausted the old man. After Blandina sponged Malchus's face, Treverius leaned close to him again. "Malchus, these murders. You travel from place to place in town. Have you seen anyone . . . anything . . . that could help us find the killer?"

The old man was quiet so long that he seemed on the verge of falling asleep.

"Let me try," Blandina said. "Malchus, a child has been killed along with the others. Can you help us find who is responsible?"

Malchus stared at the ceiling without replying.

"Have you seen anyone suspicious on the days these people died?" Treverius persisted, impatiently this time.

"Be more specific," Blandina suggested. "Give him a person's name to think about."

"Right. Malchus, today is the feast of Saint Margarita. That's my mother's name, but she's safe in the pretorium."

"Margarita?" The name seemed to rouse Malchus from his torpor. "Margarita," he mumbled, "a little pearl. Beautiful little pearl."

"What's he babbling about?"

"Your mother's name, Trev." Blandina suddenly looked up at David standing in the doorway. "That day we came to your warehouse with Penina. On the way we discovered that both your wife's name and Margarita meant 'pearl.'"

"Where is Penina now?" Treverius asked, alarmed at what Blandina was implying.

"Probably at the synagogue, cleaning the women's gallery. Sundown begins our observance of Tish be Av."

"Penina may be the target!" Treverius cried. "We've got to get over there."

Treverius overturned his chair in his haste to get outside. David and Blandina followed him, sprinting across the Via Rheni toward the domed building. The front entrance was locked. David indicated a side entrance that led to the school annex. Kicking at the lock, Treverius smashed the retainers and pushed open the door.

"Which way?" he yelled. "Where would she be?"

"To the right. This hall leads to the sanctuary." David led the way down a narrow passageway to an open door, then froze at the sill.

In the dim sanctuary space, Penina was backed against the Ark of the Torah by Aethiops, who stood in front of her with a curved sword in his hand. Startled by David's appearance, she glanced at her husband. The Black turned around. He dropped the weapon, gave a guttural bellow, and ran at the intruder the way a bull begins its charge. David leaped aside, but Treverius, behind him, received a glancing blow that sent him sprawling to the floor.

Blandina was standing just beyond. Aethiops shoved her aside and bolted through the hallway to the outer door.

David ran to Penina and held her. "I . . . I'm all right," she said, trembling. "It was that actor."

"Aethiops, but you're safe now, dearest."

Treverius staggered to his feet. His thigh felt numb from the blow, but he hobbled to the outside door and looked in both directions. The Via Rheni was empty. Judeans were indoors preparing for the commemoration and no one else was outside. Even if he knew which way Aethiops had run, Treverius realized it was pointless to try to find him in the narrow streets and warren of homes and shops. "At least now we know whom to look for," he muttered.

Nursing his bruised leg, Treverius limped back to the sanctuary. Blandina had joined David, sitting on the platform stairs while Penina told him what had happened.

"I was going upstairs to clean the women's gallery when I heard the front door open," she explained softly. "I thought someone was coming to help, but heard the inside bolt being locked and turned around. Aethiops was there with that sword."

"We'll have to tell Petranius." Treverius picked up the curved blade. "He tried to kill you with this."

"No, wait," she said. "I was frightened, of course, but when Aethiops came up to me it wasn't like a . . . a threat. He seemed to be pleading with me to get away."

"Remember how gentle he was with that old woman the day he was peddling relics?" Blandina asked.

"Nonsense, that was an act," Treverius scoffed. "The brute would have killed Penina."

"Let's get you home." David helped his wife to her feet. "It's almost sundown and father will be here to begin prayers. Don't tell him what happened just yet."

* * *

Treverius decided to confront Petranius immediately. Blandina brought the sword, wrapped in a blanket.

Pumilio was standing at the theater entrance. He told Treverius that Petranius was in his office and offered to guide him to the small room backstage.

Petranius's head was still bound with a camphor-soaked cloth to heal the thorn wounds, but his red hair was matted and unkempt above the bandage. When he looked up, creases in his sallow face were deep gullies of reflected pain.

"Ah, angel and one of my actors," he said cheerfully. "I'm working on the script for the Nativity drama."

"Petranius, we have bad news . . ." Treverius noticed Pumilio turn to leave. "No, wait, you're his companion."

"Whose companion? Bad news?" Petranius put down his pen. "What are you talking about, Treverius?"

"I believe one of your actors is involved in these murders. Aethiops."

"My friend? No, no," Pumilio objected.

"Enough!" Petranius snapped. "What do you mean, Treverius? You're limping. Has something happened?"

"We surprised Aethiops in the synagogue threatening the rabbi's daughter-in-law. It would have been another ritual killing. You were almost a victim of one yourself."

"I admit I didn't take much notice before that. Threatening her, you say? How?"

"With a sword. We've brought it."

After Blandina unwrapped the weapon, Petranius took it and ran his finger lightly over the blade. "It's ours. One we use onstage, so not terribly sharp."

"In the hands of someone as strong as Aethiops?"

"Indeed. Pumilio, bring your friend here."

"He wasn't in his room this morning," the dwarf whined. "We usually go to the kitchen together."

"For Thalia's sake, look for him." Petranius made a helpless gesture. "Friends, I don't know what to say."

"David agrees that we should keep this to ourselves for now. If people thought someone from the theater was involved in these murders, they'd burn you out."

"I'm grateful. Treverius." Petranius held up his script. "I hope this Nativity play will help . . . well, redeem us, after that unhappy ending with Stilicho."

"I'm sure it will," Blandina said. "I'm so excited about what you're doing."

"And I . . . angel." Petranius winced, then half-smiled at her.

"When you do find Aethiops," Treverius warned, "hold him in one of your animal cells and send word to me."

"I just don't understand." Petranius shook his head. "We've never had trouble with Aethiops, have we Pumilio?"

"My friend wouldn't harm a flea on a cat's balls."

"I know what we saw," Treverius insisted. "The man's dangerous."

As he left with Blandina, Treverius looked around the dingy storage area. The effigy of the Hebrew was again hanging alongside the other actors' character masks.

* * *

Treverius pictured the scene in the synagogue as he slowly limped with Blandina along the Via Trajani to the Pretorium. At the Longinus Chapel he guided her to the porch, and sat to rest his injured leg.

"At least we know our murderer. Now we have to find him before he kills again."

"Why would Aethiops do this?" Blandina asked. "What motive?"

"He's strong enough to have been a gladiator. Most of them were condemned criminals."

"But what is he gaining? These aren't robberies. And if Aethiops had tied Petranius to that cross, he would have known who it was."

"Not if the director was drugged first by that wine he drank. Still, I find it hard to believe the Ethiopian could go out and murder people for nine months without Petranius knowing about it."

"No, Trev," Blandina objected. "The poor man has enough trouble just keeping his troupe together. They didn't work last winter, or open a play in the spring."

"Aethiops could have had help from one of the other actors. Of course!" Treverius smacked a fist into his palm. "They have a room full of costumes and disguises. I wouldn't put this past that Alexandros. He was pretty offensive at the improvisation we saw in February."

"But why would they risk it? Demetrius wants to close the theater as it is. If these were robberies it would be understandable, but you've admitted there doesn't seem to be a motive." Blandina reached for his hand. "Trev, my own namesake's day is in less than two weeks."

"The martyred Saint Blandina." Treverius slipped a protective arm around his wife. "Don't worry, dove. I won't send you to the camp," he joked, "but you're not going to set foot outside the Pretorium on August first. You'll be safe. There's no disguise on earth that could get Aethiops or Alexandros past the entrance guards."

"That's not what I meant. Perhaps there's some way I could act as a . . . a decoy to flush out the killer."

"Decoy? Are you insane, woman?" Treverius pulled his arm away. "Get that idea out of your head. No, I'll not put you in danger."

"You're ordering me around again."

"Ordering you around? Hades, woman—"

"Trev," she interrupted sweetly, "then at least let me watch the Lugnasad games."

Still stubborn. "All right," he relented, "I'll get you a place on the reviewing stand with the governor. Vertiscus and Cyril will be with him."

"Trev, remember when you said you were sure the murderer would act out his motive before summer ended? Well, we finally have a suspect, not a phantom, and I thought I could do something. Don't be upset."

"Sorry I barked at you. You keep an eye on Vertiscus and the merchant at the games. I've decided to confront them after the festival and ask Demetrius to be there. We'll find out what they're up to."

chapter 21

On the day after the incident with Penina, Treverius saw four tattered members of Governor Albanus's scouting force straggle into the Pretorium. They reported that all of their comrades, including Marculf and Nathaniel, had been killed in the ambush by Gaisios. Treverius reluctantly told Blandina that she would probably never know what had happened to her father.

David came to Treverius's quarters on the afternoon of July twenty-seventh, the Feast of the Seven Sleepers, to say that Malchus had died during the seventh hour. His disciples were at the house, washing the old man's mutilated body before dressing him in a new white linen tunic.

When Treverius informed Modestus, the presbyter was averse to officiating, but finally agreed to hold an early evening funeral and bury the vexing fanatic.

While attending the service with Blandina, Treverius noticed that Malchus's disciples looked radiant when Modestus recited the words of the Nicean Creed, Et expecto resurrectionem mortuorum, which affirmed the raising of the dead. He guessed that the small group expected the shriveled cadaver to rise from its coffin as a triumphant Glorified Body dressed in a new white tunic.

It did not.

Later, Treverius heard that a few disciples had lingered in the cemetery for three days, at the mound of dirt over Malchus, in the hope that he would burst forth through the dry earth, as Christ did from the garden tomb on the third day.

Malchus did not.

Confused and disillusioned, the penitents were said to have burned their coarse clothing and dispersed. The silver quinarius of Trajanus Decius was never seen again.

* * *

Vertiscus told Cyril and Nevius to be at a final meeting he had scheduled in the mithreum for the late evening of July thirty-first, to review plans for the action he had code-named Lugos, the Celtic god honored at the Lugnasad festival. For the occasion he put on the gold-trimmed white robe and radiate crown of his Mithraic rank as Heliodromos, Courier of the Sun God. He looked in a mirror, shocked to see a reflected face sagging with fatigue. The white fringe had absorbed most of his darker hair. *I look ten years older than in October, but my goal is in sight. After tomorrow I can rest easier.*

Vertiscus was nervous and he knew the men would also be jittery on this eve of action. Incense burners, with smoldering cannabis fumes, were spaced around the benches to relax them. Hortar was back from Treveri, boasting of the Vandal victory over Marculf. *Good.* Vertiscus thought the news would bolster morale. Lupus Glaucus had come out of hiding, after the governor ordered his arrest for the attack on Malchus, to explain his officers' assignments to the men.

It was close to the fourth evening watch and dark outside, when Vertiscus saw Cyril and Nevius slip through the curtain to the main temple.

"Cyril." He forced a smile, although he was painfully tired. "I want you to meet the legionaries. Hear their plans."

Cyril glanced around. "How many men have you?"

"Here? Almost fifty, including officers who will lead the attack."

"Is this where Lupus Glaucus has been hiding?"

"Hortar is back from Treveri," Vertiscus said to distract Cyril from his question. "He's here to tell us about Gaisios's part in this."

"So the barbarian is on his way?" Nevius asked.

"In good time, friend. We'll review the mens' assignments first. Glaucus. I'm ready to proceed."

"Attention," the burly commander yelled. "We'll hear about how I won't be hidin' out tomorrow."

Laughter followed his comment. Holding the whip of Helios, Vertiscus went to the sculpture of Mithras. He wiped sweat from his forehead. The cannabis fumes were making him lightheaded and slightly nauseated.

"Officers, legionaries," he said, "it is not for every generation to be favored by Fortune, yet you here are privileged to be founders of a province, New Gothia." He indicated his guests. "Some of you have seen Cyril and Nevius in our temple, two of our most prominent . . . and wealthy . . . citizens." Vertiscus paused to let a few men applaud. "They are with us, as I have already told you."

"What about tomorrow?" a man called out.

"The day of Lugos? Glaucus, show the drawing." The commander motioned for two men to hold up a crude sketch of the game area. "This shows the front of the pretorium," Vertiscus explained. "The javelin and hammer throwing contests will be here, along the Via Praetori. They're scheduled for the third hour, immediately after the cart races, when Pretorian contestants will still be on the track outside the Germania Gate. Albanus will be on a pavilion in front of the pretorium, with Cyril and me."

"What happens then?" a legionary in back asked.

"Javelin contests." Vertiscus flicked the whip nervously. "The signal is when I hold up a board with Number One, the first throw."

"Signal to throw?"

"Y' mule's ass, listen!" Glaucus growled. "Signal to attack. My men will come out of th' basilica and surround th' governor."

"Good." Vertiscus mopped his forehead again. "Attonis. Your group will hold the guard back. Sentries under Virilo will close the Germania Gate."

Hortar chuckled. "Half the pretorians and militia will be outside, still unhitching carts. Unarmed."

"What about that Vandal in Treveri?" a man shouted. "Where will his men be?"

"Hortar, answer our comrade," Vertiscus ordered, avoiding his eyes.

"The Vandal . . . Gaisios . . . is with us," he stammered, "but . . . but he's decided to wait until we've taken Mogontium before coming."

At angry mumbling, Vertiscus waved his whip for silence. "Three of Attonis's men will ride to Treveri and be there by evening to tell of our victory. Gaisios will come to share it."

"And the loot," someone muttered.

Vertiscus let the comment pass. "After the gate is closed, Flavius's men will attack the barracks inside the pretorium. Sieze the weapons arsenal."

"Do my men kill the guards?" Flavius asked.

"That depends on resistance. They'll be unarmed, preparing for their contests."

"What about the Judeans?"

"I've thought of the Beneregesh. Most won't take part in the games, since it's not their festival. Vadomar's men will start a fire at the synagogue. When the Judeans go there to put out the blaze . . . Need I explain?"

"When do we get paid?" a man yelled. Applause and excited babble followed his question.

Vertiscus chuckled. "By evening, you'll be spending your gold in taverns and, ah, the wolf dens."

As the soldiers chortled, Hortar flung a handful of coins toward them. "That should convince hesitant comrades to join with you!"

While men scrambled for coins, Hortar handed Vertiscus a golden, twin-handled ritual goblet of wine. "Hold where you are, men," he called out, raising up the cup. After the legionaries were quiet, Vertiscus tipped out a splash of ruby wine and watched it seep into the earth floor. "A libation to lord Mithras and the great Helios, for the success of Lugos!" he cried.

"Success to Lugos!" the men responded in unison.

As soon as Hortar had led the legionaries out through the curtain, jingling coins in their hands, Cyril turned to Nevius. "We certainly had better discipline in Julian's legions."

"They may have the advantage of surprise," Nevius agreed, "yet, if this rabble is to take them, the pretorians had better be totally unarmed."

Vertiscus overheard the two. "The dice are thrown, friends. We act in the morning."

"Aren't the men a bit . . . raw?"

"Raw? Don't be fooled, Cyril. They'll fight like Herakles, won't they Glaucus?"

"I got 'em trained good."

"You'd better be right," Cyril warned. "I've staked the future on New Gothia. My warehouses are about empty. No supplies have come in from Gaul or Italy since the invasion. People are so desperate they're stealing vegetables from public gardens."

"And ready to accept my leadership, Cyril," Vertiscus pointed out. "Now, let's go complete my business of

dividing the treasure at the theater. That crippled director helped enormously by having his Ethiopian actor terrorize citizens. And by hiding the Macedonica spoils."

"What?" Cyril's complexion drained of color. "You
mean Petranius is behind these killings? Th . . . the
child's?"

"That bothers you, merchant, even though you were
so willing to blame your ridiculous Jupiter?" Vertiscus
responded in a cutting tone.

"Ridiculous? I . . . I thought you were a pagan."

"Pagan?" Vertiscus half-laughed. "After Gundstram
discovered this temple, I went along with that Mithraic
nonsense to recruit the men I needed for New Gothia."

"You treasonable bastard," Cyril spat out. "It was
Hortar who betrayed Mogontium to the Vandals for you."

"Merchant, this discussion is pointless." Vertiscus
tugged off his radiate crown and tossed it onto the altar
of Mithras. "If any of what you've heard leaves this cave,
your head and Nevius's will be spiked . . . alongside
mine . . . on top of the Germania Gate." He turned to
Glaucus. "Time we paid our crippled friend his due.
Right, Commander?"

"Not just him, I been itching t' settle with that map
maker." Glaucus's bad teeth showed in a crooked grin.
"By tomorrow night he'll be dead, and his woman'll be
sleeping with me."

* * *

Treverius and Blandina arrived early for the vigil Mass
that Modestus always celebrated in the late evening of
July thirty-first to honor the martyred Blandina.

He led his wife close to the rostrum, then looked at
the Longinus mural. The centurion stood, eternally holding his lance and gazing heavenward with his restored
eyes, but the starling that had been on the moulding
above was gone, a tiny victim of the cold winter.

"Only a few more people are here than were at the funeral for Arbitos," Treverius commented, glancing around at an assembly made up mainly of women.

"That seems so long ago, Trev. So many deaths."

"And my concern now is finding Aethiops. Murdering that child almost provoked a riot."

"Where was Vertiscus the day that crowd wanted him?"

"It's as if he wanted the governor to take the blame. He told us in February that he was ready to take over from Albanus. I'm convinced he was about to press for a recall vote on the day Malchus interrupted the meeting."

"Here's Modestus," Blandina said. "He looks so tired."

The presbyter climbed the rostrum stairs wearing a white tunic. The red stole around his neck was embroidered with crowns, a symbol of martyrdom. He leafed through Book V of The History of the Church, until he found the section about the death of the young Blandina.

"Before I begin the vigil Mass," Modestus announced, "I will describe the situation in Gaul at the time of the martyred Blandina, some two hundred years ago. Then read part of the text by Bishop Eusebius.

"Lugdunum was the capital of three Gallic provinces. On the first of August, citizens came to sacrifice to the emperor at the provincial altar, and look forward to a week of games and spectacles in the arena. These might include the torture and death of convicted criminals. On that hot summer day, the crowd was waiting for the games to begin when some spectators attacked Christians. Arrests were made. The most prominent was that of the ninety-year-old Bishop Pothinus. He was beaten by the enraged mob and died two days later. One of the arrests was of a slave girl named Blandina." Modestus opened the book. "This is how Eusebius describes the scene.

"'The fury of the crowd and soldiers fell with crushing fury on Sanctus the deacon, on Maturus, recently baptized, on Attalus, who had always been a pillar and support of the church in Pergamum. And finally on Blandina, through whom Christ proved that things which men regard contemptible are by God thought worthy of great glory.'"

Treverius slipped an arm around his wife. She had heard the story many times, but it was always unsettling.

"'The girl Blandina,'" Modestus read in a hushed voice, "'was hung on a post as food for wild beasts let loose in the amphitheater. She seemed to be hanging in the form of a cross, and through her prayers to Christ encouraged the others. In pain, they yet saw that their sister was the one being crucified for them, and when the animals were released, none of them touched her. She was taken down from the post and returned to the arena cells.'"

Modestus paused. "In my opinion, Blandina, a young slave, obeyed Paul's letter to her fellow Gauls in Asia and 'put on Christ.' For her there were neither slave nor free, for all were one in Christ."

"'On the last day of the games,'" he continued reading, "'Blandina was brought in. With her was Ponticus, a boy of fifteen. Day after day the two had been taken to watch others being tortured, and many attempts were made by the authorities to persuade them to sacrifice to the gods.'

"'Last of all, Blessed Blandina passed through the tortures. After the whips, after the wild animals, after being seared in a heated iron chair, she was put in a wicker basket and thrown into the arena with a bull. Time after time the animal tossed her, but she was indifferent to all that happened, because of the hope her faith gave her. Then she was also sacrificed. Later, the Romans admitted that they had never known a woman to suffer so much or so long.'"

Treverius noticed Blandina's trembling had increased with the reading. Her hand felt cold, and there was a tear at the corner of her eye. "Are you all right? You've heard the story before."

"I . . . I know."

"Let's go outside."

They sat on the chapel's top stair. Blandina sniffled and leaned against a column in the darkness. "I feel silly, Trev, but the reading depressed me this year. I know Blandina's death is meant to be inspiring, but with all these killings, it frightened me. I can't get the thought of little Pancras out of my mind."

"I told you that you'd be safe, even watching the games." He kissed hands that were still cold. "Speaking of the games, Blandina, David told me he's completed the mourning period for Nathaniel and the other Judeans who were killed. He's going to enter the javelin throw, and I, ah, foolishly said I'd compete too. Would you mind if I got up early and practiced with him before the games start?"

"Of course not." Blandina smiled and touched his face. "It would do you good to forget all this for a day."

"Thanks, dove. You sleep later, then come out and watch your husband make a fool of himself."

"I feel foolish myself." Blandina sniffled and brushed away a final tear. "You'll do fine, Trev."

"And you'll be fine. I won't even be far away from you. Nor will my parents. You'll be close to the governor, too. Nothing can happen, dove."

Treverius knew he was right. Blandina would spend her namesake's day in and around the pretorium, surrounded by people who loved her. Aethiops was the killer. Even if Petranius and Alexandros were somehow involved, neither of them would dare try to harm Blandina in front of hundreds of spectators at the Lugnasad games. Nor would Vertiscus act so publicly, even if he had ambitions about replacing Governor Albanus.

Treverius helped his wife to her feet to take her home. After the festival, he would force Demetrius to act like a true representative of the Augustus and, once and for all, confront Vertiscus about his seditious intentions.

chapter 22

The eve of the Lugnasad games, Governor Quintus Albanus spent another restless night. Daytime heat had displaced the coolness in his bedroom, and even the garden outside was uncomfortably warm after sundown. His leg wound throbbed continually, but he had told himself that he would oversee the games. When Remigius brought him one of Nicias's restoratives, Albanus found his secretary's suggestion of a swim in the pools of the pretorium bath appealing. He sent Remigius to ask if Demetrius would like to join him.

In the morning, while he waited for the envoy, Albanus relaxed in the tepid pool. The soothing warm water induced a sense of well-being in him and he recalled the months he had spent at Vindonissa recuperating from his thigh wound. Sophia had died of fever shortly before his injury at the Frigidus River, so he no longer had a reason to return to Constantinople. Albanus felt that his spirit and body would recover more quickly in the beauty and solitude of a remote alpine landscape, and indeed he had healed rapidly in the Rhaetian mountains. Vindonissa was again secure, the largest fort guarding the Rhine between Raurica and Brigantium.

Albanus had arrived in late September with his secretary Sebastian and the legion surgeon, Nicias. The men spent a comfortable winter in Headquarters rooms. By spring Albanus felt strong enough to join the hunting parties that ranged as far as the Rhine River, seven miles north of the camp. His appointment as Governor had come in May—at the recommendation of Stilicho, he surmised—and he had looked forward to new responsibilities that might take his mind away from the loss of Sophia.

Albanus's reminiscing was cut short by Demetrius's arrival.

"I'm grateful for the invitation, Governor," he said, throwing aside a silk tunic and lowering himself into the water. He clung to the pool's side. "This heat. The men will surely take over the public baths after the games."

"Nicias set up a medical area in the pretorium."

"You expect trouble?" Demetrius frowned. "That's right, your guards and garrison men don't exactly drink together."

"No, you misunderstood. Possible casualties from heat and injuries during the games."

"Weren't these contests Vertiscus's idea?"

"His idea to expand them," Albanus replied. "Afraid I haven't been up to that kind of planning lately."

"With what you've faced, Governor, a lesser man would have thrown down his shield long ago."

"You're being kind, Demetrius. True. Had a bad winter and spring, but so has all of Mogontium."

"But you seem well today, and your, ah, stutter is gone."

"Feel better than in a long while." Albanus turned to swim the length of the pool.

Demetrius treaded water until he returned, then commented, "Governor, you know that Vertiscus has been criticizing you at Curia meetings."

"So I've heard." Albanus was cautious, wondering if the envoy was probing him for a reaction he could report to Ravenna.

"I've complained to the Augustus, but I'm not sure if my dispatches are getting through," Demetrius went on. "I think you should take it upon yourself to replace the man as curator."

Albanus squeezed water out of his hair, then looked up. "He's done a good job administering the pretorium."

"Now you're being kind. Simply told, he wants your position."

"To be governor?" Albanus laughed at the thought. "He would have to be as demented as Amphion."

"I'm serious," Demetrius insisted. "You've been absent and have neither heard nor seen what I have."

"Such as?"

"That Lupus Glaucus, for one. What kind of commander is he? Instead of taking responsibility for what happened to Malchus, he's hiding out. I think he's doing more than trying to save his skin. And someone has to be protecting him."

"Be more specific, Demetrius."

"Very well, Governor. There may be an attempt today to arrest you and take over the Pretorium."

Instead of answering, Albanus swam slowly to the end of the pool again. Demetrius may be right. Affairs have gotten out of hand lately. He backstroked and heaved himself onto the pool's side.

"Demetrius, I'm fifty-six years old," Albanus said with a dry chuckle. "Lived a year longer than the oldest man on those grave markers outside town. I'd be grateful if you would approach the Augustus about letting me retire."

"Of course. I'll do what I can, but it would be months before you received an answer. And, Governor, you're ignoring my warning. Arrest Vertiscus, or at least let Macrianus and I question him. Cyril and Nevius, too. From what I've seen in the Curia, there's something up between those three. Furtive glances, signals. This Hortar, who brought the Vandal to you, hasn't been seen here since. What's he up to?"

Albanus sighed. "All right, Demetrius. I won't arrest Vertiscus, or bring in a magistrate, but you can question him tomorrow, after the games."

"That should be soon enough. I . . . I admit I was less than effective at the July Curia meeting, but I'm ready to face the curator now."

Remigius came in with linen towels and laid one in front of each man. "The contests will start shortly, sir." he said to Albanus. "What uniform will you wear?"

"Coolest one, Remigius. Minimum of leather and metal trappings. Do I have time for a plunge in cold water?"

"A short one, sir."

"Good. I'll see you at the games, Demetrius. You'll be seated in the pavilion with me." Albanus walked to the cold pool. "Why wait for Glaucus to be found?" he muttered to himself. "Tomorrow, when the games are over, I'll appoint Riculfius as commander of the garrison. Let Demetrius find out what he can. Cut short any conspiracy." It's good to be making decisions again, he thought, as he braced himself for the dive into chill water. Sophia would be pleased.

* * *

Vetius Modestus awoke bathed in sweat. His room was on the side of the pretorium that received the morning sun and, by the first hour, it was already uncomfortably muggy. He had slept fitfully, his mind clogged by images of Vertiscus. The man's arrogance and attempts to undermine his presbyter's authority had put him on the defensive and wasted his time refuting forged epistles, like that letter by the Apostle James, which the curator spread around marketplaces. Vertiscus's contempt toward the Church indicated sympathies for either the Arians or pagans in Mogontium. Perhaps he was in contact with leaders of both factions, fomenting dissidence to further some goal of his own.

Modestus splashed water on his face, discouraged at the thought of his twelve years in Mogontium. The temple renovation had dragged on for six of them. Now, it was effectively halted by an arrogant pagan. His dwindling congregation, mostly of women, was restless during sermons and lacked an understanding of the Divine dimension of their humanity, or Christ's message of spiritual liberation. Ancient superstitions persisted.

When he'd come to the Rhine frontier after his wife Cecilia's death, Modestus realized that he had compromised any chance for advancement. Power was in Ravenna, Rome, and Mediolanum. Bishops in those cities could barely locate Mogontium, or knew it only as an object of rustic humor. The Rhine city rated a Bishopric, but the last man to hold the office had died after Modestus arrived, and a new bishop was never appointed.

He had heard that Simplicianus had replaced Ambrose as Bishiop of Mediolanum, and that the first volumes of Jerome's Latin translation of the Testaments had arrived there. It would be good to study the works, write comments, and be responsible only to the bishop. He was fifty-three years old and had been a presbyter for twenty-eight of them. The frontier should be left to younger men.

As he dried his face, Modestus half-smiled, determined to request a transfer to Mediolanum. In the same letter he would ask Bishop Simplicianus for a Writ of Excommunication against Vertiscus for his heretical opinions. Let the bishop send a commission the hundred and seventy miles to investigate the insolent curator.

Modestus looked in a bronze mirror at the new tonsure a deacon had given him. Tomorrow, when the Lugnasad games are finished, I'll give Vertiscus notice of his pending excommunication. And report Cyril, too. Under the anti-pagan statutes of the new Theodosian Code, he could be exiled and his property confiscated.

"You should have acted months ago, presbyter," he muttered to his uneven reflection in the shiny metal disk. "Months ago, but tomorrow will still do nicely."

* * *

Treverius rose before dawn, without waking Blandina, to practice the javelin throws with David. He was already sweating when he walked to the garden and passed the atrium pool. It smelled stagnant. A sultry sky reflected off the leaden water wherever greenish scum did not coat the surface. He glimpsed a fish floating belly up under the slimy layer.

I wonder if Vertiscus will punish the slave responsible for cleaning up that mess, or is he too busy thinking of ways to embarrass Governor Albanus at the games today?

Treverius walked the corridor past the pretorian barracks, where the men were putting on short tunics, or testing their practice gear. David was waiting for him by the dining area.

"Better have a bowl of porridge," Treverius chided. "You'll need all your strength to beat me."

"I forgot about your Celtic background. The Treveri are great at bragging."

"My friend, we Celts occasionally produce."

After the two sat down, a slave brought bowls of boiled millet sweetened with maple sugar crusts. While it cooled, Treverius looked around the mess room and saw Nicias.

"David, there's the surgeon. Maybe we can get him to record distances. Did you bring the knotted cord?"

"I did. Go ask him."

Nicias agreed to help. After eating, the men borrowed practice javelins from the guards' arsenal and started across the Via Honorius toward fallow farm plots near the north wall. As he walked Treverius tested the balance of his weapon, a four-foot ash handle fitted with an equally long iron shaft that ended in a blunt point.

David chose a field that was overgrown by a tangle of ochre grasses, dry and brittle from the summer drought. He sent Nicias toward one end, then called out to him.

"That's far enough. Move to one side. These javelins have a range of about twenty-five paces, if you're good. Treverius, why don't you throw first?"

"So you can show me up? All right. Don't worry, Nicias," he yelled, "you're perfectly safe."

Treverius found the blunt weapon's balance point. With his back to a sun that had just cleared the river wall, Treverius's racing shadow mimicked the throw as he heaved the javelin into an arc. It struck the ground several paces short of being parallel to Nicias.

"Terrible, terrible," Treverius wailed. "Why don't I just throw my stylus instead!"

Nicias dropped one of the wooden end pieces, then counted knots as he came back. "One, two, three . . . five . . . eight, nine . . . twelve. Twelve paces, son."

Treverius spat in disgust. "About as far as a new recruit throws."

"But not half-bad for a cavalryman." David balanced the shaft of his weapon, leaned back, paused, then threw it hard. The javelin struck the ground in a puff of dust and skidded to a stop. Nicias jogged back, counting knots.

"Only to where it hit the dirt," Treverius called to him. "The skidding doesn't count."

"Twenty paces." Nicias bent down to pick up the javelin, then pretended to throw. "I'd like to see that black actor at the theater heave this thing."

"Aethiops?" Treverius came over with David to retrieve the shafts. "It's been kept quiet, Nicias, so I suppose you haven't heard about him at the camp."

"Heard what?"

"He's connected to the murders," David elaborated. "We found him threatening my wife Penina in our synagogue."

"Incredible. Have you spoken to Petranius about him?"

"Yes. Aethiops has disappeared."

Nicias threw down the javelin. "This is the first solid clue we have. Now, what happened with Penina?"

"Blandina and I were at David's, questioning Malchus just before he died," Treverius said. "He mumbled something about pearls that made us realize Penina might be in danger."

"We bolted for the synagague," David continued, "and found Aethiops confronting my wife with a sword. He charged through us like a wild auroch and got away."

Nicias was quiet a moment, before asking, "Have you tried to find a motive for her being attacked? Or the other murders?"

"There doesn't seem to be one, beyond terrorizing citizens."

"Why would someone want to do that?"

"I've been asking myself the same thing," Treverius admitted. "The Curia was in a panic at the last meeting. I'm sure Vertiscus wanted to recall the governor, but the incident with Malchus interrupted a vote that might have passed."

"We agreed once," Nicias recalled, "that someone educated is involved. Eliminate Cyril, although he may well be part of it with his threats of retribution. Aethiops, a mute, doesn't have the ability to mastermind this, but someone at the theater does."

"Of course, Petranius," Treverius exclaimed. "I'd almost come to that conclusion, but my wife still doesn't want to believe it."

"He would be the most likely one," Nicias reasoned, "and Aethiops is one of his actors."

"Yet it doesn't make sense. Petranius was injured in the tunnel that day, and later crucified."

"We came through the tunnel together," David added. "Petranius was knocked down when the keystone gave way. Stilicho believes he saved his life, but let's not forget that the man's an actor. And those stones were pumice. If the intent was to kill Stilicho, the heavier weight, the better."

"But if Petranius knew the arch was about to fall," Treverius said, visualizing the incident, "he could have timed his reaction."

"Petranius's signal could have been when the hammer hit the wedge. We all heard it clearly,"

"Makes sense, David." Treverius shook his head. "I guess I haven't wanted to believe he was implicated in the murders because Blandina feels sorry for him. Still . . . There's another possible explanation for what happened. What if the person responsible didn't want Stilicho killed, only wounded? That wouldn't involve Petranius."

"True," Nicias agreed. "If the motive is to terrorize citizens by showing that no one is safe, what better way than to attack Stilicho yet avoid retaliation by his men?"

"Dead, Stilicho would certainly have been avenged," Treverius speculated. "Alive, the affair would be forgotten, but the point made."

"That needn't exonerate Petranius," Nicias said. "We found him crucified, but not quite like Peter. Not head downward. I admit, he had me fooled."

"Fooled?" Treverius suddenly felt cold. "Fooled, how, Nicias?"

"In the light of how we found him. First, he was tied to the cross, not spiked. He figured on someone finding him."

"Yet he was gagged and unconscious."

"Unconscious from the nepenthes. It was a winning throw either way. If no one found him before the effects wore off, he would simply let himself down. But he knew the odds were that he would be found, at least by a cast member. It was a double win for him that it was us."

"I'm beginning to see what might have happened," Treverius said. "Petranius set up the cross on the stage with the leg and foot ropes looped into place. He put on the thorn crown, drank the narcotic, then stuffed the gag into his mouth."

"And slipped on that character mask of 'The Hebrew' we found over his face."

"Right, David."

"I didn't look at his finger tips," Nicias recalled, "but there might have been thorn pricks. Continue your speculation, Treverius."

"Petranius climbed the ladder and slipped his hands into the rope loops. After kicking the ladder aside . . . remember how close it was . . . he worked his feet into the lower rope. The vertical beam of the cross had a seat to support weight. He sat on that."

"And knew he would slump forward after the nepenthes took effect," Nicias added, "but that the ropes would keep him from falling."

"If it was all an act to divert suspicion from himself," David said, "it still doesn't clarify a motive for the killings. Why would he want those people dead?"

"He obviously isn't capable of actually murdering them himself," Treverius said. "That's where Aethiops, and maybe some of the other actors, came in. At the very least, Petranius has some explaining to do."

"Shall we confront him on the festival or wait until later?"

"Tomorrow, David. Let's enjoy the August Lugnasad games today."

"The first of August. Treverius, didn't Blandina mention at Purim that her namesake is honored today?" David asked. "Where is she?"

"Asleep. Or, more likely, having breakfast with my parents by now. She . . . Christ!" Treverius paled, realizing Blandina might be in danger. "Petranius could send for her instead of having Aethiops come here!"

Treverius bolted across the field and the Via Honorius to the front of the pretorium. David and Nicias sprinted after him. At the Via Praetori he stopped to catch his breath. Governor Albanus was standing under an awning, which shaded the spectator's pavilion, watching Demetrius direct slaves in setting up stools for the pretorium staff.

"Have you seen Vertiscus or Cyril?" Albanus called down when he saw Treverius. "The curator has the contest schedule and Cyril is to distribute prizes."

"No. Has my wife been out here yet?"

"I saw her a bit earlier," Albanus replied. "An actor came from the theater. Something about that crippled director wanting to rehearse a Nativity play before it gets too hot."

"Christ Jesus! Blandina trusts Petranius and he's lured her to him."

Close to panic, Treverius roughly threaded his way through a throng of citizens on the Via Alexander, who were coming to see the games, then ran past the Longinus Chapel and around the jog in the camp palisade where the street rose towards the theater.

When he reached the square, Treverius was winded and his side hurt. He ran into the theater entrance, hearing his footsteps echo in the dank tunnel along with those of David, running close behind him. The older Nicias was further back.

Treverius came out of the passageway, onto the lower tier of seats. The stage backdrop was in shadow, with the curtain stretched across the front to conceal the platform itself. No one was in sight. He leaned against a wooden bench to catch his breath.

A moment later David came up beside him.

"There's . . . no one . . . here," Treverius gasped.

"Perhaps . . . she's at . . . Petranius's house."

Nicias joined them. "Have . . . you found Blandina?"

"No, David thinks she may be at Petranius's. His apartment is around the back. Let's go there."

The three men had started for the exit, when they were startled by a deep, hollow- sounding voice that resonated from behind the stage curtain.

"Stay friends! Our drama soon will start.

From this mystery, the veil will part."

"Petranius?" Although the voice was distorted, Treverius recognized it. "It's the director, but he sounds so strange."

"I think I know why."

Before Nicias could explain, the creaking of machinery sounded from the direction of the stage. As the curtain slowly descended into its housing along the front of the platform, a scene of horror greeted the three men.

The nude, lifeless bodies of Vertiscus, Cyril, Nevius, and Glaucus dangled in the four sculpture niches of the backdrop. Each of their heads was covered by a caricature mask of themselves. The Macedonica treasure was heaped beneath the bodies of the conspirators in unequal piles. Even in the shadow of an awning over the stage, light glinted from the coins. Other gold and silver vessels, jewelry, and votive statuary revealed the enormity of the ancient cache.

On the stage foreground, roped to a stake set into the socket where Petranius's cross had been erected, Blandina's body slumped forward. Her head was tilted to one side. There was no sign that she was alive.

Through his shock Treverius made out an enormous figure, half-concealed in the stage shadows. It wore a mask that resembled a scowling Petranius, but the body stood erect, without the hump that deformed him. The man was dressed in a padded purple toga, decorated with a gold stripe of an Augustus, and stood on high platform shoes. His right hand held a curved sword, like the one Aethiops had dropped when he bolted from the synagogue.

"I've got to get Blandina off there," Treverius muttered through clenched teeth. He started toward the orchestra, but the mask turned to look at him.

"Stop there, map maker!" the echoing voice ordered. The figure moved awkwardly to Blandina on its high shoes and placed the sword edge under her breasts. "Remember Christina's martyrdom? Julian ordered her breasts hacked off. This Hun blade is no actor's prop." Petranius laughed in an eerie cackle. "My angel will exalt her place in heaven as a double martyr now . . . unless you sit down."

"Do what he says," Nicias cautioned. "You couldn't reach her before his sword did."

Treverius returned to the bench and slumped down. "What's that garish outfit Petranius is wearing?"

"Actors at Alexandia wore similar dress in revivals of Greek drama," Nicias whispered. "The kothurnus . . . high boots . . . and padded chiton are designed to make the actor look superhuman. The headpiece amplifies his voice. The director has cast himself as an emperor."

Petranius's voice bellowed, "That's better, map maker. Stilicho bolted from my drama, but all of you will stay until the final curtain." He stood back from Blandina and recited.

"Now sit, three friends. Yes, three.

Father, Son, and Spirit? Ah, no.
Gaul, Greek, and Hebrew, see.
Tell me, friends. Does our scene please?
Four actors there, in their final role.
Or five? My angel sleeps 'er she pleads."

Petranius's sword hand swept out in an arc to indicate the empty theater seats.

"Look around, friends, and see,
My drama is for you alone, what's more, free.
The players soon I'll introduce,
Will it be pity or relief, I now induce?"

He walked unsteadily on the clumsy boots to the body of Vertiscus and pushed it with the flat of his sword. As the corpse turned in a grotesque circle at the end of the rope, Petranius gave a mad laugh.

"Here, Pretorium Master, who would be a king.
Instead, as despised actor see him swing."

Moving awkwardly to the stiff body of Cyril, Petranius viciously poked at his chest.

"Next, pretentious pretender from the east.
He devoured wealth, on what now feast?" Petranius pointed to the corpse of Nevius, then at Glaucus.

"Fat Nevius, yapping at their heels,
"I wonder now what it is he feels?
The betrayer last, his Augustan oath,
Sold for gold, or rank, or both."

Petranius indicated the treasure under each man.

"And beneath them all in glittering heaps,
The true director vigil keeps.
It tempted our actors in time of need,
But knew they the power of mankind's greed?
Clement, Stephen. Juliana, too,
Played their part, yet no one knew.
A people terrorized, this we show,
Is easy prey for a deadly blow.
The plot's now clear. Destroy their will,
Fools shall follow all will-nill."

Turning back to the corpse of Vertiscus, Petranius stumbled and had to use his sword as a crutch to keep from falling. He recovered and wacked savagely at the curator's midsection with the broad side of the blade.

"He held us all in vile contempt,
Thought he would write the final scene,
Like Caesar's Brutus, give a final stab.
Betray Petranius and then attempt
To take the gold . . . and . . . and . . ."
He stammered over his lines, as if disoriented.

"Petranius was in a conspiracy with Vertiscus," Treverius realized, "but he must have tricked him somehow."

Petranius recovered and pointed to the conspirators.

"Yet . . . yet these a service I still do.
You see them naked, all prepared,
For resurrection and a body new.
Judged already by him they snar . . . snared."

After Petranius hesitated again, Nicias called down to him, "Blandina never did anything to you, director. She tried to help you after the crucifixion. Let her go."

"Keep talking to distract him," Treverius whispered, eyeing the backdrop. "I'll try to get above the stage."

The director's insane laugh echoed in the empty theater, muffled by the grisly tableau of the dead conspirators, then Petranius continued.

"Ah, the Greek speaks of crucifixion.
Mankind's vilest pain and grief,
here an actor's trick, but the ruse was brief.
An audience is bored if not let in."

"David," Treverius hissed, "get him to look away."

"I'll try. Petranius, that treasure behind you," David called out. "Where was it hidden?"

When the actor turned to look at the hoard, Treverius quickly crouched low and scampered for the exit.

"If you've uncovered a conspiracy," Nicias offered, "I'll ask Quintus to consider that."

"The governor may pardon me," Petranius cackled, "but I won't forgive him for snubbing my play. Or Stilicho. But wait. Hear me. I have a prophecy for the commander.

"Within a year, from the fruits of pride,
Inside a church Stilicho tries to hide.
A promise made to spare his life,
The fool believes, but not the knife!"

"Blandina did nothing to harm you," David pleaded. "Free her, Petranius."

"What, deny my angel her wish?" he replied with deadly sarcasm. "Today is her namesake's feast. What better place for her to celebrate than in heaven with the martyred Blandina. Do you recall how she died?" Petranius taunted. "Torn by wild beasts, yet that day gloriously welcomed into her Savior's embrace. Can I do less to fulfill my angel's dream?" He stepped forward and caressed Blandina's hair with his free hand. "She came to me today to read her lines. I . . . tried to probe that angel body, to see if it was flesh or spirit, but she resisted." Petranius stepped back. "She was flesh," he hissed in a voice of hate. "Like the others, she had only pity, not love, for her hunchback pet." Abruptly, a menacing snarl came from the animal cells to his left. "Albino teases Ursino." Petranius tittered. "Our drama reaches its climax."

"Arur! Damn!" David cursed. "It's the bear Treverius told me Petranius showed him." He stood and bolted down the row of seats, but when he reached the orchestra level, Petranius had put his sword against Blandina's breasts once again.

"Stop there, Hebrew," the actor warned, "lest I demonstrate Christina's fate on my angel."

David dropped to a bench. From the seat he could see the cells. Although the corridor interior was dim, he saw Albino prodding the bear with a branch and stepping back as it lunged against the bars. Then, another movement onstage caught David's eye. Blandina was regaining consciousness. She lifted her head slowly and looked around in confusion.

"Ah, my angel awakens," Petranius cried in mock surprise. "Good. There's little merit in not knowing that you're a martyr. Albino! Let our pet out."

David heard the rasp of rusty hinges. The open door to the bear's cell blocked access further in, and Ursino could only move toward the outside.

Looking up, David noticed Treverius angling along the wall behind the awning. "Impossible," David whispered to Nicias. "There are no tiles up there to drop on Petranius. And Trev can't pry a stone loose to throw down at him."

At the top of the wall that sloped to the backdrop, Treverius had the same thought. The awning below hid the actor from his view, but Blandina was far enough forward for him to see her regaining consciousness. He felt along the channel of mortar between the limestone blocks on which he knelt, silently cursing Trajan's masons for their superb craftsmanship in joining the stones. Even using his knife, it would be impossible to pry one loose in time to drop on Petranius, and the awning kept him from seeing where the actor was standing.

Treverius heard snarling. He looked down to see that a bear had shambled out of the cell passageway. It was standing by the orchestra, sniffing the air for possible danger. *It's furcing hopeless! I can't do anything from up here.* Glancing around, he saw the top of the hoisting crane. Desperate, he began crawling toward it along the narrow ledge.

Ursino blinked in the sudden brightness, then snuffled its way into the orchestra area opposite David. Standing on its haunches, the animal sniffed uncertainly, its small eyes questioning the new place.

"Ursino," Petranius called out to it. "Here! I offer you Blandina. Saint Blandina."

The yearling bear turned to the voice and deftly clambered onto the stage. At the same instant, Pumilio appeared at the cell entrance.

"No! The runt has come to watch the execution," David muttered under his breath, but saw the dwarf turn and waddle back into the dim corridor.

Ursino focused its small eyes on Blandina, snarled, and tried to assess any danger that she might pose.

David heard the sound of another cage door being opened. "Damn! Pumilio's releasing a second animal." He tugged in vain at his bench to use as a weapon. The seat was firmly attached to the flooring.

But Pumilio appeared at the entrance with Aethiops instead, frantically gesturing in sign language toward Blandina.

"Aethiops, you black satan," Petranius screamed. "You're doomed to Avernus for these murders. I should have killed you to keep you from talking." He gave a hysterical laugh. "What am I saying? You can't talk. That stunted turd Pumilio is your voice. Now he's betrayed me, too."

Aethiops saw the danger. He uttered a guttural groan, then leaped onto the stage to place himself between the bear and woman. Ursino growled a warning and lunged at the actor to catch him in a crushing embrace.

David and Nicias saw Aethiops gag at the animal's foul breath as he grappled with the creature, trying to find its windpipe in the mass of greasy fur at its throat. Ursino brought its front paws around Aethiops's shoulders and ripped through the tunic into flesh. But Aethiops ducked his head and reached up to crush the bear's larynx. Ursino gave a strangled bellow and angled its head down to tear away the powerful grip.

After tense moments of watching the struggle, David and Nicias heard the dull snap of bones being broken. Aethiops made a muffled attempt to scream, as he and the bear, still in his crushing hold, toppled off the platform. Both lay still on the stone paving of the orchestra.

"You sooty fool," Petranius shrieked, looking down at the two bodies, "you've disrupted my script. Alexandros! Open up the pipes now."

In a moment a stream of strong-smelling, black liquid oozed out of four nozzles extending from the wall beneath the bodies of the conspirators. It seeped into the piles of treasure and oozed out onto the stage.

"Smells like sulfur and the bitumen used to caulk boats," David said, looking at Nicias. "But there's something stronger."

"Naphtha, 'Greek Fire.'" Nicias replied. "It's new, used in war galley training at Constantinople."

"Alexandros, have you forgotten your lines?" Petranius screamed, as the flammable tar trickled from the treasure and oozed further across the wooden floor.

Alexandros came out of the stage wing with a burning brand in his hand, moving slowly.

"Throw the torch, you fool," Petranius shouted. "Throw the torch, then help me off the stage."

The actor dropped the flaming brand onto the nearest heap of saturated treasure. The black ooze flared into a smoky blaze that quickly ignited each pile in turn. David had fought brush fires and felt the same intense heat on his body now. The oily smoke engulfed Blandina. He was stunned to see the blaze take hold so rapidly.

"Wait." Petranius shook off Alexandros, who had taken his arm, then shuffled to Blandina on the high boots. He pointed his sword at her midsection. "Now, angel," he said with a hoarse softness in his voice, "let your Christ welcome you into his heaven."

David began a desperate run across the orchestra at Petranius, then his eye caught the blurred figure of Treverius swinging down through the black cloud, on the crane rope that held the actors' platform. The force of the arcing blow knocked Petranius away from Blandina and into one of the blazing heaps. Treverius jumped off the platform, watching in horror as Petranius gave an agonized scream and tried to stand up again on the cumbersome shoes. The flaming tar clung to his costume, while he struggled to tear off the suffocating mask. Alexandros slipped and stumbled into one of the treasure piles.

Tearing off his own burning shoes, Treverius cut away the ropes that held Blandina. She clung to the post, while he tried to pull Petranius away from the intense flames, only to be driven back by the heat. The crippled director gave a final choking scream of anguish, then lay still.

Coughing, and half-blinded by oily smoke, Treverius lifted Blandina and carried her out through the tunnel to the fountain beyond the Drusus monument. David and Nicias followed after him. In a moment, Albino, his alabaster-white face and arms blackened by soot, ran out of the entrance tunnel carrying Pumilio.

After Treverius set Blandina next to the fountain she coughed up black spittle. He dipped the hem of his tunic in the water and bathed oily soot from her face.

"That feels good, husband," she murmured, "but my head hurts terribly."

"It's the narcotic," Nicias said. "I can counter the ache with spiræ. But you're safe now."

"What happened, Trev? I went to rehearse."

"You didn't see? Thank God. Petranius tried to kill you." Treverius looked back toward the theater. A dense black cloud, billowing above the backdrop wall, reminded him of a painting he had seen at Ravenna of Mount Aetna erupting.

Blandina looked past him at David and Nicias with a weak smile. "It's said that God sends luck to fools. He sent all of you to this fool."

"You weren't being foolish, Blandina. You trusted the man."

Tears welled in her eyes. "What . . . what was that really about, Trev?"

"Petranius's final drama helped me understand, but I need to know the details." Treverius watched Albino and Pumilio walk around the theater, toward their apartment. "I'll talk to those two, but I'm taking you home now." He wiped at a spot of soot on Blandina's cheek, then helped her stand. "I'll bring the governor back to see what happened. Today is obviously the date Vertiscus chose to usurp authority and take over the Pretorium."

"Then we'd better hurry," David urged. "Even without Glaucus, the garrison still might decide to act."

chapter 23

Treverius eased Blandina past groups of gawkers on the edge of the square, who were silently watching the dense cloud spiral into the sultry sky.

"Stay away!" Treverius shouted to them. "As Tertullian predicted, the pit of Hell opened up in the theater. Not that far from the truth," he muttered to his wife, "I don't want anyone in there. As it is, rumors will spread as fast as that Greek Fire."

At the Via Praetori, most of the contestants and spectators looked in the direction of the smoke. A few officers from the garrison, who were not watching, milled about in confusion. Treverius surmised they were waiting for orders from Lupus Glaucus, and was relieved to see that Tribune Riculfius had armed his pretorian guards and stationed them around the pavilion.

"Governor," Treverius called out to Albanus. "You need to come to the theater."

"What in Hades name happened to you two?" he asked. "What's going on with that infernal smoke?"

"I'll explain when we get there. Order Riculfius to have his men disarm the garrison legionaries. Quickly."

"I've appointed him to replace Glaucus." Albanus limped down from the viewing platform. "Has this something to do with Vertiscus? I can't find him."

"Yes, and what you'll see isn't pretty. Blandina, go in and stay with my parents until I get back."

"I will not. I'm going with you."

When Treverius guided his wife and Albanus back to the theater, the fire had burned itself out. The stage backdrop was a wall of blackened limestone, the wood floor only a charred hole. A mass of molten gold and silver lay on the ground underneath and the ropes holding the four conspirators had burned through. Only shapeless mounds on smoking metal marked their scorched bodies. Nearby lay those of Petranius and Alexandros. In front of the burned stage supports, Aethiops and Ursino, singed by the blaze, were still clasped in their death embrace.

The surviving actors had lined up along the top tier of seats, but Albino and Pumilio sat in the lowest row, staring at the devastated stage. Modestus had come in, and was seated in the row behind them, next to David and Nicias. Treverius motioned for the governor and Blandina to sit alongside the men, then dropped down beside the two actors.

"Will you tell me what happened?" he urged Albino quietly.

After a long interval the actor nodded. "Vertiscus got the idea for the murders when Arbitos and the mason were accidentally killed at the temple, and Cyril claimed the wrath of Jupiter was responsible."

"Vertiscus wanted to take over Mogontium?"

"Not only Mogontium. The curator was Juliana's client. He came to Petranius and told him he had found that legion's treasure, offered him a share of it and security in New Gothia, if he helped him."

"New Gothia?"

"A rebel province he was planning."

Treverius looked back at David and Nicias. "My friends and I had determined that Petranius worked with Vertiscus to carry out the murders. What made him do so?"

"Gibber, 'Humpy,' . . . our name for Petranius . . . was from Lugdunum, not Arausio. He wanted to be ordained a presbyter, but the bishop refused to accept him because of his hunchback. Thought God had punished him."

"That's when he became an actor?" Treverius asked.

"Not right away. Lugdunum has a good library. He memorized every book in it."

"That accounts for his knowledge of the martyrs," Modestus remarked. "Too bad he didn't put it to good use."

"When Petranius couldn't be a presbyter," Albino continued, "he applied for the office of deacon. He was refused that, too. What would you have done, Presbyter?"

Modestus reddened and evaded an answer, "Christ was asked what sins a man born blind, or his parents, had committed to cause the ailment."

"Your Galilean answered that neither had sinned. But who believes him? Do you, Presbyter?" Albino rubbed at soot on his arm. "Look at me and Pumilio. A human maggot. A freak in a child's body. Would you ordain us, if you were our bishop?"

Modestus glanced away without answering.

"Did Aethiops do the actual killing?" Treverius continued, to break an embarrassing silence.

"Most of it. Gibber forced him."

"Forced him?" Blandina asked. "How could he, a man that size?"

"He gave Aethiops . . . gave us all . . . a home. He owned our lives."

"I can understand that," Treverius said, "but to force someone to kill is pure evil. Nothing can justify it."

"My secretary, Sebastian?" Albanus asked. "Neither Alexandros nor the Ethiopian were there."

"Vertiscus knew everything that happened in the Pretorium. And everyone. His gold spoke quietly."

"Bought off some of my men?" Albanus rubbed his eyes in frustration. "What a fool I was! Even joked about Sebastian being safe."

"Clement, the third victim?" Blandina asked. "Gaisios discovered him."

"Gibber told Alexandros who should die," Albino replied. "He waited near the brothel for the bargeman to come out . . . drunk. It was chance that that Vandal found him."

"We thought Gundstram might have been killed in a power struggle with Lupus Glaucus," Treverius said. "Is that what happened, Albino?"

"In a way. Gundstram reminded Glaucus that he had found the Macedonica treasure, and wanted a larger share of it, or he'd go to the governor. Glaucus strangled him, then moved the body into the house to make it look like one of the murders."

"The silver coin?"

The actor looked back at Blandina to answer. "Vertiscus couldn't resist mocking the centurion's claim to the treasure. That was his share."

"We discovered the mithreum," David said. "Did Vertiscus use the cult to recruit the garrison in support of this New Gothia?"

Albino nodded. "As a shield, he spread rumors that he was an Arian. Nevius got his friends to cause trouble at the roofer's funeral, but then it got too cold. They scattered after the Vandal attack."

"What about Juliana?" Blandina asked. "Petranius seemed so considerate of her."

"She found out about the murders. That prick Vertiscus probably boasted . . ."Albino's voice broke in a sob.

"Gibber kept to himself after that," Pumilio said, taking up the story in his high-pitched voice. "The insult by Stilicho . . . walking out on the play Petranius had written for him . . . was the final curtain. Then Vertiscus insisted that the child Pancras had to die."

"Alexandros was responsible for that murder, but after Aethiops found out he signed to me that he wouldn't kill again. When I told Petranius, he was furious. He said the Judean woman was the last victim, but she had to be killed."

"Then Aethiops was actually warning Penina?" Blandina asked. "She said it looked like he was pleading with her."

"To run away," Pumilio affirmed. "After that Vertiscus wanted my friend killed, but Gibber stalled. He locked Aethiops in one of the animal cells instead."

"Incredible." Treverius shook his head in disbelief. "Petranius staged the tunnel accident, even his own crucifixion, to divert suspicion from himself."

"You had figured out the method, map maker," Albino continued, wiping an eye. "After Glaucus surprised you in the mithreum, Vertiscus brought the treasure here. He had promised to share it with us, but his plan to recruit the garrison had gone so well that he changed his mind. And there had been enough killings to terrorize the Curia into replacing the governor and accepting his rule."

"Then Lupus Glaucus was hiding here?"

"After that prick made fun of Petranius's hunchback, he was afraid he'd be betrayed, kept telling us that he, not Vertiscus, would write the last act to this drama."

"Why did Petranius decide to make Blandina one of the victims?" Treverius asked, reaching back for his wife's hand. "She was always supportive . . . even defended him."

"Governor," Albino hedged, "during the games to-day, Vertiscus and Glaucus planned to take you hostage, massacre your pretorians, and take over Mogontium. Last night, before paying the garrison, the curator came with the others to take what they wanted of the treasure. Vertiscus gave us a few gold coins, but Petranius felt the curator had ordered Glaucus to kill him."

"How did you manage that . . . that horror on the stage?" Treverius asked.

"We're actors," Albino scoffed. "Gibber flattered the four into drinking with him to the success of New Gothia. Alexandros poisoned their wine, then we helped . . . y . . . you saw what happened to them."

"But why include Blandina?" Treverius persisted.

"Petranius's suspicions warped his mind. When she refused his advances this morning, he decided to include her in the final act. He'd gone insane."

"Why didn't you stop him?"

"We were afraid by then," Pumilio whined. "Afraid to face Gibber."

"The Greek Fire, Albino? That got here through Cyril?"

"Last year, from his agent in Constantinople. There were only four barrels, but they smell so strongly that we buried them under the stage. Alexandros was clever with machines. He set up a pump from the barrels to the stage nozzles."

"What would motivate Vertiscus to treason and murder?" Albanus wondered aloud. "I gave him a position of trust."

"An irrational need for power?" Treverius suggested. "Constantine is still defying Honorius at Arelate. Who wrote that nature had put some vice into each of her creations?"

"I don't know, but I've heard enough," Albanus said, standing up. "When the curator and Glaucus weren't there to signal their men, the conspiracy faltered. Well, the garrison is under the command of Riculfius now. I'll have him send burial details over here. What they see should end all thoughts of further sedition." The governor reached down to touch Albino's head. "Son, you and your actors will have to be confined to the Pretorium until a magistrate sorts this all out."

* * *

That afternoon Treverius brought Blandina into the seclusion of the garden. They sat under a Linden tree and tried to blot out the horror, watching gasping sparrows at a fountain take wary gulps of the tepid water. Late summer flowers, splurges of color scattered among the ochre weeds, gave the muggy air a spicy scent. Treverius always thought that August hosted a distinctive smell, one of fragrant dried grass and ripening seed pods, mingled with a mild odor of decay.

As a hot wind rustled the Linden leaves overhead, thunder rumbled in the distance. The western sky was darkening with massive storm clouds. Blandina leaned against her husband's shoulder. He slipped an arm around her.

"I'm all right, Trev. Just glad that Agilan told you where I was."

"Agilan? I never saw the boy."

"What?" She sat up and looked at him. "I told Agilan to find you and say that I had gone to the theater."

"Dove, an eight-year-old is going to stay and watch the games first. I figured out where you were."

"Then God really did look after this fool." Blandina brushed at oily soot on her arm that her bath had not washed away. "It's hard to believe these horrors were all part of Vertiscus's skewed ambition. Would his New Gothia have succeeded?"

"Constantine hasn't been dislodged from Arelate, and he's more accessible from Ravenna than Germania is. A rebellious leader isn't a new situation in Roman history."

"Yours was a literal deus ex machina rescue. Trev."

"A 'god from a machine'?" He chuckled. "I'm hardly a god . . . just lucky that hoisting crane was there. Actually, if Plautus had tried to end one of his plays that way he would have been hooted out of the theater."

"I'm so sorry about Aethiops. He saved my life, too."

"Blandina, the man murdered people," Treverius countered. "Yet, in a sense, I suppose saving you could be construed as an act of love. It's said that God forgives much for love." He leaned over and kissed black hair that smelled of his favorite Artemesia scent. "Dove, you need to forget all this."

Blandina nodded and brushed a blond curl away from his forehead. "You should have Ageria cut your hair. And, oh, by the way, it was Sextus Propertius who wrote that Nature had conferred some vice on each created thing."

"What a memory, woman." Treverius watched the birds a moment, then thought of the curator. "Vertiscus was correct in one respect. Honorius needs to assign more legions here if he wants to hold on to his Germanic provinces. A new tribe of Franks was reported crossing the Rhine at Colonia and—"

"Shush!" Blandina put a finger to his lips. "I have a different future in mind, Trev. How would you feel now about having a child?"

"Now? I . . . I think I'd like being a father. I know I've hesitated, yet I really can't think of many times in the past when it wasn't too dangerous to start a family."

"Then I have a nice surprise for you. Remember when we made love in that pool near the Nava?"

"You mean?"

"Trev, if our child is a boy, may I name him after my father? I know 'Cingetorius' is a mouthful, but perhaps a diminuative . . . like Getorius."

"Getorius it is!" Treverius exclaimed. "I . . . I'm really pleased. Ah, shouldn't you be resting? Let's go inside, it's about to rain, anyway." He chortled in delight. "So, I'll be a father. When exactly? Have you picked a midwife yet?"

"Calm down, Trev." Blandina laughed. "And yes. She thinks in March or April."

"Dove, that's wonderful. 'Of all light-hearted men—'"

"'None is lighter-hearted than my Treverius is today,'" Blandina paraphrased. "See, I know some of Catullus's poems, too."

"His nicer ones, I hope—"

A rumble of thunder sounded closer now. As Treverius helped Blandina up and prepared to lead her indoors, the first drops of rain spattered onto the Linden leaves and designed dark, irregular circles on the terra cotta tiles around the atrium pool.

The wetness, with Nature's promise of renewed life for her created things, would be welcome.

The End

photo © Lynne Lawlor

Albert Noyer's career includes professional work in commercial and fine art, teaching vocational art in public schools, and teaching art history. He lives in New Mexico, where he is currently working on his next two books. You can find out more at www.users.uswest.net/~aanoyer